Roger Armbruster

Three Marias

A Sicilian Story

LEGAS

© Copyright Legas 2013

No part of this book may be translated or reproduced in any form, by print, photoprint, microfilm, microfiche, or any other means, without the written permission from the copyright holder.

Library of Congress Cataloging-in-Publication Data

Armbruster, Roger, 1939-
  Three Marias / Roger Armbruster.
     pages cm
  ISBN 1-881901-92-0 (pbk.)
  1. Women--Italy--Sicily--Fiction. 2. Italians--United States--Fiction. 3. Italian American women--Fiction. 4. Italian American families--Fiction. 5. National characteristics, Sicilian--Fiction. I. Title.
  PS3601.R555T48 2013
  813'.6--dc23
                                    2013003022

Acknowledgements

My gratitude to Geoffrey Aggeler, Ph.D., whose editing, professionalism, encouragement and steady hand guided me in the completion of this book. Thanks to Bill Dougherty for allowing me to bore him with the early drafts, his research and firm, but kind insistence, that I remain honest and not take short cuts.

Thanks also to Gaetano Cipolla, Ph.D., for tirelessly correcting my Sicilian, and bringing the book to print, Karen Bohner for her good cheer through tedious revisions, and Corindo DeCollibus in assisting with the final draft. A special thanks to Carl Mills, MD. Finally, thanks to my granddaughter, Olivia Russell, who, three years ago insisted; "*Nonno*, you gotta write a book!"

Cover design by Olivia Russell

For information and for orders, write to:

Legas

P. O. Box 149
Mineola, NewYork
11501, USA

3 Wood Aster Bay
Ottawa, Ontario
K2R 1D3 Canada

legaspublishing.com

Dedication

To my children and family, past, present, and future.

Table of Contents

PART I

CHAPTER 1	7
CHAPTER 2	15
CHAPTER 3	22
CHAPTER 4	27
CHAPTER 5	31
CHAPTER 6	37
CHAPTER 7	43
CHAPTER 8	47
CHAPTER 9	53
CHAPTER 10	59
CHAPTER 11	66
CHAPTER 12	71
CHAPTER 13	78
CHAPTER 14	84
CHAPTER 15	90
CHAPTER 16	96
CHAPTER 17	100
CHAPTER 18	105
CHAPTER 19	110
CHAPTER 20	117
CHAPTER 21	121
CHAPTER 22	124
CHAPTER 23	130
CHAPTER 24	135
CHAPTER 25	138
CHAPTER 26	141
CHAPTER 27	145
CHAPTER 28	149
CHAPTER 29	155
CHAPTER 30	159
CHAPTER 31	163

PART II

CHAPTER 32	168
CHAPTER 33	177
CHAPTER 34	182
CHAPTER 35	186
CHAPTER 36	190

CHAPTER 37 194
CHAPTER 38 198
CHAPTER 39 201
CHAPTER 40 205
CHAPTER 41 208
CHAPTER 42 213

PART III

CHAPTER 43 218
CHAPTER 44 223
CHAPTER 45 226
CHAPTER 46 230
CHAPTER 47 234
CHAPTER 48 237
CHAPTER 49 243
CHAPTER 50 248
CHAPTER 51 252
CHAPTER 52 257
CHAPTER 53 262
CHAPTER 54 268
CHAPTER 55 273
CHAPTER 56 279
CHAPTER 57 284
CHAPTER 58 290
CHAPTER 59 295
CHAPTER 60 299
CHAPTER 61 303

CHAPTER I

Giuseppe Caiozzo urges the stubborn donkey up the dusty Corso Garibaldi of Castellammare del Golfo between the rows of old flaking plaster houses with worn terra-cotta roofs and wind beaten wooden doors. The ornately painted cart moves slowly on wobbly wheels away from the harbor toward the outskirts of the village and the precisely planted, exactingly terraced vineyard.

The grapes in the hills of Mount Inici have enjoyed an excellent summer, nurtured by a warm Sicilian sun, ample rain and a mild Scirocco breeze promising a successful autumn harvest. They have matured to plump ripe during the year just as the breasts of the young girls in the village are peaking and swelling full in adolescence waiting to be plucked. He smiles the smile of a lecherous man who has more on his mind that day than gathering grapes.

At thirty five Caiozzo is certainly not old, even now in the Castellammare of the early 1890's. But he is venerable and wily enough to have earned the right to affect the title 'Don' before his given name because of his years of experience and expertise in the business of growing and tending the grapes. The true Don, Angelo Bono, is not offended by the usage and finds it amusing. He understands it was bestowed on Caiozzo with a wink and a nod by the locals and carries no weight.

"Yes," Bono will remark laughing, "he is a 'Don,' the 'Don of the Dirt'. But don't underestimate him. I have had many business dealings with him and know he is also shrewd and skilled enough for cagey negotiations with the land owners around the issue of profit sharing."

Caiozzo helps himself to a more than modest share of the loaf and always pays himself before the workers. He makes enough *lire* to bury half in the ground beneath his mother's chicken coop and still live very comfortably before whisking the crumbs off the table into the waiting hands of the grateful workers. "I give them enough to feed their families and earn their gratitude," he will say, "but not so much to encourage greed, or worse, ambition."

To describe Caiozzo as frugal would be to understate. The man tosses one *lire* coin around like an iron sewer cover and watches his money with the eye of a hawk protecting her newly-hatched chicks. His success in amassing hoarded wealth is not only a product of knowledge and cunning, but also comes by strokes of fate with the premature deaths of many young men in the village, eliminating competitors just as their own ambitions were maturing.

Malaria was rampant in Sicily, reducing the young as well as the old to grey wisps of humanity shivering with sweat and fever. They died helpless under dirty, moth-eaten blankets as the insidious disease wasted their poor bodies to paper thin skin and bone and the stench of decaying flesh fouled the air. Assassination took the lives of others in an atmosphere of vendetta dating back centuries and rivaling the air borne scourge on the island. Those men who did not succumb to disease or assassination were often criminals and assassins themselves. Between 1890 and 1950, eighty percent of Castellammare's male population had spent time in jail, thirty percent for murder. Those who, like Caiozzo, were not struck down by one of these events were able to take full advantage and prosper, economically, politically and in social standing. The dearth of eligible young men coupled with the availability of women in the village also assured his enjoyment of fleshly pleasures, gratifying an insatiable libidinous appetite with frequent and reckless abandon.

The cool of the early September morning is already giving way to thick, rising heat, providing an excellent foundation for the winged malaria agents of death to begin their day's work. Caiozzo pulls the rumpled straw hat down just above wild, bushy eyebrows, shielding against a blood orange sun breaking in the East, but allowing enough visibility for dark, narrow eyes to survey and calculate everything around.

He knows the nuance and gesture of every movement and the potential danger of shadowy figures lurking in the gloomy alleys, a skill acquired and carefully nurtured by successive generations of Sicilians. Under the heel of Greek, Roman, Arab, Norman, and Spanish conquerors, they had become a people perpetually suspicious. "Trust no one," was the cautionary message the old men and women in the village, the story tellers, passed on from generation to generation. It was as endemic as the DNA which produced the dark eyes and the olive tinged skin and seemed to hover in the very air the Castellammarese breathed.

When the centuries of invaders had finished and Garibaldi ousted the Bourbons, the legacy of suspicion did not depart with them. The eyes turned to the government in Rome which took more freely than it gave, and the Church in Rome, which filled its coffers with *lire* the people could ill afford, and offered empty platitudes repeated in the pulpits every Sunday: "Trust in God, my child, and remain pure in your hearts and deeds." To this day, many elderly Sicilians bless themselves with holy water but bitterly recall a childhood when the Church turned a blind eye and a deaf ear to their pleas for relief from poverty and health related sufferings.

The anger and sense of desertion were not limited to Church and State. They were also directed at the mainland population who regarded Sicilians as indolent mutants who would rather steal than work for their bread. They were called "*mezzogiorno*," a derogatory expression applied to a people only willing to work half a day, forfeiting the right to assistance or compassion. Their dialect was considered a cacophony of gibberish which borrowed words from centuries of invaders, corrupting the mother tongue.

"These people are not Italians but some bastards from the desert in Africa. They have no right to call themselves Italians," was the verdict too often heard from the North.

Enrico Conte, the oldest and most gregarious story teller in the village repeatedly told anyone who would listen with colorful and exaggerated language: "For more than 2000 years we were at the mercy of invaders who stole our souls and made poor serfs of us. Fate has not been our friend. Even the map of Italy has predestined us. The toe of the mainland points directly at the heart of Sicily and our own *paesani* kick us out into the middle of the Mediterranean Sea. We are the poorest place in Europe so we must fend for ourselves. We must do whatever is necessary to provide for our families."

Suspicion and mistrust festered and infected relationships between neighbors and even within families. "Love thy neighbor" was not a compelling mandate. What people lived by were cautionary warnings:

Stay away from sick doctors
Men who don't speak
Dogs that don't bark
People who go to church twice a day
And quarrels with those who are bigger than you.

Conte blamed this suspicious and fearful mind-set on the invaders but he neglected to acknowledge the positive contributions of at least one group of occupiers, the Arabs.

Around 827 BC, the Arabs, sensing the potential commercial attraction of the little town's harbor, settled in with an indigenous population known as the Elimian, of whom history has recorded little. They named the town "Al Madarig," the steps, perhaps because of the severely inclined main road which served the trade traffic in and out of the village. The Arabs established an emporium where goods, produce and fish could be sold and shipped to the mainland, vastly improving the economic life of the natives as well as providing an organization and structure which were missing.

They improved agricultural practices and diet, and the architecture of many churches and buildings reflect a discernible Arabic cast. Sicilian affinity for *couscous* and *cassata*, an iced cake, and the wailing, dirge-like quality of some of the music is further testament to the Arabic cultural influence.

Caiozzo had scant knowledge of or interest in the historic particulars of the village of his birth. He had worked the vineyards alongside his father since he was seven and assumed the role of breadwinner at age ten when his father died. Other than the welfare of his mother, a steady supply of wine, and enough *lire* to retain his place as the darling of the local whores, he had few questions or concerns which did not directly affect his daily routine – nor was he aware of such matters as hygiene and personal appearance.

Recently, however, he found himself lingering before his reflection in the murky, cracked mirror hanging on the kitchen wall, increasingly troubled by his appearance. He noticed the unsightly strings of wheezing nose hair dangling from flaring nostrils, becoming one with an unattended handlebar moustache. A sinister scar curled from the corner of his lower lip just below his chin, the result of a stupid quarrel orchestrated by stupid men with a broken wine bottle. A toothpick hung from his mouth, chewed and shredded limp by uneven brown teeth, discarded only when it became splintered and soaked with saliva and then replaced by the lit remnant of a thin, wrinkled cigar which produced rings of smoke that smelled like a death certificate. He was short and thick, crusted and sunburnt with fingertips the size of walnuts. His clothing was more sleep and wear than wash and wear. At a glance he was indistinguishable from the other men who toiled in the vineyard.

But Caiozzo was a boss, a *capo*, not a laborer. His crew of some thirty men and a few good women duly followed him up the sun-baked corso four miles to the vineyard, most on foot. A fortunate few were blessed with a ride on the unsteady back of an aged, struggling donkey with a bloated belly, frothing at the mouth and tormented by a mass of swirling vermin.

On the first day of the autumn harvest, the procession brought a large turnout of villagers from their mean little houses; shabby, shirtless and wine-soaked men, drunk in delusion and denial with little prospect of ever earning a decent wage to support their families. Women with dark rings under hollow eyes stood lowly and quietly obedient at their sides while hungry, crying infants sucked at dry breasts. Older children wrapped themselves around their mothers' legs like limp, discarded rags.

The wet, heavy eyes of the women would turn to the flat ground of the cemetery surrounding the Church of San Giuseppe. Their somber, weary faces were etched with anger and despair, and they wondered how much longer, how much time they might have, before their own children would succumb and be put to eternal rest in that soil of sorrow. Their toothless husbands with cigarettes stuck to parched lips smiled mindlessly and applauded wildly like children at a circus as Caiozzo and his crew passed. He acknowledged the cheers and tribute with the theatrical flourish one might expect from a Pope or a King on one of his balconies. "*Grazzii, grazzii tantu. Tuttu va beni.* Thank you very much, all goes well," he assured the villagers.

But Caiozzo himself was not completely assured.

Born in a land with roots buried deep in superstition and Greek myth, where unexpected forces of nature could devastate a crop, he purchased a divine insurance policy. Caiozzo doubled his offering at Sunday Mass, and lit a candle at the church each day before the work began.

The men were satisfied with the performance as they had been the year before and the year before that. Those without work resignedly stumbled to the tavern to drink bad wine cheaply and excessively and were soon drunk passing yet another day with nothing to show.

The women returned to their homes to begin the daily routine of kneading the dough into rounds and loaves of bread to bake in their wood burning ovens. They always made more than was necessary, selling the extra loaves to the passing gentry. Along the way home, the women would lift their spirits with derisive humor at their husbands' expense; *"Il tacchino, l'asino e l'uomo sono tutti e tre fratelli,"* they joked. "The turkey, the ass, and the man are all three brothers."

The bread was a staple attending a meal of watery stew made with what could be salvaged at the dock before the fishermen took the most and the best of the daily catch across the Strait of Messina to be enjoyed in the kitchens of Rome and the North. The scene was similar in every house in the village. The women made do with what they had, a potato to thicken and garlic and an onion to season. On odd nights, a few sardines were boned and crushed into tomato sauce, and occasionally escarole or swiss chard floated in a plate of warm olive oil. The hungry children fought with each other at the wooden tables, clutching warm, crusty bread in tiny fists and quickly devouring the evening meal. Wee eyes of appreciation met the loving eyes of a mother who was grateful she could provide well for her children that night. At the far end of the table, a man with glazed eyes sat quiet and alone stuffing himself with both hands, his silence broken only by an occasional burp or an involuntary release of moaning flatulence.

In the autumn evening the women sewed by the fire making warm leggings and hats for the children. Winter would soon bring the dreaded *colpo d' aria*, a cold, wet wind which pierced the skin and left the furrowed land creased and cracked like the faces of the men who farmed it. It would sit lifeless and barren, without a potato or a trace of a leafy green for the soup or stew. Until then there would be food on the table. The husbands staggered to bed with full stomachs as the women spun the yarn and wool until the fire became cinders and the room grew dark and chilled. The next day, with what little *lire* was available, they purchased cloth from the outlawed black market vendors supplied by "The Friends," or stole what they could from the stalls when the merchant wasn't looking. With little assistance from the government, their poverty forced them into larcenous behavior that followed scripts circumventing the written law. The law did not protect them so why should they abide by it? Even *Padre* Pietro the fat, pink village priest, was sympathetic and ignored the eighth commandment. He offered absolution in confession with a mild scolding and five Hail Mary's. A man of some education, he rationalized the soft penance by shrugging his shoulders and referencing a quote from the Greek historian Thucydides: "The strong do what they will; the weak do what they must." The priest's motive, however, was less than pure. It was very much in his interest not to discourage the stealing too forcefully. If his parishioners fared poorly or did not survive, it would be reflected in the collection basket and then on his kitchen table and reduced wardrobe.

Most Sicilian women were, of necessity, excellent seamstresses and could thread the eye of a needle with the precision of William Tell. They could also insert that same needle into the exposed genitals of unsuspecting sleeping husbands who had strayed that night and violated the marriage vow. "Be aware," Caiozzo warned his men, "these Sicilian women can turn on you in an instant and become as dangerous and unpredictable as a child with a rifle in his hands."

Caiozzo had no such concerns. His obsessive attention to work and filial duty to his mother, an accepted requirement of all good Sicilian sons, had precluded marriage and considerations of raising a family. But with the years advancing, his position secure, and a tidy nest egg safely concealed, he was seriously considering a search for a wife. It might be nice, he thought, to return from a long day's work to a clean, warm home, enjoy a good supper and, later, the welcoming arms and dewy thighs of a young woman in the comfort of my own bed. The more he considered the advantages, the more appealing the prospect became. Finally, with the same resolve that led him recently to purchase a fine young mule at the livestock fair, he decided to begin his search for a wife.

Late one afternoon at the tavern stinking of grapes gone sour, Caiozzo ordered a bottle of his reserved wine and sat alone at a dark corner table. He dismissed attempts of the regulars to engage in conversation and, under a veil of thick blue smoke licking up the walls, ruminated over how he would tell his mother of his decision. He drank quickly, shuddering at the prospect of contending with operatic histrionics and extravagant expressions of grief. After an hour passed, a bottle of wine emptied, and courage summoned, he decided the best approach was simple and direct and made his way through the shadows of an early September evening along Via Canale to his mother's house. The sun was slowly settling behind the hills yielding to a long, lean stretch of flat purple and grey clouds like a body in repose. He blessed himself and prayed it was not the omen of an old woman fainted or, worse, the victim of a heart attack.

Sofia Caiozzo, stout and sturdy, sat nestled comfortably in her padded chair. Her response was about what he had expected.

"Ah yes, Giuseppe, I knew one day this time would come. But truly, I wish it came after I closed these tired eyes forever."

"Mamma, for God's sake, bite your tongue. These are selfish and hurtful words. I have worked in the vineyard since age seven and now at thirty five have neither a wife nor even a bastard child. I can't believe God gave me life only to spend it wedded to the labors of the vineyard. Can you not be happy that I would find someone to share my life, give me children and you grandchildren and ....."

"Yes, yes," the old lady interrupted, waving her hands, "she's gonna share your life, she's gonna share your home and bear your children... and she's gonna share your money too. And you'll give me grandchildren? Why? I don't need the worry and the sorrow for more children. I grieved enough when I buried your sister and brother before they could walk," she lamented. "Then one year later the sweat and fever came and took your poor father before we had a chance to make more children," she moaned.

"But Mamma," Giuseppe implored, "we can't undo those losses. I will always be here for you, take care of you and....."

"You can guarantee that, eh," Sofia said sarcastically, arching an eyebrow. "Your ear has a direct line from God's lips? Each time the fever came to this house I lit a candle every day and kneeled faithfully so long on the cold stone at the statue of the Madonna that my knees got the bone disease. And what good did it bring? I still lost two children and a husband and am half a cripple myself. Sometimes I think the saints made a trick and put *lu mal'uocchiu*, the evil eye on our family."

Giuseppe listened patiently to this sorry old story but could constrain himself no longer. "*Basta mamma*, enough," he exploded. "I too have lived these tragedies of the past. Your losses are also my losses. But we have enjoyed good fortune. We are well-positioned with land we own, and I have a secure income which puts more than stale crusts of bread on the table. Do you not eat better than anyone in the village? Fresh fruit and vegetables, and meat twice a week from the butcher? And most important, we both have our health. Surely your prayers at the statue of the Madonna are being answered now. You have no reason to complain," he added reproachfully. Sofia felt ashamed and silently put her hands between her knees and looked down. "Mamma," Giuseppe continued, "I seek your blessing but, with or without it, I will begin my search for a suitable woman to share my life."

Sofia breathed deeply and spoke with quiet resignation. "Yes, and I'm sure your quest will not be long or difficult." She caressed his face with both hands. "There are few enough men left in this village and none more *beddu* than you, *miu caru*.....and secure with the *lire*," she demurely added. "There are many women to choose from who would eagerly accept your proposal with the approval and encouragement of their families seeking to improve their destiny. But be careful, my son. Choose wisely lest you marry someone who, by her wicked behavior or her family's questionable history or conduct, brings you shame and drives you to financial ruin."

"Yes mamma," Giuseppe agreed. "I'm aware of these concerns and have given them careful thought. They are foremost in my mind."

He felt he had successfully placated his mother and rose quickly, fearing that a prolonged discussion might reverse the outcome. He kissed her on the cheek and walked toward the door and turned. "But before I leave, what is foremost on my mind, is attending to the chickens and feeding them this bag of corn meal I brought."

"Ah, dear son," the old lady said smiling and clasping her hands together. "You care for those chickens the way a good mother cares for her children."

"*Veru è*, Mamma, truly I do. But I attend to them well only for your sake."

"For my sake," she responded with affected surprise. "Why for my sake Giuseppe?"

"Mamma, those poor widows would not be buying eggs from you every Sunday after Mass if they didn't come from healthy, well attended chickens," he said with a wry knowing smile.

"No, Giuseppe, don't say that," she laughed as he walked out the door. "Don't say that."

CHAPTER 2

Caiozzo was sure his mother was right. He did have his choice of any unmarried woman, young or old, in this village of desperate females. He was aware of the obsequious behavior and the furtive smiles of the single women whenever he passed them strolling around the Piazza Europa on Saturday evenings, or standing on the steps of the church after Sunday Mass offering a *bedda comparsa*, their best form and dress for consideration. Yes, he thought suspiciously, they smile sweetly, but their intentions are poorly disguised. The gleam in their eye is not for me, but for the *lire* they see sprouting from my pockets like asparagus from the dirt. My *lire*, which will bring them a lifetime of comfort and security. I must remain patient, prudent and cautious as mamma advised or risk losing all I have worked for and attained over the years. An impulsive decision for a guarantee of a hot meal, clean underwear and nightly pleasure could lead to ruin.

That evening he sat sipping good grappa at his kitchen window framing the spectacle of a full, pale moon, breaking the dark and illuminating the silver-green leaves of the olive trees and their gnarled branches, bent like the limbs of the old men in the village. He considered his options like a king at his court looking over his stable of available maidens.

The young girls are firm and attractive, he thought, and ripe for a sexually experienced man, and most have a fine dowry which their parents assembled to induce a good marriage. But many seem flighty, foolish, and unpredictable, with no sense of purpose. And as I move from May to December, I wonder if I can always satisfy a much younger woman. The humiliating horns of the cuckold could appear over my front door and I would earn the title, *curnutu*. The older women in the village are more easily satisfied, dependable and grateful and don't ask for much when you give them pleasure. Jenna, the butcher's daughter, is pleasing enough, except for her nose which is rather large and fleshy. And she can become moody with a sour disposition. Yolanda has an ample dowry but an ass to match, the width of my mother's old cow. Gina's full bosom is the object of fantasy with the young as well as the old men in the village, but her dull wit reflects a brain the size of the one in the head of the canary she keeps caged in her kitchen.

Despite the potential risk with a younger woman, Caiozzo realized none of the older women excited him. In truth, he wanted someone young, someone on the threshold of womanhood, ripe and ready to be initiated by an experienced older man. Yes, there was the possibility of being cuckolded as the years passed and he was in his dotage. But that would be many years in the future. In the meantime, he would have had the pleasure of coupling with a firm, young, virginal body and, having a youthful companion, might even retard his aging process. So it might be, he mused, if he could find a young woman who had been properly raised and instructed in the duties of a good Sicilian wife.

Caiozzo poured a second glass of grappa, felt the clear, strong drink burn its way to the base of his throat and thought more about the young girls in the village. The bell in the church tolled eight, a monotonous, dull clang which hung in the thick night air, marking the conclusion of the Tuesday night novena. He had an image of his mother standing on the steps of the church, gossiping with the other women before returning home. They were all devout matrons and many had young daughters properly raised. One of them came to mind, Maria, the young daughter of Nino and Amelia Pepitone. Caiozzo saw the family at Mass every Sunday but, until recently, had not noticed Maria's transition from the awkward phase of being an undeveloped child to ripening young womanhood. His contact with the Pepitones had always been limited to a perfunctory, "Good Morning," at Mass or a passing nod of greeting in the village. The families had nothing in common, and Caiozzo thought Pepitone snooty and aloof, a man who offered nothing from which he might benefit. Until now.

The Pepitones were a modest, private family who had endured more than their share of tragedy over the years. Maria was referred to in the village as, *la bambina dei miracoli*, the miracle child, because she was born a full ten years after Antonio, her only surviving sibling. During that period, *la signura* Pepitone had miscarried six times and delivered two still-born infants, an epic tragedy still discussed by the perpetually mourning cadre of bun-haired village women, invariably draped in black.

Nino Pepitone was a gentle, supportive husband who never faulted his wife for the miscarriages or stillbirths of the two infants. This was remarkable, considering how many insensitive, ignorant Sicilian men known typically for their coarseness and cruelty, would hold their wives accountable if the cock did not crow precisely at daybreak or the pitiful cry of a sick child disturbed their sleep. Moreover, they adhered to an old Italian proverb which holds that the more a woman is beaten like an egg, the better she becomes. In sharp contrast, Pepitone's reputation as a husband, father and neighbor was peerless. He was known as an honest merchant and respected for the superb quality of his craft as a tanner from Palermo to Siracusa. He attended to his work with the skill and pride one might expect of a third generation artisan.

Three or four times a year he made the three hour journey by train to Palermo to purchase skins and other necessary materials, and to sell his finished products at the bustling market on Via Roma. He timed his visits for the spring, summer and autumn seasons when the streets of the city teemed with tourists from as far north as Britain and as far east as Austria. The locals could not afford the price of his merchandise and the family depended mostly on brisk sales from vacationers and commissions.

Maria had accompanied her father since she was twelve years old and as the selling season approached, her excitement and anticipation grew. She looked forward to the opportunity to quit the provincial confines of the village and, for a few days, immerse herself in the excitement and cultural vitality of a city hosting people from all over Europe. She also learned more about her native land passing along the streets of Palermo among buildings shaped by diverse influences reflecting the Island's history. Seeing how the architecture had become so distinctive made more of an impression on her than any lessons her six years of school provided. It also offered the opportunity to spend time with her brother, with whom she shared a loving and close relationship, despite the difference in their ages.

Antonio had completed the tenth grade and left Castellammare years earlier to pursue his dream of writing and teaching. He published a thin volume of poems and a few short stories which sold poorly, not surprising since the literacy rate in Sicily barely nudged forty percent. The government did not mandate education and the peasantry, suspicious of intellectual pursuits, did not expose or encourage their children. Sofia Caiozzo spoke for most when she admonished her young son years earlier: "Reading and schooling are only for the idle gentry, Giuseppe. Use your time and energy productively with your hands in the soil, rather than your nose in a book. Nobody puts *lire* in your hand for reading." The children could learn what was necessary about simple arithmetic and history from the village story tellers or at the feet of family members. And this could be achieved without the threat of contamination by inconvenient or embarrassing truths. Intellectual rumination would only lead to confusion and, perhaps, insanity, and questioning threatened the balance and stability of the family and the community. Increasing knowledge could well increase sorrow. Some exposure to music, painting and sculpture were not considered a threat unlike academic subjects. The arts could be appreciated purely as an experiential exercise which did nothing more than indulge and massage the primary senses.

The Pepitones were an exception and strongly supported their son's career choice. However, Nino was beginning to worry about his son. He heard gossip in the marketplace that certain people in high places in politics, the *carabinieri* and, "The Friends of Friends" were complaining that the young man was becoming a stone in their collective shoe. Many of Antonio's essays were critical of the collaboration among the politicians, the police and "The Friends." Antonio went so far as to accuse them of being, "Three fingers of the same dirty hand, a coterie of power hungry profiteers who controlled and victimized the poor peasants."

"Be careful of what you say and write," Nino warned his son. "People are talking and you may be courting danger. Write less harshly and concentrate more on your stories and securing your teaching position, which puts *lire* in your pocket. Be discreet and don't put into writing words which may bring upon you the angry reprisal of powerful, unscrupulous men."

Antonio smiled dismissively and tried to ease his father's concerns with the confidence and spirit typical of youth. "Papa, you worry too much. Your generation doesn't understand that many things have changed since the unification of Italy. There is a new mood in the air championed by my generation. We are no longer subject to the oppression of foreign invaders and now have a legal system and a constitution to protect our rights. You are stuck in a time when there was a potential enemy behind every tree."

Nino gently placed a hand on his son's shoulder. "Yes, Antonio," he agreed, "some things have indeed changed. But the specters of evil and greed will always be with us, lurking behind that very tree you speak of. The invaders have gone but we must now contend with....." Maria stood by, quietly listening to the conversation but her patience was exhausted. She smiled and tugged at her brother's hand. "Come, Antonio. It's getting late and we have much to see and do today. And papa, the day is too beautiful to spend worrying about such things. You are wasting precious time yourself as the *lire* you seek ends up in the pockets of the other vendors. Go make your wages and enjoy the day."

Pepitone smiled at his daughter's words which seemed both wise and naïve and returned to his stall. But he was far from assured and the worry stayed with him.

Antonio enjoyed taking his sister around this vibrant city, the intellectual capital of southern Europe during the 11th and 12th centuries, and beamed at her curiosity, the intelligent questions she asked and the comments she made. At the Archeological Museum, Maria was struck by the prehistoric collection of panels illustrating Orpheus with Wild Animals, from the 3rd Century B.C. She was pensive and saddened observing the examples of Etruscan funerary art and turned to Antonio.

"I have heard of the Etruscan people who were in Italy before the Romans but mysteriously disappeared. What happened to them?," she asked Antonio.

"No one knows for sure Maria, but many writers of history say the Etruscans were victims of mass genocide at the hands of the Romans."

"How brutal! But why would the Romans do such a thing?," she asked.

"That too is uncertain *beddu*. But then, who can reasonably explain the motive for brutality?"

Maria then expressed disappointment that the Doric frieze of the Greek temple at Selinunete was not the original, a mere reproduction, but was satisfied by Antonio's sage explanation: "Maria, the original frieze belongs at the remains of the temple on the land where it was constructed, not behind the walls of a building." At the puppet museum they cavorted and giggled like naughty little children, mimicking the fierce faces and bent limbs of the Norman-inspired Sicilian puppets, dangling awkwardly from strings.

They were very hungry after the museums and Antonio bought a bag of colossal red cherries, some figs and a large piece of goat cheese, which they ate at the Botanical Gardens while enjoying an ensemble performing arias from various operas. Antonio was particularly interested in hearing the libretto from Mascagni's one act opera, *Cavalleria Rusticana*. He proudly told Maria that the work was based on a play written by the Sicilian, Giovanni Verga.

"A Sicilian writer," Maria gushed, "just like you Antonio."

"Not quite, *cara*, not yet," he responded with a smile.

Before returning to the market and the rendezvous with their father, Antonio took Maria to a bookshop he knew on Via Papireto which had a few scarce translations of famous British authors. *Signor* Luchino, the owner, was happy to see his old friend and extended a warm greeting. Luchino was happy to see anyone walk through his door, a musty place so empty and quiet you could hear the tiny feet of mice scurrying along the bookshelves. Yes, indeed, only last week he had purchased a fine leather-bound translation of Charlotte Bronte's *Jane Eyre* from an inebriated student whose immediate priority was a bottle of bad red wine rather than the company of a good book. "For you, Antonio, only five *lire*, a miraculous price for such a fine work in such fine condition." The inevitable bargaining began. "Your generosity is overwhelming," replied Antonio, "but all I have is a paltry three *lire* to spend. I must save the rest, for we have not eaten all day and, as we speak, I hear my poor sister's stomach growling with hunger." Maria turned and put her hand to her mouth to stifle a giggle. "Ah, a full day of fasting is it? And how do you explain the red stains which dot your clean white shirt, Antonio?" Luchino asked, smiling. Antonio's face reddened and he looked aside in embarrassment. "Ha! You are a scoundrel, my friend," exclaimed Luchino, "but put four *lire* in my hand and be off with your sister to enjoy a good supper and the work of the celebrated Bronte sister at my expense." They laughingly embraced and bid each other farewell.

Antonio saw his father and sister off at the train station when the sun was still high enough in the sky to light the tracks and the countryside on the way back to Castellammare.

"We can expect you two weeks from this coming Sunday?" Pepitone asked his son with the gentle hint of a command. "Papa, since I have been at Palermo, have I ever failed to sit with the family for dinner one Sunday every month? You needn't keep reminding me. It is not a chore or obligation I feel, but a pleasure I look forward to every month. *La famigghia è tuttu*, the family is everything, papa."

Nino smiled. "Good, good! And you know how happy it makes your mother." He embraced his son and Antonio leaned forward and kissed his sister on both cheeks.

As Maria mounted the steps of the car she turned and shouted to her brother, "And bring me another book by the English writers, if you can get one at a good price from Luchino," she giggled.

"But, Maria," Antonio said wide-eyed, "you have not even started the first chapter of the Bronte book you have in your hand."

"Yes," she loudly called back as the train inched along the track, "but by the time we reach Castellammare I will be long past the first chapter and in two days will have nothing to read." Antonio stood with his hands in his pockets, a smile on his face and nodded. *Chi bedda carusa!* What a beautiful kid, he was thinking, what a beautiful kid.

The newly purchased locomotive from the Fiat company in Milano chugged along smoothly belching grey smoke from the stack, effortlessly pulling the train through the seaside resort of Mondello. The sun worshippers from the North were slowly leaving the beach, moving across the sand like old, spent turtles. They searched for a cool place to relieve seared skin which had gone from flat white to blistered red.

Maria stopped reading and ran her slender fingers along the soft leather of the book, pausing to ask her father, "Papa, do you make leather bindings for a book like this.?"

"Ah no, Maria, not me," he replied. "That is not my kind of work. It belongs to the men in the North who run big machines and turn out hundreds of bindings a week."

"Oh! And today papa, did you turn out any *lire* from the market?" she asked mischievously.

"Surely I did, Maria, surely I did," he said laughing. I sold pouches, purses, belts and small briefcases to important men who carry important papers from place to place. Yes, I sold most of the items we brought and even secured a commission and an advance for a large set of luggage which, alone, can keep us quite comfortable for a couple of months. If we are prudent, of course."

"For months?," she asked in amazement. "Is that not a lot of *lire* for one person to pay for a few pieces of luggage, papa?"

Pepitone was troubled and looked down for a moment, then turned to his daughter. "I know what you are thinking Maria," he said. "You are a sensitive and perceptive girl and may be upset that so many of our neighbors suffer badly from want while we are blessed with good fortune. But that is how things are. You know we do what we can. Your mother, good woman that she is, gives food, and clothing which you have outgrown to the families, and we make a generous offering in the poor box every Sunday at Mass. I only pray the *lire* does not stick between the fat, stubby fingers of *Padre* Pietro," he added with a deep sigh.

Maria turned and looked out the window. She was startled by the long, desolate shrill of the train whistle piercing the quiet early evening like a desperate, pleading voice. The train slowly passed through miles of fields thick with vineyards, and trees profuse with oranges, lemons and olives. The flat, furrowed ground in front of the trees yielded rows of purple cabbage, green zucchini and bright red tomatoes so full they bent their stalks and drooped to the ground. Beyond the trees the land inclined and got rocky, and Maria saw shepherds wearing stocking caps and carrying long sticks, and barking dogs running around and in between the herds of sheep and goats. On the right the land gently sloped to the sea dotted with fishing boats, heavy with their catch, pushing through whitecaps on their way home. And in Castellammare and other small villages in Sicily, Maria thought, the bread was always scarcer than the children who often went to bed hungry.

CHAPTER 3

Early Saturday evening after the work in the vineyard was finished, Caiozzo walked into Bartolo Fontana's barbershop off Corso Garibaldi.

"Don Caiozzo," Fontana exclaimed, "I was about to close my shop and join the family for supper this Saturday." He ceremoniously put his broom in a corner. "But for you, I make an exception. The family can wait," he expansively announced.

"Enough, Bartolo, *basta*," Caiozzo scoffed. "Your tongue is so far up my ass it tickles my tongue."

"Ah Don Caiozzo, always with the funny line and the poetic image," Fontana laughed. "What can I do for you this evening? I haven't had the pleasure of your company for at least two months."

"Yes, no, I mean," he snapped impatiently and said, "Fontana, I need you to take your time to make neat this mess of unkempt hair and get rid of the unsightly threads poking out of my nose and ears."

"Yes, Don Caiozzo, I see. You have a harvest like the brown wheat growing wildly in the fields."

"Enough with your poetic goat shit talk," growled Caiozzo, "Get on with the business and do your job."

"*Subbitu*, immediately," responded Fontana. "And may I assume your urgency is a matter of attendance at a wedding, or God forbid, a funeral tomorrow?"

"You may assume nothing, you imbecile. But, if you must know, mamma said that my appearance is becoming an embarrassment to her at Sunday Mass. So to make her happy tomorrow, I'll present myself with a haircut and a clean-shaven face, which, if you will kindly get on with it, I will provide.

"Of course, of course," Bartolo replied, knowing full well this was not Caiozzo's motive. Caiozzo had escorted his mother to Mass for years with a bad appearance and never thought twice about it. Now he is suddenly concerned?

Barbers everywhere know everything that goes on in their domain, even more than the village busybody *chiacchiruni* or priest. Rumors, speculation and outright lies circulate in and from the barbershop like hair flying from the tongs of a sharp scissor. Bartolo knew that the bachelor Caiozzo was on the hunt for a wife. The news of his intention had spread like wild fire throughout the village.

Bartolo tied a fresh cape around Caiozzo's neck and soaked and soaped his greasy black hair. His fingers dug deep into a scalp of dry skin and scab which had accumulated over weeks of neglect. He rinsed the hair with warm water and towel dried it, freeing flakes which fluttered to the cape like dirty snow. He combed the hair straight back and cut evenly, eliminating knots of bramble. Bartolo then removed the cape, snapped it clean and replaced it. He massaged Caiozzo's face with a hot towel to soften the stiff whiskers and followed with lather. Fontana then produced an ominous-looking straight razor and sharpened it on a thick leather belt, lickity split, and then began shaving with the precision of Da Vinci putting the smile on the face of the Mona Lisa. He gently patted with cool witch hazel and dramatically stepped back, removing the cape, to admire his work.

"And so, *Signore*, finished," Bartolo exclaimed proudly, as Caiozzo left the chair. "And now you are even a more handsome man than when you walked into my shop, if that is, of course, possible," Bartolo effusively proclaimed.

A grinning Caiozzo stood admiring the improvement in his appearance as he inspected the cut and shave in the mirror.

The barber did an excellent job, he grudgingly admitted to himself, and I must reward him well. The grin disappeared as he turned to Bartolo. "Yes, yes, thank you," he responded tersely, pressing *lire* into Fontana's hand.

"Ah, most generous, Don Caiozzo," Fontana thanked him, mock bowing at the waist. "And good luck tomorrow at Mass," he slyly added with a knowing grin. Caiozzo disappeared into the dusk and did not hear the last of Bartolo's farewell as the disappointed barber counted his *lire*.

"And on your way home, Caiozzo, may an asp bite you on the balls you stingy bastard."

Caiozzo stayed home that evening avoiding the tired spectacle at the Piazza Europa and the drunken fellowship of the tavern. He was intent on putting his best face forward for his carefully scripted plan to engage the Pepitones and Maria. He looked in the mirror somberly and ran his fingers over his skin, parched and dry like the soil in the vineyard when the rain didn't come. Nothing could improve the effects of years of weather and labor which had aged the face ten years. But he could control the presentation. At least he was clean-shaven with neatly trimmed hair, and unsightly growth did not curl from his cavities. On his next visit to Palermo to meet with the landowners, he vowed to consult a dentist to restore woefully neglected brown-stained teeth.

Caiozzo laid a fresh set of underwear and socks on a chair and hung a recently washed shirt on the back. He rummaged through a pile of clothing in his closet and found a pair of trousers, somewhat wrinkled, but free of stains from the vineyard or other unmentionable places. He cleaned the dirt and dust off his shoes and buffed them to a respectable shine with a rag dipped in melted candle wax. Caiozzo stripped, and scrubbed himself with a bar of coarse soap and rinsed with rosemary, floating in water warmed on the iron stove in the kitchen. He laughed heartily as the clean, pleasant aroma enveloped the room and exclaimed out loud, "Caiozzo you old artichoke, you have not smelled this good since the midwife delivered and cleaned you with her sack of herbs." He slipped naked in the dark under a clean sheet his mother had insisted on giving him, grinning like a contented infant, or a wolf sensing the prey.

The Pepitones arrived at the church exactly five minutes before the Mass began. They took their seats three pews from the altar. The second pew was always occupied by Don Bono and his family, the Mayor, Caiozzo and his mother, and other village dignitaries. The first pew remained unoccupied, the silly vestige of a long-held village superstition turned tradition, that it was reserved for the Spirit of the Holy Family and the apostles. Caiozzo and his mother arrived a few minutes later. To her surprise, he took her by the arm and insisted they sit five rows back, rather than their customary second row pew with the village dignitaries. She fussed at first then looked up at her son with his neatly-trimmed hair and clean-shaven face intently staring at the Pepitone family. Sofia instinctively divined her son's motive and quietly acquiesced.

Padre Pietro gravely droned on about the wages of sin, particularly sins of the flesh, a topic in which he had an inordinate interest. He freely cited Dante's *Inferno* as the inevitable destination of trespassers bound for dire eternal punishment. His harangue left the men sleeping, the women yawning, and the children terrified.

Caiozzo's eyes were stone-fixed on Maria Pepitone, sitting between her parents and listening with quiet reserve and respect to Pietro's homily.

Following the sermon and the passing of the collection basket, which always lightened the priest's manner, bringing a smile, the Pepitones rose as one to receive Holy Communion. As they returned, Caiozzo was struck by Maria's natural beauty, unadorned by cosmetics. Her curly black hair casually peeked from under a kerchief, framing unblemished lustrous skin and perfectly proportioned features. Her prayers of thanksgiving after Communion were offered with restrained dignity, without the affected exaggerated piety of so many other parishioners.

When the Mass ended, a smiling *Padre* Pietro in a fine silk robe, walked down the center aisle to the front door to await the departing congregation. Caiozzo quickly grabbed his mother's hand and hurried behind the priest, much to her annoyance. He wanted to be at the entrance, when Maria and her family arrived for his blatantly contrived meeting. Caiozzo boldly reminded the priest of the generosity of his offering and broadly hinted that it be mentioned as the Pepitones approached. Like everyone else, the priest was aware of Caiozzo's spouse hunt and understood his intent. He was not only happy to oblige but actually enjoyed his part in the charade.

"Good morning, Don and *signura* Caiozzo," the priest greeted them. "And a beautiful morning the Good Lord gives us, made more memorable, *signura* by the charity of your son, once again," he said, his voice rising slightly. "This good man," Pietro continued, patting Caiozzo's shoulder, "has learned the lesson of St. Paul very well."

"Thank you, *Padre*. But are we not our brother's keepers? We do what we can," Caiozzo said seriously, shuffling his feet in a gesture of false humility.

"Indeed! Indeed! And here standing beside you is the Pepitone family, also generous and kind members of our parish," the priest said.

Caiozzo turned with a surprised flourish and gushed, "Ah, *signura* and *signor* Pepitone. So good to see you again," he said extending a hand. The stunned couple looked at each other askance as they returned the greeting.

"Yes, and, a good morning to you Don Caiozzo and *signura*," Pepitone returned. Sofia silently acknowledged the greeting dismissively with a nod and pursed lips. Caiozzo then turned to Maria with a feigned, wide-eyed expression and exclaimed, "It cannot be! Is, is this your daughter, Maria, the little girl I gave almond candies to when she was no higher than my knee?" Maria had a vague recollection of once receiving sweets from the filthy hand of a foul-smelling man at the piazza.

"It is, *signor* Caiozzo," Pepitone replied. "Alas, she does what all our children do, grows up too fast and too soon before our very eyes."

"*Com'è beddu*, how beautiful," Caiozzo said softly, taking Maria's small hand in his palm and gently patting it with the other. Maria felt an instant revulsion as she looked up at Caiozzo's smiling face which seemed more a leer than a smile. She recalled a nursery tale Antonio read to her when she was a child. The fable, which may have originated in Italy, of a young girl dressed in red, lost in the woods, and accosted and devoured by a drooling wolf.

"So Maria, and how old are you now?" Caiozzo asked with mounting interest.

"I have just passed my 16th birthday, *signor* Caiozzo," Maria blankly replied. "Ah, just turned sixteen. Happy birthday, my dear. And at sixteen, with your beauty and charm, you must turn the heads of many young boys in the village," he remarked, probing.

The Pepitones were visibly uncomfortable with the direction of Caiozzo's remarks as Maria, lost for a response fidgeted nervously with her scarf, blushed and weakly said, "*Signor* Caiozzo, I, I, please....." Pepitone immediately interceded, firmly but respectfully. "Ah, *signor* Caiozzo, Maria has many interests and pursuits natural for a girl her age. But presently, boys are not among them." Caiozzo silently nodded in assent and *Padre* Pietro, feeling the embarrassing tension, excused himself to engage another family. Even Sofia Caiozzo's sensibilities were shaken at her son's obvious bungling efforts, and moved to end it.

"Giuseppe, I'm going to the *pasticceria* now to meet the other widows for coffee and cake," she said clutching her basket. "Yes, mamma," he said turning to her with a wink and a smile. "You go ahead to have coffee and cake with the other widows."

"Don't forget," she admonished, waving a finger in the air. "We eat today at three o'clock. Don't be late. *Addiu signore, signura* and Maria."

"*Addiu, signura* Caiozzo," the Pepitones replied in unison.

A chuckling Caiozzo turned back to the Pepitones.

"I let mamma go on thinking she is fooling me," he said throwing a thumb over his shoulder. "Her Sunday ploy of coffee and cake with the widows. Ha! How funny!"

The Pepitones looked confused as Amelia asked, "What do you mean, *signor* Caiozzo? I don't understand."

"The basket, *signura* Pepitone. Did you not see my mother clutching it as a mother cradles her child?" he asked.

"Yes, I saw," replied Amelia. "But what has that....."

"Eggs, *signura*, eggs," he impatiently interrupted. "She has eggs in that basket and sells them to the poor widows every Sunday after Mass to put a few miserable *lire* in her pocket. Why, I don't know," he continued. "Surely she doesn't need it. As I'm sure you're aware, I am quite capable of taking good care of my mother," he said boastfully clasping his suspenders and puffing his chest.

"Of course, Don Caiozzo. We are all sure that is true," Pepitone restively said, tiring of the burlesque. "Unfortunately we must end our conversation and be on our way. My son, Antonio, arrives on the 11 o'clock train from Palermo and we must be at the house to greet him."

"Your son. Antonio is it?," Caiozzo said placing a hand on Pepitone's shoulder.

"Yes, I've heard tell of that name from some of my associates in Palermo. The young man is making quite a reputation for himself. Please give him my regards."

"Thank you, I, I will," replied a puzzled Pepitone as he slowly backed away.

"And *signor* Pepitone," Caiozzo called after him. "We have been neighbors in this village for years but hardly know each other. Perhaps we could share a glass of wine at the tavern or a coffee at the *pasticceria* if you prefer."

"Yes, well, thank you," Pepitone called back. "My days are quite busy with this new commission I secured. But it is something to consider. *Ciao signor* Caiozzo."

"Yeah, *ciao*," Caiozzo responded with quiet irritation.

He has no intention of considering anything, Caiozzo thought. That high-minded tanner thinks he and his family are too good for me. I can sense it in his tone. But I won't be so easily dismissed, he determinedly vowed.

CHAPTER 4

Amelia Pepitone's brow wrinkled and her teeth gripped taut lips as she busied herself in the kitchen preparing the Sunday dinner of roast goat, marinated potatoes and sauted escarole. Nino sat at the table silently watching his wife, wringing his hands, and uncharacteristically, drinking a late morning glass of grappa. Both were absorbed in thought about the encounter with Caiozzo but Amelia was particularly concerned. She reflected on a conversation she recently had with Celestina, the butcher's wife, in the village.

"Amelia," Celestina asked, "have you heard that the bachelor Caiozzo is on the hunt for a wife?"

"No, Celestina, I have not heard. Nor does it interest me. Why should I have an interest in Caiozzo's affairs,?" Amelia asked, puzzled.

"Well," Celestina responded with the glee of a gossip who had juicy news to impart, "the talk in the village is he may be interested in your Maria."

"What?" Amelia snapped in wide eyed surprise. "That is laughable. A man his age with his sordid reputation seeking the attention of my Maria? Well, he can seek all he wants but it will come to nothing. Maria is not for him. And you can tell that to the busy body *chiacchiruni* in the village when you next see them, Amelia said dismissively."

Amelia bid Celestina a curt, "Addiu," and went on her way. The idea was so preposterous to her she gave it no further thought and even forgot to mention it to her husband. But now, because of the morning encounter with Caiozzo on the church steps, she felt compelled to relate her conversation with Celestina to Nino. He responded with surprising calm, and attempted to minimize the significance of and any connection between the two events, arousing Amelia's anger.

"You sit there calmly drinking grappa, following this morning's encounter and after I tell you that Caiozzo may be stalking our daughter," Amelia said whispering.

"Amelia, you are overreacting," Pepitone responded quietly. "We don't know for certain this is true. It is not the first time, nor will it be the last, that the village *chiacchiruni* have manufactured a rumor for their perverted pleasure and, more often than not, their cackling means nothing."

"Nino, I cannot believe you," Amelia angrily began, when the door in the small hallway swung open.

Antonio walked in, smiling, carrying a bouquet of bright yellow sunflowers in one hand and a copy of Jane Austen's *Mansfield Park* in the other.

"*Ciao*, Mamma, Papa, Maria!," he boomed with the genuine enthusiasm of a son happy to be home with his family.

"*Ciao beddu, Ciao* Antonio," the parents called back as they moved from the kitchen to the hallway and embraced their son. A smiling Maria bounded out of the salon and wrapped her arms around her brother's neck, kissing him on both cheeks.

"What beautiful flowers," Maria gushed. "And what's that you have in your other hand behind your back?" she playfully asked her brother.

"Nothing, Maria, what, ...nothing at all," he teased, circling and frustrating his sister as she tried to reach around him and snatched at empty air.

"Antonio," Amelia pleaded smiling, "stop tormenting your poor sister."

"Amelia," Nino said taking her hand, "this is what brothers and sisters do. Have you forgotten?," he reminded her wistfully.

"All right, all right *principessa*," Antonio relented, handing the book to Maria.

"Oh'," Maria exclaimed, "Jane Austen, *Mansfield Park*. I know of this book. *Grazzii, frati*," she said kissing his cheek. "And did you make a good bargain with Luchino?," she asked with a laugh.

"Any price is a bargain if it is for you, Maria," he answered warmly. The parents smiled, gratified to see their children so devoted to each other, as Nino massaged his wife's shoulders. His hands dropped to his sides as Amelia abruptly turned and went back to the kitchen proclaiming, "I must complete the preparation for dinner.

And you, my dear Nino," she said, turning to point at her husband, "must, of course, finish your early morning glass of grappa." He smiled sheepishly and dropped his chin as he walked out.

Maria and her brother sat in the salon as she thumbed through the pages of *Mansfield Park* and Antonio read the Sunday newspaper. Breaking the silence, she asked her brother, "Antonio, why is it the British have women who write stories, stories about heroic women, and here in Sicily, we have neither?"

Antonio dropped the newspaper on his lap and reflected a moment before replying.

"That's a fine question with an unhappy answer," he responded. "Unfortunately, Maria, our country does not value reading, or education in general, especially for women. Other countries in Europe and in America approach the 20th century with the promise and hope of a new day but we, in Sicily, are mired in stupid tradition and bound by foolish attitudes."

"But is it possible," Maria asked hopeful, "that such women as Jane Eyre and Fanny Price could really exist?"

"Yes Maria," Antonio said smiling, "if something can be imagined, it can become reality. The Bronte sisters and Jane Austen could see beyond the horizon, and give women everywhere cause for optimism."

The dinner was uncomfortably quiet without the usual laughter, interesting discussion and gossip. Maria finished quickly, asked to be excused, and went into the salon to read.

"So," Antonio drawled looking perplexed at his parents, "what is the problem here? What is wrong? My instincts tell me you are hiding something and I insist that you tell me."

An uneasy silence pervaded the room as Amelia glared at her husband then exploded with anger.

"Tell him Nino," she said, "tell your son what happened today on the steps of the church after Mass."

"Amelia, please," Pepitone implored. "Let us finish our meal, this fine roast goat you prepared, without discussing some odd, isolated occurrence."

Antonio put his fork down and looked at his father with distressed interest.

"So what happened at the church today, papa?" he asked.

"It's nothing Antonio, nothing. Your mother is reading...."

"Nothing papa? Then why are you quarreling, with mamma close to tears, and Maria excuses herself before we have finished our meal?"

"Well," Amelia explained, worried, "I am very upset by what happened today outside the church. That Caiozzo whom we haven't exchanged more than twenty words with all these years is suddenly very friendly. He engages us in conversation after Mass, then invites your father for coffee. Does that not seem strange to you Antonio?"

"Well, yes, perhaps," Antonio replied, "but maybe he's just offering you friendship after all these years. Maybe he's really a decent fellow who just wants to get to know you better."

"My dear Antonio," Amelia said shaking her head, "for an intelligent young man you are very naïve. There is nothing decent about him. He takes advantage of people to fatten his purse and uses young women shamefully for his pleasure. No Antonio, the wolf does not change his ways. I am suspicious of his motive and his intent, and I am very angry with your father for failing to make it clear that he wants nothing to do with Caiozzo. He should have refused that man's invitation outright," she said glaring at her husband.

Nino looked aside, cradled his chest in his arms, and nervously shifted in his chair.

"Amelia, please," he timidly began, "I did not want to make him an enemy by insulting him. And as you recall," he hastily added, "I never made a commitment to meet with him." Pepitone reached out to pat his wife's arm saying, "Amelia, in a week this will all pass and be forgotten."

"No Nino," Amelia quietly said, pulling her arm back, "this is like thunder on a clear day rumbling in the distance. I fear it may be the beginning of something very unpleasant. That man is uncomfortably persistent and has the odor of evil about him." Amelia was thinking about the *chiacchiruni* rumor which they did not share with Antonio. She rose abruptly and went into the kitchen to make the espresso and plate the *cassata*.

Antonio moved closer to his father and whispered.

"Papa," he said, "do you remember two weeks ago in Palermo when you warned me about evil lurking behind a tree? Perhaps you should heed your own warning and give this incident more consideration," he advised.

"Don't you think I have," Pepitone testily replied. "It has been on my mind all day and even compelled me to take a drink before noon to quiet my nerves. I made little of it because I did not want to show concern and alarm your mother and sister. But I need time to think this through," he said tensely. "I cannot act in haste and anger a man like Caiozzo who has a strong place in this village and powerful connections in Palermo."

"I understand, Papa," Antonio said nodding with concern. It saddened him to see his parents so upset and he reached for his father's hand.

"Whatever I can do..."

"I know, my son, I know...Ah!," Pepitone broke off, forcing delight, "but here is your mother with the coffee and *cassata*."

CHAPTER 5

Nino Pepitone was a very precise and orderly man. He arose every morning at exactly seven a.m., one half hour after Amelia, who was already pressing the coffee beans and slicing the bread in the kitchen. He shaved, scrubbed with soap, rinsed, dried with a fluffy towel, and put on a fresh set of underwear. He tied a cravat around the collar of a clean white shirt and slipped the tails into trousers with dangling suspenders. Black sox and sturdy work shoes completed his dress for the day.

Pepitone's small shop on Via Minore was clean, tidy and organized, and, in an instant, he could put his hand on whatever he needed in the way of treated skin, tools or stitching thread. The sewing needles and cutting instruments were neatly arranged according to size and function. Nothing was wasted, neither time nor material. He established a strict schedule for the completion of each piece and, nearly always, the merchandise was delivered as promised. His work habits reflected the kind of man he was as a husband, father, and good Christian neighbor. Undisturbed and secure in his daily routine, he believed that God was in His Heaven and all was right with the world....Happy in his work, blessed with a devoted wife and children, he was a contented man. Like Job, he was perfect and upright, a man who feared God and eschewed evil, and he had no reason to suspect that his world, like Job's, was about to be upended.

Every morning at ten o'clock Pepitone locked the door of his shop and walked the five minutes to the *pasticceria* for a cappuccino and a *cannolu*, allowing himself exactly one half hour. He smiled as he felt the wet build in his mouth, anticipating the crisp brown shell filled with creamy ricotta and specks of chocolate or pistachio nuts, the perfect mid-morning break which satisfied him until one o'clock and his main meal taken at home with Amelia and Maria.

Caiozzo had been stewing over his abrupt and disappointing encounter with Pepitone on the church steps. Determined to create a situation where he could spontaneously meet Pepitone again, he ordered Mosca, one of his three *citrulli* (a deprecating Sicilian word for jerk), to shadow Pepitone and report his daily activities. Since Pepitone's schedule never varied, this was an easy assignment, even for the feeble-witted Mosca. He followed Pepitone for two days from 8 a.m. to 7 in the evening and gave Caiozzo a remarkably full and accurate account.

A few days later, Caiozzo hitched the mule to his cart and left simple but exact instructions to the three *citrulli*, Lorenzo, Ciuto and Mosca, regarding the work and supervision of the men during his morning absence from the vineyard. Mosca, the dullest of the three, was preoccupied, nibbling on a piece of cheese with the strange and irksome habit of frenetically massaging his fingertips as he ate, earning him the nickname, "Fly," or Mosca. Caiozzo glowered as he repeated the instructions for the inattentive Mosca, threatened him with a beating and finally, exasperated, turned the mule down the road toward the village, throwing his hands in the air and cursing the poor dimwit's ancestors with a string of obscenities.

In the village, Pepitone approached the *pasticceria* and was surprised to see Caiozzo there in an animated, one way conversation with the village butcher, Cenna, whose brow was creased and expression bewildered. As Caiozzo turned to greet Pepitone, the butcher took the opportunity and quickly walked away, shaking his head and muttering, "That man's mouth moves, he speaks, but he says nothing."

"*Signor* Pepitone!," Caiozzo exclaimed extending a hand. He feigned great delight in this supposedly unexpected encounter. The color drained from Pepitone's face as he took the hand and forced a cordial reply.

"Good morning Don Caiozzo. I'm pleased to see you again."

"What a fortunate coincidence," Caiozzo said. "I took some time off from the vineyard to conduct necessary business in the village and here, here you are. You know," Caiozzo said leaning forward conspiratorially, "the success of our business not only depends on the actual hands-on work we do, but also in the behind the scenes maneuvering. But good business man that you are, I'm not telling you something you don't know," he said winking.

"Quite true," Pepitone dryly agreed.

"Well now, come and allow me to buy you that coffee I promised," Caiozzo said placing a firm arm around Pepitone's shoulders and guiding him toward the entrance of the *pasticceria*.

"Thank you, Don Caiozzo, but my time is very limited," Pepitone replied nervously. "I always return to my shop by 10:30 and it is already half near that hour."

"Nonsense, my friend," Caiozzo said tightening his grip. "We all need a little extra time away from our labors and, ha!, your skins at the shop are long past the form when they could run away from you."

"Yes, but really, I...." Pepitone weakly responded.

Caiozzo's eyes glared and his face hardened. "But I insist," he imposed.

"Well, I, I guess a few minutes more can't hurt," Pepitone reluctantly agreed.

"Good, good," Caiozzo said smiling warmly again.

At Caiozzo's suggestion they took a table by the window.

Cheerfully, Caiozzo said, "I like sitting here looking out at the people in our little village passing and going about their daily business."

Yes, thought Pepitone nauseated, you like to know everybody's business. Keeping your thumb on the pulse of the village gives you the knowledge you require to exercise control and sustain your power.

"So Nino…may I call you Nino?" Caiozzo asked. "Formality is wearisome and seems dated as we approach a new century."

"If you prefer," replied Pepitone.

"I do, I do," Caiozzo said, determined. "And please refer to me as, 'Giuseppe'. This 'Don' business is nothing more than an empty label which, for reasons that escape me," he said modestly shrugging, "the neighbors have conferred."

"As you wish. Thank you D…Giuseppe," Pepitone replied.

"Now," Caiozzo began, "when we last spoke on the steps of the church, you mentioned you were engaged in a commissioned work. May I inquire what it is?" he asked. Pepitone hesitated for a moment then, reluctantly answered.

"When I was in Palermo last month…"

"Yes, you make frequent trips to Palermo. Three or four times a year isn't it?," Caiozzo interrupted.

Pepitone was astonished that this man knew so much about his movements, astonished and annoyed. And when he thought about the incident on the church steps and the rumor Amelia had conveyed to him about Maria, he became anxious as well.

My god, he thought, this son of a bitch knows my every move and time table.

"When I was last in Palermo," Pepitone repeated, "I was fortunate to receive a commission on a detailed set of luggage, which may take three or more months to complete. So, you see, my day is full and my time strictly budgeted," he added hastily.

"*Bravo*, Nino. But it is a time consuming and a laborious task for which I hope you will be well rewarded. Ha! If you don't mind my saying, you have your work cut out for you."

Pepitone cringed and his instinct was to ignore the stupid pun, but he thought better of it and smiled.

"I hope you have not underpriced your pieces," Caiozzo said leaning forward. "I hear the sellers in Palermo, thieves that they are, have significantly increased the price of their skins, a move which could hurt your profit."

"Yes D…..Giuseppe. I have also heard these rumors. But I am satisfied with the price I paid," Pepitone answered.

"Because, you know," Caiozzo said ignoring Pepitone's response, "I have a few contacts in that business in Palermo. If you wish, I could have a word with them and perhaps you might strike a better bargain and increase your profit."

Does this man never stop his prodding and interfering? Pepitone wondered. And does he take me for a fool? Yes, he'll have a word with his contacts, pay 110,000 for 120,000 *lire* worth of skin, sell it to me for 115,000 and pocket the rest."

"Thank you very much for your generous offer," Pepitone said, "but the Buontempos and my family have been doing business for generations. I am content with the price and the quality of the goods, and would rather maintain my relationship with that family."

"I understand," Caiozzo said smiling, "but remember, misplaced loyalty should never put a good profit at risk."

Pepitone's discomfort became unendurable as he felt his underarms moistening and the immediate urge to flee.

"But now, *signor* Caiozzo," Pepitone said draining and placing his empty cup on the saucer, "I beg your indulgence. Thank you for the coffee but I really must return to my shop and continue work on the commission. I am already behind schedule."

"Of course Nino, of course. As we sit here I can hear the animals howling for your attention," Caiozzo said laughing.

Again with the witless remark, Pepitone thought.

"Yes, well, in any case, I must go. Thank you again Giuseppe."

Pepitone rose from the table and walked quickly toward the exit. His body stiffened when, from behind, he heard words delivered in a manner that turned his skin cold and made the hair on his neck rise; "I will see you again soon Nino." There was an audible menacing edge in Caiozzo's voice.

Pepitone closed his shop early that afternoon and hurried home through the blistering midday heat, arriving sweat-soaked and shaken.

"Nino!," Amelia exclaimed, "you're early. The *minestra* is not yet even ready and ...*Diu miu*, my God," she said laughing, "did you fall into a well?"

"Where is Maria?," Pepitone asked nervously.

"She's at the Stuffas visiting with Agata," Amelia replied.

"Why Nino, what's wrong?" You don't look well and your face is as pale as flour," Amelia said putting her hands to his cheek.

"Sit down, Amelia, please," Nino said.

"Let me get you a cup of cool water," Amelia offered.

"Amelia," Pepitone shouted, "will you please sit down."

"Nino," she demanded, shaken, "what's wrong?"

Pepitone ran trembling hands along his thighs as he sat and collected his thoughts.

"Amelia," he said, "I think your fears about Caiozzo may be justified. I confess I also had concerns after our conversation with him on the church steps. I didn't say anything to spare you more worry. But events this morning have convinced me that your suspicions may be quite correct."

Amelia breathed heavily and she slowly sank to a chair. His words made her sick with apprehension.

"Why, what happened Nino?," she asked.

"This morning,...this morning, when I approached the *pasticceria* to take my morning coffee, I found Caiozzo at the entrance talking with the butcher, Cenna," Pepitone replied.

"Yes, and,?" Amelia asked anxiously.

"This was a sham, Amelia," he said, his voice rising, "a carefully planned scenario for an encounter with me. He knew my schedule exactly, and was waiting for my arrival."

Her voice began to quiver.

"How can you be so sure? Perhaps it was just a coincidence," she hoped. Amelia knew it was not a coincidence but was trying to allay her mounting fears.

"It was pathetically obvious," Pepitone continued. "Caiozzo used Cenna as a prop so his intent would be obscured. I could see it was a one way conversation, with Caiozzo talking and waving his arms at Cenna like a madman." Pepitone's agitation grew as he went on, recalling the incident.

"The butcher looked bewildered and, as soon as Caiozzo turned to greet me, Cenna used the opportunity to make a hasty retreat, without so much as an *addiu*. Caiozzo then practically forced me into the *pasticceria* under the pretense of sharing a cup of coffee.

Amelia, he knew too much about my business and schedule. The trips to Palermo, the increase in the price of the skins, matters which should be of no interest or concern to him. He even offered to broker an arrangement whereby I might purchase material at reduced cost form his connections in Palermo."

Pepitone suddenly paused and reflected, then whispered, "Palermo."

"What, what about Palermo?" Amelia asked.

"Last Sunday on the steps of the church, Caiozzo referred to Antonio, mentioning his growing reputation, 'making a big name for himself' were the words he used. I did not think he even knew Antonio's name much less where he lived and the nature of his work. But there he was relating our own son's activities to us. My God, this man's tentacles reach everywhere," Pepitone moaned.

"What else happened at the *pasticceria* today, Nino?" Amelia asked.

Pepitone shook his head and resumed his account.

"I thanked Caiozzo for his offer, declining it of course, made my excuses, and got up to leave. I thought I was safely free as I neared the exit until I heard words that were ominous and chillingly delivered," Pepitone said as his voice trailed off.

"What words, Nino,?" Amelia asked with mounting concern.

Pepitone looked vacuously past his wife as he uttered Caiozzo's threatening words: 'I will see you again soon, Nino.'

"Amelia," he said, beginning to break, "it sounded like the voice of doom. I have never felt so weak, so helpless and intimidated. A malevolent force seemed to drain the strength from my body," he said suppressing a sob.

Amelia rose from the chair and went to her husband, gently caressing his head at her breasts as she tasted salt from the tears running down her cheeks. Pepitone wrapped his arms around Amelia's waist and they held each other tightly, quietly sharing the same terrible fear. And Nino heard the echo of *Padre* Pietro's words and understood their meaning too well;

"The strong do what they will.

The weak do what they must."

CHAPTER 6

It was two weeks since the village encounter with Caiozzo, and Pepitone stopped going to the bakery for his morning coffee. Instead he walked ten minutes in the opposite direction to his home on Via Bovia to be with Amelia and Maria. It added a half hour to his work day but he hoped he could elude Caiozzo altogether. He had, in fact, heard nothing more from Caiozzo but remained vigilant nevertheless.

The Pepitones did not want to alarm Maria with their concerns but urged her to be cautious at all times. When visiting the village, she must always be in the company of a friend. And she would have to discontinue her solitary walks to the outskirts of the village where she enjoyed sitting and reading in her own little pastoral retreat. They had also suspended attendance at Sunday Mass giving Maria the excuse that her father and *Padre* Pietro had a falling out over the distribution of the *lire* from the poor box.

"Yes," Maria confirmed, "I remember, papa, your mentioning concern about the *Padre* and the *lire* on our return from Palermo last month. But is there something else wrong, papa,?" Maria asked sensing that her parents were concealing something. "You are restricting my activities more than you did last year when I was fifteen. It seems strange and almost funny," she said forcing a laugh.

"Maria," Pepitone began solemnly, "Luongo, the captain of the *carabinieri*, was in the shop yesterday to purchase a billfold to hold the new paper *lire* the government is beginning to distribute. He told me he was receiving reports from the surrounding villages of bands of marauding gypsies stealing from and terrorizing locals and tourists."

"I have heard nothing of this, papa," Maria said wondering.

"No, Maria, and you won't," Pepitone replied. "And please do not mention any of this to your friends. Luongo shared this with me as a courtesy and swore me to secrecy. If this information gets out it may cause panic and hurt the tourist trade on which so many of us depend. It is a threat that will pass. Gypsies never stay in one place. They always move on. In the meantime, you must be very careful. You will promise won't you,?" he entreated.

"As you wish, papa, *ti lu prumettu*, I promise," Maria responded.

Amelia overheard the elaborate fabrication from the kitchen and entered the salon grinning. She threw her arms around her husband's neck and said with a mischievous smile, "Nino, I never suspected your talent for weaving so convincing a tale. From now on I must watch you more closely," she teased. They hugged and enjoyed a much needed moment of laughter.

"What's going on in there,?" Maria called.

"Nothing for your young ears to hear, *beddu*. Your silly father just made a joke," Amelia responded.

. . .

Caiozzo ripped a large piece of bread from the heel of the loaf with his teeth, and stuffed his mouth with a chunk of goat cheese and black olives. He spat, arching the pits of the olives a few feet away with the skill of a man practiced over many years, washed the bread and cheese down with a long draught of red wine, and wiped his mouth clean on his shirt sleeve. By the manner in which he ate, Lorenzo was not sure if he was watching a man who was very hungry or very angry. Caiozzo began to rant.

"That damn tanner is successfully avoiding me," he said to Lorenzo who was sitting quietly on the grass with his arms wrapped around drawn knees.

"He no longer," Caiozzo continued, "takes his morning break at the *pasticceria*, the door of his shop is always locked, and the shutters on the windows are closed, although I can hear movement inside. And the family has not been at Sunday Mass for two weeks," he added.

Lorenzo picked on a few blades of grass, tossed them, then coolly opined, "Perhaps, Don Caiozzo, your approach has been too timid. You are a man who sets his sights on a goal, acts boldly, and always accomplishes his mission, by whatever means necessary. You may need to take more aggressive action in this matter, Don Caiozzo," Lorenzo suggested, leering.

Caiozzo rolled and lit a cigarette, slowly inhaled, and pensively looked at Lorenzo with a crooked smile.

"You know, Lorenzo," he said with his eyes brightening, "occasionally you surprise me with your observations and counsel, unlike the other two who think as often as a clam. Yes, yes. A good peg to hang an idea on. I will give your words careful consideration. But come now, we have work to complete," he said rising, patting Lorenzo on the back.

Lorenzo smiled with the satisfaction of a young son praised and preferred by a proud father, validating his status over his brothers.

Good neighbor Stuffa had been out hunting rabbit early Sunday morning and appeared at the Pepitones' door with a neat kill.

"Ah Enzo, *bon giornu*, and what have we here?" Amelia exclaimed. "Yet another example of your fine marksmanship," she said.

"It is as you see it, *signura*. But more importantly, it is for your table and family to enjoy."

"Enzo, you are too kind," Amelia replied. "I couldn't,...I..."

"Nonsense," Enzo said producing two more from behind his back. "There is more than enough for my family."

"A very good day for the hunter," Amelia said, laughing. "Please, please come in."

"Only for a moment Amelia. I have been out all morning and, *la signura* has expected me home long ago."

"An *espresso*, or *cappuccinu* and *biscottu*?" Amelia offered.

"*Cafè no, biscottu, no, grazzii*," Stuffa answered. "But perhaps a little grappa to warm my chilled bones,?" he asked.

"Of course," she said, laughing.

"And where is Nino," Stuffa asked looking around the kitchen.

"Oh, Enzo," Amelia replied, "he works so long on the Palermo commission that I let him sleep longer on Sunday. We even miss Mass," she said, obviously a little embarrassed.

"Yes, I know." Stuffa replied, settling into a chair. "We have noticed your absence." Amelia ignored the remark, placed a glass of grappa on the table and changed the subject.

"So, all is well with your family,?" Amelia inquired.

"Yes, *tuttu va beni*, all is well," Stuffa replied. He then leaned forward, pulling himself away from the back of the chair and looked directly into Amelia's eyes.

"Amelia," he said, "*la signura* and I are worried. We hear whispers in the village, disturbing talk about your family and troubles with this Caiozzo character."

"Enzo, you hear whispers from crazy old women who have nothing more to do than gossip," she snapped. "There is no problem…everything is fine."

"Amelia, I take you at your word," Stuffa said. "But if there's anything I can do, anything at all…,"

"Thank you Enzo, but all is well," Amelia interrupted smiling.

"*Allora*, so then," Enzo said draining his glass. "I'll be on my way before I myself am skinned like the rabbit. But Amelia, if…"

"Thank you again Enzo, you are a good and faithful friend and this family is appreciative," Amelia said, embracing Stuffa. "But," she paused for a moment, "Enzo, could you please see Maria home before two o'clock,?" she asked. He smiled and reached out to pat her lightly on the shoulder; "I will Amelia, *ciao*."

As Stuffa walked up Via Bologna to his home he considered Amelia's odd request to see Maria home. She had never asked this and seemed nervous and fearful, he thought.

It was a very fine rabbit, full and round but young enough to be tender.

Nino will be so pleased, Amelia thought. I'll prepare it *cacciatore* in honor of the hunter.

She carried the rabbit by the ears to the cutting block outside. The sharp knife cut through the neck with one pass. Amelia skinned, cleaned out the entrails, split and washed the pieces with cool water from the well. She patted it dry with a towel, brushed with olive oil and placed it in the wood burning oven to brown.

As Amelia walked toward the kitchen to finish cooking the tomato sauce, she was startled by a voice from the shadows of the trees.

"*Bon giornu, signura* Pepitone."

"What, who's there?" she exclaimed.

Caiozzo moved slowly into the sunlight, peeling an orange with his teeth and spitting the skin on the ground.

"We have missed you at Mass the past two Sundays, and I have not seen your husband at his usual place every morning in the village. I was concerned. I hope all is well," Caiozzo said.

"What are you doing here? What do you want, Caiozzo,?" Amelia demanded.

"Caiozzo? I recall telling your husband he needn't refer to me as, 'Don,' but I don't remember giving you permission to disrespectfully address me by my family name," Caiozzo replied.

"I don't care what you remember. Get out of here. Leave now...or,"

"Or what?" Caiozzo shot back. "I am not here to discuss anything with you. This is business between men. Now where is your husband?" he demanded.

"He's not available to you," Amelia replied defiantly.

"Not available? Then make him available, *signura*. It's in the best interest of your family," Caiozzo said, with deadened menace.

Amelia was numbed but too fearful to speak.

"Amelia, who are you talking to?" Pepitone asked as he staggered out the door rubbing his eyes. Amelia ran to her husband and hooked his arm.

Seeing this unwelcome visitor in his home, Pepitone gasped, "Caiozzo,".

"I thought we were on a first name basis, Nino," Caiozzo said finishing the last of the orange and wiping his hands on his trousers.

"Where is Maria,?" Pepitone whispered to his wife.

"She's at the Stuffas with Agata," Amelia whispered back.

"Nino, tell your wife to go into the kitchen and stir that wonderful *condimento* I smell cooking before it sticks and burns. We have business to discuss," Caiozzo said.

"Do not assume you can come to my home and order my wife about, Giuseppe," Pepitone snapped. "And we have no business to discuss," Pepitone raged as his face turned crimson and the veins in his neck swelled.

"Yes we do, Nino, yes we do," Caiozzo said calmly, beckoning Pepitone to him.

"Nino?" Amelia looked at her husband.

"Please, Amelia, go inside. It's best that I handle this without you here," Pepitone replied.

"But Nino, I....."

"Amelia, please," Pepitone insisted gently.

Amelia left with her face in her hands, sobbing.

Pepitone walked slowly toward Caiozzo, ignoring his extended hand.

"Let's sit here on this bench," Caiozzo patted it, "where the cool of the shade can temper the heat of the moment."

"What do you want? Why do you haunt me, Giuseppe? Have you no decency? Do you not see the anguish you inflict on my family?"

"That is not my intention, Nino. I have no wish to cause trouble for your family," Caiozzo said.

"Then how do you explain your behavior?" Pepitone demanded.

"Nino, I know you are a wise and perceptive man," Caiozzo said, "and although I am not a made member of 'The Friends of Friends,' my connections are well-known."

"Oh! You do not wish to cause trouble, but you threaten me with your nefarious connections," Pepitone countered caustically.

"Not at all," Caiozzo said. "I merely mention this, as I did previously when we had coffee in the village. I wish to offer you an opportunity to grow your business, your profit, and secure your family's future."

"Secure my family's future?" Pepitone echoed mocking.

"Yes, simply, if you pay less for your material and extend your market, which I can assist you with, you cannot but help increase your profit."

"I have need of neither," Pepitone said. "But I am confused. Your bothersome and intimidating behavior, and your presence here today are nothing more than a benevolent desire to help a man you hardly know?"

"*Bravo*, Nino. I'm impressed," Caiozzo said nodding his head.

"What then," Pepitone asked, "would you want in return? You are not known as a man who gives favors away."

"Nino," Caiozzo began, "it is no secret that I have decided to marry. The *chiacchiruni* in the village have been talking about nothing else, and it is the main topic in the barbershop of that weasel Fontana. I will come directly to the point, with all due respect. I am here to ask for the hand of your daughter in the Blessed Sacrament of marriage."

"My daughter," Pepitone choked, although he'd sensed it was coming.

"There is no one in this village, or anywhere else," Caiozzo continued, "whom I would rather have as my wife than Maria. Her beauty, intelligence, good humor and spiritual qualities are..."

"I don't need you to remind me of my daughter's qualities, Caiozzo," Pepitone said, cutting him off.

"...are unmatched," Caiozzo continued, unfazed. "I can offer your daughter a lifetime of protection and security and help you grow your business tenfold."

"So," Pepitone said, "you are asking me to sell my daughter to you in return for your offer of a lifetime of protection and security."

"Sell, offer," Caiozzo said waving his hand. "These are ugly words, Nino. I prefer, 'mutually beneficial arrangement,' which is, as you know, a common practice among our people. Arranged marriages have taken place in Sicily, in all of Italy for that matter, for centuries, and we are none the worse for it."

"*Veru*, quite true," Pepitone replied. "But as long as I breath, I will never consent to this *infamia* and give my daughter to you."

"Measure your words carefully, Nino. Your breath may run out sooner than your resolve," Caiozzo grimly admonished.

"Again with the threats, Giuseppe. This is not the Sicily of old. You can't go around intimidating people to bend them to your will," Pepitone thundered.

"Nino, you are reading too many of your son's articles in the *giurnali*, the newspaper. Some things have not changed in Sicily," Caiozzo said rising from the bench. "Think it over. Discuss it with your wife and daughter. But no one else," he warned, "especially that 'fine marksman' neighbor of yours, Stuffa."

As he was leaving, Caiozzo turned to Pepitone and, in an unmistakably threatening tone said, "I'll see you again in one week, Nino."

"Fuck you, Caiozzo, fuck you," Pepitone shouted as Caiozzo walked away.

CHAPTER 7

Amelia had been listening at the door and fell into her husband's arms crying uncontrollably and stammering.

"He...he... he mentioned Stuffa to you in his warning, Nino. Caiozzo was here all morning," Amelia said, clinging to her husband and trying not to break down.

"What are you talking about, Amelia?" Pepitone demanded, holding her close to him. She pushed her husband away and forced him to look into her eyes and said trembling, "Stuffa was here this morning with a rabbit for us. I praised him for being a 'fine marksman,' and that was the way Caiozzo described him to you this morning."

Pepitone paused to reflect then flatly affirmed, "He was here all morning, well before my encounter with him..."

"Yes, yes, Nino, don't you see?" she said, vexed by his slowness in grasping the awful truth." He was watching and listening from the woods and the bramble, like a hunter stalking prey. I was moving in and out of the kitchen and left the door open and the shutters unhinged. He heard every word of my conversation with Enzo."

Pepitone slumped into a chair and put his head in his hands as Amelia stood over him nearly beside herself with rage and fear. "We suspected his intentions, and now this outrageous proposal. What are we going to do, Nino?" Amelia demanded. "What are you going to do?"

"I don't know, Amelia," Pepitone responded weakly. "I don't know. Let me think for a moment."

Seeing his weakness intensified her rage and fear, but she was able to collect herself and view the situation rationally. What was called for was decisive action. In a cool, deliberately calm voice she told her husband, "The time for thinking is long past. We must act now before it is too late." He could hardly argue with her.

"All right, all right," he agreed, restively. Yes, he needed to act resolutely. "Tomorrow, before I open the shop, I'll go directly to Luongo at the station and..."

"And what?" Amelia demanded. "Tell Luongo that Caiozzo is a madman obsessed with our daughter and he stalks us and comes to our home early on a Sunday morning and scouts us from the woods? And what will Luongo do as he considers our complaint? I'll tell you what," she continued, "he'll tell you that Caiozzo is just an overzealous suitor whose only infraction is trespassing. He'll ask you what other law he has broken and you will not have an answer. And even if you did, what would the courts do? Give him a stern lecture, a warning and a fine? Would that solve our problem, Nino?"

Pepitone stared into space, listening to his wife, unable to contradict anything she was saying and unwilling to cross her in this state of maternal outrage. Her question was rhetorical. He didn't try to answer it and Amelia continued.

"The law in Sicily has always ignored these stalking incidents by determined men, and the benumbed and dull-witted villagers of Sicilians have always clung to and honored these barbaric traditions of the past." It was apparent, even to Pepitone, that their son, Antonio, had inherited his capacity for fiery eloquence from his mother.

"What would you have me...?"

"Have you do?" Amelia interrupted. "Do you remember a few years ago when those speculators from Napoli approached Stuffa with an offer to buy all that land he owns above the vineyard?" she asked.

"Yes, of course," Pepitone answered. "Stuffa refused to sell."

"Yes," Amelia acknowledged, "he refused to sell despite pressure and threats. And the land is still his today. And the Neapolitans disappeared and were not heard from again."

"Yes, Amelia," Pepitone said, "I remember. But Stuffa had the backing of his cousins, important people from Alcamo and..." He paused, tilted his head and asked, "What are you thinking, Amelia?"

"Nino," Amelia began deliberately, "we have known Enzo and Nina for many years. Their daughter, Agata, and Maria have grown up together. They are good and trusted neighbors. Enzo didn't come here this morning just to give us a rabbit for our table."

"What do you mean?" Pepitone asked.

"Enzo told me he heard talk in the village of some problems we are having and asked me if all was well."

"What did you tell him?", Pepitone asked.

"Tell him, tell him?," Amelia answered, "why nothing of course. I didn't want to get him involved. But I know he doubted me. He kept offering his assistance and, before he left, he turned very serious and emphasized, 'anything, anything I can do,' in his offer."

"Then it is possible Caiozzo overheard everything in your conversation with Enzo," Pepitone said.

"Possible?", Amelia said, "assuredly it is so. I think Caiozzo was close enough to touch me," she added chillingly.

Having listened to his wife speak her mind at length, Pepitone took his time formulating an appropriate response. Finally, realizing her intent, he said, "Amelia, I know you want to act immediately and decisively. Maybe Caiozzo should fear you," he added in a vain attempt to lighten the moment.

"But we need to decide wisely what we will do. If we don't choose wisely, we may bring disaster on ourselves and, God forbid, also on Maria." He then put a finger to his lips, "Hush now," he said, "I hear Maria coming. We can continue this discussion tonight on the bench outside when Maria goes to bed."

They embraced tightly, both yearning for reassurance. Amelia closed her eyes and felt some relief as she clung to the hope that they could find a resolution, while Pepitone tried to convince himself that matters weren't beyond his control. There had to be a way to deal with Caiozzo.

. . .

Vendemmia, the gathering of the grapes, was in its fifth and final week and the landowners, anxious to complete the harvest before the weather turned against them, pressed Caiozzo to double the work force, a boon for thirty more families who might see enough *lire* to last them through Christmas. Caiozzo was forced to suspend acting on his plan to obtain the object of his desire, and this gave the Pepitones more time to develop their defense.

Stuffa had now been thoroughly apprised of the situation, a revelation he hardly needed. He devised a strategy involving his cousins from Alcamo, three fearless and resourceful men willing to work for little *lire* on behalf of their relative.

Stuffa himself was, by any account, fearless but wise and prudent as well. Before bringing his cousins to Castellammare, Stuffa requested and was granted an audience with Don Angelo Bono. Bringing armed men from a neighboring village could easily be misinterpreted as a belligerent act of ambition, triggering a bloody conflict. Stuffa wanted to make it clear to the Don that his action would not be prompted by ambition or any desire for power. Nor would he act without the Don's approval.

"I appreciate, *signor* Stuffa, the respect you show coming to me with this, this Caiozzo situation," the Don said in earnest.

"It could not be otherwise, Don Angelo," Stuffa assured him.

"Yes, good, good," the Don said scrutinizing the man before him. Satisfied, he dismissed the bodyguard from the room.

"And now we may speak freely," he said to Stuffa. "I have, of course, heard of Caiozzo's pursuit of this…this,"

"Maria Pepitone," Stuffa interjected.

"Yes, this Pepitone girl," Bono reiterated. "Ha!", the Don erupted laughing, "his pursuit is like that of a clumsy old fool, a bull in heat seeking the sexual favor of an unwilling young heifer. It is both comical and regrettable, a man of his standing in the village behaving like a *cafone*," Angelo said shaking his head.

"Yes, and if I may add, Don Angelo, injurious to a gentle, respected family of our village who have suffered many personal tragedies and yet produced two children of worthy and fine character."

"Yes, well perhaps at least one," Bono caustically corrected. "As to the boy, this..."

"Antonio," Stuffa offered.

"Yes, this Antonio, about him I'm not so convinced. But that is a discussion for another time," the Don said.

"Let me say this *signor* Stuffa. As you know, Caiozzo and I have engaged in numerous business transactions over the years, but he is not a member of my family, or any other on this island as far as I know. I have no interest in his personal life and, certainly, no interest in the fortunes of the Pepitone family. As long as their dispute does not disrupt the peaceful activity of our village, or interfere with my business, I don't care in whose favor this matter is resolved. But I respect and applaud your friend Pepitone's resolve in protecting his daughter and, within reason, he is free to do whatever is necessary. However, allow me to warn you. Caiozzo is not a buffoon. He is a clever and cunning man, but also quite reckless and unpredictable. He can be as dangerous as an asp hanging from a tree, and equally deadly. Stay vigilant, one step ahead and, remember that an ounce of prevention is worth far more than a pound of cure.

"And now," Bono said rising form his chair and extending his hand, "thank you again for coming and I wish *bona furtuna* to you and the Pepitones in this matter."

"And thank you for your time and wise counsel, Don Bono," Stuffa replied taking the Don's hand.

Stuffa related the particulars of his meeting to the Pepitones, emphasizing the Don's promise not to take sides. Bono's interest and suggestions offered the couple some hope that, with Stuffa's support, Caiozzo would be thwarted. Hopefully, he might abandon his quest for their daughter and search elsewhere.

CHAPTER 8

On the morning of the first Saturday in October the town bustled with activity preparing for the annual *festa* that evening celebrating the conclusion of a successful harvest. The farmers guided their carts from the fields, loaded with fruits, vegetables, flowers and wheels of cheese into the Piazza Europa. The women baked bread and *cassata* and made fresh pasta from flour and eggs for sale, and set tables up alongside the farmers' produce. Local artisans displayed earthenware, costume jewelry and woodwork, and a few desperate farmers brought worn mules long past their value, available for sale at any price.

Pepitone put a small stand out near those of the other artisans and hired Jenna, the butcher's daughter, to attend it. He didn't expect to sell to the locals who did not need and could not afford his fine work, but knew tourists attended the *festa*, and he might realize a few sales or even secure a commission.

Ciuto and Mosca rolled two casks of Caiozzo's reserved wine over the uneven cobblestones of the piazza. He sold the good vintage grape for half a lira a class, which induced the customer to purchase a bottle for three lira. The bottle, of course, contained the dregs, netting Caiozzo a nice profit.

An out of step, poorly coordinated brass marching band in tattered military uniforms and silly feathered caps, rehearsed, producing discordant sounds, as young children mimicked, whirled and raced about in that unscripted play typical of childhood. In a far corner alley with good acoustics, the church choir practiced a medley of religious and Sicilian folk songs and, at the harbor, the Valachi family assembled their elaborate collection of fireworks for the grand finale at midnight.

But the most popular concession of the *festa* was always the *gelatu* stand owned by Don Angelo Bono.

The velvety chocolate and fruit flavored delicacy was a rare treat for the children of Castellammare and especially appealing to the young girls who deliberately dipped their spoons into the cup, nursing the *gelatu* as it melted and glided down their throats.

The popularity of Bono's attraction, which always effected a long line, made it imperative that the stand be placed in the far corner of the piazza near the Via Nasi to allow a free flow of pedestrian traffic. Bono enjoyed a monopoly on the sale of *gelatu*. He was the only one in the village able to afford the cost of the scarce ice, sugar and natural flavorings. To curry favor among the villagers he sold it for only one half lira a cup and gave the melting remains away at the conclusion of the *festa*.

"Let the poor families indulge their deprived children," he would command expansively.

Bono relished his sense of power as a mafia don. And he well appreciated that most Sicilian dons came from the dirt, surviving years of struggle, devious maneuvering and brutality. They did not inherit the trappings of the gentry, the soft hands and manicured fingernails, and their swollen and blistered feet had bled into rotting, dirt-caked shoes, unlike the gentry whose feet were cradled in supple leather.

Bono honed his natural born skills of observation and listening quietly with a keen ear to the machinations of the bosses supervising the men in the fields in which he toiled as a young boy. He hadn't read Machiavelli but quickly learned how to acquire and maintain power. It was a matter of prompting fear without arousing hatred. Brutality, law breaking, even occasional murder, while not condoned outright by the people, were soon forgotten and denied, as long as their property was secure.

Bono would agree with the celebrated Florentine that men more quickly forget the death of their father than the loss of their patrimony. You bind them to you by largess, dispensing favors and rewards that will be remembered and embellished, becoming embedded in local myth.

Bono always punctuated his performance at the *festa* by donating his profit to the church for distribution to the villagers. *Padre* Pietro in turn, anxious to maintain Bono's benevolence, made a great show of charity by distributing a goodly sum to the parishioners, but not before he enacted a service charge. Everyone in Sicily with power or authority managed to fill his coffers at someone's expense.

At the vineyard, the harvest was completed by noon and Caiozzo sat sweating at a table in the afternoon heat, a Beretta within easy reach, and Lorenzo with a rifle at his side. A stack of *lire* sat waiting for distribution to the workers, the fifteen percent the landowners allotted. Caiozzo customarily gave the workers ten percent to share, but the harvest was exceptional and he was feeling magnanimous. With a great flourish, he theatrically announced a one half percent increase, and full remuneration for the half day of work, creating near-riotous jubilation of grateful workers, hugging and dancing in the fields. Lorenzo turned and looked at Caiozzo who nodded and smiled, knowing word of his generosity would spread like the second coming of Christ in the village. Caiozzo and Bono drank from the same cup.

After he had apportioned the ten and a half percent and dismissed the workers, he placed his share in a bag and harnessed two of the horses from the vineyard to a large wagon and set off to his mother's chicken coop to make his deposit.

Sofia greeted her son with a sly smile and a cynical observation.

"Ah Giuseppe," she said. "Here to feed cornmeal to the chickens again?"

"Sì, Mamma," he answered, "But I cannot remain long. I have much to do before the *festa* begins tonight."

"What task could you possibly have that is so important?", she asked, probing suspiciously. "The harvest is completed and you have obviously allotted the profits to the workers," she added with a twinkle in her eye. "At least let me make you a nice espresso before you leave," Sofia offered.

Caiozzo agreed and took the opportunity to bury his share in the chicken coop while his mother brewed the coffee. He fended off his mother's questions and hastily drank the espresso with the promise that he would see her at the *festa* later that evening.

Caiozzo returned to his apartment to wait for Lorenzo and the other two to finalize his plan. He pulled the cork from a bottle of his reserved wine and filled a cup with the smug certainty that history and opportunity were his allies that night.

Marriage by abduction or marriage by capture was a common practice in Sicily, a barbaric vestige of Arab influence and of Romulus, legendary founder of Rome, who provided wives for his citizens with the rape of the Sabines. Over the centuries the practice was adopted by spurned suitors who felt justified in kidnapping women they desired to redeem their tarnished honor and respect, an act which enjoyed the tacit approval of the law, the church, and the community. An unmarried woman spending the night in the home or company of a man was assumed to have engaged in sexual activity and, to avoid village condemnation of shame and disgrace, was forced to accept a *fuitina*, an immediate, "rehabilitative marriage," or suffer being labeled a whore.

Village attention would be occupied by the events of the *festa*, allowing an excellent opportunity for Caiozzo to carry out his plan. Even the *carabinieri* would relax their surveillance as they stole sips of wine, which Caiozzo made available, in the dark alleys.

Caiozzo would not be involved in the actual act of the kidnapping. He planned to make himself obvious in the piazza, selling his wine to establish an alibi and avoid initial suspicion and questioning when Maria's disappearance was discovered. He knew, however, at some point he would become the prime suspect and Luongo, with pressure from Pepitone, would demand an interrogation and a search of his apartment. Caiozzo was prepared for that eventuality and his scheme and timing were well-conceived.

"Lorenzo," Caiozzo sternly admonished, "I depend on you to listen carefully and follow my instructions exactly." He hesitated and glanced uncertainly at Ciuto and Mosca, droopy-eyed and wide-mouthed like children first learning their alphabet.

"Just before sunset you will take the wagon and the two horses to the alley off Via Nasi and secure the animals to the hitching post. In the wagon you will find a rag to cover Maria's mouth, rope to bind her hands and feet, a rug and a blanket. And bring a jug of water and some fruit. Bono's *gelatu* stand is at the bottom of Via Nasi, and, at some point in the evening, Maria will want the treat. None of the young girls can resist it. There will be many distractions as she waits on line and, when she leaves the stand and passes near Via Nasi, move quickly. Pull her into the alley, gag her mouth, tie her hands and feet and bind her in the rug. Ciuto, you drive the horses up the Corso Garibaldi to the vineyard shed and, Lorenzo, you and Mosca remain in the back with Maria. During the confusion following Maria's disappearance, I will slip out of the piazza and take the narrow path through the woods and wait for you at the shed."

Caiozzo paused, clasped his hands together and breathed deeply. He looked at the three men and said gravely, "And I warn all of you. Do not show Maria any disrespect or engage in any conversation. And not a drop of wine or grappa is to pass your lips."

They winced then wilted under Caiozzo's harsh gaze.

The sun slowly slipped under the horizon and hissed into the blue-green Mediterranean. Lanterns flickered like fireflies and gaslights on posts lit the dark water of the harbor, twinkling like dancing faeries. Early arrivals, families with children in tow and whispering lovers, clutching shoulders and waists, made their way to the piazza. The Pepitones dallied at their home.

"Papa," Maria said. "You have not even washed or shaved and you look and smell like a gypsy. The Stuffas will be here any moment. Is this the way you want our neighbors to see you?"

"No, no, Maria," he replied. "I would never present myself with a *mala figura*. I'm attending to that as we speak."

"I would hope so, papa," Maria responded with feigned petulance, "I would hope so."

Pepitone shaved, washed under his arms and put on a clean shirt as they waited for Stuffa, his wife and his cousins who arrived shortly. They walked down Via Bovia in the middle of the gathering crowd. One of the cousins led the way, flanked by the other two. All three had pistols tucked into their pants under loosely fitting shirts. Maria and Agata locked arms, giggling and teen gossiping as their nosey parents strained to hear the conversation.

"Maria," Agata confided. "Not a word to anyone, but Ruggero asked me what time I would be at the *festa* tonight. I think he wants to invite me to the youth dance next week at the parish."

"Ruggero?," Maria responded wide-eyed. "Ruggero *lu beddu* with the straight brown hair and the perfect Norman nose? Oh you she wolf," Maria said laughing, playfully punching Agata's shoulder. "I'm so jealous."

"But Maria," Agata said placating her friend, "Rano has an interest in you."

"Yes," Maria said wrinkling her face in revulsion, "Rano! You get the fellow whose father is the mayor of the village and who is named after a prince of Sicily, and I get the son of a father who makes his living peddling toads to the chemist and old ladies with bad knees, and names his son after a frog."

The two friends embraced in laughter as their parents looked at each other bewildered.

They arrived at the top of the piazza near Bono's *gelatu* cart and Maria and Agata carried on like spoiled children because the stand was not yet open for business.

"Maria, Agata, please," Stuffa scolded, "the evening has not yet begun. Patience, there is more than enough time for the treat and plenty enough for both of you." The girls scowled with displeasure.

The piazza was coming alive as venders hawked their wares and bargained with perspective customers, keeping a watchful eye out for shoplifters. Old women in black sat on benches like crows strung together commenting critically on this or that dress of the young girls or the pair of shoes they wore or the manner in which they walked.

Wood fires in troughs crackled under layers of sweating sausage, peppers, onions and fennel, and golden balls of *zeppole* bobbed in vats of bubbling oil, producing a haze of aromatic grey smoke drifting through the piazza like low, slow-moving clouds. Gypsy fire-eaters ate fire, juggled, and tumbled as their children aggressively begged for *lire*, and the village women protectively clutched their purses.

Every table in front of Zuffolo's *salumeria* and Ferrara's *pasticceria* was occupied with families devouring sausage and peppers on thick crusts of bread or stuffing *cannolu* into their mouths. Their children, with tomato sauce caked on their mouths, ram amuck, shoving and punching each other as proud fathers encouraged and saluted the action with raised glasses of wine, and frustrated mothers screamed threats and obscenities. At the opposite side of the piazza at Pace's smaller *pasticceria*, other parents sat quietly reminding their children to dab the residue of ricotta from the corners of their mouth, and lovers sat staring into each others' eyes and sipping anisette. The old ladies remained on their bench sharing a basket of chestnuts and offering comments about the strolling walkers who soon became the spectators, while the erstwhile spectators, took their place on the stage, subject to scrutiny. And so it went, *comu in Sicilia*, like a concerto without a conductor or a play without a director. Sicilians do not require a director. They are all natural born actors.

After blessing Bono's *gelatu* cart, *Padre* Pietro led a religious procession, complete with a suffering Christ hanging off a heavy wooden cross, carried by six superbly sculptured young men with as much lust in their eyes as piety in their hearts. The procession was preceded by a band offering a monotonous droning of funereal-like music, and an altar boy with a box hung from his neck into which the villagers tossed a lira or two. The procession made a complete circle around the piazza and ended where it began. The *Padre* immediately relieved the alter boy of the box and cloistered himself in the middle of six, previously designated intrepid nonnas who escorted him to the rectory. Don Angelo Bono smiled and nodded in accord, but nevertheless, assigned two armed men to follow the group.

Ruggero saw Maria and Agata waiting on line at the *gelatu* stand, waved enthusiastically, and elbowed his way toward them.

"*Ciao* Agata, *ciao* Maria," the handsome young boy greeted them.

"Oh *ciao* Ruggero," Agata replied pretending to be surprised.

"*Ciao* Ruggero," Maria joined sing-song with a slight coquetry in her voice.

"So," Ruggero said, reaching for some topic of conversation, "we have a beautiful night for the *festa*."

"Yes, very beautiful," Agata agreed, "and very crowded," she added.

"Yes, very beautiful and very crowded," Maria mimicked teasing. Agata shot her friend a nasty look which produced an equally nasty tongue-thrust from Maria.

"So have you...," Ruggero started to ask.

"Did you see..," Agata began at the same time.

They lapsed into laughter as Maria impatiently rolled her eyes. Ruggero looked at Maria then asked, extending a timid hand to Agata.

"Agata, could we speak alone for a moment?"

"Of course," Agata said, arching her shoulder seductively as she looked back at Maria.

"*Va*, go, go," Maria smiled. "Do you want *ciocculattu* or *limuni*?," she asked her friend.

"Maria," Agata said, "*cioccolattu*. For us it has always been *cioccolattu*."

Maria inched up the line, casually looking back and smiling at Agata and Ruggero holding hands. One of the cousins moved along outside the line, always keeping Maria in sight, but then was distracted by a passing, smiling Gina whose low cut blouse revealed more cleavage than it concealed. The two fell into flirtatious chit-chat.

"I thought I knew all the handsome young men in this village. How is it I missed you?" she asked seductively.

"Ah, *signorina*," he replied, "I am not a Castellammarese. I am here from Alcamo, visiting my cousin. But had I known of the beauty of the women of Castellammare, I surely would have made a visit sooner," the cousin gushed.

The mutual flattery was most gratifying and the two were soon engrossed in each other, making plans for a liaison when the *festa* concluded at midnight.

CHAPTER 9

One of the timeless fears parents everywhere share is the sudden disappearance or abduction of their child. This is the ultimate catastrophe. Whatever can happen to a parent, himself or herself, is nothing compared to the loss of a child. They are here before us one minute, warmed by the sunlight of security, full of innocence and promise, then, like a snowflake melting in a warm palm, they vanish. Our worst fear has been realized, and we are left utterly bereft.

Maria took a cup in each hand from the vendor and turned left to avoid the crowd in the middle of the piazza to make her way back toward Agata and Ruggero. She laughed at the sight of the young couple oblivious to their surroundings, deep in intimate conversation with eyes fixed on each other. She stopped in front of the deserted Via Nasi to lick the melting *gelatu* from her wrists whereupon two pairs of strong hands came out of the darkness and seized her arms, dragging her back into the alley. Dropping the cups, Maria tried to scream but was quickly silenced by Lorenzo covering her mouth with a coarse rag and tying it to the base of her neck. Mosca began binding her hands, but Lorenzo stopped him.

"No Mosca, you and Ciuto hold her. I'll bind the hands and feet." They placed Maria, face up, on the rug and Lorenzo folded the sides over and secured it with a rope. Mosca and Ciuto hoisted the struggling Maria on their shoulders and the three, led by Lorenzo, made their way up the short Via Nasi to the wagon just above the Church of San Giuseppe. The brutal operation was quick and efficient and took less than two minutes. Mosca and Ciuto began celebrating, laughing and congratulating each other, prompting an angry, *stati zitti*, "shut up," from Lorenzo. "This mission is far from accomplished."

As the trio turned a corner approaching the church, Maria began twisting in an attempt to free herself. By the time they reached the steps of the rectory, she had managed to loosen the rope and slide out the back of the rug landing ass-bruised and dazed on the cobblestones, writhing and attempting to rise. An irate Lorenzo issued a profanity-laced tirade as Ciuto and Mosca began squabbling loudly, one accusing the other of the blunder, then venting their rage physically, tearing at each others' shirts and trading wild punches and kicks like two drunken brawlers. Lorenzo tried to intervene but was rewarded by a misdirected blow to the nose from Ciuto, followed by a mouth gouge and flying fists from behind delivered by the nitwit Mosca who was unsure of whom he was hitting or why. The fracas was loud enough to bring a breathless *Padre* Pietro running from the rectory to quell the hostilities.

The four men stood wordless, looking at each other, then at Maria who was still attempting to rise. The priest looked down at Maria and saw the terror in her eyes. What these men were doing was monstrous, something no one, certainly not a priest, should permit to happen. But even as he heard this small voice reminding him of what he ought to do, he looked up and encountered the baleful countenance of Lorenzo. Fear quickly silenced the voice of conscience as Lorenzo's dark burning eyes mirrored a heart capable of murder. In no uncertain terms he made the priest understand what was expected of him, nothing less than complete cooperation.

"*Nun dicissi nenti, Patri, nenti di chistu*, speak nothing of this. Tomorrow when the sun rises, we will be at your door with Don Caiozzo and the girl. You know what your duty will be. Do you understand me, *Padre*?" Lorenzo asked.

"*Capisciu*," the frightened priest replied. Looking down at Maria, he stifled the pity she aroused and told himself that what was happening could not be prevented by a village priest. It was beyond his control. He gave Maria a perfunctory blessing. A warm trickle made its way down his leg as he left the scene, but he consoled himself with the thought of what he would gain if everything played out as he guessed it would. Tomorrow, he reflected, I will certainly have a sacrament to perform and some *lire* to put in my pocket.

After the priest had gone, the three abductors calmed themselves and focused on their task. Lorenzo retied the cord around Maria's wrists and ankles and carried her to the wagon. They placed her in the middle of the wagon bed, climbed in and settled on either side of her. Ciuto secured the rear gate, unhitched the horses, took his seat and whipped them up the Corso Garibaldi for the thirty minute ride to the vineyard and the shed.

Lorenzo pinched his bleeding nose with a bandana and cursed a repentant Ciuto as the wagon rumbled up the corso. A full autumn moon shed enough light to allow Ciuto to maintain a steady pace, but they slowed as they reached the top of the hill and the tired snorting animals balked at the touch of the whip on their steamy backs. They crossed over Via Umberto, well beyond the village, and entered a dark twisting road leading to the shed about one mile away. Lorenzo loosened the rope around Maria and pulled the rug from her face. It was a meager gesture of compassion, but she welcomed the relief the cool night air offered. He then removed the rag from her mouth, raised Maria's head and put the jug of water to her lips. She rejected it, turned her head to the side and expelled mucus and dry specks of dirt. When he offered her water again she refused it, prompting him to say,

"Whatever you prefer, princess, whatever you prefer."

It is astonishing, often frightening, to see how an unexpected, sudden event can change the course of one's life forever.

As Maria looked up at the stars against the dark, cloudless sky, she sensed that her life was about to change completely. The stars would be the same but she would never again be the young girl who sat with her parents on cool summer evenings or walked to the village with Agata, joking about Rano, the frog boy, or accepting an invitation to dance at one of the parish youth gatherings. She wept quietly as she anticipated the loss of everything dear to her. If only there were some way to prevent it. She seethed, thinking about *Padre* Pietro's lack of action and wondered why he hadn't tried to help her. She prayed she could be rescued and remain as she was, a happy young girl. Time and change, so it seemed, only brought more sorrow than joy. She thought about the John Keats poem "Ode on a Grecian Urn," which Antonio had once read to her, and yearned to be the fair youth who never changes, sitting under trees that never lose their leaves.

Fear was giving way to quiet rage and then reflection. She recalled the incident with Caiozzo weeks earlier on the church steps, her feelings of discomfort, her parents' odd behavior and the strange prohibitions they placed on her activities and the sudden appearance of Stuffa's three cousins from Alcamo. What was happening to her now was precisely what had been feared. Now she looked closely at the two men beside her in the wagon and remembered seeing them with Caiozzo in the village. Everything became clear to her then. Caiozzo was the malignant force behind this terrible event. Her abductors were working for him.

At first she had feared that they intended to use her for their own pleasure, but as she came to realize they were following Caiozzo's orders, she guessed, barring a miracle, an even more miserable fate awaited her. She was in Caiozzo's power. That much was clear. What he intended to do with her she could only guess in the light of the stories she'd heard about how young Sicilian women were abducted and forced into marriage. But such incidents occurred elsewhere on the island. As far as she knew, nothing like this had been reported taking place in Castellammare. But perhaps it had and there had been no report. In matters involving family honor a veil of secrecy was drawn if necessary to avoid shame and maintain reputation, which was honor itself. And of course it was a given that a family was shamed and dishonored if any female member was reputed to have lost her virtue. Maintaining family honor was a sovereign imperative, and forced marriages to preserve appearances came about as a result of it.

Such topics were not discussed in the Pepitone home, an impenetrable bastion of security. Not so impenetrable and not so secure, Maria thought, as tears streamed down her face. Why hadn't she been told that she was in danger? By keeping her ignorant, her parents had made her more vulnerable. And now she was in the power of a man who had aroused instant revulsion and whom she dreaded having to meet again. The wagon bounced over the rocks of the last few yards to the shed and an expectant Caiozzo.

The shed was a windowless, crudely constructed building of irregular stones, a worn tile roof and a dirt floor. Ladders, buckets, and rusting tools of the vineyard trade hung on the walls and the dank, musty smell of a subterranean tomb fouled the dead air. Caiozzo sat waiting on a rickety chair at a long table, sipping tepid water and eating grapes pulled from clusters. A corner lantern provided enough light for the room but was not visible from outside.

Caiozzo heard the wooden wheels of the wagon clattering over the road and walked out into the dark as the panting horses appeared, struggling up to the shed. Ciuto pulled the horses to a halt as Caiozzo secured them to the hitching post. Lorenzo and Mosca gripped Maria's arms so tightly as they walked toward Caiozzo that she could barely move, but she continued twisting to free herself.

"Release her," Caiozzo ordered. His eyes coldly moved from her feet, up her body like a man appraising a piece of livestock purchased at a fair. Maria turned her head, avoiding his gaze, and dabbed her wet eyes with a handkerchief. The last time they had met on the steps of the church, he had felt compelled to be deferential. Clumsy and embarrassed, he'd tried to present himself in a respectable manner, and he'd felt the disdain in the Pepitones' response to him. Now he had their daughter, and there was no need to be deferential. When one had power, one was superior. It was immensely gratifying.

"Maria," Caiozzo began, assuming a reasonable tone, "this is not the way I wanted it. I offered your father..."

"Offered?", Maria turned and defiantly cut him off through tears.

"What do you mean 'offered'?", she demanded.

"I offered your father an arrangement common to our people which, had he accepted, would have avoided this unnecessary unpleasantness and given you and your family a lifetime of protection and security."

"Offer? Arrangement?" Maria responded scornfully. "I am a person, not wares to be bartered for. And my family and I do not need your protection."

Ciuto's snicker was cut short by Caiozzo's glower.

"Maria," Caiozzo replied calmly, "if that were true, you and I would not be in this place, at this time, talking as we are." He continued in the manner of a master instructing his student.

"Your father is a just and decent man, an honest man who has lived a good life. But, as you see, even these virtues do not enable him to oppose the interests of someone in a position of power. That is the way of the world. People must submit to what they cannot oppose. In this case, it will be in your interest and that of your family to submit to what you cannot oppose."

"Do you believe...do you believe," Maria asked sobbing, "that my father is the kind of a man who will do nothing, that he will just abandon me to you? You know, you know Stuffa and his cousins will join him and be here shortly and...and then..." Her voice trailed off, revealing false optimism as the tears flowed.

"Maria," Caiozzo said, "Stuffa and his cousins have already failed. Their task was to prevent this situation from occurring, not trying to reverse it. Despite what you might hope for, a counter offensive is unthinkable. I know Don Angelo Bono well enough to know he would never permit retaliation from Stuffa and your father. It would disrupt his business interests and disturb the tranquility of the village. And it would endanger the lives of at least three sons of Castellammare and the three men from Alcamo, possibly triggering a bloody war with that village. No, Maria, you must accept the fact that a rescue is impossible. What is happening to you has happened to young village girls in Sicily for centuries. It may not be openly encouraged, but it is an accepted norm, nevertheless, a custom that binds young women and their families."

Maria could not believe that she was without any recourse. Surely the law would protect her. "My father will report you to Luongo. You are breaking the law," she said desperately. Caiozzo chuckled indulgently and snuffed out her last glimmer of hope.

"The law, Maria? The law in Sicily is as effective as the toothless old men in the village who must swallow their bread and pasta without chewing. It is meaningless, an idea people like your brother write on a piece of paper. The real law in Sicily, Maria, is written by Don Bono and other men like him."

Caiozzo broke off, turned abruptly and walked toward Lorenzo.

"Did you bring a jug of fresh water," he asked.

"I have it here in the wagon," Lorenzo replied.

"Get it, and the rug, and bring Maria to the shed," he ordered.

"And hurry, I have already wasted too much time. Spread the rug in the corner near the lantern and cover it with the blanket," he said.

"Now Ciuto, listen carefully. You and Mosca, God damn you imbecile, Mosca," Caiozzo broke off and shouted, "stop nibbling on that fucking cluster of grapes and pay attention." The startled dullard dropped the grapes to the ground and listened mindlessly, as an irritated Caiozzo continued.

"Each of you," he said to Ciuto and Mosca deliberately, "circle the shed in opposite directions every fifteen minutes. Mosca, you go this way," he said with dramatic exaggeration, pointing to his right, "and Ciuto, you go this way," he directed to his left. "*Capiti*, do you understand?" he demanded, fixing each of them with a threatening gaze.

"*Sì, sì, Don Giuseppe, capemu*, we understand," they nodded in accord, gaping stupidly.

Caiozzo released a deep sigh as he returned to a grinning Lorenzo.

"Lorenzo," he said quietly, "keep a sharp eye on those two but don't leave the door unattended. And look in at Maria every half hour or so. I will return from my apartment at sunrise and we'll all go to the church where, if you have done your job, *Padre* Pietro will be waiting to perform the ceremony.

"It is taken care of, Don Giuseppe. It is all arranged with the *Padre*," Lorenzo assured.

"*Va beni*," Caiozzo said as he walked toward his horse. He suddenly stopped and returned to Lorenzo, thrusting a finger into his chest.

"And remember what I said, Lorenzo," Caiozzo reminded him sternly: "*Cu tuttu rispettu a Maria*, with all due respect to Maria."

CHAPTER 10

When Maria did not return, Agata and Ruggero walked up toward the front of the line looking for her. As they passed Via Nasi, Ruggero pointed to chocolate *gelatu* melting from two cups laying on the ground. They looked quizzically at each other and Agata asked a classmate if she had seen Maria.

"Yes," the girl answered, "she was here just in front of us but then..."

"Then what?" Agata asked.

"I don't know. I didn't see her again," the girl responded.

Cousin Francesco, realizing his negligence, broke off his conversation with Gina, ran to the front of the line, looked around, then pushed his way through to the other side where he encountered Agata and Ruggero.

"Agata, where's Maria?" he asked breathless.

"I don't know. We were wondering the same thing," Agata said. Francesco wiped the beads of sweat from his brow, as Ruggero called his attention to the melting gelato on the ground prompting a groan and exclamations of anguish.

"Oh, *Diu miu*! My God! No! *Merda*! Shit!"

"Francesco, what's the matter?" Agata demanded with mounting concern.

"Agata," Francesco said, ignoring her question, "go and bring your father, my brothers and *signor* Pepitone here immediately."

"But what...," Agata began.

"*Subbitu, subbitu*, immediately," Francesco bellowed. He then turned to Ruggero.

"You, young man, help us here. Go up Via Nasi and the adjoining alleys and see what you can find." Ruggero looked at Francesco and hesitated.

"Please," Francesco implored, "we're looking for Maria." Instantly, Ruggero disappeared up Via Nasi.

Agata zigzagged through the piazza past surprised strollers to *pasticceria* Pace where her parents and the Pepitones were enjoying their cappuccinu, waving her arms frantically and calling to her father. Stuffa, followed by Pepitone, ran toward his daughter and clasped her shoulders.

"What, what happened, Agata?" he asked gently shaking her.

"Is it Maria?" a worried Pepitone asked.

"Oh, I don't know," Agata replied through mounting tears, "we can't find Maria, and Francesco told me to bring you to him immediately." The women, biting down hard on their knuckles, joined them and Amelia, ashen-faced, asserted. "It's about Maria, isn't it?" Her legs began to betray her and Pepitone steadied his wife.

"Amelia," Stuffa said taking charge, "she probably just wandered off with one of her classmates. "Nina," he said to his wife, "take Amelia and

Agata back to the *pasticceria* and wait for us there. I'm sure we'll joint you in a few minutes with an embarrassed and apologetic Maria in tow."

"Nino?" Amelia sought confirmation from her husband.

"Do as Enzo says, Amelia," Pepitone responded.

A crowd had gathered like moths to light, and uninformed speculation already began to ripple through the piazza. Stuffa, Pepitone and the two other cousins pushed their way toward Francesco.

"Ah *stunatu*, shithead," Enzo flung at Francesco. "What the hell's the matter with you? You were given a simple order, not to let Maria out of your sight, and you fucked it up," Stuffa said, as Pepitone glared at him with more anxiety than anger in his eyes.

"Enzo," Francesco pleaded with extended hands, "I swear, I turned away for only a minute, and when I looked back, she was gone." Ruggero returned and informed the group that his search turned up no sign of Maria.

The crowd of nosey on-lookers had swelled and was pressing closer and questioning, as if it was their right to know what was occurring. They began to disperse as Luongo and his deputy, Turi, arrived, waving their arms and shouting, "Go, leave, all of you…get out of here."

Luongo, having heard all the gossip about Caiozzo's quest and the rumor that Maria was in his sights, suspected that what Pepitone feared was coming to pass. He ignored Stuffa and spoke directly to Pepitone, who was clearly beside himself with worry.

"What happened, Nino?" he asked, speaking gently and voicing concern.

"It's Maria, Vincenzo, Maria, we can't find her," he said putting his hand over his forehead.

"Ok, ok, who saw her last and where?" Luongo demanded, looking around.

"I guess it was me," Francesco offered, stepping forward tentatively. "I was looking after her. She was waiting in line for the *gelatu*, and I had her in my sights and…and I turned for just a moment…"

Luongo cut him off sarcastically. "You were some protector. Distracted for just a moment, were you and, when you turned back, puff," fanning his fingers from his mouth, "she was gone, just like that."

"*Capitano*, I…I"

"*Basta*, enough," Luongo interrupted shaking his head. "Turi," he said to his deputy, "round up all the *carabinieri* you can find who are still sober and can walk. We will begin by scouring every foot of the village."

"What?", Pepitone cried, "scour the village? Why are you wasting time? You know damn well why she is missing and who is responsible," he said.

"Nino," Luongo returned softly, "we know nothing for sure at this point, but must begin somewhere. After all, your daughter may have taken a walk to the harbor, or some other place, for a private adolescent moment with one of her classmates."

Luongo stepped back to avoid Pepitone's weak, flaying blows to his chest as Stuffa restrained his friend.

"Take your wife and go home now and comfort each other. I will assign a *carabiniere* to stay with you as we continue our search and make all necessary inquiries," Luongo said.

Hours after the *festa* ended and all inquiries were made, Luongo and Turi went to the Pepitone home to advise them of the status.

Amelia was prostrate on her bed as Nina pressed towels drenched with cool water to her forehead.

"So what news do you have of my daughter and her disappearance?" Pepitone demanded.

"Regrettably, nothing," Luongo responded, avoiding Pepitone's angry gaze.

"Nothing?" Pepitone repeated, "nothing. And have you questioned that *facci di mortu*, that face of death, Caiozzo,?" he demanded.

"Not yet. We are going to his apartment after we leave here," Luongo replied.

"His apartment? His apartment?" Pepitone said incredulously. "You seriously underestimate this man. Do you think he is stupid enough to bring Maria to his apartment?" Pepitone raged.

"We both damn well know where he is keeping her. Why have you not gathered a force and gone to that filthy shed he keeps in the vineyard and freed my daughter?" Pepitone pleaded.

"Nino, I told you earlier in the village. We know nothing for certain and must proceed one step at a time, and this is the next step."

"You are stalling, Vincenzo," Nino charged. "You are stalling because you have some part in this treachery, and know, that once the sun rises and..."

"Watch your accusations," Luongo shot back through tight lips. "I am the law and I won't have you telling me how to go about my work."

Luongo softened as he heard Amelia's pitiful sobs from the bedroom and saw Pepitone go limp in a chair murmuring, "The law...the law."

"Nino," he said kindly, "I am doing all I can but there are some things that even I..."

"Yes, yes," Pepitone said waving his hand in disgust. "The law of which you speak, however, is not the law written in your manual. It is found etched in the very fabric of this island by men above your law, and it demands our total submission. I understand now, Vincenzo, I understand," a despairing Pepitone said.

Luongo's head sank to his chest and he silently patted Pepitone's shoulder as he and Turi walked out the door.

"Let's return to the station," he said to Turi. "Maybe something has turned up which we missed earlier." The deputy nodded his head and shrugged his shoulders.

A light from one window of the station on Corso Garibaldi broke the dark and Luongo knew that at least someone was on duty earning their *lire*.

They entered a small hallway leading to a room that was Luongo's administrative office. At one end, on an elevated platform, was a desk with a name plate prominently displayed. Behind the desk was a comfortably padded chair. On either side of the desk and slightly below it were small work tables and chairs. The light from the gas lamp flickered, casting eerie shadows on flaking plaster walls with religious pictures of the Madonna and the burning heart of Christ hanging askew. A wooden crucifix framed by dried palms was nailed to the wall behind Luongo's desk. The heavy stale air smelled like the inside of a wood-burning oven which had not been cleaned for months.

"Any new developments?" Luongo asked the duty officer sitting at one of the tables.

"Nothing. Not a trace of anything. All is quiet," he replied, as a loud gurgling roar suddenly erupted from one of the two cells behind the room.

"What the hell is that?" Luongo asked surprised.

"It's Rienzi, *Capitano*, the vineyard worker Caiozzo put in charge of his wine sale when he left," the officer said chuckling. "He drank more than he sold, became loud and abusive and was vomiting on the shoes of his customers," the officer laughed holding his sides. He collected himself and continued.

"One of Don Angelo's men suggested we get him out of the piazza and lock him up. So, here he is."

"I hope you put a pail in his cell," Luongo said.

"I did, *Capitano*, I surely did," the officer answered proudly.

"Good work," Luongo said, "Now finish the job and dump the vomit outside before the stench chokes us all."

"Yes, sir," the officer replied losing his smile and wrinkling his nose.

Luongo sat at his desk and aimlessly flipped through some official papers and reports of complaints. He laughed quietly as he read the weekly grievance of the widow Nardino about the peeping Tom who came to her window every Saturday night when she was bathing. He would not need to be at her window, Luongo thought. With her girth he could be a kilometer away and still enjoy a good look. Luongo placed his head on the desk of strewn paperwork and slept for a half hour.

. . .

Caiozzo was awakened from a deep sleep by a pounding on the door. He glanced out the window and saw the black sky fading to the soft, azure blue of a false dawn.

"Who is it?" Caiozzo asked.

"*Polizzia*," Luongo announced. "We need to have a few words with you, *signore*."

"One minute," Caiozzo said, splashing water on his face. He pulled the creaking door open and greeted Luongo with a familiarity which always irritated the captain.

"Vincenzo!" Caiozzo exclaimed. "And deputy Turi. Well," he said, "It's either a little late or a little early for a social visit. I can only assume this is official."

"It is, Giuseppe, very official and very serious," Luongo replied. "Earlier this evening, Maria Pepitone, daughter of Nino and Amelia, disappeared from the *festa* at the piazza."

"Yes, I know," Caiozzo responded solemnly, "what a tragedy. Her parents must be sick with grief. But you are not here in the middle of the night to inform me of something I know nothing about, other than what I heard at the *festa* while pouring wine when this unfortunate incident occurred. So how can I help you?" he asked.

"Giuseppe, let me get right to the point. Everyone in the village knows you have been seeking a wife. I have spoken with the Pepitones, and they have informed me of your actions during the past few weeks, actions of intimidation and threats in your pursuit of their daughter."

"Ah, Vincenzo," Caiozzo responded, scratching his head, "Pepitone and his wife have overstated and overreacted to my overtures regarding their daughter. I don't deny my interest in her. But I merely pointed out to them certain advantages and benefits Maria and the family would secure if a marriage could be arranged between us. Is it not our custom in Sicily to arrange marriages that will serve the families involved? I confess I may have overstepped my boundaries one Sunday morning when I foolishly went to their home, the transgression of an overzealous suitor. And for that I am truly sorry. Some heated words between Pepitone and me were exchanged, but they were due to nothing more than a mild misunderstanding. I have not spoken to Pepitone for weeks."

"Not even at the *festa* this evening?" Luongo asked.

"Not even this evening," Caiozzo responded. "In fact," he added, "I turned my wine stand over to Rienzi, one of my workers, and came directly home. It had been a very long day and I was tired and in need of sleep."

"I see," Luongo said, looking past Caiozzo into the apartment, "So you know nothing of the disappearance of Maria Pepitone?"

"Must I repeat myself Vincenzo?" Caiozzo irritably responded. "Nothing more than the rumors I heard at the piazza before I left at about 8:30."

"So you wouldn't object, then, if we came in for...," Luongo began.

"I surely would object," Caiozzo indignantly responded. "What reason and what legal authority would you have for searching through my home?"

"You needn't be so defensive, Giuseppe. Just routine police investigation," Luongo said.

Caiozzo noted light beginning to break in the East and calculated that Luongo's search could work to his advantage by stalling the search for Maria.

"You know Vincenzo," he said, "your presence here and your insinuation tests my patience and good nature. But I have nothing to hide. It's all very demeaning, but yes, yes, you may search about as freely as you wish," he said stepping aside and inviting them in.

"May I offer you dedicated men of the law an espresso or, perhaps, a grappa?" Caiozzo asked winking.

"*Grazzii*, no," Luongo responded, "we are still on duty."

"Of course, of course, still on duty," Caiozzo replied.

Predictably, they found nothing in Caiozzo's small quarters and walked toward the door.

"Thank you for your cooperation, Giuseppe," Vincenzo said shaking his head with a wry knowing smile.

"And thank you for your professional conduct," Caiozzo returned. "As a resident of this village, it is very reassuring to enjoy the thoroughness of our *polizzia*. And if I may be of further assistance..."

"Yes, yes," Vincenzo interrupted cutting the air with his hand. "*Bona notti*, Giuseppe."

"And *bona notti* to you...*Capitano*."

Outside, Luongo, shaking his head, turned to the deputy and said, "That Caiozzo is among the most cunning and sly men I ever met. He must have been nursed at the teats of a fox."

"You might be right, Captain," Turi smiled and agreed. "After all, his mother is Sofia Caiozzo."

Luongo's morning visit was convenient for Caiozzo. The early hour gave him time to wash, shave, change his underwear and make himself presentable to his prospective bride.

Following Caiozzo's orders, Lorenzo had arranged with *Padre* Pietro to meet the group at the church at 6 a.m., one hour before the first scheduled Mass at 7 a.m. The Marriage Sacrament would take no longer than fifteen minutes, avoiding an uncomfortable encounter with early arrivals at the church.

Caiozzo put a wash cloth, towel and some soap in a saddle bag, along with a loaf of bread, a piece of goat cheese and some figs. He brewed a pot of coffee, spiked it with a drop of grappa, and contentedly sat on the bench outside his front door. He watched the sun peak over the horizon, evicting the night shadows. He finished the espresso, fed and watered the horse, and galloped up the corso Garibaldi toward the shed. This was, he thought, my day of resurrection, my day of redemption, and the start of my new life as a respected man in the village with a lovely young bride of a good family, and the prospect of fatherhood.

The three lounging *citrulli* sprang to attention as they heard the hoofs of Caiozzo's horse coming up the rocky path.

"*Tuttu va beni*, all is well?" Caiozzo called out.

"*Sì, tuttu va beni*, Don Giuseppe, "Yes, all is well," Lorenzo responded. Caiozzo dismounted, took his saddle bag, and walked to the shed.

Maria was lying on her side, her face to the wall, as Caiozzo entered. He placed the saddle bag on the table and walked toward her.

"Maria," he said, reaching out to stroke her hair. "I brought..."

The girl turned abruptly, grasped his hand, and bit down hard between Caiozzo's thumb and forefinger, drawing a stream of blood, and producing a scream which echoed throughout the vineyard.

"*Figghia di na strega*, daughter of a witch!" Caiozzo shouted as he brought the injured hand to his mouth.

"What, what happened?" Lorenzo asked as he frantically entered the shed. Caiozzo composed himself and said, "Nothing, nothing, I just jammed my hand against the table."

"But it's bleeding Don Caiozzo," Lorenzo said.

"I told you it's nothing. I must have broken the skin when I hit the table. Bring me a wet rag and some grappa," he ordered.

"I'm sorry, Don Giuseppe, we have no grappa. Don't you remember your warning last night?" Lorenzo asked.

"Yes, Ok," Caiozzo replied, "just bring me the wet rag." He bound it tightly around the wound to stem the flow of blood and stormed out the door, still swearing. Lorenzo looked at Maria with raised eyebrows and offered her some bread and figs. She walked to the table, drank some water and washed her face, ignoring the offer of food.

"Take something, *signorina*, you will need something to keep your strength up today."

"Nothing, my strength comes from my faith and my heart," Maria responded firmly.

"Lorenzo, *subbitu*, bring Maria here. We are already behind schedule," an angry Caiozzo called, as the two left the shed.

"You, Lorenzo, sit in the back with Mosca and Maria. Ciuto, harness my horse to the rear of the wagon," he ordered. "I'll sit with you in front."

The wagon kicked up a cloud of dirt as it made its way down the rocky road to the church of San Giuseppe.

CHAPTER 11

Wearing a fine silk vestment, the fat pink smiling priest was at the door of the church when the wagon pulled into the deserted Via Nasi. *Padre* Pietro hurried over to meet it, hoisting his garment above his size six shoes to avoid tripping, and extended a hand of greeting and congratulations to the groom. He prudently refrained from asking questions about the bloody wrap on Caiozzo's hand.

"Welcome, so the happy day is here," the priest said smiling.

"*Ciao, Padre*," Caiozzo coldly responded.

"Ah, Maria, I'm glad to see that you are ready for this blessed event," he said, ignoring the fact that just a few hours before, he had seen her struggling desperately to resist abduction. Maria stood blank and disdainfully unresponsive. Disregarding the slight and her contemptuous expression, he rubbed his hands together and said cheerfully, "Well then, let us be off to the chapel and celebrate this holy union."

As they walked through the cool dark church, Maria suffered a momentary loss of faith and wondered where God was at that moment. They arrived at a small side chapel to the right of the main altar, guarded by a statue of St. Joseph.

Pietro began a litany of dry perspectives and the requirements of marriage sacrosanct to the teachings of the Church. As he rambled on, Caiozzo broke in and demanded he get to the point where the vows are exchanged.

"*Capisciu*, I understand," the intimidated priest said, "but, as you know, Don Caiozzo, receiving the sacrament of Holy Communion is a prerequisite to the Sacrament of Marriage and must, of course, be preceded by a confession."

"I have nothing to confess which would require me to kneel in the confessional with you, *Padre*," Caiozzo replied, and it was clear that he wouldn't be hampered by any ritualized nonsense.

Maria spoke up then, and it was equally clear that on that one point she agreed with her captor. Confessing to *Padre* Pietro would be ridiculous. "My only sin," she said, "if that is how you wish to define it, may be declared publicly; I have nothing but hate and contempt for this man who has abducted me and would steal my innocence." Caiozzo was silent and expressionless, staring unblinking at the priest. Her loathing meant nothing to him and was clearly no obstacle.

"Well then," a befuddled Pietro said after a gravid silence, "since you, Don Giuseppe have nothing to confess in the presence of God, and you, Maria, publicly acknowledge your sin of trespass, I absolve you both; *Ego te absolve in nomine patri et filii et spiritu sancto,*" he solemnly intoned. "And now you are ready to receive the sacred host that is the body and blood of our Blessed Lord and Savior Jesus Christ."

He went up the steps to the side altar where he had placed a covered chalice and brought it back to where they were standing by the communion rail. Removing the cover, he gave them each a host reciting, "*Corpus Domini nostri Jesu Christi custodiat animam tuam in vitam aeternam. Amen.*"

Caiozzo sucked the host off his tongue, chewed and swallowed it immediately. Maria let it slowly melt in her mouth, silently prayed for forgiveness for her lapse of faith, and beseeched the Almighty for help.

"To continue," Pietro said, "do you Giuseppe Caiozzo take Maria Pepitone, under God, as your rightful..."

"Yes, yes, I do, I do," an imperious Caiozzo cut him off. The priest then turned to Maria.

"And do you, Maria Pepitone, take Giuseppe Caiozzo as..."

"Take him? Take?" Maria responded choking with rage. "I have not taken this man. He has taken me according to some barbaric norm which seems to be sanctioned by Holy Mother Church."

"What is your answer?" the priest demanded, ignoring the outburst.

"The Church, Caiozzo and you, *Padre*, have already answered for me," she responded with disgust.

"So then," Pietro said looking at the three *citrulli*, "in the absence of anyone who might protest this holy union, I now, under God, pronounce you man and wife."

Yes, Maria thought, but not much of a man and much less a wife than he or you can ever imagine. Turning to Caiozzo, the priest started,

"You may now kiss..."

"No he may not," Maria anticipated as she turned and quickly walked back up the aisle alone, followed by a strutting Caiozzo and the three *citrulli*.

Caiozzo caught up with Maria on the steps outside the church, the same steps on which she stood weeks earlier with her parents during the fateful encounter with Caiozzo. Her defenses began to crumble in the swelling heat and she felt herself passing into a surreal world, alone, afraid and traumatized by the events of the past 24 hours.

As her legs began to betray her, Caiozzo caught her elbow to prevent a fall. She looked up at him with wet, sorrowful eyes and dry, parted lips, and weakly murmured, "Why?"

Three aged prune-wrinkled women on their way to Mass wearing their ubiquitous black dresses, stopped and observed the pitiful sight. They were aware of the events of the previous evening and, life long members of the village, knew what had just occurred inside the church. They blessed themselves, nodded empathetically, and wondered if the final public humiliation of blood-stained sheets would hang from Caiozzo's window the following day.

Caiozzo led the group back to his apartment where he dismissed Ciuto and Mosca, but asked Lorenzo to remain.

"Tomorrow you may take the day off with pay," he offered as an inducement. Lorenzo was delighted. He welcomed the pay and was gratified to be serving Caiozzo during this momentous event.

Maria sat at the table in Caiozzo's cramped apartment, her head on her hands and closed her eyes. Exhausted, she fell into a deep sleep and awoke with a start about a half hour later to the sound of coffee beans being crushed in a mortar. Wordlessly, Caiozzo poured cool water into a cup and placed it in front of Maria. She hesitated, then despite herself, grabbed the cup with both hands and drained it in one gulp, quenching her thirst and restoring moisture to her dry, sour mouth. He poured more water into a bowl and placed it on the table with a bar of soap and a cloth, then walked out and sat with Lorenzo on the bench.

"Lorenzo," he said looking at his pocket watch which read 7:20, "sometime this morning Maria will need to go to her parents' house to gather clothing, personal items and, maybe, her dowry. I want you to accompany her in the wagon and assist her in retrieving her belongings. But, under no circumstances, enter the Pepitone house, and do not answer any questions they may have or engage in any conversation. Take my pocket instrument and mark the time, returning here by 3:00 pm. You might also take a jug of water, some cheese and figs. I'm certain the Pepitones will not offer you anything."

Caiozzo returned to the kitchen as Maria furtively stuffed a piece of cheese in her mouth.

"Good," Caiozzo said smiling, "you need to eat something after this wearisome, stressful night." She responded to this clumsy show of concern by tossing a fig across the table.

"Maria," Caiozzo said with feigned solicitude, "I'm going to permit your return to the house of your parents for a few hours to assure them that you are well and in no danger and to allow you to take your dowry and everything you need as we begin our life together. Lorenzo will, of course, assist you."

Maria felt nauseated and choked hearing the words, 'life together.'

"Permit, allow?" she responded in disgust and went on sarcastically, "How generous of you, Caiozzo."

"Maria!," Caiozzo snapped at her, unable to contain his anger, "my Christian name is Giuseppe, and I demand that you respect and address me as such."

"Demand?" she replied, "you would be more successful demanding that the sun rise at midnight. And as for respect, I more respect the wolves that stalk and devour their prey in the woods than I do you."

Caiozzo's face burned blood red as he stormed out the door and shouted to a lazing Lorenzo, "Hitch the horses to the wagon, take her to the Pepitones, bring her back at 3:00 o'clock, and let us end this bothersome shit now!"

As the cart with Maria and Lorenzo disappeared over the hill toward Via Bovia, Caiozzo mounted his horse and rode in the opposite direction to his mother's house on the far side of Via Umberto.

"So, *bravo*!" Sofia greeted him comfortably embedded in her padded chair with folded arms. "*Bravo*, you have successfully achieved your goal. A beautiful young girl, a virgin, no doubt, from a respected family in the village. Congratulations." While her congratulations were sincere, her tone was also faintly mocking.

"Mamma, I...I," Caiozzo began stammering.

"No need to explain anything to me, Giuseppe," Sofia said absolving her son. "I have lived my entire life in this village and am well-acquainted with the accepted way you pursued and attained the bride of your choice. I knew," she continued, "of your intentions weeks ago when I looked into your eyes that day at Mass and saw your determination. But you look troubled, my son. Are you not happy, at least satisfied, with your prize?" She prodded.

"My satisfaction," Giuseppe replied, "is tempered by fears of what might occur in the future. I know what can happen when young women marry older men, how they may wander and seek pleasure with men closer to their age."

"Who will know better than you,?" his mother asked caustically. "You are twice her age and, as the years pass and your fire smolders and turns to ash, hers may just be beginning to rage."

"Thank you very much for your kind words of advice and consolation mamma," Caiozzo coldly returned.

"I'm sorry I can offer you neither, Giuseppe," she said. "This is the course you have chosen, and you must now live with your decision. But," she continued, "you may have yet another problem to consider with this young girl."

"And what would that be?" he asked, exasperated.

Sofia measured her words.

"Giuseppe, this young girl comes from a family which has never conformed to the ways of this village. The father is not a man of the soil and comes from more than forty years of artisans who made their living pandering to the gentry. The mother, Amelia, has Norman blood and spent part of her childhood educated in France living with well to do relatives. And, as you know, Antonio, Maria's brother, is a teacher and writes for a newspaper in Palermo, and he encourages his sister to read, a skill she quickly learned in her six years of schooling. She was a difficult pupil, constantly requiring reprimand from the good sisters because of her tendency to question and challenge authority during lessons."

Caiozzo was astounded at the scope of his mother's knowledge of the history of the Pepitone family, particularly Maria.

"How, mamma, did you come to all this information about the Pepitone family?" he asked his mother.

"Giuseppe," his mother said with a sly smile, "the weekly meeting with the other widows after Sunday Mass affords more than *café* and *cannoli*. Speaking little, but listening with the third ear and watching with the third eye, yields much information which can be useful, and few things in life are more valuable than good information. But why are you so surprised, Giuseppe?" she asked. "Where do you think your talent comes from?"

Caiozzo's head fell to the back of the chair and his hands dropped to his sides.

"And all these years, mamma, without knowing it, I was learning at the feet of a master," he replied mocking.

"Be aware, Giuseppe, that your little Maria is an educated, willful and feisty young girl, not easily dictated to and controlled. But I'm sure you have already discovered that for yourself," she said, looking at the blood-stained wrap around his hand.

CHAPTER 12

Maria didn't wait for Lorenzo to bring the wagon to a full stop. She jumped from the seat and ran to the door calling to her parents with a mixture of joy and distress.

"Amelia," Nino shouted to his wife in the bedroom. "It's Maria, Maria is here."

Amelia emerged skeptically, rubbing swollen eyes, then seeing her daughter, cried out, "Maria, *me figghia, me figghia, grazzii a Diu*." The three hugged in a protracted embrace of sobs and wet kisses before settling on the divan in the salon. Maria sat between her parents, whose hands held hers so tightly she voiced a mild complaint.

"Are you all right?" her mother asked breathless.

"I am not physically injured if that is what you mean," she replied. "But, as I'm sure you know," she said beginning to choke, "I was taken by three of Caiozzo's men from the piazza last night and brought to a shed in the vineyard where Caiozzo was waiting and...," she paused sobbing, "held overnight until this morning."

"Did he? Did he?" Pepitone began as Amelia bit down on her knuckles.

"No papa, no," she interrupted turning toward him. "He never touched me. He didn't stay at the shed but returned this morning and he, his three workers and I went to the church where *Padre* Pietro was waiting."

"Oh Diu miu, my God!," Pepitone exclaimed, then quietly murmured, *fuitina*, rising from the divan and punching the plaster wall, leaving fragments on the floor.

"According to *Padre* Pietro, who speaks for the church," Maria said with a bitter sigh, "I am now the wife of Giuseppe Caiozzo."

Maria's words hung in the air like clouds portending a violent downpour and left the parents speechless.

An agitated and guilt-ridden Pepitone pulled his daughter to him and began to sob, crying, "I'm sorry Maria, I'm so sorry."

"We suspected for weeks that Caiozzo might attempt this action. That's why we took the precaution of involving Stuffa and his cousins. But we were not attentive enough at the *festa*. We allowed ourselves to be lulled into a false sense of security," he said, his voice rising to a woeful lament, "with this calamitous result," Pepitone moaned.

"Maria," Amelia said through tears, "please try to understand we did everything possible when we realized you were missing. We tried to enlist Luongo's help but his search was half-hearted. He gave us some weak bureaucratic excuse, but we now know his real reason for not being more aggressive was his fear of crossing Bono. When he found out you were missing, Bono made it clear that he wouldn't tolerate an aggressive search which might lead to war if any of the three men from Alcamo were injured or killed by men from Castellammare. He was concerned that a war would disrupt his business interests...his business interests, more precious than the life of an innocent child," she exploded. "Oh, my Maria, my poor Maria!" she cried, embracing her daughter.

"Mamma, papa, I know that you did all you could to prevent this awful thing from happening, and I don't blame you for Luongo's failure. But if I had known that Caiozzo was stalking me I might have been on my guard at the *festa*. I know you were trying to protect me but you should have told me that I was in danger," she moaned, disappointed.

"I know, I know," Pepitone sighed as he sank into a chair castigating himself for not having had more resolve and demanding that Luongo mount an attack to free her.

"Papa," Maria said, "it could never have happened."

"How can you be so sure?" Pepitone asked puzzled.

"Last night Caiozzo told me exactly what Bono's warning to Luongo was which led me to end all hope of being rescued: Bono would never risk disrupting the harmony with surrounding neighbors to...to," she sobbed, "rescue an obscure little village girl. Mamma, papa," Maria continued, trying to console them, "that evil man could not be stopped. The police, Bono and even the Church were helping him, and he was very much aware of that fact. He triumphed but he may yet live to regret it someday," she added cryptically.

Maria's words were perplexing and did nothing to comfort her father. But Amelia took a small measure of hope from what she heard, a note of defiance and determination not to be broken. My daughter, she thought, may have more strength and wisdom than we imagined and may yet survive this misfortune.

. . .

With an idiot's grin fastened to his face, Antonio could hardly contain his joy as he sat on the train for the two and a half hour trip to Castellammare and Sunday dinner with his family. His delight was the result of the events of the previous week during which he was shown a review written by Giovanni Verga, one of Italy's premier fiction writers, describing him as, "..a long-awaited, fresh, exciting voice on Sicily's literary landscape." By a strange coincidence, two days after the review circulated, he received a note from Elio Zappa, chairman of the literature department of the University in Palermo, inviting him to discuss a position as an assistant professor. By week's end, Antonio accepted an offer of 1200 *lire* a month, almost double what he was receiving at the high school where he was teaching. The flexible schedule at the university also permitted him more time to spend on his writing, an activity the university strongly encouraged. Antonio eagerly anticipated sharing the news of his good fortune with his parents and sister.

The smile left his face and his warm feelings were extinguished as he approached his parents' home and saw a man armed with a rifle standing near the door.

"Who the hell are you and what are you doing here?" Antonio demanded.

"Go inside, Antonio, and your parents and sister will explain everything," Lorenzo told him laconically.

"What?...what are you...how do you know my name?" Antonio asked trembling. Too anxious to wait for an answer he pushed past Lorenzo and burst through the door, frantically calling, "Mamma, papa, Maria." He found them in the salon huddled on the divan in an obvious state of distress. The eyes of all three reflected anxiety and sadness.

A slumping Nino got up and embraced Antonio and sought strength and solace from his son but was unable to offer the comfort and strength of a father. Antonio held his father for a moment then sat down next to Maria who clung to him wordlessly with her head on his chest and began to weep.

"What, what's happening here with my family?" he asked in anguish.

"Antonio," Amelia began slowly, "last night at the *festa* Maria was abducted by three of Caiozzo's men, abducted from under us, and held captive overnight at his vineyard shed. And this morning..."

"Abducted, held captive overnight," he shouted. He thought for a moment then quietly uttered, *fuitina*. "So, so, that's what all your concerns were about last month. Why didn't you say something to me, why didn't you tell me?" he asked with rising anger. "Damn it, am I not a member of this family? Don't I have a right to know if there is trouble concerning my own sister?"

"Antonio," Maria broke in softly, "mamma and papa went to great lengths with elaborate tales to hide their concerns from both of us. They didn't want to create alarm and, by handling it secretly with Stuffa's support, they honestly believed they could prevent...this, this." Maria couldn't finish and began to sob again.

"And that, that thug out there with the rifle," he pointed, "is he one of the abductors?" Antonio asked, burning with rage. He got up quickly and walked into the kitchen, returning with a large butcher's knife in his hand.

"Antonio, what are you doing with that?" Amelia screamed hysterically.

"What am I doing, mamma? I'm going to stop this madness now and, after I end the scum outside, I'll take his rifle and put Caiozzo where he belongs."

"Are you *pazzu*?" Amelia shrieked rushing to block her son's exit and grabbing his wrist with both hands.

"Antonio, no, please," Maria implored, joining her mother to restrain him while Pepitone sat irresolute, paralyzed in his chair. Dazed, Antonio looked at his mother then at his pleading sister and dropped the knife to the floor. Amelia shoved him on the divan and slapped him hard across the face.

"Are you crazy?" she repeated. "Don't you see the likely outcome of such an action? Even if you succeeded in killing Caiozzo, I might have my daughter back, but I would surely lose a son in a vendetta, or retribution from Bono, or the hangman's noose. Yes, our Maria is the victim of a cruel and brutal act, but she is alive, and I will still be able to hold her, feel her warmth, breathe her scent and hear her voice. What do I embrace, if my son is under the dirt in the cemetery, a cold hard stone?"

"Your mother is right, Antonio," Nino joined in. "And, and," he hesitatingly added in a pathetic attempt to relieve his guilt, "Maria will, at least, be secure and protected under Caiozzo's roof." Maria closed her eyes and looked away from her father, and Antonio's angry response was halted by Amelia's fingers pressed against his lips. She looked at her husband in amazement, as though she'd never really seen him before. She couldn't believe the words she heard and her disappointment and grief was overwhelming. She realized she had lost more than her daughter that day.

Maria set the table and sliced the bread as her mother stirred the *pasta ca fasola* and put out a platter of cold meat. She realized that she had not eaten a meal in more than twenty hours and the familiar aroma of the thick, bubbling *minestra* made her mouth water and offered some comfort. As it was with most Sicilian children, mamma's food always satisfied more than just an appetite.

"How long will you stay, Maria?" Nino asked, looking at his pocket watch which showed 1:30.

"I heard Caiozzo tell the one outside that we should return by 3:00 o'clock," she answered.

"So then," Antonio said as he recovered his senses, "we have an hour and a half to begin to develop a family plan by which you can endure this wretched situation with that beast."

"Well," Pepitone began, "I think..."

Amelia raised her hand toward her husband. "Don't interrupt, Nino" Amelia said softly but sternly. "What are your thoughts?" she asked Antonio, as Pepitone slipped quietly back in his chair. Antonio glanced at his father, paused for a moment to reflect, then said, "We all know that Maria is an intelligent, free-thinking young woman who is not afraid to speak her mind. You recall, even as a pupil in school, she was known to be outspoken and questioned authority, much to the chagrin of the good sisters," he said, smiling and reaching out to touch her hand. "Maria must use her strength and take the initiative by immediately establishing guidelines, making it clear to Caiozzo that this family will never abandon her and that she will not give in to his intimidation or attempts to completely control her."

"But how does Maria accomplish this?" Pepitone asked. "After all, she will be…"

"Nino, Amelia exclaimed, "let Antonio finish," she said, and Pepitone fell back in his chair.

"First, and very important," Antonio said to Maria, "he cannot deny you the right to visit your parents. Inform him now of your intention to spend every Sunday and all holidays at the table of our family, his presence excluded, of course. He will be hard-pressed to deny you because, when word of his refusal circulates among the neighbors that he will not allow you to see your family, he will anger the villagers who hold this right inviolable. He will not want his image to suffer. Also, offer the animal a carrot by letting him know you have no objection to one of his *citrulli* accompanying you and standing outside the door in the heat, the cold or the rain as you enjoy the warmth and comfort of your family."

Maria's eyes brightened and her smile widened as she felt a surge of empowerment at Antonio's words, lessening the gloom and despair she felt earlier. She leaned toward her brother, kissed him repeatedly on the cheek and said with resolved determination, "Yes, *frati*, I will do as you say, I trust your judgment completely and I'm confident that things will go better for me if I follow your directions."

Amelia smiled for the first time all day as she left her chair and held her son's head close to her breast, saying, "Antonio, your words lighten the heavy heart of your mother, make sense, and give us hope that not all is lost."

"Yes, yes, very good, Antonio. I had the very same thoughts and was about to express them," Nino said pouring a second glass of wine.

"Yes," Amelia said expressionless turning to her husband, "I'm sure you did, Nino."

"So," Amelia continued, "we can have hope that our Maria will be able to at least salvage and protect her dignity, and maintain ties with her family. "Nino," she suddenly ordered, "clear the table, brew the espresso and slice the *cassata*. Maria and I have women things to discuss which are not for men's ears," she said leading her daughter into the bedroom.

The mother and daughter retreated to Maria's bedroom and sat on the bed as Amelia took her hand.

"Maria," Amelia began, "tonight you will experience…"

"I know, mamma, I know, I am well aware of all the particulars and know what to expect," she said with disgust. "Agata and I have been talking about this for the past three years."

"Of course, Maria, how silly of me to think that you and your friends have not discussed sexual matters. But," Amelia continued, "this is not the time or the man you have chosen to give yourself to in marriage. He has taken you and, despite what the church may say, you are under no obligation to willingly discharge wifely duties. What will occur will not be an act of love but the satisfaction of physical pleasure for a beastly man who seeks to use and control you. Retain at least a small measure of self respect and dignity by turning your back to him and avoid his lecherous eyes. And here," she said, reaching into her pocket, "take this rosary which has been with the women of our family for generations, clutch it tightly in your hands and concentrate on where you have come from and where you may yet ascend to. You know, Maria, I take some comfort when I think of the words you spoke earlier in the day about evil triumphing, but perhaps only temporarily."

"I'm glad you recall those words, mamma...I believe that truly, and, with God's help, I can live with this nightmare."

Amelia smiled and hugged her.

"Now, Maria, as to your dowry. We will not give you any monies or articles of value, you understand why, of course."

"Of course," Maria replied.

"These will remain in the house for your use only, whenever you need them. Take the fine linens, towels and any other personal items which may comfort you, but I will exclude frilly and lacy undergarments. And take your long cotton and flannel nightgowns so..."

"I know, I understand mamma," Maria said, embarrassed.

"Yes, of course you do," Amelia replied gently stroking Maria's cheek.

A series of knocks and a voice from outside the front door startled them.

"*Signura, signura,*" it called.

Amelia went down the hallway and opened the door.

"What do you want?" she coldly asked.

"Ah, *scusi, signura,*" Lorenzo said, "but I was calling for *la signura* Caiozzo. We must leave now."

Maria and her mother finished packing the dowry into a small leather trunk Pepitone had made for his daughter years earlier. As she put the Bronte and Austen books in the trunk, Antonio entered the bedroom and dropped a rare anthology of selected English poems alongside the two others. He embraced his sister and called her attention to one work in particular, *To Althea from Prison*, by Richard Lovelace, quoting from the last stanza;

Stone walls do not a prison make,
Nor iron bars a cage;

Minds innocent and quiet take
That for a hermitage;
If I have freedom in my love
  And in my soul am free,
Angels alone that soar above,
Enjoy such liberty.

"Remember these words and the truth they express," Antonio said to his sister, "and remember always that your family will never desert you."

The parting was wrenching for everyone, but particularly difficult for Nino, who could not contain a paroxysm of heaving sobs, as he clutched his daughter tightly in his arms and had to be pried away by Lorenzo. Antonio glared menacingly at Lorenzo and was gently but firmly restrained by Amelia.

"Please, *signura*, we must go now," Lorenzo said, taking Maria's arm and placing the trunk in the back of the wagon. From her seat, she turned and kept pensive eyes on her family until they were out of sight and the wagon disappeared down the road.

CHAPTER 13

The cold came early to Sicily in 1892 and the night frost damaged the lemons and oranges so badly that many landowners suffered unexpected losses as the fruit withered and dropped from the trees and the day lost its sweet fragrance.

Maria sat on a chair in the corner of the small bedroom staring at the open trunk with linens and clothing hanging over the side. A chest with two empty drawers ajar was against the wall, but Maria could not bring herself to put her possessions in the same space occupied by Caiozzo's underwear. The kerosene lamp offered some heat, but barely enough to halt the appearance of goose skin on her arms. She walked to the trunk and took one of the sweaters Amelia had knitted, and lovingly rubbed it against her cheek. She slid her arms through the sleeves and buttoned it to the top. She then put on a pair of knit leggings with foot pockets and returned to the corner chair with the anthology of English poetry Antonio had given her that morning. She turned to the Lovelace poem, concentrating on the last stanza; "Stone walls do not a prison make...," when she heard Caiozzo in the kitchen cursing the packet of damp kindling wood which did not hold a flame in the stove. The front door slammed and Caiozzo returned a few minutes later cursing the "thieving bastard of a neighbor," who charged him three *lire* for a bundle of dry wood.

The small apartment began to warm and Caiozzo called to her from the kitchen.

"Come in here, Maria, where it's warm and have some spaghetti my mother prepared." Maria ignored the offer and was grateful she had eaten well at her parents' home that afternoon. Even if her stomach cried out for food, she thought, she would never eat anything that the mother of that monster prepared. She sat reading next to the kerosene lamp until the slurping in the kitchen suddenly stopped and the light went out. She knew the moment she dreaded was coming and quickly extinguished the lamp, pulling her knees to her chest in a sitting fetal position.

The soft pale light from a cold moon slipped through the window, revealing Caiozzo's silhouette as he removed his shirt and trousers, and fell heavy onto the bed. After a few moments, his voice broke the silence.

"Come to bed now, Maria," he commanded. "The bond of marriage has been sealed by the Church. You are my wife and nothing will change that."

Maria did not respond and quietly dropped her feet to the floor, closed her eyes and feigned sleep. She felt his presence looming over her in the dark like an evil specter.

"Come now, Maria," he said placing his hand at the small of her back. "This little charade of yours will not work," as he swept her up in his arms and laid her on the bed. She quickly turned on her side facing the wall as her mouth dried and her eyes moistened. She wrapped the rosary beads around the wrists of her clenched hands and silently began reciting the Hail Mary. She felt Caiozzo's fingers fumbling to unbutton her sweater and heard the snap releasing her brassiere, then felt the straps pulled from her shoulders. He tugged at the top of her leggings and pulled them down past her buttocks, massaging her vagina with one hand and her breast with the other. Maria stiffened, continued her prayers, and gripped the bellows of the sheets, biting down on the corner of the pillow as Caiozzo entered her. She smothered any vocal issue despite her disgust and his foul, heaving breath drifting past her nostrils.

Caiozzo was satisfied quickly and released her, falling onto his back, then into a deep sleep. Maria waited for a few minutes then left the bed, went into the kitchen, shuddering and quietly weeping, and thoroughly washed herself hoping that the sperm had not found its mark.

...

The next morning Caiozzo abruptly woke to an empty bed and, fearing a desertion, ran into the kitchen. He was relieved by the scent of fresh-brewed coffee, poured a cup and walked outside where Maria was sitting on the bench.

"Well, Maria," he said, puffing, satisfied, "I'm happy to see you continuing your wifely duties," as he saluted her with his coffee cup. Maria paused for a moment, turned stone-faced, then said:

"Last night you took what you wanted, but understand I did not, nor will I ever, freely, give myself to you. You have violated my body, but my thoughts are unstained and my soul remains pure. How will you explain your lecherous actions when the time comes to save your soul?" she demanded. He gaped in amazement and disappointment, having foolishly assumed she had willingly submitted to him. Before he could respond, she continued;

"I will cook because I must eat, I will clean because I refuse to live in filth. But I will never put my hands on your body in a loving embrace, or on your dirty clothes. Let your mother attend to this need as she has for these many years, or pay the women in the town to wash the stains off your underwear. And know this, Caiozzo, I will spend every Sunday, and every holiday at the home of my parents." Caiozzo responded with a string of invectives, but Maria remained adamant.

"Rage all you want, Caiozzo," Maria replied, defying him, "but if you dare place any restrictions on visits or engagements with my family, your prohibitions will be the topic of conversation on the steps of the Church every Sunday, and your mother will have many questions to answer as she sits with the other widows at the *pasticceria*."

Determined to recover a vestige of self-respect and honor as a newly-wedded man, he stormed into the bedroom and tore the blood stained sheets off the bed. Returning to the kitchen, he hung the sheets out the window, a vulgar display in accord with a Sicilian custom, proving to the villagers that his bride was a virgin on the day of the wedding.

Undaunted, Maria turned and looked at Caiozzo with scorn.

"And what do you think that proves?" she asked sarcastically, then answered her own question. "The neighbors can just as easily suspect that your mother will have one less chicken to feed today as believe that the blood on the sheet comes from a virgin bride. I have heard it would not be the first time such a ploy would have been used in this village."

Reflecting on his own experience with women in the village, Caiozzo knew Maria's words rang true. His head shook uncontrollably and the veins in his neck swelled like pasta boiling in water. Reeling at the words and unable to offer a keen response, he mounted his horse and shouted a lame, "Vaffanculu," as he rode off in the direction of the tavern.

Sofia Caiozzo slept fitfully the week following her son's marriage to Maria. Although *fuitina* was a widespread, if not encouraged, manner by which a man might satisfy his need for the woman of his choice, she was concerned that public sentiment, particularly among women might hold against Giuseppe because of his reputation for scandalous escapades with married women, shady business dealings, and the animosity most villagers felt toward him, not to mention the sympathy many felt for the Pepitone family, who were well liked in the village. She decided to forgo attendance at Sunday Mass and coffee with the women at the *pasticceria* for at least a few weeks to avoid embarrassing questions and allow the gossip to abate.

But she was feeling even more uneasiness about the prospect of a rival whose presence in her son's life might command more of his time and attention, diminishing her place, a concern quite common in Sicilian mothers. Considering Maria's contempt for Caiozzo, her fears were groundless. While she was well aware that her daughter-in-law loathed her son and wanted nothing from him, it was inevitable that he would force her to bear his children, and, with the added expense of supporting a family, he might be inclined to withdraw some of the support she had come to expect. Despite his philandering and other indulgences, he had always provided well for her but the circumstances had changed. She needed to protect her interests.

Sofia was aware of her son's habit of secretly feathering his nest with substantial portions of his salary and bonus money that he buried in the ground under the chicken coop. Ah! She thought, chortling to herself, did he really believe he could fool his mother with that ruse of feeding the chickens?

The more she thought about the buried money, the more concerned and determined she became to obtain an account of his holdings. If he lied and tried to tell her that he could not afford to maintain her standard of living, she could then confront him with the truth, but first she needed to know exactly how much wealth he had stashed away. Her comfortable life style was at stake.

Sofia rose early on a damp, dark late autumn day and was encouraged by the dense clouds yielding a steady sprinkle of rain. Good, she thought, the rain will soften the ground making the dig easier. She dressed warmly in a sweater, leggings, and a sheepskin coat, pulled rubber boots over her feet, then put a flop cap on her head. She ignored the ache the damp brought to her swollen knees and walked gingerly over the rain-slicked ground to the small shed behind the house, took a bag of corn meal and a shovel and went to the chicken coop. She opened the gate and went in, standing at the entrance and scattered the corn meal at her feet summoning the chickens in the manner of country folk; "*Pila, pila, pila,*" she called, as the hungry flock gathered pecking around her. The rest of the coop was now clear and she could begin her hunt unobstructed. As Sofia moved forward, her feet became entangled among the flapping covey and she lost her balance on the slick ground, screaming as she landed head first on the tip of the shovel producing a surge of blood down her face. Sofia never regained consciousness and her crumpled, rain-soaked body was discovered later that morning by a passing neighbor, Tatada who, after determining that she was dead and covering her, hitched his mule to his cart and hurried to the church to report the deadly accident to *Padre* Pietro.

Tatada and the priest then returned to the house and carried the body to the salon where they spread a dry blanket and placed Sofia on the divan. *Padre* Pietro then administered the sacrament of Extreme Unction, the sacrament for the dead, and ordered Tatada to go to the home of the widow, *la signura* Mortuannu, inform and return with her.

Infants entering life in Sicily were delivered by a midwife, and the poor departing souls were attended to by people like *la signura* Mortuannu whose family had enjoyed a brisk business in Castellammare for decades. Embalming and other preservative measures of mortuary science were not available in the small villages at that time and preparation of a body for the wake, the church service and the burial was handled exclusively by the skilled and knowledgeable *signura*.

Wearing her solemn funeral face and bearing her sack of scented soaps, dried herbs, cloth and other necessary items, the widow arrived and promptly took command.

"*Padre*," she said to the priest, "I must wash, prepare and dress *la signura* in clean clothes now. Your presence, with all due respect, is not necessary."

"No, of course not," the priest replied. "My task now is to go to the home of Don Giuseppe Caiozzo and deliver the sad news," he said sighing, "and comfort him in his time of grief."

"Yes, and if I may suggest, *Padre*," the *signura* added, "you might first stop at the work shop of Giovanni, the carpenter, and see about a coffin. He always keeps two or three about and we will need one as soon as possible."

"But *signura*, shouldn't we wait for Don Caiozzo to make that arrangement?" the priest asked.

"We could, but in my experience, the family of the deceased is always grateful that these unhappy details have been attended to, freeing them to grieve without distraction."

"Yes, I see, *signura* Mortuannu," the priest replied. "I will do as you suggest."

"Tatada," he asked, "may I impose on you to take me to the home of Don Caiozzo?"

"*Padre*, I am at your disposal for as long as you need me," he replied, happy to be a participant in the dramatic event.

After stopping at the workshop of Giovanni the carpenter and ordering the coffin, they arrived at Caiozzo's apartment on Via Giglio just as he was saddling his horse for the ride to the vineyard for the morning inspection.

"Ah *Padre*!" Caiozzo exclaimed as the cart pulled up. "I was just on my way to the rectory to pay you for the service you provided last week, an unfortunate oversight on my part." Caiozzo reached into the purse hanging from his belt, took the priest's hand, and dropped a generous ten *lire* in coin into his palm. Pietro looked appropriately solemn as a bearer of sad news and Caiozzo took his expression to be one of displeasure, prompting Giuseppe to ask, "What *Padre*, not enough?" he said laughing, as he reached into his purse again. Pietro grasped Caiozzo's hand, held it tightly and said, "This is not why I am here this morning, Don Giuseppe."

"What the...what is it?" Caiozzo asked puzzled, tilting his head.

"These matters are never easy and it pains me to tell you that, this morning, Tatada here found your poor mother..."

"Found, found, what do you mean?" Caiozzo interrupted.

"...found your mother," Pietro continued, "lying on the ground in the chicken coop at her home."

Caiozzo's eyes widened and his jaw tightened as he asked, "Is she all right, is she injured...is, is she..."

"Regrettably," the priest shook his head and sadly replied, "*morta*."

"Oh, no, Santa Maria," he cried, throwing his head back and clasping it in his hands as he rocked back and forth. Maria was in the bedroom when she heard her name mentioned and slipped behind the half-open front door.

"What happened, what happened,?" Caiozzo asked anguished.

"I'm so sorry," Tatada said, stepping forward, "but this morning as I was passing your mother's home, I noticed a form on the ground in the chicken coop. I went in to investigate and found your poor mother on the ground. I felt her pulse but...but, she was already gone, lying in the middle of scattered corn meal with a shovel at her side. She must have slipped while feeding the chickens and fell, causing a mortal wound to her head."

"Corn meal, shovel," Caiozzo murmured, then erupted in hysterical sobs and laughter.

Tatada and the priest looked at each other, and Pietro whispered, "shock."

"Oh, *Diu miu!*" Caiozzo exclaimed, "I must go to her now."

Pietro held his hands up and said, "No, Don Giuseppe, now is not a good time. We have taken the liberty of sending for the widow Mortuannu, who is tending to your mother as we speak. We have also arranged for the...the...her final resting place to be delivered to her home this afternoon by the carpenter, Giovanni, so that the widow may complete her preparations. I will alert the parishioners of this sad time so they may go to your mother's house to pay their respects this evening. I will also schedule a Mass for noon tomorrow before..."

"Yes, yes," Caiozzo said absently.

He looked at the *Padre* through sad red eyes and uttered, what were probably the most heartfelt words anyone in Castellammare ever heard from Caiozzo.

"*Padre*, your words and deeds have my undying gratitude. I will never forget your kindness and compassion," he said embracing Pietro.

Always eager to be on Caiozzo's good side, the priest was gratified to hear these words. "I must go now," the priest said, "for I have many arrangements to make and much work to do."

"Yes, *Padre, e grazzii tanti ancora*, thank you again," Caiozzo replied.

CHAPTER 14

Maria hurried back to the bedroom as she heard Caiozzo approach the door and sat, putting her face in a book. He stood in the doorway watching Maria read and ignoring his presence. Finally, he said, forcing back tears, "I'm sure you heard the sad news *Padre* Pietro brought this morning. Can you not, at least, offer a word of condolence for my loss?" he asked.

Maria slowly placed the book on her lap, thought for a moment, and vacantly looked directly at Caiozzo, replying, "The death of a mother is among the saddest moments in our lives, but not as sad as the loss of a child. I am too preoccupied, thinking about my grieving parents and their loss, and my own," she added "whereby I am deprived of the cheer of my family and the promise of a life of my own choosing. I cannot join in your bereavement," she said, sharply, returning to her book.

Caiozzo hesitated for a moment, shuffled his feet, then asked, "Will you, at least accompany me to the funeral Mass tomorrow?"

Without looking up, Maria brusquely answered, "Only if I'm dragged."

Caiozzo stifled an angry response, turned and walked outside, mounted his horse, and rode, lamenting, to his mother's house.

Sofia's wake, funeral Mass and internment in the cemetery at the church of San Giuseppe alongside her husband and two children followed a familiar Sicilian script and was well-attended by Castellammare's sorority of widows. The old women dressed in perpetual black wailed, prayed aloud and cried copiously at the open coffin, then again on the walk from the church to the cemetery, following a brass band tediously rendering lugubrious funeral music.

As the coffin was lowered they formed a line and, one by one, went to Giuseppe, reached up clasping his face with both hands and tenderly kissed him on each cheek. Lagging behind the other mourners were the three *citrulli*, striving gamely to summon tears of grief. Caiozzo was very moved by the show of affection for his mother and the sympathy expressed for his loss. Fortunately, he didn't hear the widows expressing their real sentiments as they made their way to the *pasticceria*.

"Her hand rarely found the bottom of a purse when it came time to pay her share at the *pasticceria*," one said.

"And if ever it did," said another laughing, "it was probably because she was holding someone else's purse."

"And her sauce was a disgrace," a third added. "She was too lazy to peel the tomatoes, and the skins floated on top like discarded laundry."

But the last comment delivered by the widow Alfia was the most cutting, producing an eruption of cackling among the group.

"Her home was so dirty it was rejected by the two pigs she kept in the pen. I think the only time the broom left the corner of the kitchen was when the *strega*, the witch, needed it to fly her to the Village for a loaf of bread."

After the service ended, Caiozzo rode to his mother's house that was now his, off Via Umberto just below the vineyard. He wept quietly, as he wandered pitiably through the empty rooms and missed his mother more than he could have imagined. He went into her bedroom and sat on her bed, the same bed he had crawled into for comfort as a frightened trembling child the night his father died when he was ten. He suddenly realized that he was now completely alone; the only person who had stood between him and the cold void of a world without love was gone, and there was no one to whom he could turn for succor.

He got up, went into the kitchen, and found an open bottle of wine. He poured some into a cup and drank, ignoring the sour taste hinting the wine was turning to vinegar. He poured a second cup and continued his walk through the rooms, rousing a vivid memory here, a vague recollection there.

A prudent consumption of wine can often spur the imagination, and prompt ideas and thoughts which might, otherwise, not have materialized. Caiozzo looked around and considered the dimensions of the house which had a second floor with three bedrooms and a main level with a large kitchen, an indoor *furnu*, and a dining area adjoining the salon. By Castellammare standards, it was palatial.

His spirits lifted as he imagined a house echoing with the sound of children, playing, laughing and running about teasing each other, his children who would love and respect their papa. A yearning for fatherhood was one of his motives for abducting Maria but, so far, she had shown no inclination to be a willing partner or please him in any way. He resented her cold refusal to attend his mother's funeral, but was unwilling to create a spectacle by dragging her to it. He remembered his mother's prediction that Maria would not easily bend to his demands. She had shown her strong will and spirit when she established the future parameters of her relationship with her family. Caiozzo was willing to make some concessions but, on one point, he was adamant; Maria would fulfill her duties as a wife, satisfying his physical needs, and deliver children to fill the empty rooms of the house.

Maria showed no reaction when Caiozzo told her of his plan to move them into his mother's house. "Whatever you prefer," she uttered, disinterested. She concealed her relief that the spaciousness of the house on Via Umberto would give her the luxury of some privacy and distance from the closeness to Caiozzo which the small apartment had forced her to endure. Maria also looked forward to enjoying the pastoral setting on the outskirts of the village where she had always enjoyed reading her books. This sudden event was the only occurrence of an otherwise horrible week which offered Maria a modicum of solace.

Caiozzo decided to make the move immediately so he would be close to his buried money, a charge which produced no argument from her as she began packing. He then rode to the tavern where he knew he would find Lorenzo and the other two who had retreated there after the funeral. He instructed them to take the wagon and go to his apartment, get his clothes, disassemble the bed and bring his other few possessions and Maria to the new residence.

Maria sat at the kitchen table as the three went about their work. They were interrupted by the appearance of Meno, the landlord, who, despite the absence of a lease, demanded to know where Caiozzo was and what was going on. He suspected he was about to lose his monthly twenty *lire* rent money. Lorenzo collared the landlord, pulled him aside and coldly said, "Meno, some things are better off left as they are. I don't think it is in your interest to question Don Giuseppe or pursue this further. But, if you insist, you may follow us and speak to him yourself."

Meno meekly retreated without another word.

With the wagon packed, Maria climbed up next to Lorenzo and asked him to stop at her parents' home so she could advise them of the move and also obtain her own clothes chest. Her plight was still deplorable but less so than when she awoke that morning.

April was a cruel month in 1896 as the driving rain beat relentlessly for days and the wind howled like a hungry wolf at the door of the Caiozzo house. But when it finally stopped and the sun broke through, Spring was everywhere – in the sweet air, in the hardy crocus growing wild between the rocks on the side of the road and in the small cultivated gardens of the houses where asparagus shoots pushed up through the dirt.

After two miscarriages in four years, Maria became pregnant. With her belly full with her first child, she was confined to the bed during the last days of her pregnancy as a precautionary measure. Amelia came every day when she was sure Caiozzo had left for the vineyard, bringing meals and fresh-baked bread. In the four years since her daughter had been forced into the marriage with Caiozzo, not a word had passed between the Pepitones and Caiozzo.

Amelia bathed her daughter, swept the room and prepared a *minestra* for the afternoon meal and a mushroom *frittata* for the evening supper. She fumed as she cooked, knowing that Caiozzo would also eat well that evening. But there was no recourse; her daughter needed to be nourished.

Large-breasted, jovial neighbor Nena Tatada, the midwife, came to assess the stage of the pregnancy, and authoritatively proclaimed,

"One, two days at the most. Maria should not be left alone now. So, so, *signura*, after you leave, I'll wait until Caiozzo returns from the vineyard. When the labor comes, whoever is here, ring the large bell hanging over the front door. I am nearby, less than a kilometer away. We will keep a large pot of water heating on the stove, clean clothes, towels and a washbasin at the bedside."

Satisfied with Nena's thorough preparations, Amelia went upstairs and kissed her daughter goodbye.

"*A dumani, bedda,*" till tomorrow she said.

"*A dumani, mamma,*" Maria replied smiling.

Late that night a loud clang pierced the still air and the midwife quickly waddled across the dark field, a lantern in one hand and a satchel in the other. A nervous Caiozzo met her at the door and the two ran up the stairs to the bedroom. Nena determined that the contractions were two minutes apart and sent Caiozzo downstairs.

"*Va, va*, go, go," Nena ordered, "and bring the pot of hot water." Caiozzo returned and placed the pot on a side table.

"*Allora*, so" the midwife said, "Now leave and go downstairs. I will call you when the baby arrives."

"The baby," Caiozzo responded, "A boy no doubt."

"Whatever you say," Nena replied dismissively.

In less than half an hour, Nena's voice boomed, following a series of screams.

"*Signor* Caiozzo, come, come," she shouted, "come and meet your son."

"My son, my son," he murmured as he hurried up the stairs and paused in the bedroom doorway looking dazed and bewildered.

"Come in, don't be afraid," Nena beckoned as she washed the baby, "the little fellow needs to get the scent of his father now."

"Little fellow," Caiozzo repeated softly, "My prayers have been answered." He looked down at the bawling, scrappy boy with a dense shock of black hair, wrinkled and cranky after his nine month confinement in dark, cramped quarters.

"This one will be a handful," the midwife predicted as she counted fingers and toes, laughing, "at least eight pounds, and his tiny fists already clenched, punching the air, and legs moving like he will walk before he crawls."

"Yes, yes," Caiozzo gushed proudly.

He looked at Maria and saw the faint smile fade from her face.

"And Maria," he asked as an after thought, "*tuttu va beni*, all is well?"

"Yes, Caiozzo, all is well," she replied absently.

Her head fell back to the pillow and she tried to deny his presence as she woefully thought, in four short years I have gone from an innocent young girl to the forced wife of a man I detest, to motherhood. I don't know who I am or how I feel about being a mother. The time went by so quickly, she mused, yet, in that period, events which I could not control have changed my life forever.

The christening took place quietly at the church of San Giuseppe one week later, attended only by the Pepitones and the three *citrulli*. Caiozzo instructed the priest to make the service brief to minimize the possibility of an ugly exchange between the Pepitones and himself. Caiozzo was not concerned with Amelia, whose efforts were spent seeing to the welfare of her daughter, or with Nino whose daily consumption of the grape had made him an amorphous figure fading into a dark corner of family activities. It was Antonio who engendered uneasiness, with his cold, stony glare when they passed each other in the village on a few occasions.

Caiozzo naturally wanted the child named after him, but Maria would have none of it.

"One Giuseppe Caiozzo is more than enough for this village," she told an angry, ranting Caiozzo. Maria remained inflexible and Caiozzo relented with one stipulation;

"My son, then, will not carry the name of your father or your brother," he declared. "This village has no need for another Nino or Antonio," he proclaimed, pleased with his lame attempt to trump Maria's words. Maria remembered what her brother had suggested about offering, "a carrot to the animal," and a compromise was reached; the child was christened, "Carmelo."

Following the christening, Maria suggested to Caiozzo that she spend a few weeks at her parents' home so her mother could assist her with the chores of caring for a newborn. He refused at first then reconsidered, recalling the previous week of a baby crying through the night and a weakened Maria who required attention during the day. Besides, he thought, what did he have to fear;? Where would a mother with a newborn flee?

Caiozzo spent his nights for the next three weeks at the tavern, unmercifully boring the patrons with accounts of his son's birth and his invaluable assistance in the delivery, and regaling them with grossly exaggerated accounts of his son's development in just one week.

"He has already grown one inch and weighs almost two pounds more than he did at birth. I'm certain he'll look like Michelangelo's David before his sixteenth year."

Maria moved back to her parents home and Amelia Pepitone's maternal instincts were obvious as she fed, bathed and carried her grandson about. Maria welcomed the attention her mother gave to Carmelo and the support she felt. But she saw nothing from her father, who maintained his distance, either sitting in the salon or keeping long hours at his shop and scarcely acknowledging his grandson's presence. Maria wondered if her father's guilt and shame made him unable to face her and quietly wept as she saw her once close relationship with him deteriorate.

When Maria returned to the house on Via Umberto after three weeks, Caiozzo was astounded by his son's rapid development in that short period. He had indeed gained three pounds and grown nearly an inch, dimensions confirmed by Nena who had weighed and measured the child.

"I knew it, I knew it," Caiozzo crowed as he picked Carmelo up and walked a kilometer in each direction up and down the road, parading him like a prince in front of his neighbors. Without family or friends to speak of, this was the only venue Caiozzo had to show his son off.

On New Years day in 1897 as Amelia was preparing the traditional lentil and sausage dinner for the holiday, she turned from the stove and was stunned to find a smiling Carmelo grasping his mother's hand and taking baby steps in her direction.

"Oh *Diu miu*, my God!" she exclaimed with outstretched arms as the baby toddled toward her.

"But this baby is months ahead of schedule," Amelia said in amazement.

"The midwife was right, he never did crawl," Maria said laughing.

"Nino," Amelia called out to her husband sitting in the salon, "come here and see the surprise little Carmelo has for us."

A disheveled, bent Pepitone slowly entered the kitchen nursing a glass of grappa, looked dolefully at his daughter then down at Carmelo, forcing a smile.

"So, he stands already," Pepitone stonily observed. "Soon he will be out in the woods with his father shooting rabbits and birds," he added caustically, showing no warmth or feeling for his grandson. He then embraced and kissed Maria before returning to the salon.

Maria looked sorrowfully at her mother who pulled her close and said,

"He still blames himself for what happened. Give him time, Maria," Amelia said, but they both knew time would not change how Pepitone felt.

Despite himself, with no children of his own, the bachelor Antonio was seduced by his nephew who charmed him with his dark staring eyes, wide smile, and acrobatic moves which ended in his lap with tiny fingers playfully slapping his cheeks and pulling his moustache. Antonio returned the gesture with the familiar Sicilian practice of an uncle with thumb and forefinger, pulling down on his nephew's cheeks to the child's squealing delight.

As the months passed to another year, Antonio began spending two Sundays every month in Castellammare, and it was clear his nephew was the reason. The bond between Antonio and Carmelo had blossomed due in no small part to Nino's forfeiture of the expected role between the nonno and the grandchild. The strengthening relationship was not lost on Caiozzo who repeatedly grumbled to Maria, "That damn brother of yours is coming between me and my son, and has too much of an influence on him."

I certainly hope so, I certainly hope so, Maria thought.

CHAPTER 15

During the next few months Caiozzo intensified his efforts to breed more children, repeatedly imposing himself on his unresponsive, disgusted wife. In the late spring of 1897, Maria missed her cycle, and on a rainy day in February of 1898, she delivered her second child.

"Only a girl," a disappointed Caiozzo announced to his friends at the tavern.

Maria, as she was christened, was five weeks premature, a scrawny, sickly baby who cried and coughed her way through the night and required the constant attention of Maria, Amelia and the midwife during the day. Nena was so convinced that the child would not survive she suggested to Giovanni, the carpenter, that he consider fashioning a small coffin as it was just a matter of time. But little Maria survived and became known as, *"La seconda bambina dei miracoli,* the second miracle baby" after her mother.

Her health and strength improved over the next few months, but her growth was clearly stunted. Still, she was an exceptionally beautiful little girl, proportionately correct, alert and animated.

Caiozzo, much to his surprise, found himself bonding strongly with little Maria, as she came to be known, and watched proudly as the little girl who had defied the odds ran with her brother and rivaled Carmelo when it came to standing her ground with other village children. Despite the disparity in size, and appearance, it was obvious they were cut from the same cloth, fiercely protective of and devoted to each other.

One evening at the supper table little Maria asked her mother for a cup of water.

"I told you a hundred times before, no water with the pasta. It bloats and plugs the stomach and makes the passing difficult," Caiozzo snapped.

"But, papa, the sauce is salty and makes me thirsty," Maria implored.

"*Basta*, enough, did you hear what I just said? *Stai zitta*, shut up now and eat."

Little Maria narrowed her eyes and tightened her lips and looked directly at her father.

"*Tu stai zitta* now and eat," she returned, thrusting her tongue, stuffing her thumbs in her ears and wiggling her fingers at him.

An enraged Caiozzo pushed his chair back, got up from the table and reached for his belt as little Maria rushed behind her mother. Carmelo quickly rose and stood between his mother and father with small fists clenched, as Maria waved a threatening finger at her husband and said, "*Non tuccari sta picciridda*, Caiozzo, don't you touch this child."

Caiozzo stared dumbfounded at his family defying him then silently turned, picked up his chair, and resumed eating, thinking with a measure of pride, my God, these children of mine have more balls than all the lions in the jungle.

From 1899 to 1902, Maria disappointed Caiozzo with three more daughters, prompting him to complain, "My wife fails me. She can produce only one son out of five and the bread grows more scarce with each child. And that one son, he is as close to his uncle, her brother, as he is to me."

Actually, as the years passed, both Carmelo and little Maria came to appreciate that their father, if nothing else, was an influential and successful man in the village and they realized that their comfortable lifestyle and status was a result of his industry and cunning. The significance of the neighbors and villagers addressing him as, "Don" was not lost on them either.

On the morning of Carmelo's tenth birthday, Caiozzo called his son to the wagon and unfolded a blanket containing a gleaming Belgium-made lupa rifle. Carmelo's eyes widened and his jaw dropped as he shouted, "Papa, papa, *grazzii*, thank you. You knew what I wanted and you got it for me."

"*Silenziu*, quiet, your mother doesn't need to know right now," he advised his son conspiratorially. "She would object but it's time you learned the ways of the hunter and how to properly handle a weapon. My papa taught me when I was only eight years old." He said nostalgically.

Little Maria had been quietly listening and observing from the doorway, and slowly and deliberately, walked over and confronted them. "I know what that is and I know where you're going. You're going to kill some rabbits with that new gun you bought Carmelo for his birthday," she said sneering at her father.

"Shush, Maria," Caiozzo said looking toward the door.

"Shush, papa?, then take me too," she demanded.

"Out of the question, Maria. You're too young and, besides, you're only a girl," he responded.

"Yeah, too young and only a girl," Carmelo joined his father.

"Only a girl, only a girl," little Maria echoed both of them sarcastically. She then burst into a prototypical Sicilian princess screaming fit, jumping up and down, and shouting.

"I want to come! I want to come! I want to come!"

"For Christ's sake, quiet," Caiozzo implored as his wife came to the door.

"What's going on there" Maria demanded.

Little Maria abruptly stopped her histrionics and looked stone-faced at her father.

"Caiozzo," Maria said, "if you're taking Carmelo someplace and little

Maria wants to go, please take her, for God's sake, and relieve me of at least one day's burden of caring for five children."

"Papa?" little Maria asked, wide-eyed, thrusting her small neck forward. Caiozzo looked at his wife then at Maria.

"All right, all right," he said throwing his hands in the air. "Both of you, get in the wagon. *Ma sta picciridda è na rumpiscatuli*, but this kid is a big pain in the ass," he mumbled as he took his seat.

"By the way, where are you taking them?" Maria shouted.

"Fishing," Caiozzo yelled over his shoulder, "I'm taking them fishing."

Maria's misgivings about her children using guns were ignored and, under their father's tutelage, Carmelo and little Maria became proficient in the use of firearms. Little Maria was relegated to using the small Beretta because of her age and diminutive stature. Nevertheless, she impressed her father and brother with her marksmanship as she blew the necks off wine bottles from five feet away with remarkable consistency.

Her mother was less impressed and bemoaned her failed efforts to interest her daughter in the joys of reading and more gentle pursuits, but was not surprised when Carmelo announced, with the blessing and to the relief of Mother Superior Caterina, the Principal, that he was quitting school. Carmelo had decided that working for wages in the vineyard with his father and spending his spare time in the piazza with his friend Bartolo Fontana, the barber's son, was more rewarding and productive.

"All I earn at school," he said snickering, "are callouses on my ass from the wooden benches and I'm bored with the daily warnings of dried up, wrinkled virgins in gloomy black habits warning me of the wages of sins of the flesh."

As Caiozzo had hoped, Carmelo was becoming an almost perfect specimen of ideal Italian manhood. By his twelfth birthday he was almost five feet, eight inches tall, gargantuan by Sicilian standards, broad in the shoulders and narrow at the hips, with a long mane of shiny black hair which flowed like a swift stallion on the soccer field. He was the object of desire of the young girls in the village and the object of envy of his male friends who could not compete with his athletic skills, quick tongue, and equally quick fists. Unrivalled by any peer, he emerged as the ordained leader of Castellammare's youth.

The differences in their interests and lifestyles didn't diminish Carmelo's close relationship with his uncle. At least once a month he accompanied his father and Lorenzo to Palermo, where Caiozzo tended to the business of exchanging his buried coin for the newly distributed more convenient paper *lire*. He avoided the local bank in Castellammare where he feared his transactions might start the tongues of the bank tellers and the manager wagging.

Caiozzo never wanted to put his business on the table.

During these trips he left Carmelo off at his uncle's apartment, where the boy spent the day with Antonio enjoying the attractions of Palermo as his mother once had. Caiozzo and Lorenzo meanwhile spent the remainder of their day looking at the four walls of a hotel room, entertained by a couple of Palermo's *buttani*. Since the birth of the fifth child, there had been virtually no activity in the Caiozzo bedroom, much to Maria's relief, and the monthly trips to Palermo offered Caiozzo a much-needed outlet for his physical needs.

Carmelo did not share his mother's interests in Museums but was excited by a university production of Luigi Pirandello's one act play, *L' epilogo*, The Epilogue, which Carmelo took him to. Antonio was delighted by his nephew's sudden interest in the theatre and arranged for them to attend another production the following month. Carmelo's interest did not diminish and, after the performance, he enthusiastically told his uncle,

"Oh, *zio*, this really excites me. This is what I want to do. It seems very natural for me and I'm sure I could do it well," Carmelo insisted.

Despite Caiozzo's initial vehement opposition, Carmelo persuaded his father to allow him to spend a week in Palermo with his uncle to attend an acting workshop offered at the university.

"All right, all right, go if you must. Go and waste your time with idle, mindless bull shit," he relented, growling. "But if you return and start acting like a *finocchiu*, I'll kick your ass out of this house on the spot. I won't have a fag living under my roof," he warned. Maria, of course, was delighted and supported her son's interest.

But it did not go well, much to his uncle's and mother's disappointment. Carmelo enjoyed the role-playing and acting scenes, the experiential essence of the craft, but had no patience for the classroom lectures and reading assignments. He dropped out before the week ended, telling his uncle, "I don't need acting lessons, *zio*. We Sicilians learn to act in the piazzas and streets of our villages. That is our stage. We are naturals," he said as he brushed his hair and admired his chiseled profile in the mirror.

"You might have something of a point there, Carmelo," Antonio conceded smiling and shaking his head. "But it seems to me you don't really want to be an actor or you would be willing to do the necessary work to attain that goal. You just want to be a star."

. . .

On one of his trips to Palermo, Caiozzo encountered Tommaso Baldi, an old acquaintance and low-level figure in the Bonanno family. Don Bono had died a few years earlier and, after a power struggle with the Felice Buccellato clan, Salvatore Bonanno emerged as the new Don in Castellammare, with Stefano Magaddino as his trusted *consiglieri*.

Baldi had just come from the Palermo docks where he was fortunate enough to come upon ten boxes containing gramophones in the hull of a British freighter, conveniently left unguarded. The new technology was in much demand by Palermo's gentry. Baldi knew he could realize a nice profit, and the ten boxes mysteriously disappeared.

"Giuseppe," he said hoping to entice Caiozzo into a quick purchase, "you have four young girls. Wouldn't they love to have one of these wonderful new machines?"

"Ah!" Caiozzo dismissed the idea scornfully, "my girls have no need of the foolish gadgets of the new century. They are perfectly content to learn the business of becoming good Sicilian wives and don't need the distraction of these stupid machines. And," he added, "I certainly have no need to spend money on contraptions I don't understand." Caiozzo's interest in the new technology of the 20th Century was limited to marveling at the electric street lights which were beginning to appear in Palermo.

"I understand," the cagey Baldi pressed on, pandering to Caiozzo's ego. "But think of the esteem and gratitude you would receive from your daughters as you presented them with something so unique in the village of Castellammare. You would become their hero, and they would be the envy of all their friends. And...and" he added, winking and whispering into Caiozzo's ear, "this contraption as you call it, would be so compelling that your daughters would rather remain at home than sneak off to the Piazza Europa where all those horny young bastards stand around sniffing at every young girl who passes." Baldi's words hit the mark. Caiozzo looked at him with narrowed eyes and tight lips, remembering his own history as a young boy and, now, learning about the exploits of his son.

"Twenty five *lire*," Caiozzo impulsively blurted out.

"Twenty five *lire*?" Tommaso exclaimed. "But where is your pistol Giuseppe?" he asked.

"Pistol, what pistol, what the hell are you talking about Tommaso?" he demanded.

"Well, Giuseppe, when you try to rob somebody, you usually have a pistol," Baldi said. "Fifty and not a lira less."

"For fifty *lire*, Tommaso, your wife would have to kiss my ass while your sister services me with her mouth at the other end," Caiozzo scornfully laughed.

"You have not changed, Giuseppe," Tommaso said with a mixture of anger and amusement. "Forty *lire* and I'll give you two wax disks of Verdi and Puccini's operas."

"Thirty five, Tommaso. You have a quick sale here and will be lucky to sell the remainder in six months," Caiozzo countered.

"First, you try to rob me outright," Baldi moaned, "then you insult my wife and sister and now, the final pain, you drive a knife through my heart. All right you cheap, miserable bastard," Tommaso capitulated, taking Caiozzo by the arm and leading him to a small, windowless store in a dark alley.

"And don't forget the two wax disks," Caiozzo reminded him.

. . .

As Baldi predicted, Caiozzo was greeted by the girls with the frenzied joy and gratitude Caesar enjoyed returning to Rome from the Gallic wars. But when the excitement ended and they removed the gramophone from the box, Caiozzo and the three younger girls stood helpless, baffled by the machine, uncertain how to work it. Wordlessly they looked puzzled at each other. Little Maria quietly walked to the machine, cranked the handle and placed a disk on the spinning turntable and lowered the arm. The crackling sound of a soprano's voice emanated and Puccini's *Madame Butterfly* filled the room.

"She did it! She did it!" the girls clapped and jumped with joy, "Little Maria made the beautiful music come from the machine!" Caiozzo looked proudly at his daughter with a twisted smile as his wife stood in the doorway beaming broadly with hands clasped as though prayers had been answered. This little one, Maria thought, is capable of anything. I never know what to expect form her.

Caiozzo certainly didn't expect what was to come. Three or four times a week his salon was the gathering place for a bevy of screaming, laughing and crying teenage girls emoting to the music of Verdi or Puccini. Maria occasionally joined her daughters and their friends making Caiozzo rue the day he bought the gramophone and cursing Baldi as he stormed out the door.

"And next month, girls," Maria taunted loud enough for Caiozzo to hear, "and for months after, I'm sure *zio* Antonio will be bringing many more disks from Palermo, and we will soon have a wonderful music library to enjoy every day."

CHAPTER 16

Mother Caterina had become aware of the daily gathering of young girls at the Caiozzo house and, like everyone else in the village, was aware of the existence of the gramophone. She fretted over the possible negative influence the themes of the music, sex and violence, might have on impressionable young girls. As a native of Sicily, she could understand, if not condone violence. But sex, sex. Now that was another matter. It was, and in some quarters remains, the Big Sin. If Mother Caterina had read Dante, she would have learned that lust is the least deadly of the seven sins. But in her celibate mind it was the most deadly, more corrupting than pride itself.

"*Signura* Caiozzo," Mother Superior called as she approached Maria on the church steps after Mass one Sunday, "may I have a word with you?"

"Of course, Mother, and how are you today,?" Maria asked politely, suspecting the worst.

"*Signura*, this is a most delicate matter but I feel I must address it with you honestly and directly," Mother Superior solemnly said.

"Of course, Mother, I would expect nothing less."

"*Signura*, it has come to my attention, reported to me by Sister Alfonsa, that the girls in Maria's class gather at your home two, perhaps three times a week, to listen to music on your...your..."

"Gramophone," Maria offered.

"yes, yes, on the gramophone," Mother Superior responded. "As sworn guardians of the virtues, and indeed the souls, of these innocents, I must tell you of my concerns about the preoccupation of these children, and the dangers of their listening to this music, concerns which I have expressed to *Padre* Pietro, dangers which may morally corrupt them and put their souls in imminent peril."

"Morally corrupt them,?" Maria responded indignantly. "They are enjoying wonderful music with lyrics which speak of love and the human condition, written and composed by Italy's finest artists. Does the Church have no room for art? If you, the *Padre* and the Church are so concerned with moral corruptibility perhaps you should remove every copy of the Bible with its sordid tales from the school and insist that every family in the village shred and burn them to light their stoves. Apparently you have forgotten the words of St. Augustine, Mother: 'Those who sing pray twice.' I don't recall the good Saint excluding themes of love."

"You leave me no alternative," Mother Superior angrily snapped to Maria. "The *Padre* and I have already discussed our duty if you did not listen to reason. We must," she said gravely, "expel your daughter from the San

Giuseppe School, without hope of reinstatement if you do not change your opinion, and properly supervise your daughter. I must add, however, I am not completely surprised at your response. As I recall, when you were my student before I became Mother Superior, you were a difficult, impertinent pupil whose endless questioning and arguments bordered on heresy and were a distraction in my class. I could clearly see over the horizon what I might expect from your daughter," she sternly remarked.

"Could you, Mother?" Maria responded, coolly. "I never realized you were capable of seeing the horizon," she said as she turned and walked away.

That night Maria spoke to her daughter about the encounter with Mother Caterina and told her of the decision for expulsion if changes were not made regarding her interest in the music.

"Mamma," little Maria said, "I can read, write and count well enough and, if the only way I can remain in school is to give up my interest in something I truly enjoy, I would rather give up the mindless dull rantings of Sister Alfonsa."

Maria accepted her daughter's decision with mixed emotions. Little Maria's problems never affected the standing of her younger sisters who were considered ideal students, quiet, humble and pious. Their presence was noted by Mother Caterina every Sunday at the Communion railing and she wondered how the three younger children could be so different from their siblings.

Their public persona was consistent with their private lives: the girls had little interest in socializing, avoiding the piazza, preferring the domestic tranquility of the home, helping their mother with the chores and spending their spare time knitting, weaving and sewing. The family was always stylishly outfitted. The girls even turned out extra socks, hats and mittens from left over materials and distributed them to the children of poor families in the village.

"I have four daughters," Caiozzo grumbled to his friends at the tavern, "the oldest gets put out of school for corrupting the morals of her classmates, and the three youngest go around the village like missionaries giving clothing to the poor." He was bewildered by the difference in the personalities of his two older and three younger children. At times, a gnawing question gripped him and he wondered if he was, indeed, the biological father of the three younger girls. They all had rather fair complexions he thought, and a tint of red in their hair not unlike Turi, the deputy, who had been promoted to *Capitano* after Luongo retired. Had he been cuckolded, or worse, were three of his children the consequence of his wife's sexual transgressions?

Ultimately, Caiozzo was able to quiet his fears by concluding that Maria would not have had time to engage in sexual adventures. She delivered Carmelo and little Maria in less than four years, and the demands of two active young children on a 20 year old mother would have made it difficult for Maria to have an affair. And, he reasoned, where would Maria have carried out her secret rendezvous? Castellammare is a small village and the sexual indiscretion of his wife would have been noted with gossip sweeping through the piazza and the alleys like a hot sirocco wind. Caiozzo also assured himself that Maria would never have compromised her personal moral standard. She had integrity and would not want to bring shame and disgrace to her family.

The winter of 1912 was particularly brutal, and countless numbers of infants, children and the elderly fell victim to pneumonia, consumption and other respiratory ailments. Grazia and Stella were home-bound for a month, and Maria did not visit her parents during that period. Amelia came everyday with broth and medicinal herbs to help nurse the girls back to health.

Two weeks before an early Easter, their fevers quit, and the sun broke through bringing much needed warmth to the chilled air. Grazia and Stella immediately began work completing Easter outfits for the family. It was unthinkable that any of them would attend Easter Sunday Mass without something new and bright to celebrate the Resurrection and the coming Spring season.

Caiozzo was stunned when his daughters presented him with a finely tailored linen shirt and matching cravat, and Maria was delighted with her new, flower patterned dress. Carmelo slipped a pastel colored, cotton sweater over his head and, pleased with the fit which complimented his well-toned physique, pranced around the salon like Beau Brummel.

Maria reluctantly agreed to attend Easter Mass as a family, after which, she and the children planned to join her parents and Antonio for Easter dinner.

When the service ended, the children kissed their father goodbye and walked to their grandparents' home with their mother as Caiozzo made his way to the tavern. They had grown up with the estranged relationship between their father and grandparents and stopped asking questions or seeking explanations years earlier. The circumstances of their parents' marriage were unknown to them and remained a family secret for decades.

It had been a month since Maria had seen her father, and she was horrified at his physical condition. Nino Pepitone had deteriorated to a shell, sitting listless in a corner chair. His dark hair had turned snow white and his skin was a ghastly ashen grey. He looked like a specter about to vanish into the air. Maria bit hard on her lip as she approached him, bent down and kissed his forehead, placing her hands on boney shoulders where the flesh seemed to have melted like snow on a warm spring day. Pepitone looked up at his daughter with sunken, sorrowful eyes and quietly mouthed,

"*Mi dispiaci, Maria. T'amu sempri.*"

"*Anch'iu, papà*, I will always love you," she replied fighting back tears. Maria turned to the children who were silently staring and said,

"Come, all of you and give *nonnu* a kiss and wish him Happy Easter."

They came hesitantly, one by one and kissed Nino, who managed a weak smile, a pat on the hand and a "*Grazzii, niputi.*"

After a somber Easter dinner, Antonio asked Maria to join him outside.

"Maria," he began, "we must prepare ourselves..."

"I know, I know," Maria tearfully interrupted. "He spent the last twenty years with guilt and shame eating away at his heart and soul, and drank himself into this deteriorated condition."

Antonio pulled Maria close to him and the two comforted each other in a long, silent embrace, dreading the worst.

CHAPTER 17

Nino Pepitone's vital organs started to quit and within two weeks he was buried in the cemetery at the Church of San Giuseppe. Amelia was now free, released from the burden of caring for a man for twenty years whose physical, emotional and spiritual breakdown had left her drawn and haggard. She felt guilty but relieved that she no longer had to attend and be exposed to a man whose life had become consumed with self-pity.

For nearly a year she breathed freely, taking pleasure in simple things, buying gifts for her grandchildren, enjoying coffee and *dolce* at the *pasticceria* and engaging in idle chatter with the baker when she bought hot, fresh-baked bread.

But Pepitone's chronic malaise had exacted a heavy physical toll on her and, two days before Christmas, Amelia collapsed while shopping in the village for the holiday dinner, grasped her chest, and died before horrified onlookers.

Turi, saddled his horse and rode to the Caiozzo house on Via Umberto. He dismounted, removed his hat and walked slowly to the front door, opened by a smiling Maria.

"*Capitano!*" she exclaimed, "have you come to wish us a Merry Christmas?"

Turi did not respond but his solemn, pleated face foreshadowed an unhappy message.

"*Signura* Caiozzo," he began, "I'm so sorry..."

"No, no," Maria sobbed, as she put her hands to her mouth, "don't tell me, please, not again," she cried falling limp into his arms as he gently stroked her head.

"What the hell is going on here?" Caiozzo demanded as he came to the door and pulled Maria away from Turi.

"Don Giuseppe, Don Giuseppe," please," Turi implored with outstretched hands.

"*La signura*'s mother, she collapsed in the village,...and...and, we were not able to revive her." Maria broke loose from Caiozzo, ran crying into the kitchen and sat at the table with her face buried in her hands.

Little Maria and Stella heard Turi's account and came into the kitchen in tears. They stroked Maria's back as Giovanna nudged past her legs and curled into her lap.

"The neighbors," Turi continued to Caiozzo, "saw *la Signura* clutch her chest and fall forward. She must have died instantly."

"Yes, I see," Caiozzo answered gravely, "and where is she now Turi?" he asked.

"I sent for the new priest, *Padre* Marco, and he came immediately to administer the Sacrament. I then summoned young *la signorina* Morteannu who came with her brother in the wagon and they took *la signura* Pepitone to her home. Will you order the coffin?" Turi asked, "or would you rather I informed the carpenter, Giovanni?"

Caiozzo thought for a moment, then replied, "Yes, Turi, *grazzii*, I think that would be best. And if you would, please, pass the word along that *la signura* will be waked in her home this evening. I'm sure the neighbors will want to pay their respects to a woman of her standing in the village."

"I will, Don Caiozzo," Turi replied.

"*Allora*, so then, thank you again for your assistance, Turi," Caiozzo said.

As he returned to the village, Turi reflected on the impact of the death of two parents on Maria in less than a year and he never forgot about her abduction and forced marriage twenty years earlier. He had always felt guilty that he was not able to do something to save her, but he had been restrained by Luongo's command. For years Turi despised Luongo and was angry that he refused to act more decisively on Maria's behalf. But now, as *Capitano*, he could appreciate that Luongo's hands were tied by Don Angelo's edict. He ran his fingers across the badge on his chest and thought in disgust, this thing is a meaningless joke. He was grateful, however, that he could be of some service to Maria in this moment of her grief.

...

Following her mother's service and burial, Maria sat quietly in the salon and waved off her children's' attempts to comfort her. She thought about how quickly the years had passed since her marriage to Caiozzo, the changes in the village and the deaths during that period: Caiozzo's mother, Don Angelo Bono, Cenna the butcher, and now her parents. The unfortunate Mosca met an untimely and ironic end when he swallowed a chicken bone and choked to death, and Ciuto drowned after diving from a cliff into the Mediterranean trying to impress a group of vacationing English school girls. Bartolo Fontana, the barber, died after a dissatisfied customer plunged scissors into his neck during a senseless argument, and his son, Bartolo Jr., Carmelo's best friend, sold the shop soon after and migrated to America where he worked in a barber shop on Kenmare Street on Manhattan's lower east side, a heavily populated Southern Italian neighborhood. *Padre* Pietro was elevated to Monsignor for all his good works, and transferred to the beautiful, Norman-inspired Duomo in Monreale.

Agata and Ruggero married and moved to Bologna where the young man completed his medical studies at the University and established a practice, and the Stuffas sold their home and moved to Florence, where they could be close to their daughter, and bought a small pensione on the outskirt of the city.

Caiozzo, who was well-positioned financially, shortened his work day and delegated more responsibility to Lorenzo. He assigned Carmelo the title Assistant Supervisor, insuring that he would still have his eyes and ears in the daily operation of the vineyard. Caiozzo continued to prosper but had to deal with an unexpected expense when the Bonanno family, which had succeeded Bona, suggested he pay a ten percent tribute to insure that vineyard operations would continue smoothly. He wisely agreed to the demand without objection and reasoned this was a fair tariff for doing business in the village. Besides, he had accumulated more than 50,000 *lire* during his thirty five year tenure at the vineyard. He did not want the Bonanno family snooping around his financial affairs. If they discovered his true worth, they might well demand retroactive compensation.

. . .

In May, 1915, Italy, sensing an opportunity for land acquisition and status, joined England and France in the Great War and sent a million ill-equipped, ill-trained and poorly-led troops to the Dolomites on the Austro-Italian border. The population on the mainland of Italy was fiercely divided as to the merit or necessity of Italy's military adventure, but on the island nearly 2,000 miles from the hostilities, Sicilians overwhelmingly opposed the country's involvement. Ever the pragmatist, Caiozzo echoed the prevailing sentiments of his fellow citizens:

"This war has nothing to do with us. We are an island of poor people, concerned with getting up every day, going to work and earning enough to put bread on the table to feed our families. Besides, the government in Rome never gives a damn about us. We have never been more than a bothersome hangnail on the toe of Italy. Fuck them and their military adventure!"

Fate did fuck them, and, by the end of the war, Italy lost more than 600,000 men.

Life on the island did not change significantly, and Sicilians suffered no more during or after the war than they had in the past. The collusion among the politicians, the police and the Friends of Friends continued, and the stranglehold on the peasantry saw no relief. Antonio's decades long attempt to effect change through his writing, teaching and political activism had accomplished nothing and now, at 49 years of age, the frustrated writer and teacher decided to become more proactive and seek political office. Despite the misgivings and admonitions of his advisers and supporters in the university and the reform press who urged him to run for a city council seat, Antonio announced his candidacy for *Sindaco*, Mayor of Palermo.

"If my candidacy is successful" he reasoned, "I am in a much better position to effect change from the seat of power, rather than as an obscure member of the city council." His announcement immediately garnered the support of students, not only in Palermo, but also in Syracusa and Messina. The administrators of the universities, while not openly opposed to his candidacy, were tepid in their support, fearing a political backlash from the powers which held the purse strings. The writers, Giovanni Verga and Luigi Pirandello were impressed by Antonio's idealism and the enthusiasm of the students and, with the backing of Palermo's intelligentsia, rallied to the cause with statements of public support and financial assistance. More important, his eloquent and fiery message stirred the historically apathetic electorate and bred concern not only within Palermo's power structure, but across the Strait of Messina, even resounding in Rome. He was emerging as an influential voice not only in Sicily, but in other small, Southern Italian cities and villages. His campaign was gaining traction with unexpected and almost lightning speed.

The demands of the campaign as well as his position at the university made it impossible for him to continue to visit the family at Castellammare on a monthly basis. Antonio and Maria agreed that maintaining the Pepitone family home was an unnecessary burden and expense and they agreed to sell it to Turi, who had expressed an interest, for a modest L400, with the stipulation that Antonio could rent one of the bedrooms and receive his family whenever he returned to Castellammare for a visit. Turi sensed a bargain and a deal was struck. Maria and the children did not see Antonio for nearly two months and they looked forward to a family reunion. Carmelo was especially proud of his uncle's aggressive leadership in the opposition attack on the corrupt forces dominating Palermo. He bragged openly about Antonio's courage, while Maria and little Maria were impressed by his efforts to include equal rights for Sicilian women in his platform.

Antonio had given Maria excerpts from a volume of the works of Susan B. Anthony, the American, whose voice for the Womens' Suffrage movement in America resounded throughout Europe. Much to her delight and surprise, she found her daughter reading the literature and announcing to her mother,

"It's true what you and *zio* Antonio always said, mamma. There are things taking place beyond this island which confirm a woman's right to equality and to be treated with respect and dignity."

"Yeah," Caiozzo sneered, overhearing the conversation between Maria and her daughter, "you and that trouble-making brother of yours will soon have this little one parading around with a mob and a sign in her hand calling for a revolution and a destruction of a system which has served Sicily well for centuries. Besides," he added, "she's only sixteen years old. What the hell does she know?" Maria glared at Caiozzo with unwavering defiance and answered, "She knows much more than a poor, obscure village girl is supposed to know. She has a mind of her own and is not afraid of men like you. She's ready to fight and I promise you, Caiozzo, this little one will never become a helpless pawn to be used in the games that evil and manipulative unscrupulous men create."

Caiozzo glowered at his wife and his jaw tightened.

Little Maria's lips parted slightly and her eyes narrowed as she looked at her mother quizzically, digesting her words, then at her father whose face burned crimson as he avoided her gaze.

"Grazia, Stella, Giovanna, come," Maria called, "it is past noon and *zio* Antonio will be waiting for us." She turned and walked to the foot of the stairs, calling to her son.

"Carmelo, we're leaving now. Take the pot with the sauce and the *ragù*. We'll take the pasta, the *pani* and the *insalata* and meet you at the house."

Caiozzo sat at the table, head down, rotating his fingers.

"Did you at least leave something for me to eat?" he asked like a rejected child.

"It's on the stove," Maria answered curtly as she moved toward the door.

"Thank you very much *cara*," Caiozzo responded sarcastically. "By the way," he asked, "will Turi be joining the family for dinner today?" Maria stiffened, turning slowly shaking her head and replied, "Caiozzo, twenty four years ago you were only a miserable fool. Now you are a miserable, pathetic old fool."

CHAPTER 18

A few minutes after 11 p.m., one evening in early spring, Maria heard the front door open and close quickly. She put her book aside, got up from her reading chair, and walked to the hallway calling,

"*Ragazzi, ragazzi*? kids, kids?"

"*Ciao*, mamma," the girls responded nervously as Maria approached them.

"So, did you enjoy yourselves at the dance?" she began, then suddenly stopped and asked, perplexed, "where is your sister, where is Grazia?"

"She, uh...," little Maria began, then stopped.

"I've told you a hundred times," Maria interrupted, "when you leave this house you leave together, and when you return, you return together, especially at night. Now where is Grazia?" she demanded.

"For God's sake," little Maria spoke up irritated, "she's sixteen years old mamma, and she stopped to talk with a classmate."

"A classmate?; What classmate?" Maria inquired suspiciously as Stella slipped into the shadows, and put her fingers to her mouth.

"I'm not sure. I, uh, I think it was Giacomo Vitale," little Maria answered haltingly.

"You're not sure but you think it was Giacomo Vitale?" Maria repeated raising her voice in anger, prompting Caiozzo, who overheard the exchange, to call from the salon.

"What the hell's going on there. Get in here, all of you," he commanded. Stella's eyes rolled to the ceiling as they followed their mother into the salon.

Caiozzo sprang to confront his daughter like a vulture spying a carcass.

"Now stop stalling and tell us now where your sister is," he demanded.

Little Maria stood silent, lips trembling, glaring back at her father.

"Now, damn it," Caiozzo shouted, pounding his fist into his palm. Despite her promise to Grazia not to tell their parents anything, little Maria did not know what to expect from her father and yielded out of fear.

Grazia and Giacomo had been secretly involved with each other for almost a year and had fallen in love. Aware that a marriage would not be permitted by her parents, they decided to elope and orchestrated an abduction, fleeing with the assistance of Vitale's friends to the remote village of Monte Scardina and the home of Giacomo's demented but accommodating aunt. Wisely, they did not tell Grazia's sisters of their intended location and planned to return to Castellammare the following day, when custom and preservation of family honor would demand a *fuitina*, a rehabilitative marriage.

"*Diu miu, Diu miu*," Maria cried in anguish as the color drained from her face.

"Mamma, mamma, please," little Maria pleaded trying to comfort her mother. "Grazia told me to tell you she is in no danger and that she and Giacomo made this decision together."

"And did she tell you where they were going?" Caiozzo angrily demanded.

"By all the saints in Heaven, papa, no. But even if she did, I wouldn't tell you," little Maria answered him defiantly, regaining her courage.

A strange calm came over her mother as she turned to Giuseppe and said, "Caiozzo, go now to the station and tell Turi what has happened and..."

"Are you *pazzu*, Maria, are you crazy? Tell Turi what? To ride up and down the coast and into the hills and burst into every house looking for a young couple who have eloped?"

Maria sank into a chair rubbing her hands together then looked up at Giuseppe and agreed bitterly, "Of course you're right, Caiozzo. This time the village *Capitano* truly would not know where to begin to look."

Little Maria and Stella looked puzzled at their mother as a grim-faced Caiozzo stormed into the kitchen and filled a cup with grappa.

"Don't worry, mamma," Stella said trying to comfort her mother, "Grazia told us, for sure, they would come to the house tomorrow morning and explain everything."

"Tomorrow morning," Maria weakly murmured as she turned wet eyes toward Caiozzo.

...

Maria rubbed the sleep from her eyes and winced, stretching after an uncomfortable night on the divan in the salon. She walked into the kitchen, lit the stove, then went outside with a pitcher and primed the well pump. She returned and poured some water into a basin and the remainder into a kettle and placed them on the stove to warm as she crushed the coffee beans in a mortar. When the water had warmed she removed her top and soaped and rinsed her face and body and made the coffee.

No one stirred and the only sound was Caiozzo's wheezing snore echoing through the house. Maria walked out the front door with her coffee and looked, expectantly, up and down the deserted road as puffy morning clouds drifted by like pink cherubs at play in the sky.

Maria finished her coffee and returned to the kitchen and sliced the bread. One by one her family came down the stairs and ate their breakfast in icy silence, absent, to no one's surprise or concern, Carmelo.

Shortly after 11 am Grazia and Giacomo walked timidly into the kitchen arm in arm, with Grazia clutching a small bouquet of spring flowers.

"Mamma, papa," Grazia greeted her parents, smiling nervously, followed by a whispered, "*Bon giornu signore, signura Caiozzo*," from Giacomo who stood uncertain with his large, workman's hands to his chest. Little Maria, Stella and Giovanna sat still at the table as Maria and Giuseppe leaped to their feet.

"What have you done you foolish child?" Maria asked in anguish.

"Don't you realize the consequences, what the village talk will be?" Caiozzo demanded in a rage.

"We have done nothing wrong, mamma, and there will be no village consequences for you to worry about, papa. *Padre* Marco married us, not an hour ago, at the Church of San Giuseppe, the same church in which you and mamma were married."

"Married," Maria gasped, choking back tears, "only a child, just 16 years old."

"Yes, mamma, the same age as you were when you married papa," Grazia returned. "And I am not a child," she continued, "I'm a woman, a young woman, yes, but old enough to make the same decision you made when you married papa. Were you wiser at 16 than I?" she asked. Maria sighed, and Caiozzo left the room.

"You know, mamma," Grazia continued, "I have listened to you and *zio* Antonio and little Maria here talk endlessly about a woman's right to make her own decisions and enjoy equal rights like that lady in America. Now I make a decision in my interests, and it seems you and papa condemn me for it."

"I knew it would come to this," Caiozzo said as he returned with a full cup of grappa. "You and that *finocchiu* brother of yours poisoning their minds with that women's rights shit," he said to Maria.

"Poisoning, papa?" Grazia responded caustically. "I think the only poisoning that occurs is when men establish customs and make laws that force women to do things against their will."

Maria swallowed hard and looked away as Caiozzo coughed, expelling a stream of grappa from his nostrils, and left the room again, red-faced and ranting.

"What about that, mamma?" little Maria said. "It seems my sister makes a very good point." Maria could not refute Grazia's remarks and, as she looked at the faces of the two young people with their hands tenderly entwined, she thought wistfully, I see something here which I have once experienced, only briefly, a long time ago. She softened, and her anger and distress began to fade.

"Grazia, Giacomo, I can see you love each other and I am truly happy for both of you. But could you not have waited at least another year until Giacomo has established himself in some profession or trade. Remember,"

Maria said, smiling slightly, "the faster the children come, the thinner the sauce gets."

The young couple looked at each other and Grazia slowly responded.

"*Veru*, mamma, that is true. But Giacomo is already eighteen years old and has been learning the trade of a mason with his father for three years."

Caiozzo had composed himself and re-entered the room authoritatively exclaiming, "Yes, yes, *signor* Vitale. I know the name. Well-established and well-regarded in the village," he said nodding his head affirmatively.

"Mamma, papa," Grazia began hesitantly, "there is something else I must tell..."

Maria covered her heart and her eyes widened.

"Grazia, *figghia mia*, are you with child?" she asked pained.

"No, mamma, no," Grazia responded laughing, "but, but..."

"Grazia, please let me, *cara*," Giacomo interrupted raising his hand.

"*Signore* and *signura* Caiozzo, the opportunities for masons are plentiful in America. My oldest brother, Michelangelo, left Il Golfo not four years ago and already has a successful mason business in New York. He has sent for me and I cannot refuse him because he is my brother, and also because I can earn twenty times what I make working in our village. I must leave within a month and I did not want to be separated from Grazia. That is why we decided to elope." A quiet enveloped the room until Caiozzo responded.

"So what you're telling us, Giacomo, is that you and Grazia rushed into this marriage to insure that she would accompany you to America."

"No, *signor* Caiozzo, I'm telling you that I love your daughter and she loves me, and we want to be together, respecting of course, the commandments of Holy Mother Church."

Caiozzo turned and looked out the window. He saw the roof of the shed in the vineyard at the top of Mount Inici and remembered how he had acquired a wife. Love, he thought, what a troublesome, useless bit of make-believe.

Maria smiled and replied warmly, "I understand Giacomo...I understand."

Grazia, sensing Giacomo had won the day, broke in enthusiastically.

"And mamma, papa," she said, "this is not only an opportunity for Giacomo, but there is also something for me."

"What?" Caiozzo asked skeptically.

"Tell us," Maria urged her.

"Well, Giacomo's brother has already offered to help us establish a shop where I can make interesting clothing for the fine ladies in New York and have a business of my own."

Little Maria had enjoyed some furtive, near intimate encounters with a Vitale cousin who shared with her some secrets of the family's business, threw her head back and rolled her eyes.

The cousin had babbled to little Maria that, before he died, Don Bono sensed the lucrative potential in the booming construction industry in America and sent Michelangelo Vitale to New York with a valise full of money to establish a concrete business and explore any other opportunities, legal or not. Caiozzo noticed his daughter's reaction to her sister's enthusiasm and wondered, does this little one know something? Ever skeptical, Giuseppe had no doubt about Vitale's motive. He knew Vitale had been a member of Bono's family and that they would entertain any prospect to establish a foothold in New York, including using a simple Castellammare girl to help achieve their end.

Maria wanted to believe the optimistic account she heard from Grazia. One of her daughters would at least have a chance to escape the provincialism and restrictions which limited opportunities and held Sicilian women in bondage for centuries. She moved forward and embraced them.

"All right, all right, I'm convinced," she said, resigned, "you have my blessing and may the spirit of the Madonna watch over and protect you."

"Yes," Caiozzo added sarcastically, looking at Giacomo, "and may the spirit which guides the third eye and ear always be with you."

"What blessing, what spirit?" Carmelo asked as he sauntered into the salon. "What's going on here?"

Little Maria took it upon herself to explain the particulars to her brother, adding,

"If you had not stayed out all night and come home stinking of cheap wine and cheap perfume, you would not have to ask," she said, mocking him.

"*Statti zittu*, shut up, squirt," he said as he moved slowly toward an apprehensive Giacomo, pulled him aside, placed a finger under his nose, and whispered,

"If this goes well with my parents, it goes well with me. But know this. If you ever treat my sister disrespectfully or, God forbid, harm her, be assured I will be on the first boat to New York, find you, cut your balls off, stuff them in your mouth and leave you on 'Broodaway' for everyone to see."

"No, never," a frightened Giacomo replied, "never."

"Good," Carmelo said laughing as he embraced Giacomo and Grazia.

CHAPTER 19

Antonio boarded the train to Castellammare, full of the enthusiasm he had felt years earlier when he came to tell his parents of his teaching appointment at the university. Now he had accomplished a nearly impossible feat, forming a coalition and support for his mayoral candidacy between university students whose fingers turned pages in books and the peasants whose fingers dug into Sicily's dirt producing food for the island. He wished his parents were alive to enjoy his success.

The steamy, dirty car was empty except for the police officer who lounged over two seats sweating alcohol through his rumpled uniform. He grinned an idiot's drunken grin offering wine from his flask as Antonio passed.

"No, *grazzii*," Antonio said smiling as he made his way to the rear of the car, and sat at a brown-streaked window. He reached into his canvas bag and took a long swig of water from a bottle then lifted a paper jacket containing a recording of Bach's Brandenberg Concerto. He smiled knowing that his sister and the girls would be pleased with this fine addition to their music library.

Antonio had last visited the village two months earlier when his sister prepared a small wedding dinner for Grazia and Giacomo. He was happy that his niece and her husband seemed very much in love and had the good fortune to migrate to America. But, like Caiozzo and little Maria, he harbored some concerns about the legitimacy of the Vitale family's business interests in New York.

The train issued three short whistles indicating its departure and groaned forward, then halted abruptly, snapping his head back. Antonio looked out the window and saw a portly priest limping and waddling quickly toward the train with raised hands. The priest mounted the steps of the train and stood breathless, taking a large bandana from a black satchel and wiped the profusion of sweat from his forehead and neck. He made his way slowly down the aisle on unsteady, chubby legs, wrinkling his nose in disgust as he passed the drunk police officer.

"*Bon giornu, Padre*," the officer slurred smiling.

"*Sì, bon giornu*," the priest replied curtly, as he looked at Antonio and shook his head. Antonio shrugged his shoulders and nodded in return.

"Do you mind?" the priest approached and asked pointing.

"Please, *Padre*, of course not," Antonio answered extending his hand.

"Ah!" the priest sighed as he fell heavy into a seat opposite Antonio. "It is much too hot for early spring, and I am getting much too old for these itinerant trips to remote villages to celebrate the Mass for those without a priest," he laughed, wiping his face again.

"May I offer you some water, *Padre*?" Antonio asked. "It is not very cold but at least it's wet."

"Oh! You are a life-saver my son," he said reaching for the bottle with a fleshy hand, and taking a long draught. "Thank you, thank you," he said finishing and wiping his mouth with his hand.

"I have not seen you on this route before *Padre*," Antonio commented.

"No, my son, I am on my way to Scopello for the first time. Usually my orders take me to the villages east and north of Palermo. But, orders are orders, and I must do what I am told. And you, do you regularly take this train west along the coast?" the priest asked.

"Yes, quite regularly, *Padre*. About every six weeks to visit my family in Castellammare," Antonio answered.

"Yes, yes!" the priest exclaimed, "I have heard of this village. Very well known for its' excellent seafood and," he added winking, "for its tightly controlled, tranquil atmosphere."

The *Padre* paused for a moment then tilted his head slightly.

"You know, you look very familiar, my son, I'm sure I have seen your face before. Perhaps on the stage at one of the university productions?" he asked.

"No, no," Antonio responded laughing, "I have no talent for the stage."

"Not that stage but, perhaps…ah!, I know now," he said as his face broke into a broad grin of recognition. "You are the young man seeking the office of Sindaco, Mayor of Palermo," he said pleased with his recognition. "Pepitone, isn't it? Antonio Pepitone?" the priest said extending his hand.

"You have unmasked me, *Padre*…."

"Forgive my rudeness, *signore*. I am *Padre* Franco. And what an honor to meet you, *signor* Pepitone. You know," the priest said hushed, leaning forward, "I am more than a few years older than you and of another generation which does not take to change easily or graciously. But between you and me, I am most impressed by what I hear in your platform and, if you will respect my secret," he said looking about, "know that you have the vote of at least one of Palermo's clergy," he said, laughing.

"You honor me with your support, *Padre*," Antonio said moved, "and your secret is safe with me," he added, smiling.

The drunk officer in the front of the car had fallen asleep and dropped his flask spilling the wine which had gone sour in the heat, filling the car with an odious stench.

"I cannot tolerate this any longer," the annoyed priest said to Antonio.

"Join me outside on the platform where, if you have paper and tobacco," he said hopefully, "we may enjoy a smoke in the clean air."

"Certainly, *Padre*," Antonio said rising as the priest reached for his satchel.

"Surely you needn't bring your satchel with you *Padre*. I'm certain it is safe here."

"Antonio," the priest responded. "I am set in my ways. It has never been my practice to leave the host and chalice unattended in a public place."

"Quite so, quite so," Antonio agreed.

They stood on the platform taking in the fresh breeze as Antonio rolled a cigarette and handed it to *Padre* Franco who thanked him, smiled and put the cigarette between his lips. Antonio was startled by the sound of the heavy steel door opening behind him but, before he could turn, his arms were grabbed and pinned against his back.

"*Ora, ora*, now, now," he heard the officer frantically yelling as the priest took a large butcher knife from his satchel, covered Antonio's mouth with one hand and plunged the knife deep into his abdomen and drew it up quickly, exposing organs along its path. Antonio's eyes widened in surprise and pain, but his scream remained muffled under the priest's firmly pressed hand. He drew the blade back down, removed it and threw it over the railing and Antonio limply dropped to the floor as blood gushed from the wound.

The two stood wordlessly looking down at Antonio as the last gasp of life left his body. The officer then queried, "*Mortu?*"

"Sì, sì," Franco returned, curling his lips in a sneer, "*veru mortu*, truly dead, even though his eyes remain open." The priest removed his bloody vestment and tossed it. They lifted Antonio's body and dumped it over the side and watched as it rolled and came to rest at the bottom of a small embankment. They waited for a couple of minutes as the train slowed around a curve just before reaching Mondello, and leaped into the brush through a field where a man in a wagon slowly chewing a wrinkled cigar waited dispassionately.

Maria scrubbed and rinsed the sand off the clam shells and lowered them in a bucket into the well where the cool, dark water kept them fresh. Little Maria had taken an interest in cooking and enjoyed helping her mother prepare the dinner. She basted the chicken, browning and crackling in the outdoor *furnu*, with an olive oil, butter, lemon and rosemary mixture, and seared the antipasti of sausage, onion, fennel and peppers on the open flame.

"Don't burn the peppers," Maria cautioned her daughter as she kneaded the dough for the bread.

"I know what I'm doing, Mamma. The peppers must sear enough so the skin can be easily removed," little Maria replied, "or we will have digestive problems, burping and farting like mules."

"*Basta* with that talk," Maria said chiding her daughter and laughing.

Giovanna put a disk on the gramophone, playing scenes from Puccini's *Tosca*, accompanied by little Maria's thin, but pleasant, soprano voice. Stella sat in a corner of the kitchen sewing, smiling and gaining weight just inhaling the scrumptious aromas emanating from the outdoor stove. Carmelo was still sleeping but had returned from his escapades at a respectable midnight hour the previous evening in anticipation of his uncle's visit, and Caiozzo had left early in the morning for a day of hunting with Lorenzo. He was not expected back until late in the evening. Maria persuaded Antonio that it would be more convenient for her if he came to the house on Via Umberto for dinner.

By 11 a.m., the preparation for dinner had been completed, and Maria and her daughters sat around the kitchen table dunking crisp almond *biscottu* into large steaming cups of cafélatti while loudly accompanying the lyrics to Puccini's *Turandot*. An annoyed Carmelo came into the kitchen complaining about the off key singing and went straight to the stove, pouring a cup of black coffee with unsteady hands, ignoring the muffled giggles of his sisters and his mother's sarcastic remark.

"Well, well," Maria said to the girls, "we have the rare honor of your brother joining us for breakfast this morning," she said.

"Where's *zio* Antonio?" Carmelo wanted to know, ignoring his mother's remark.

"I'm sure he'll be here shortly. The train, as usual, was probably delayed at the station in Palermo," Maria replied.

"Probably," Carmelo agreed, suddenly turning to little Maria who sat staring with a mischievous smile and hands tucked under her chin, "And what are you looking at?" he asked irritably.

"Oh, excuse me," little Maria teased, feigning an apology, "I didn't mean to stare. I was just wondering who enjoyed the pleasure of your company last night. Was it the widow Nardino's daughter with the ass of a horse, or Rita, the pharmacist's wife with the breasts of a sparrow?"

"You see, you see, mamma, how this one constantly taunts me," he whined.

"...how this one constantly taunts me, " little Maria echoed mimicking.

"Little one," Maria said, suppressing a laugh, "*basta!*"

When Antonio failed to arrive by 1 p.m., a concerned Maria sent Carmelo to the train station to inquire if a malfunction or, God forbid, an accident had occurred on the line.

"No, *signor* Caiozzo," the station master told him, "the train from Palermo arrived on time, only thirty minutes late at 11:30."

"Did you see anyone get off the train?" Carmelo asked.

"No one," he responded, "In fact, the train was empty."

"Has there been, perhaps, a cable for my family from the Palermo station?" Carmelo asked.

"No, nothing," the station master responded. "I have been on duty since 8 a.m. and nothing has come over the wire."

"*Grazzii*," Carmelo said and walked away returning home.

"This is not like your uncle," Maria said. "He is always punctual."

"Maybe he was detained in Palermo by some last minute campaign business," little Maria suggested.

"No, *cara*," Maria said, "if he was going to be delayed he would have cabled to let us know of any change."

. . .

At mid afternoon Turi made one of his surprise Sunday visits to headquarters to make sure the desk sergeant was sober and had properly designated the force of three officers in the village. As they discussed the assignments in Turi's office, they heard three loud discharges that sounded like gunfire and rushed into the street with drawn pistols. They watched as a motorized ambulance belched its' way down Via Garibaldi and rolled to a stop in front of the station. Turi read the lettering on the truck, *Città di Mondello, Polizia*, Mondello City Police, and recognized the chief, Mario Ardolino, emerging from the passenger side

"Mario, nice to see you again. It's been awhile," Turi said shaking Ardolino's hand.

"Maybe not so nice when you see what I brought you, Turi," Ardolino said gravely. He moved to the rear of the truck and opened the doors revealing a black body bag on a stretcher. He reached in and pulled the zipper down, exposing the contorted, ghastly gray face of Antonio, and continued down to the blood-caked death wound which ripped open the torso.

"My God; my God," Turi exclaimed turning away and retching.

"Of course, you know this man," Ardolino asserted as Turi dabbed his wet eyes and wiped his mouth clean.

"Yes, yes," Turi sighed, "Antonio Pepitone, a son of Castellammare and the man seeking the office of Mayor of Palermo. And a monthly guest of mine," he added.

"A railroad worker discovered the body alongside the tracks this morning, just outside Mondello. In all my years, I have never seen a murder this brutal," Ardolino said.

"Murder?" Turi responded sarcastically, "It looks more like an assassination. Someone ordered it" he said bitter and angry.

"Well, I wouldn't speculate on that, Turi, and you'd be well advised to keep your suspicions to yourself. Anyway, it was probably gypsies."

"Gypsies," Turi responded incredulously. "Very incompetent and careless gypsies," he observed. "They left his pocket watch and his pouch with *lire* behind."

"Maybe," Ardolino returned, shrugging his shoulders.

Turi composed himself and turned to his deputy.

"Vito" he said, "go to Lucia Morteannu and tell her to come immediately. Then go to the church and return with *Padre* Marco," he instructed. They moved the body out of the heat and placed Antonio in one of the cells where it was cooler.

Before departing, Ardolino told Turi that the responsibility of the investigation would be handled by his department since the murder occurred in his jurisdiction. Yes, Turi thought cynically, some investigation it will be.

Truthfully, he was relieved he would not have to become involved and would avoid a confrontation with Bonanno. He suspected Bonanno had at least prior knowledge of the crime and may have, in fact, ordered the assassination of Antonio with the sanction of the other Sicilian families.

Turi anticipated a large turnout of public mourners in Castellammare during Antonio's wake and funeral service but was not concerned about a violent backlash. Palermo's university students and the intelligentsia were not prone to such action. Carmelo, however, was another matter. His hot temper and reputation for impulsive acts could pose a problem, a *vendetta* leading to another *vendetta*, resulting in bodies showing up in every alley of the village. *La compana di la morti*, the ring of death, continues to surround Maria and her family, and may yet toll again, Turi reflected sadly.

. . .

Lucia Morteannu stood patiently as *Padre* Marco administered the last rites, then moved forward to examine the body. She winced visibly then announced,

"The preparation will take longer than usual, *Capitano*, at least one, maybe two days. His face has deep lacerations and is badly bruised and there is much work to be done on the body. We can keep the body in the wine cellar where it is cool and get some ice from the fishermen to help in the preservation."

"Thank you, *signorina*," Turi replied staring down at Antonio's face, marred when he was thrown from the train. *Padre* Marco saw Turi's pained expression and placed a supportive arm around his shoulder.

"I know this loss must be difficult for you, Turi. You and Antonio had grown close during the time he spent with you in your home every month," the priest said.

"Yes, *Padre*, we came to realize we had many things in common. We trusted each other and shared many confidences. He was a close and valued friend," Turi replied, choking back tears.

"And now duty demands that you must go to *la signura* Caiozzo once again and inform her of the death of another family member, this time the result of a brutal murder," the priest said, shaking his head.

"*Padre*, I....I don't know how to...how I can bring Maria and her family more tragic news."

"I know this is difficult for you, my son, but I also know you have been close to the family over the years, and la signura would expect nothing less from you," the priest declared perceptively.

"*Padre*?" Turi responded anxiously and turned to Marco.

"It's all right, it's all right," the priest said patting his shoulder, "I know your intentions have always been sincere and honorable. I will accompany you to the Caiozzo home and, hopefully, together we may help Maria and the children through this difficult time."

CHAPTER 20

Death always brings difficult, onerous tasks, which the living must attend to on behalf of the deceased. Antonio's death was an assassination involving a person of some celebrity which occurred on the state controlled railroad. News of the event had already been picked up by Palermo's newspapers and would run in the following day's edition. Turi and *Padre* Marco were dreading the logistical nightmare the throng of public mourners would present for Castellammare, particularly for the Church of San Giuseppe. The *Padre* suggested that the wake and the funeral service both take place in the church to consolidate the crowd and minimize the chaos.

"What do you think, Turi?" he asked.

"*Padre*?" Turi responded and turned anxiously to Marco.

"Yes, I...I guess so," Turi said indifferently, as he guided the horse along the rocky, dusty Via Umberto. Suppressing thoughts of the unpleasant task which was ahead, Turi occupied himself with the petty concern as to when the village council would allocate the necessary funds for the purchase of a motor lorry and bring his police department into the 20th Century.

The late afternoon shadows settled on the road and his absent musing almost let the horse pull the wagon off the road into a ditch.

"Your mind is wandering, *Capitano*," the *Padre* observed.

"Yes, *Padre*," Turi admitted, as they neared the Caiozzo house. "I wish I were someplace else, anyplace, in my office maybe, tending to a neighbor's silly complaint about the family feud next door, or pushing official papers across my desk."

They climbed down from the wagon, hitched the horse, and slowly walked toward the door, where they were greeted by a surprised Carmelo.

"*Bon giornu*, *Padre*, Turi," he said inviting them in, "what can we do for you?" he asked.

"*Bon giornu*," the priest and Turi responded weakly.

"Who is it, Carmelo?" Maria anxiously called from the kitchen where she sat sipping espresso.

A puzzled Carmelo escorted them in and Maria immediately stiffened as she looked at them. The color drained from her face as she slowly rose, and brought her hands to her mouth.

As *Padre* Marco solemnly explained the reason for their visit, Maria's piteous, heaving sobs of grief erupted into shrieks of rage.

"All this dying, all this never-ending damn hateful dying!" she cried pounding her hands on the table. "I don't know how much more I can stand, and I'm afraid there will be more to come. There's always more to come. This island breeds sorrow and death, and the only time we are truly happy here is when we are young. And I'm not young anymore," she continued with tears streaming down her cheeks, "and I'm afraid, afraid for my children and afraid for myself." Carmelo moved toward his mother and held her tightly.

"I feel so alone, so helpless and empty," she sobbed slipping limply and exhausted onto a chair.

"You are not alone," *Padre* Marco said, placing a gentle hand on her shoulder. "God is always with you, giving you hope and the strength to carry on for your family and…"

Maria exploded in a torrent of blasphemous sarcasm.

"God is always with me? Always with me *Padre*? Then I wish he would confer his presence on someone else. I have had more of his attention than I need since my sixteenth year. I feel I am a plaything in the hands of a mad entity who manipulates His helpless creatures for amusement."

"Maria!" the priest exclaimed horrified, "your words are blasphemous."

"Don't speak to me of blasphemy, *Padre*, it is God who defiles His creation," she retorted bitterly.

"Maria," the priest said, acknowledging her grief, "I can see you are overcome with sorrow. But when this terrible time has passed and your heart is not burning with anger, we can speak again. Our Lord is always merciful and forgiving. Until then, receive this blessing," he said, making the sign of the cross, and know the presence of our Lord and Savior, Jesus Christ, is always with you, my child. Meanwhile, with your accord, I offer the church for the wake, as well as the service, to make it easier for you to accommodate the expected crowd wishing to pay their respects to your brother. Turi," he then asked, "may I impose on you to…?"

"Of course," Turi replied, "of course."

Turi turned and looked at Maria and their eyes met mirroring mutual affection and Maria's gratitude for his presence. Turi fought the impulse to comfort her with an embrace and quietly murmured,

"*A dumani*, Maria, till tomorrow."

"*Sì, a dumani*, Turi," she returned with heavy eyes.

. . .

Stella and Giovanna tearfully embraced their mother, but little Maria sat alone, hard, impassive, staring at the wooden crucifix on the wall. "Again," she murmured, "again the stench of death permeates this cursed family." Carmelo, uncharacteristically quiet and calm, followed Turi out the door.

"Turi," he called, "can I speak with you for a moment?"

"Yes," Turi replied, shrugging his shoulders, turning to meet a stone-cold face of restrained anger.

"Do you have any idea who is responsible for this butchery of my uncle?" Carmelo asked.

"No, honestly I don't," Turi lied. "All I can tell you is that Ardolino, the chief of police in Mondello, thinks it may be the work of gypsies."

"Gypsies," Carmelo repeated, thoughtfully stroking his chin and nodding facetiously, "Yes, of course. Well, that should be easy enough to verify. All we have to do is get a description of the passengers who bought a ticket for the 8 a.m. train from Palermo and..."

"Carmelo," Turi impatiently interrupted, "I told you this incident is not in my jurisdiction. Ardolino from Mondello is handling the investigation, and I advise you not to snoop around and interfere. He has the authority and the badge."

Carmelo was seething and his cool melted.

"Fuck you, fuck his authority and fuck his badge which you can stuff up your ass!" Carmelo shouted at Turi, bumping against his chest.

"Carmelo, please, please, stop this," the *Padre* implored, pulling Carmelo away from Turi. "Your family has suffered a terrible loss and is in the throes of grief. Please, do not add to their misery."

Turi walked over to the wagon as the still night was disturbed by the sound of hooves breaking the stones on the path.

"What the hell is happening here?" Caiozzo demanded as he dismounted, looking around.

"Don Caiozzo," the *Padre* responded, "passions are running high in your home tonight with the tragic news of the death of your wife's brother, Antonio."

"Antonio dead!" Caiozzo exclaimed, shocked. "What happened, *Padre*?" he asked.

"Antonio Pepitone's horribly mutilated body was discovered on the train tracks between Palermo and Mondello this morning, the apparent victim of a murder," the priest responded.

"Apparent victim of a murder, *Padre*? Papa," Carmelo raged through tears, "they butchered *zio* like a pig, and now Turi is saying it looks like the work of gypsies."

"Those were not my words, Carmelo," Turi corrected, raising his hands. "I told you what Ardolino, Mondello's police chief told me. The incident occurred outside my jurisdiction, and I have nothing to do with the investigation," he said, turning to Caiozzo.

"Oh, yes, the investigation, the goat shit investigation," Carmelo caustically interrupted.

"*Statti zittu*, shut up, Carmelo!" Giuseppe said, angrily rebuking his son.

"I told your son, Don Caiozzo," Turi said sensing an opening, "that there was nothing we could do here, and advised him not to interfere, for his own good. I'm sure you understand my meaning, Don Giuseppe."

"Fuck you and fuck your advice, Turi!" Carmelo screamed moving toward him. Caiozzo grabbed his son's arm as Turi and the *Padre* turned and walked away.

"Don't worry about what's good for me, Turi!" he shouted after them. "I'll see justice done and have satisfaction, one way or the other."

The girls were drawn outside by the fracas and watched from the shadows as their father pulled Carmelo to him and smacked him across the face.

"What the hell's the matter with you?" he demanded. "Are you stupid or deaf? Did you not hear Turi's warning to stay out of this?"

"Papa," Carmelo said unblinking and ignoring his father's words, "I have a very good idea as to who is responsible for this assassination..."

"Carmelo, for Christ's sake!" Caiozzo said, "stop."

"Papa, let me finish, please," Carmelo implored, continuing his scenario with the vehemence of a man obsessed. "Now, the assassination has the handprint of Pietro Magaddino all over it. He is well-known as a man who settles disputes and has his way with a large knife he always carries with him. That is why he's referred to as, *lu macillaiu di lu villaggiu*, the village butcher. His physical appearance is unmistakable, stocky with a slight limp and, if the ticket agent in Palermo can confirm that a man answering to this description boarded the train..."

"So, now I know that you are crazy as well as stupid and deaf," Caiozzo broke in. "Pietro Magaddino is the brother of Stefano Magaddino, *consiglieri* to Don Salvatore Bonanno. Must I paint you a picture?" he asked.

"The picture you paint, Papa, contains the message that justice cannot prevail in Sicily," Carmelo answered bitterly.

Caiozzo's eyes rolled to the back of his head. "The picture I'm painting, you fool, is that, in Sicily, power trumps justice, perhaps no different from anywhere else in the world. These men who hold power define justice, Carmelo. *Testa dura!*" he said banging his fist on his head, "you are thick-headed. You sound like your uncle, and look where that got him. This conversation is finiri, ended, do you understand?" he demanded, turning and walking into the house, leaving Carmelo alone in the descending dark.

Little Maria moved slowly from the shadows and walked to her brother. She took his hand and rested her head on his chest.

"You know, *frati*, papa is right about one thing. A few men have all the power and, whoever, or wherever they are, they define justice. You must be very careful about what you say and to whom," she advised.

CHAPTER 21

Don Salvatore Bonanno folded his arms across his chest as he stood on the small balcony of his office in the village observing the throng of mourners snaking through the narrow streets of the village.

"I hope this thing was not a mistake," he said turning to his *consiglieri*, Stefano Magaddino.

"Mistake? What do you mean by mistake, Don Salvatore?," he asked.

"What I mean," the Don replied petulantly, "is pray we have not created a martyr here, that we have not committed an action which will stir the people and ignite their fervor, causing us more problems in the long run. He may be more dangerous to us in death than he was in life," the Don said, stroking his brow.

"You may put that concern to rest, my Don," Magaddino assured. "What you see there," he said pointing to the crowd, "is the spectacle of public mourning, a happening among people everywhere who have a need to demonstrate in a common cause and dramatically flaunt their grief. Let them wallow and comfort each other in their moment of mutual sorrow," Magaddino went on cynically. "In a week Antonio Pepitone will be old news. In a month they will hardly recall his name, and in a year he will be a forgotten footnote in Sicily's history. That is how these things always play out."

"Pray you're right, Stefano," Bonanno said skeptically, "and I also expect that my name will not be associated in any way with this…this thing," he added sternly.

Bonanno never used the words 'murder' or 'assassination,' even with his closest advisor, and forbade the usage with his capos when they were in his presence.

"We have taken all necessary precautions, Don Salvatore," Magaddino guaranteed. "The thing occurred well outside our village, in the jurisdiction of Mondello, and will not be connected to you. My brother, Pietro, made certain of that. And," he smiled reassuringly, "the investigation will be conducted by Chief Mario Ardolino, a friend of ours, and Turi, who occasionally has peculiar notions as to his responsibilities and allegiance and can be troublesome will have nothing to do with it."

Reassured, the Don placed a hand on Magaddino's shoulder, and said, "Good work, Stefano, very thorough. And convey my thanks to your brother. He will, of course, be compensated for his work."

. . .

Don Salvatore strove mightily to protect his perceived reputation as nothing more than an influential business leader in the community, although one would have to be born cursed with the brain of an imbecile not to know that he commanded one of the most powerful and successful criminal families in Sicily, a brother in a fraternity of hard, treacherous men. But like his predecessor, Angelo Bono, he was regarded in Castellammare as a grandfatherly figure who generously dispensed favors, offered sound counsel and tried to settle disputes amicably. His obsession with maintaining a respectable public personae was consistent with his private life-style. He lived comfortably, but not extravagantly, on ten acres of olive and lemon trees just east of the village in a comfortable house inspired by English Tudor architecture. It would have been more at home in the rain-sodden peat moss of England's lake district rather than Sicily's dusty, dry climate. The Don was an unabashed Anglophile whose obsession with the stereotypical trappings of British respectability and civility was even reflected in his choice of clothing. His wardrobe consisted exclusively of custom-made clothing tailored by Dunhill of London, and his sturdy footwear was cobbled by the venerable Macauber and Son, boot maker to the kings for centuries.

"*Sempri vistutu cu eleganza*," always elegantly dressed, the village parishioners remarked to each other as he emerged smiling from his right-hand drive 1913 Stellite driven by Nunzio, his chauffeur and bodyguard. He had considered the purchase of a Rolls Royce but yielded to his wife, Teresa's prudent advice.

"That would not be a wise choice, *caro*. It is not consistent with the image you worked so hard to cultivate, and might engender resentment among the villagers...or worse, the envy and suspicion of your colleagues."

Teresa's appearance reflected her sensitivity in this matter. She eschewed the high fashion of the times and stayed within the parameters of understated style and good taste, unlike the wives and mistresses of the other Dons who embraced and paraded every new trend.

As far as anyone knew, Bonanno was a faithful husband and devoted father of two grown children, Ricardo, who was studying law at the University of Florence, and his sister, Lisa, a student of fine arts at the same school. If Bonanno engaged in any sexual indiscretions, it was concealed with as much diligence as the Pope's sexual habits and preferences.

The Don tried to impart the salutary effects of fidelity to his capos.

"The business we have chosen is dangerous and stressful enough without adding sexual adventures with women, to whom, in the heat of passion, we might violate our oath of *omertà*, placing this thing of ours in serious jeopardy. And," he pontificated solemnly, "it also violates the holy vow of matrimony, bringing shame and disgrace to our wives and children."

"My Don," Magaddino joked in private, "we are not running an English boarding school here and you, with all due respect, are not a headmaster."

"*Veru è*, true," Bonanno replied chuckling, "but perhaps Sicily could do with a few stern English headmasters. They have turned out men whose country has successfully ruled the world for centuries. But, of course, you're right, Stefano," he said sighing, "it is impossible to prevent men with power and money from taking advantage of their allure to young, attractive women who constantly throw themselves at them. They are in such abundance that many of the men even cheat on their mistresses. I can only hope they trust the head sitting above their shoulders to dictate their actions, rather than the one below their waist," he joked, wrinkling his brow.

CHAPTER 22

Padre Marco delivered a compassionate and stirring eulogy, recalling Antonio's odyssey from "....A simple son of Castellammare to his life as a writer, teacher and fearless champion of the disenfranchised, a man who loved god, his family, and was devoted to the ideals of truth and justice. He was silenced by the dark forces of evil, but his message will resonate and light the way for future generations of Sicilian men and women to take up the cause and continue the fight to rid our land of this vile *infamia*, and the men who perpetrate their wicked ways through fear and intimidation."

The mourners erupted into enthusiastic and sustained applause, accompanied by chants of, "*Viva Antonio, Viva Padre Marco,*" as the priest left the pulpit and moved toward the first pew where Maria sat with her family. She rose as he approached and pulled the black veil aside revealing swollen eyes and tear-stained cheeks.

"*Padre,*" she said earnestly, "*grazzii tanti*, thank you very much for your kind and comforting words. They made me realize how fortunate I am to have a brother like Antonio, and how very proud I am to call myself the sister of a man who fought for justice and refused to surrender his principles. And I want to apologize to you for the blasphemous words I spoke last Sunday and ask for your forgiveness."

"Maria," *Padre* Marco gently replied taking her hand, "it is not me to whom you should apologize. I think you know where to direct your contrition. But it was not the words you spoke in anger which troubled me. It was your sense of despair, a malignancy which can eat away at us and destroy our potential to enjoy the gift of life. Blasphemous words can always be recalled, but a wasted life, a much greater sin, can never be retrieved. Even though I am newly assigned to the parish of San Giuseppe, I am well-aware of the circumstances of your marriage and what you have endured, the deaths of both parents within a year, and now, your beloved brother. But your quest for enlightenment and your intellectual curiosity has never wavered"

"*Padre?*" Maria wondered how he could know so much.

"Mother Superior Caterina felt compelled to discharge her Christian duty and apprised me of your history and your questionable attitude toward Holy Mother Church and child-rearing practices," he replied, winking. "I believe the path you have chosen is the right path. Do not abandon it. Antonio would expect nothing less from you. Some day your grandchildren, and God willing, your great grandchildren will look back on your life for inspiration. Follow your bliss and do not disappoint them....or yourself."

. . .

The Don had dispatched Magaddino to the church to gauge the mood and the reaction of the crowd, and the *consiglieri* returned with a disquieting report.

"You look tired and troubled, Stefano," Bonanno observed. "A glass of wine or some of this fine Scottish whiskey" he asked.

"Yes, thank you, Don Salvatore" he replied, "perhaps we should both have a glass of that fine Scottish whiskey."

"What are you saying?" he asked turning abruptly and putting the bottle down.

"Well," Magaddino answered, "I think some of the concerns you expressed earlier may have merit, Pepitone aside. We may yet have another problem with this priest...this *Padre* Marco."

"What about him?" the Don asked puzzled.

Magaddino gave him an accounting of *Padre* Marco's fiery eulogy and the reaction of the crowd.

"I haven't seen anything like it in our village since the day Garibaldi ousted the Bourbons and unified Italy," he responded. "They applauded and cheered for almost ten minutes, followed by chants of, *Viva Antonio, Viva Madre Marco*. In less than an hour, this priest may have laid the foundation for a new leader to emerge, one who wears a collar and stands on the shoulders of a dead martyr. And," Magaddino continued, "he already has a base and an accepted pulpit to preach his cause. He needn't spend time and energy cultivating the support of the masses."

"I am interested to hear what you advise, Magaddino."

"What I advise, my Don, is to move quickly and decisively. Cut the head from the snake now and flood the fields before the seeds have a chance to germinate."

Bonanno swallowed a long draught of whiskey, put the glass down hard on a table, and thought for a moment.

"Stefano," he said dryly, "I have always trusted and valued your advice, but, in this matter, I cannot agree with the solution you propose."

"Respectfully, what then do you propose my Don?" Magaddino asked.

"Tomorrow," Bonanno replied, "we must meet in Palermo with the heads of the other families. We will leave Castellammare one hour earlier than usual so that I have time to visit and have a word with Bishop Leone."

"And that will?" Magaddino began.

"And that will," Bonanno responded irritably, "end our problems with this *Padre* Marco."

"If that is what you prefer."

"Prefer, Salvatore? It is not what I prefer. It is what I insist," he declared.

The following week Maria received a note from *Padre* Marco which read, in part,

"I am sorry I was not able to bid you farewell in person, but was commanded to report immediately to the office of the Bishop of Palermo.

I have been ordered to the front, in the Dolomites between Austria and Italy where this senseless massacre plays out every day. I'm sure you know my personal feelings about this mad war, but our men are entitled to the spiritual comfort of their religion and, of course, I must fulfill my vow of obedience. We can never predict what is ahead for us but are guaranteed that sorrow and disappointment, as well as joy and happiness, will be part of our lives. It never ends well but we must continue to do the best we can for ourselves and those we love.

Remain true to yourself and the word of our Blessed Savior.

Yours in Christ, Marco"

That Sunday the newly assigned priest, *Padre* Vecchio, an octogenarian, struggled up to the pulpit to deliver his first homily at the Church of San Giuseppe.

The news from America was encouraging and a smile broke Maria's grieving face as she read the letter from her daughter. Grazia and Giacomo had settled into a small, one bedroom apartment in Manhattan's east Greenwich Village, an area bustling with immigrants from eastern Europe as well as southern Italians.

"It's so exciting mamma. Living next to me is a Jewish family from Poland, next to them people from Russia, and across the hall, Neapolitans, and they are nice enough, mamma. I don't understand why papa was always so critical and suspicious of the Neapolitans.

"Giacomo is working steadily for his brother, Michelangelo, in the concrete business and brings home thirty American dollars a week. That's six hundred *lire*, mamma. I have a job as a seamstress at fourteen dollars a week in what is known as the garment district, and a few commissions for custom made dresses. Giacomo gets annoyed with the clatter of the sewing machine.

"Yes mamma, I have a machine that sews, and Giacomo smiles and is happy when I give him half of what I earn. You weren't aware, but little Maria, Stella and I always knew you told papa that providing for the family cost more than it did, and you secreted *lire* like a squirrel preparing for the winter. I learned your lesson well.

"I miss you all and, yes, I miss our Castellammare with its quiet, slower pace, the narrow streets winding down to the Piazza Europa and the harbor with the beautiful sunsets, and the sweet toll of the bell of San Giuseppe calling us to Mass on Sunday morning. I will always cherish those memories of a young Sicilian girl, but I also look forward to becoming a modern, Italian-American woman.

Cu amuri pi tutti, Grazia"

Maria shed a tear of happiness and pride as she lovingly rubbed the letter against her cheek.

...

Ardolino's investigation dragged on through the autumn of 1915 for appearances. Finally, a week before Christmas, to no one's surprise, he announced Antonio's murder was, indeed, the heinous work of gypsies. Any hope of bringing the perpetrators to justice was doomed, he concluded. They had, in all likelihood, fled the island, and were safely encamped with a band on the mainland. The case was closed

Turi informed the family of Ardolino's findings, moving Carmelo to storm out of the house screaming expletives as he headed for the tavern and foolishly drank himself into a stupor, vowing to personally pursue an investigation and bring the killers to justice.

Early the following Sunday morning, he took the vineyard lorry and drove to the Palermo railroad station, parked, and walked through an empty terminal to the ticket booth, greeted by a pale, bookish-looking young man.

"*Bon giornu*, may I help you, *Signore*?" the agent asked.

"That depends on whether or not you are on duty every Sunday morning, and how accurate your memory is," Carmelo responded, forcing a smile.

"*Signore*, I am on duty every Saturday and Sunday morning from 7 a.m. to 5 p.m., and, as a student of history at the University, I can tell you that my memory is flawless," he proudly replied.

"Good...good," Carmelo said, surprised by the agent's ready response. "Then I'm sure you'll recall Sunday, 15 May of this year when Antonio Pepitone was murdered on this train line between Palermo and Mondello."

"I do, *signore*, I certainly do. How could one forget the day cowardly forces of evil took our beloved Antonio Pepitone from us?" he dramatically responded. "But what has taken you so long to question me about that day?"

"What?, what do you...?," Antonio began, puzzled.

"I would have thought the *polizzia* would have approached me sooner," he interrupted.

"Yes, well, you understand," Carmelo replied, having instantly perceived that the clerk mistook him for a police officer, "these things cannot be rushed. We must proceed carefully, one step at a time. I'm sure you understand."

"*Sì*, I do," the agent responded.

"Now then," Carmelo continued officiously, "exactly how many gypsies did you sell tickets to?" he asked.

"*Signore*? Sell to gypsies? Gypsies do not purchase tickets," he declared. "They are as clever and quick as the fox and always manage to sneak on the train. If there were gypsies present, I never would have seen them. I can only vouch for three passengers that day; our own Professor Pepitone, a drunk uniformed police officer who didn't pay, they never do, and a portly, odd-looking priest who limped to the train and narrowly made it aboard." A priest and a drunk policeman. Who would suspect? Carmelo thought?

He thanked the agent, turned, and hurried to the exit.

"I hope I've been helpful to you," the agent shouted after him.

"*Sì, sì,*" Carmelo replied, waving a hand over his back, "*grazzii tanti.*"

. . .

Little Maria awoke to muffled voices outside and quietly slipped down the stairs and sat in the dark under the window in the salon.

"I've told you repeatedly, Carmelo," she heard her father warn, "to end this dangerous pursuit of yours. The matter has already been settled with Andolino's investigation. Your careless talk and threats of vengeance for Antonio's death have not escaped Magaddino's ears. You are antagonizing men who think nothing of committing murder to achieve their end or protect their interests. You have painted a bull's-eye on your forehead, and it is only because of my business dealings with Bonanno that you haven't joined your uncle in the church graveyard."

"But don't you see, papa," Carmelo insisted, ignoring his father's concerns, "the ticket agent in Palermo clearly identified Magaddino and his cohort as the only other passengers on the train, and…and, isn't it curious that Magaddino has not been seen in the village since the murder? Don't these two facts point to Magaddino as the murderer?," he asked.

"All right, all right," Caiozzo yielded with mounting irritation and impatience, "suppose what you say is true, suppose he is the assassin. What the hell do you think you're going to do about it? Track him down like a hunter and kill him? Fool, then you will become the hunted one."

"I will not have to track him down, papa. At some point he must return to the village. He is totally dependent on his brother, and has nowhere else to live and make his earn. I can wait," Carmelo coldly replied. He may have been remembering an old Sicilian proverb: Revenge is a dish best served cold.

Caiozzo dropped his head to his chest, stroked his jaw, and thought for a moment.

"Carmelo," he said quietly, "sadly, it appears I cannot dissuade you from this reckless course you are plotting by pointing out the certain dire consequences you will bring upon yourself. But," he added in a rare moment of sensitivity, "think of the effect on your mother and sisters, who have already felt the cold hand of death take the lives of three loved ones only years apart."

Carmelo was silenced and stunned by his father's uncharacteristic expression of concern, something he himself had not considered.

"Papa, I..," he began.

"*Sugnu assai stancu*, I am very tired," Caiozzo interrupted, "We can continue this conversation tomorrow, and I pray that a good night's sleep will clear your head, my son."

Maria remained crouched under the window until her father passed by then went into the kitchen where Carmelo was pouring a glass of wine.

"Pour one for me, *frati*," she said sitting. They drank the sweet, white, Sicilian Marsala wordlessly until little Maria broke the silence.

"I heard you and papa talking outside, and I am worried. Do you think papa is right? Do they really have a bull's-eye painted on your forehead," she asked.

He looked at her, smiled, and reached over pinching her cheek.

"Everyone has a bull's-eye on their head," he said fatalistically. "We're born with it. No one escapes death, little one. The trick is to make the shooter miss as often as possible, do what is right, and enjoy the gift of life."

"So what will you do about this Magaddino thing you and papa talked about?" she asked.

"Maria, you and I have been close, trusted and protected each other since we were children. But now I must insist that you remove yourself and forget what you heard tonight. This is the business of Sicilian men and, the less you know, the better," he advised.

"Yes, yes, of course," Maria responded, irritated by his condescension. "Everything in Sicily which is important is the business of men. But the decisions you men make, for better or worse, affect the lives of Sicilian women and their children, and we have nothing to say about it."

"Ah, my sister," Carmelo said cracking a smile, "always the rebel and, unmistakably the *niputi*, the niece of Antonio Pepitone."

"Don't you dare talk down to me, Carmelo. Even you have no idea of what I am capable of," she warned.

Carmelo regarded her thoughtfully.

"*Veru è*, true, I don't," he had to admit.

"I'm glad you give me that much credit," she said, rising and walking toward the door.

"Maria," he gently called to her.

"What?" she demanded, turning, showing her palms and looking at him impatiently.

"I was just thinking. Saturday, we have no work at the vineyard. I could borrow the lorry and we could drive to Palermo early and spend the day as we did with *zio* Antonio when we where children."

"Really?" little Maria exclaimed, delighted by her brother's proposal.

"Really," Carmelo affirmed.

"Oh!, how I would love that!" Maria exclaimed, walking back to Carmelo, hugging him and kissing his cheek.

CHAPTER 23

The summer had been warm and dry and passed into an autumn when the grapes stressed, yielding a bountiful harvest and a good pay day for Caiozzo, Carmelo and Lorenzo. Carmelo had persuaded his father to guarantee the workers an increase to fifteen percent of the share and a five and a half day work week for the following year, to encourage them to remain in Castellammare rather than join the tens of thousands of Sicilians who were abandoning the island for the opportunities in America.

"If we don't make it more attractive for them to remain, papa," he advised, "our work force will be thinner yet next year, and we will be forced to hire gypsies to help pick the grapes. And they steal more than they harvest," he added.

Caiozzo was miffed, but could not refute his son's logic. In fact, he was relieved that Carmelo had taken an interest in the business and had not mentioned Magaddino for weeks.

The cold came with the winter and a light snow settled on the peak of Mount Aetna and draped it like a lace doily on the arm of a chair. The Christmas season was particularly difficult for Maria, who profoundly felt the loss of her brother. She realized she was the last Pepitone, alone, and with no living connection to her childhood.

Maria placed her copy of Jane Austen's *Pride and Prejudice* on the small table next to her chair and left the salon to join her daughters in the warmth of the kitchen to help little Maria and Stella prepare the Christmas Eve fish supper of clams, *gamberoni* and *baccalà*. As she passed the front door, Maria heard muffled voices and opened it to a startled Giovanna, and a wide-eyed, frightened young boy with blazing red hair.

"Oh, mamma!" Giovanna nervously exclaimed, "this...this is Roberto who is from Catania and is here with his family visiting his Nonna for the Christmas holiday and..."

"Yes, yes, slow down," Maria replied lowering her hands, "It's all right, *cara*, it's all right."

"*Bon Natali, signura* Caiozzo," Roberto choked in a voice somewhere between childhood and adolescence.

"And *Bon Natali* to you...Roberto, Maria said smiling as she tilted her head quizzically. "That is a handsome head of hair you have there, young man."

"*Grazzii, signura*, but I wish it was on someone else's head," Roberto said sadly. "I am teased a lot by my classmates who tell me that I was probably stolen by gypsies in Ireland, brought to Sicily, and left on my parents' door."

"He gets teased a lot, mamma, a lot," Giovanna emphasized.

"Yes, Giovanna," Maria said smiling, "I heard. Well, Roberto, I think your hair is fine, very distinguished, and very fine," Maria assured him.

She looked at Giovanna and said, "*Cara*, go inside and get your shawl and muffler. It's very cold out here."

"Yes, mamma," Giovanna said relieved and grinning.

"Well, Roberto, it's been very nice meeting you. Perhaps you can stop by later or tomorrow and enjoy some hot chocolate with us."

"Oh! Oh! I would like that very much, *Signura*, thank you. And very nice to meet you," he called as Maria made her way to the kitchen chuckling to herself; - very unusual, a Sicilian boy with red hair.

Maria was relieved that the young red-head was gone when Caiozzo returned home a half hour later and walked into the kitchen, complaining as he poured a cup of grappa.

"I don't know why I let those two talk me into this," he said to no one in particular. "Another ten *lire* for each worker just because it's Christmas. And after I already agreed to increase their share to fifteen percent and shortened the work week by a half day. Do I look like the English St. Nicholas?" Caiozzo asked.

No, you don't look, or act like any saint, Maria thought.

"Where is Carmelo?" she asked.

"Where is Carmelo?" Caiozzo repeated. "Where do you think he is? He's at the tavern with the other big shot getting his ass kissed by the *poveri*, the poor grateful workers who will want to canonize him by the end of the night."

"Oh papa, stop complaining. You jump over *lire* to get at *soldi*, pennies," little Maria said. "Carmelo is establishing good will among the workers, which will bring you dividends in the long run. He knows how to do business in the 20th century. You even fought with the vineyard owners when they replaced those rickety old horse-drawn wooden wagons with motorized lorries which helped increase efficiency and production this harvest."

"We didn't need those damn motor carts," Caiozzo grumbled.

"No, papa, you...you didn't need those motor carts because you don't know how to drive, and refuse to learn," little Maria said reproachfully, as her mother and Stella smothered their laughter.

"And I suppose, wise ass, you do," Caiozzo returned, pleased with his retort.

Little Maria hesitated for a moment, smiled and looked at Stella whose hands were pressed to her mouth, and said, "As a matter of fact I do, papa, Carmelo has been teaching me."

"Ah," Caiozzo exploded frustrated. "There's no end to what you know, is there little one? Maybe you should meet with the syndicate owners. Maybe they will discharge me and give you the job of supervisor," he ranted storming out of the kitchen.

"Maybe I will, papa," little Maria called after him as Stella doubled over in laughter, and her mother quietly clapped her hands and whispered, "*Brava*" to her daughter.

Carmelo returned home as the late afternoon sun quit over the Mediterranean and went straight to his room, barely acknowledging the family. Maria looked at her daughter, poured hot water into a cup of tea leaves and said, "Take this to your brother, little one. He will probably need something to help clear his head and calm his stomach before we sit for Christmas Eve supper."

Maria knocked three times on Carmelo's door before he finally responded.

"What?" he growled.

"It's me, Maria," she said as she opened the door and walked to the bed where he was lying on his back with arms folded over his eyes. She put the cup of tea on the night table and sat on the edge of the bed.

"What's wrong, *frati*?" she asked, placing her hand on his arm. He rose slowly, staring expressionless at his sister, and said, "He's back, the assassin has returned in time for the holiday. The son of a bitch walked into the tavern like Garibaldi and tossed *lire* around like a farmer seeding his field."

Maria's face tightened and her eyes narrowed as Carmelo continued.

"He then pointed at me, turned, and said to the *barista*, the bar keep, 'Give a bottle to the tough guy there, a bottle of his father's reserved wine, as he sneered and winked at me. He was taunting and challenging me, Maria," Carmelo said in anguish.

"What did you do?" Maria asked.

"What did I do? What do you think I did?" Carmelo responded angrily. "I ran over to him intending to put my hands around his throat, but was restrained by Lorenzo and some of the vineyard workers. As they pulled me out the door I heard…I heard him laughing," Carmelo said between sobs. "He said, 'come back when your friends aren't here to protect you, tough guy, and we can finish our business.'"

Little Maria seethed as she listened and felt her brother's pain, thinking, this pig, this assassin whose place near a seat of power allows him to publicly flaunt his murderous deed and humiliate my brother. He does not deserve to live.

Carmelo dried his eyes, composed himself, looked at his sister, resolved, and said, "I can't let this pass, Maria, whatever the consequences. This beast who slaughtered *zio* will never stop torturing our family unless I stop him."

"Carmelo, please," Maria implored, "think of what papa..."

"I don't give a goat shit what papa said," he interrupted, slamming his fist on the night table and knocking the cup to the floor. "I will not allow that animal to drag our family's dignity and honor through the dirt."

Maria picked up the pieces of the cup and put them in her apron, sighing as tears rolled down her cheek.

Carmelo reached over and took Maria's head, resting it on his chest.

"What would you have me do, *beddu*?" he asked quietly. "I am a Sicilian man, born with the curse of pride which demands vengeance to protect my honor."

"Pride," Maria said, "a very dangerous sin which has led centuries of men to the grave."

"Little one," Maria called, "let your brother rest, and come down here. I need you in the kitchen."

"Wait," Carmelo commanded, grasping her hand, "say nothing to mamma about this. I don't want to worry her."

"Of course not, Carmelo," Maria replied. "But you know, papa will find out what happened at the tavern today."

"Yes," Carmelo agreed, "but you let me worry about how to handle that," he said, as he fell back on his pillow.

. . .

Maria primed herself for the New Years Eve dance held at the parish hall as Stella lay in her bed, flatulently distressed with a swollen belly as a result of a week of too much holiday food.

"I wish I was coming with you," she mourned to her sister.

"Yes," Maria responded with scorn, "if you had put your fork more often on the table than in your mouth, you would be joining me."

"Oh!" Stella moaned, "you are such a cruel sister."

"No, Stella," Maria replied, "just honest."

Caiozzo walked into Carmelo's room where he was putting the finishing touches on his hair and straightening his cravat.

"I hope you're not going to the tavern tonight," he cautioned his son.

"No papa," Carmelo replied, "I would not want to be in a place where pigs gather. Vito, Turi's deputy, has imported some girls from Palermo, and we will celebrate the new year at his house.

"Good, good," Caiozzo said, relieved but skeptical. "Enjoy yourself, have a good time and return home safely at a respectable hour," he admonished.

"And what," Carmelo asked sarcastically, turning to his father, "is a respectable hour on New Year's Eve?"

"Before the cock crows, smart ass," Caiozzo answered as he walked out the door.

"I guarantee, the cock will crow long after I am in bed sleeping soundly before you, papa," Carmelo shouted back.

Maria finished braiding her daughter's hair and said, "Now, go wish your sisters *Bon Annu*, Happy New Year, and apologize to Stella for your harsh comment," Maria ordered, waving a finger.

"Yes, mamma," little Maria promised, always ready to please her mother.

She returned to the salon and reached for her shawl and purse.

"Wait," her mother said, "turn around."

"What now, mamma?" she asked, as her mother fastened a gold chain with a beautiful, hand-carved cameo around her neck.

"Oh, mamma, it's so lovely," she gushed, fingering the piece. "Didn't this belong to Nonna Amelia?" she asked.

"Yes, *cara*, and to her mother before that. Now it belongs to you, a link joining the generations of the women in our family."

"Thank you, mamma," Maria said with moist eyes as she kissed her mother on the cheek. "But what about you? What are your plans for tonight?"

"Oh! Very exciting," Maria joked. "First I must soak the lentils in water, then stuff the sausage meat in the casing in preparation for tomorrow's dinner..."

"Mamma!" little Maria exclaimed sadly.

"..... and then Giovanna and I will go to neighbor Tatada's home for a glass of prosecco, coffee and cake where I will enjoy the spectacle of Nena's grandson, Roberto, and Giovanna making eyes and flirting with each other."

"And papa?" little Maria asked sadly.

"He was invited, of course, but I don't know," or care she thought, "what his plans are," she said dismissively.

"Anyway, please don't dally too long after midnight, and make sure that Vitale cousin sees you home."

"I will, mamma, *Bon Annu*," little Maria said, embracing her mother.

CHAPTER 24

Turi had no plans for New Year's Eve. His on and off relationship with Zinna, the pharmacist's widow, was at a new low and going nowhere.

He went to the station early to relieve Vito, allowing the young man to return home and complete his preparations for the party that evening.

"Now, Vito," Turi admonished, "make sure those young imports from Palermo are on the early train back tomorrow. I don't want a pile of missing person reports on my desk."

"*Capitano?*" Vito asked, feigning surprise.

"*Basta*, enough with the horseshit, Vito," Turi replied throwing his hands in the air. "I know all about your recruitment for tonight. Just make sure all the girls get on the early train to Palermo tomorrow."

"*Sì, Capitano,*" Vito quietly acquiesced, and left quickly with a "*Bon Annu*, Happy New Year."

"*Sì, sì, Bon Annu,*" Turi returned.

The cold night came, and the gas lamps and a few newly installed electric lights broke the dark. Turi hung a note on the door of the station house indicating he was at Savino's restaurant and would return by 8:30. He walked down Via Garibaldi, past early revelers to the restaurant, thick with smoke, love struck couples, and happy families engaged in animated conversation.

"*Bona Sira, Capitano,*" Leo, the proprietor, greeted him. "Your table awaits you at the window, as always. *Subbitu*, immediately," he said to the busboy, clapping his hands, "set the Captain's table."

As Turi sat, Leo leaned forward and whispered conspiratorially, "Tonight, we have for you a nice *Branzino*, taken this very day from the sea, sautéed in olive oil, white wine, and herbs, served with rosemary roast potatoes and arugula salad," he revealed, mincing his thumb and forefinger.

"Good," Turi said, "I am persuaded."

"And a demi of white wine?" Leo asked, "after all, it is New Year's Eve, Captain."

"Yes, Leo," Turi responded, "I'll take a demi of white wine, *grazzii*."

The waiter was at his table immediately with a basket of warm, thick-crusted bread, a wedge of goat cheese, olives, and a small bottle of white wine.

Turi suddenly realized how hungry he was and dribbled some olive oil into a saucer, dipped the bread with a piece of cheese, chewed and washed it down with the crisp chilled wine. Bread, cheese, olive oil and wine satisfied, he thought, a poor, but acceptable substitute when you are alone.

A pretty young woman with fashionably cut short black hair and skin white as newly fallen snow, entered the restaurant and looked around with darting, nervous eyes.

"*Signorina*, over here," Leo motioned. With keen eyes still surveying the room, he bent down and whispered, seating her at a corner table. "*Signor* Amato sends his regrets and has instructed me to inform you that he is unavoidably delayed, but assured he will be here shortly."

Leo looked at Turi, shrugged his shoulders, and ordered the waiter to bring the young woman an aperitif with some bread and cheese.

She looked too young, too pure and too innocent, and, aware of Amato's standing in the Bonanno family and his reputation with women, he hoped she would be well treated and not be humiliated or, worse, violated that night. That man is not for you, he was thinking, and he reflected on Maria.

How he wished Maria could be there with him that evening, laughing and dipping the bread, and sipping the wine, and he could hold and protect and love her and make things right.

. . .

Turi woke early the next morning on a bed in one of the cells to a furious pounding on the station door.

"All right, all right, I'm coming," he yelled irritably, rubbing the sleep from his eyes. Opening the door, he was confronted by Pannini, the baker in an obviously agitated state.

"What is it, Pannini? Are you so intent on kissing my ass that you bring me cake and bread for New Year's day breakfast?" he asked.

"Nothing smelling so sweet, *Capitano*," Pannini replied. "I am here to tell you of the foul-smelling body of a man I discovered not ten meters from the door of my shop early this morning."

"What?" Turi exclaimed as his eyes widened and his jaw dropped. "What are you saying?" Turi asked incredulously.

"What am I saying?, What am I saying," Pannini repeated. "Are you deaf, or still drunk from last night?" the baker wanted to know.

"Ah! A hell of a start to the new year," Turi said, reaching for his coat and hat, and strapping his holster to his waist.

"Do you recognize the man?" Turi asked as they hurried out the door.

"Oh yes, *Capitano*, oh yes" Pannini slowly answered. "It is...was..., without doubt, *senza dubbiu*, the body of Pietro Magaddino."

"Magaddino!" Turi exclaimed. "Oh shit, it gets worse!"

"You didn't touch the body or move anything, did you, Pannini?" Turi asked as they ran to the scene.

"No, no, Captain, nothing," Pannini answered. "You will find it... Magaddino, exactly as I discovered, not five minutes ago, undisturbed.

As they turned off Via Garibaldi, Turi saw his deputy in the distance walking slowly toward them.

"Come with me!" Turi yelled waving his arm, prompting Vito to break into a fast trot.

Three nonnas in morbid black with hands clenched to their mouths and chests stood a few feet from the body, looking down and mumbling prayers.

"All right, all right, ladies, please, please, move away, move back, he ordered, approaching to survey the ground. He crouched beside the body and saw a clean entry to the temple, looked to either side, and picked up two shell casings.

"Oh! Oh!" he heard Vito behind him. "It's Magaddino, Pietro Magaddino!"

"Yes, yes it is, Vito," Turi coolly replied as he rolled the casings in his hand.

"You have two casings there in your hand, but I see only one wound, *Capitano*."

Turi slipped his hand behind Magaddino's head and raised it.

"That's because the mortal wound" he said pointing to the base of the neck, with a blood soaked hand, "entered here."

Turi continued his examination of the body and lifted a hand. He noticed a white circle around the middle finger. Perhaps a finger from which a ring was taken, he guessed. A broken gold chain dangled from Magaddino's bloody neck. It looked as though someone pulled a crucifix or medallion from the chain. Also, absent was a *lire* pouch, or wallet, suggesting that, too, was stolen.

Turi stood up shaking the casings in his hand.

"What do you think, *Capitano*?" Vito asked. "The work of gypsies?"

"Maybe," Turi pensively responded.

"But you're not convinced?" Vito asked.

"No, Vito, I'm not convinced of anything," Turi drawled. "But that is as good a place as any to begin."

CHAPTER 25

Turi arrived at the appointed hour, was frisked, and then ushered into Bonanno's office by the bodyguard, Nunzio.

"Good of you to come," Bonanno greeted Turi, smiling and extending his hand. "It's refreshing to see people punctual for their appointments these days," the Don said.

"How could it be otherwise, my Don?" Turi responded.

"Please, please, sit," Bonanno said pointing to a chair. "So, *comu ti senti? Tuttu va beni?* How are you, all is well?" he asked.

"Yes, thank you, all is well," Turi responded.

"Good, good, so then, let's get down to business. I understand you think this unfortunate Magaddino incident is the work of gypsies," Bonanno stated.

"Well," Turi hesitated, "with the evidence we have it appears..."

"Appears," Bonanno interrupted, "appearances can be deceiving, and no more so than in Sicily," he said laughing.

"This is true," Turi agreed.

"So then, it is possible that the perpetrator was, indeed, not a gypsy as you suggest, but perhaps, perhaps a rogue member of our own village, an incensed grief-ridden troublemaker, let us say, intent on obtaining justice for an action he believes dishonored himself or his family."

"Anything is possible, Don Bonanno," Turi quietly agreed.

"Yes, yes, exactly," Bonanno said, pleased. "Therefore, I would expect your investigation, to explore every possibility thoroughly, satisfying my associate Stefano Magaddino's questions, and avoiding the possibility of vendettas which would only bring harm to our village. I hope you find that the gypsies are responsible, but, honestly, we cannot blame them for everything. We must also look closer to home for the culprit," he suggested, raising his eyebrows.

"Yes, Don Bonanno," Turi said, "Of course that is part of my plan."

"Good *Capitano*, you understand my point exactly," he said tapping his finger on the desk.

The Don rubbed his chin and reflected for a moment. Then he went on to add, "Now, as a sworn protector of the safety of all our Castellammare citizens, you have the grave responsibility of investigating every possible explanation of this...this incident, your personal feelings aside," he said and fixed a knowing gaze on Turi.

"Don Bonanno?" Turi queried.

"Do not test my patience," Bonanno suddenly responded sternly, "you know what I'm talking about. I'll say no more."

Turi dropped his head to his chest, and twiddled his thumbs.

"Yes, my Don, I do," Turi replied, quietly.

"Good, so then," Bonanno said smiling again as he rose from his chair and placed an arm around Turi's shoulder, "my associate, Stefano Magaddino, his family and I, can depend on you to bring this investigation to a successful conclusion within, let us say, within two weeks," he declared, "and the assassin will hang for his crime, and justice, and the legal system will prevail."

"I will do my best, Don Bonanno," Turi said as he walked to the door with Bonanno's arm draped around his shoulder.

"No, *Capitano*," Bonanno snapped, "you will do what is necessary in the interest of justice, and we will avoid any further ugliness from occurring in the village which will harm our image, and disturb my interests, *capisci*?" he asked, "do you understand?"

"I understand," Turi responded.

"*Addiu*, go with God," Bonanno called as Turi walked out the door.

"*Grazzii*, Don Salvatore," Turi replied as he left.

The Don's message was chilling and ominously clear. Despite concerns for his own safety, Turi knew he couldn't abandon Maria again and resolved to alert the family to the danger they faced.

Giuseppe," Turi implored, "I know we have not been on the best of terms all these years, but I must warn you of the danger your son faces."

"What danger? Caiozzo asked. "It's clear gypsies killed Magaddino, just as they killed Antonio. All the evidence points to that."

"It may be clear to you, but THEY don't think so. I'm not going to get into specifics, but I have met with Don Bonanno, and he and Magaddino believe, without a doubt, that Carmelo is the assassin," Turi said.

"That's ridiculous," Caiozzo countered. "My son was at Vito's house, your own deputy's party, that night."

"That's true," Turi said, "but he didn't arrive until 9 p.m. and left shortly after midnight, giving him enough time to commit the deed."

"He didn't do it. He told me he didn't do it, and I believe him," Caiozzo insisted.

"Believe what you want," Turi said, "but understand that those who believe differently control the game and make the rules."

"So what are you suggesting, Turi?" he asked.

"What I'm suggesting," Turi said, hesitating, "is that you get Carmelo out of Castellammare, out of Sicily and, perhaps, out of Italy as soon as possible. And, maybe," he added, "the rest of the family, too."

Turi's message was disturbing but not surprising.

Caiozzo looked up at the pale blue sky framing puffy white clouds, then back at Turi. It was the only time he had ever seen fear mark Caiozzo's face.

"Thank you for your time and advice, Turi," he replied earnestly. "I will give this very careful consideration." "Giuseppe," Turi implored gravely, clutching his arm, "you don't have time for careful consideration. If you don't act quickly, I can assure you that this case will be resolved within two weeks, one way or the other," he warned. In the interest of...your family, you must act immediately.

CHAPTER 26

For all his brutish failings and insensitivity, Caiozzo was adept at accurately assessing a situational danger which could affect his family. He heeded Turi's advice and moved quickly and decisively. Boarding an early train to Palermo the next morning, he was determined to do what was onerous but necessary. He walked into the *Banco di Sicilia*, sat at the manager's desk, and signed the necessary documents converting forty of his fifty thousand *lire* to five thousand American dollars. He then requested that the manager arrange cabling the exchange to the Bank of America, founded by an Italian, establishing an account.

Satisfied that his money was secure, he went to the land acquisition company of Terra Ferma, and negotiated the sale of the house, furnishings, animals and property for a scandalously low five thousand *lire*, with the understanding that he and the family could remain in the house for up to thirty days. Yes, he thought, counting the *lire*, they plucked me cleaner than a newly slaughtered chicken, but he knew he had no choice. He had to get the family out of Sicily immediately. Retaliation by the Magaddino family, swift and brutal as an attack by wolves, was certain if they remained.

As he left the realty office he felt sad and empty. Caiozzo had made decisions which would forever change their lives. He was forced to abandon his childhood home, and his family was being driven from the only place they had ever known. Their life in Sicily would become a distant and cloudy memory. He felt some resentment and anger toward his son, but a father's love for his children and concern for their safety outweighed his choler.

It was past noon and Caiozzo's stomach began growling in protest. He walked in the cold and wind down Corso Vittorio to Casa del Brodo, a small, good inexpensive restaurant known only to the locals. The restaurant was warm, busy and crowded with merchants and professionals in animated conversation between mouthfuls of food.

Aldo, the owner recognized Caiozzo, smiled and waved him to a small table near the kitchen.

"It's been a while, *Signore*. In town for business or pleasure?" he asked, leering.

"Ah, Aldo, my friend, I only wish it were at least *mezzo mezzo*, half and half," Caiozzo replied.

"Well," Aldo said, "in that case, I can only hope the business brings you a nice return. *Lo stesso*, the same as usual?" he asked.

"*Sì, sì, lo stesso*, Aldo. You still make the best marinara sauce outside my dear departed mother's kitchen."

"And a small plate of *carni vugghiuta*, boiled meat on the side?" Aldo asked.

"*Va beni*, very good Aldo," Caiozzo responded.

He devoured the steaming hot plate of spaghetti bubbling with Romano cheese and dipped the pieces of boiled meat and bread into the remaining sauce, washing it down with a good, crisp red wine. Caiozzo patted his expanded stomach contentedly, but couldn't resist the lure of Aldo's fresh-made cassata and a cup of hot espresso.

As he sipped the thick black coffee, he looked out the window at the passers-by, the citizens of his Sicily, buffeted by a furious wind, and thought wistfully, this will probably be the last time I see this, and I doubt I will ever enjoy a meal this good in a restaurant in America.

Caiozzo was aware of the cargo ships which regularly brought cotton, wood and other materials to Italy from America. Rather than return empty, the steamship companies offered passage at a modest fare to Italians wanting to immigrate to America. Two or three of these ships could always be found docked at Palermo or Napoli.

Caiozzo pulled his collar up and wrapped his scarf around his neck against the howling wind, then walked down Via Garibaldi to the port where the office of The Star Line Company was located.

"Yeah?" a grubby, churlish man asked as Caiozzo approached the counter.

"Yeah!" Caiozzo echoed irritably, letting the agent know he didn't appreciate the disrespectful greeting.

"And what can I do for you?" the agent coldly asked, giving Caiozzo the once over.

"What you can do for me is, first show some respect, and then give me a schedule of January departures from Napoli," Caiozzo demanded.

The bold response startled the agent; his manner softened, and he quickly became cooperative.

"You said, Napoli?" the agent asked surprised. "But we have a ship waiting here in Palermo..."

"I said Napoli," Caiozzo returned through clenched teeth leaning forward.

His plan was to hire Santino, the old dean of Castellammare fishermen to secretly ferry the family to Napoli. It would be a difficult twelve hour trip by fishing boat, but they would have a much better chance to avoid alerting Magaddino to their exodus than they would be embarking from Palermo. Caiozzo was semi-literate but could read well enough to decipher a schedule. Fortunately, Star Line had a ship departing Napoli in ten days, 12 January, 1916. The timing was as good as he could expect.

"All right, then," Caiozzo said to the agent, exhaling heavily. "I want six tickets for the ship leaving Napoli on 12 January 3 p.m. for...for America... first class."

"First class?" the agent exclaimed.

"First class," Caiozzo repeated.

He chose first class reasoning security would be tighter and, generally, the trip would be far more comfortable than steerage where the passengers were confined in the hull like rats and had to sneak up to the deck for a breath of fresh air.

The agent took a minute to calculate, looked at Caiozzo, then solemnly announced, "That, *Signore*, will be, will be, he swallowed hard, "five thousand four hundred *lire*."

Unblinking, Caiozzo peeled off five one thousand and four one hundred *lire* notes with the same ease as if he were skinning a peach on a warm summer day, and dropped the money on the counter.

"I will return in a moment," the agent said, nervously scooping the *lire* up and taking it to another room where there must have been a safe. Then he returned and placed the tickets on the counter.

Caiozzo watched as the agent stamped and certified them. "Now," he said assuming a cordial, helpful manner, "the ship will depart from Napoli at 3 p.m. on 12 January. The crossing will take 10 days, weather permitting, and arrive in New York on 22 January at 10 a.m. Be aware that all passengers will be detained and interrogated by American government officials, and you will be required to take a physical examination. Do you have any questions?" he asked.

"No...uh, yes..., where can I make a...a cable?" Caiozzo asked.

"Make a cable?" the agent queried. "Oh, you mean send a telegram," the agent corrected.

"Whatever the hell it's called," Caiozzo growled.

"I can do that for you," the agent replied helpfully. "Who are you sending it to, and what do you want to say?" he asked.

Caiozzo slowly unfolded a wrinkled piece of paper from his pocket, and quietly read:

Grazia Vitale

45 St. Mark's Place

New York, New York, USA

He then stood motionless and looked blankly and embarrassed at the agent.

"All right, all right, I'll help you," the agent said. "You want, Grazia is it?" he said confirming the name, as he wrote, "Grazia Vitale to know you and the family will be arriving in New York on 22 January at 10 a.m., and you want her to meet you when the ship docks. Correct?" the agent paused. "May I suggest, *Signore* that you add, 'please make arrangements and reply'?"

"Yes, yes, that's good," Caiozzo said, brightening.

"And how would you like it signed?" the agent asked.

"Papa, just Papa," Caiozzo quietly answered.

The agent wrote the message down and went to the wireless to transmit it. He returned with a copy and said, "You can return in two days to confirm that the telegram was delivered, or we can forward the confirmation and reply to your..."

"No, no," Caiozzo interrupted alarmed, "I...I will return here in two days for the confirmation and reply."

"Whatever you prefer, *Signore*," the agent said.

"*Grazzii*," Caiozzo gratefully replied, pushing a two *lire* note to the agent.

"Ah! *Grazzii a Lei*, thank you, *Signore*," the agent said smiling. "And have a good trip," he called, as Caiozzo walked out.

The cold air hit his sweat-soaked face and neck and a chill ran down his body. He crossed the street and went into a dark, foul-smelling café dense with smoke, past a sleeping drunk and men with cracked grey faces arguing loudly.

"A double grappa," he called to the waiter, taking a seat and putting two *lire* on the table.

"Three *lire*," the waiter said, placing the glass on the table as he studied the ceiling.

Thieves, they're all fucking thieves in this city, Caiozzo mumbled to himself as he drained the glass with an unsteady hand.

"*Cameriere*, waiter," he called, raising his glass, "bring me another."

He wiped the dry, salty sweat from his face and neck, dropped his head to the back of the chair sighed, and downed the second drink.

In one day, he thought, I have separated myself from the only life I have known for fifty-nine years. I live in an unfamiliar century which I don't understand and I'm going to a foreign place called America when I can barely read or write in my own language."

"*Un' altra ancora*, one more," he shouted to the waiter.

CHAPTER 27

Caiozzo boarded the 5:30 train and immediately fell asleep waking as it pulled into Castellammare. His lips were parched and his mouth felt like the bowel of a gravel pit.

"Domenico," he asked walking into the station office, "have you a bottle of water, perhaps?"

"*Sì, sì*, yes," the agent replied, "but, Don Caiozzo, with all due respect, you look like a fig that was too long in the sun, dried, and went bad."

"Yes, well that damn wind and cold in Palermo hit me in the face all day," he answered, gulping the water and splashing some on his face.

"Don Caiozzo," the agent said, concerned. "My son is here in the back. He can take you home in the cart," he offered.

"Thanks, no," Caiozzo said, "I slept on the train and could benefit from a nice long walk to clear my head."

The cold clean air was a relief and he looked up at the sky punctuated by stars glittering like sequins on dark velvet with a full ivory moon lighting the path. He thought about the next step. Tomorrow he would go to the dock and speak to Santino about taking the family to Napoli. He didn't anticipate a problem. Santino was a tough, crusty, tight-lipped old man who hated Magaddino from the days when he was a two-bit hoodlum who tried to muscle him.

"I told him," Santino once confided to Caiozzo laughing, "if you ever try this shit with me again, I'll skin your ass, slice the pieces of flesh like *calamari*, and sell them to the fish mongers. Then everyone in the village can have a piece of you."

The house was quiet and cold when Caiozzo arrived home. He walked into the kitchen, put a small packet of wood in the stove and lit it. He took a plate of sausage and potatoes from the ice box, sliced some bread, and ate quickly, savoring the mildly marinated potatoes, a nice compliment to the spicy sausage. He then walked up the stairs to the bedroom and slid shivering under cold sheets and pulled the heavy wool blanket to his neck. He heard Maria turning restlessly in her bed on the far side of the room.

After Giovanna was born fourteen years earlier, sexual activity ceased, but at least his bed had been warm and not empty. When Grazia married and left for America, Maria had Carmelo move her daughter's bed into the master bedroom and established her own space. Caiozzo had his less frequent sexual needs satisfied by Palermo's whores and offered no protest. The children had guessed long ago that their parents' marriage was celibate.

Caiozzo slept deep and woke late as the sun streamed through the window and warmed the room. A good omen, he thought, smelling the aroma of fresh-brewed coffee. He walked down the stairs past the salon where Maria sat reading, into the kitchen and poured a cup of strong coffee and steaming milk. Alone at the kitchen table he was struck by how quiet the house was. Carmelo was at the vineyard with a small group of workers cleaning and repairing tools, little Maria was working at the *pasticceria*, Stella was at Conte's Bella Figura clothing shop helping with the spring fashions, and Giovanna was at school. Not bad, he thought. The marriage was a failure, utterly loveless but all the *picciriddi*, the children, are industrious and turned out well. With everyone gone, it was a good time to inform Maria of the plan.

Caiozzo walked into the salon with his coffee and sat opposite Maria on the divan.

"*Bon giornu*," he said.

"*Bon giornu*," Maria responded without looking up from her book, a translation of Thackeray's *Vanity Fair*.

"I need to speak with you," Caiozzo began, "about a very important matter, a decision I have made which will probably affect all of us for the rest of our lives."

"Then speak," Maria replied caustically and without interest. Still reading she went on to add, "You never needed to consult anyone before about a decision you had already made."

"Maria, for Christ's sake, put that damn book down and listen to me," Caiozzo exploded, "this matter affects Carmelo and the girls."

When she heard the children mentioned, Maria dropped the book to her lap and regarded Caiozzo more seriously.

"What are you talking about?" she asked.

He hesitated, breathed deeply and said, "I'll come directly to the point. Turi confided to me that Stefano Magaddino is convinced that our Carmelo is responsible for the murder of his brother, Pietro, in reprisal for Antonio's assassination. Bonanno has ordered Turi to conduct and conclude a swift investigation which, undoubtedly, will lead to Carmelo's arrest. Once he is arrested, he will probably never see a trial by jury, whatever good that would do," his voice trailed off.

"My God!" Maria gasped, clasping her hands to her face, "they can't do that...can they?...will they?" she asked in desperation.

"I assure you, Maria, they can, and they will. Carmelo will be arrested and, assuredly, found guilty."

"What, what can we do?" Maria asked horrified, rising and nervously pacing around the room.

"Maria," Caiozzo ordered, "please sit down and listen to me carefully. I have made a difficult but necessary decision which I believe will, will save, not only Carmelo but perhaps our family."

"What? What?" Maria anxiously asked.

"We must leave Sicily immediately for America," he said looking away to the crucifix on the wall.

"What? Maria gasped, sinking into the divan, "leave Sicily immediately?" she repeated his words as though she couldn't really believe what she heard.

"Now I know what a terrible shock this must be for you," he continued, trying to calm her and soften the drama of the moment, but..." The rest of his words were lost and Maria heard only his droning voice as fear for her son conflicted with a rush of excitement at the prospect of leaving Sicily immediately for America. Her heart pounded wildly. Reading the works of the Bronte sisters, Jane Austin and Susan B. Anthony left her with the desire to some day quit the restrictive confines of the island for Britain or America where a better quality of life and opportunities for women were more readily available. Maria got up and went into the kitchen, returning with a small glass of grappa to quiet his nerves.

Poor woman, Caiozzo misinterpreted, she is understandably distraught and hysterical, and now, has taken to drink.

Maria composed herself as she sat down, slowly sipping the grappa.

"So, Caiozzo," she asked, looking intently into his eyes, "what plans have you made?"

Caiozzo's brow furrowed briefly, then he provided a detailed account of the arrangements. Maria regarded him thoughtfully, impressed by his care and efficiency but was not really surprised. As she well knew, he was tenacious when he put his mind to achieving a goal. Indeed, the course of her life had been the result of his tenacity. She thought of that warm summer night twenty four years earlier at the piazza and the *festa*, and the families laughing with their children, and Agata's rendezvous with Ruggero, and how happy and silly they all were. And how, suddenly, everything changed when she was pulled into a dark alley, and the *gelatu* fell from her hands and melted on the warm stone. She recalled the taste and texture of the filthy rag stuffed into her mouth and, to this day, could not eat anything with a coarse texture.

How strange, she thought, now I must depend on the guile and determination of the man who stole my life, to save my children and myself.

Maria recovered to hear the explanation for the Napoli departure and the reason for the first-class accommodations. He thinks of everything, she reflected, grudgingly.

"Now," he continued, "we cannot tell the children of our plan until the day we depart. And once we tell them, they must remain in the house and have no contact with their friends. Careless slips of the tongue can put us in mortal danger."

"But won't Carmelo be in danger for the next ten days?" Maria asked.

"I don't think so," he answered. "Turi, and he is as you know very reliable, . . . assured me that Bonanno has forbidden Magaddino to take action until Carmelo is arrested and convicted. That will take at least two weeks and, by that time, we will be half way across the ocean. Nevertheless, keep Carmelo close to you by assigning him tasks around the house. He could never resist your demands" he said, smiling.

"Now I must go to the dock to speak with Santino," he said rising.

CHAPTER 28

Santino was a small, wiry man, comically ill-proportioned with a large head on a slender body. Bags of accumulated fat hung under his eyes, and a large knobby nose protruded from the center of his face, once leading Caiozzo to remark, laughing, "Santino, if that nose of yours was full of *lire*, you would never have to work another day."

Santino's calloused hands, fingers and mean scars were witness to fifty unforgiving years of hauling fish from the sea with thick coarse line. On good days, after he had his weekly bath, he smelled like fresh brine. On bad days his body and clothing smelled like rotting fish.

"I realize," Caiozzo told Santino, "that what I'm asking might put you in a dangerous position. And if you refuse, I will understand, and there will be no hard feelings."

"Giuseppe," Santino guffawed, "I have lived my life on the sea for more than fifty years and have battled fish more dangerous than Magaddino. I have no fear of that ass-kissing pipsqueak, and, as for Bonanno, we have been friends since childhood. He would never give me up to Magaddino. But," he added solemnly, "the trip you speak of is more than 24 hours, round trip, not considering the cost of the *benzina*, the petrol. I must, therefore, have 2,500 *lire*"

A considerable amount of money, Caiozzo thought, but well worth it when weighed against the family's safety and Santino's risk.

"Now, Santino said, "listen to me carefully. The next two nights will be very dark with no moon and some rain, and the streets will be empty," he predicted.

"Tomorrow night put Maria's trunk in your cart, cover it and..."

"Trunk? What trunk, what the hell are you talking about?" Caiozzo asked.

"*Calma, calma,* relax" Santino said. "Undoubtedly Maria will have a trunk filled with items she could never leave behind. You must get that trunk on board before the night of our departure. You cannot be dragging it through the streets of the village."

"But Santino," Caiozzo interrupted, "if there is a trunk, I can put it in the wagon with my family on the night of our departure."

"Ah yes, *stupitu*," Santino exclaimed, "And of course," mocking Caiozzo's stupidity, "you will not arouse any suspicion taking your family on a midnight ride in your wagon?" he asked facetiously.

"I did not think of that," Caiozzo responded embarrassed.

"All right, then," Santino continued. "On the night of 11 January between 10 and 10:30, your family will dress in the clothes they will wear on the ship and each carry only a small valise with a change of clothing and personal items. You will leave first, making sure the house remains lit. Maria and the three girls will follow 30 seconds later, then Carmelo. I needn't tell you to be armed."

"No, you needn't," Caiozzo responded gravely.

"Tell Maria not to bother with food or drink. I will have all the necessary provisions on board."

"Santino, how can I begin to..."

"You can't," Santino interrupted. "Not only have I known Bonanno since childhood but I have also been well-acquainted with Nino Pepitone and his family. He was a fine man, a credit to our village, and he and his wife, Amelia, raised two wonderful children. I am happy to do what I can to assist Maria, the children, and you to safety. Go now and make your last minute plans. I will see you tomorrow night when you bring the trunk."

Caiozzo rode to the vineyard to check on Carmelo. As long as he was with a group he would be safe. Even crazy Magaddino would not attempt an assassination, violating Bonnano's edict. Also, he would have to kill every witness, an act which would surely result in mortal consequences for him.

. . .

Maria was already making preparations for the trip. As Santino predicted, she was filling a steamer trunk with linens, sheets and blankets, together with a priceless dinner table setting which had been in her family for three generations, along with a few other family heirlooms. The books of Austen, Dickens and other British and American writers inscribed by her brother were of special importance to her, and she lovingly placed them on top of the other items.

Maria was relieved and gratified that Caiozzo had made first class reservations, accommodations for one state room for herself and the girls, the other for Carmelo and himself. Ten days at sea without a private toilet and shower would have been unbearable and made her shudder.

As she walked through the rooms of the house, she reflected on the furnishings which would be left behind. No matter, she thought, none of this ever belonged to me. I was forced to accept them as they came with the man I was forced to marry. They mean nothing to me. In less than a month in America, I will make all my own choices.

. . .

That afternoon as Maria entered the *pasticceria*, she heard her name called from a table in the rear.

"Maria, Maria, over here!" Dina Fontana called to her.

Maria was surprised to see her. She walked smiling to the table, embraced Dina, and sat down.

"When did you come back from America? She asked surprised.

"Just two days ago," Dina answered.

"So, oh my God!," Maria exclaimed excited, sensing an opportunity for a first-hand description of life in America. "Please, Dina, you must tell me everything."

"Yes, yes," Dina responded, "but first, before I forget, my brother Bartolo told me to make sure that I give his warm regards to his dear friend, Carmelo."

"I will tell my son," Maria assured her.

Dina went on to give a rambling, non-stop account of her visit to America.

"I stayed, of course, with my brother, the confirmed bachelor," she laughed, "in a place called the Bronxa, which is very near the City of New Yorka. Now he works in a barber shop in...in Via Kenmare, but he is looking to buy a shop of his own. And...and, once he buys a shop," she said excited, "he will send for me, and I can live in America, and work with him as a manicurist."

"I am happy for you Dina, but please, please, I am so interested, tell me what life is like in America."

Dina paused, then began professorially.

"Well, Maria, first, you can go anywhere in the City of New York on a motorized bus, or a train that rides on rails above the street for as long as you want for five cents. That's only five *soldi*, Maria. And there are stores everywhere, big stores, small stores, where food, clothing or furnishing can be had from early in the morning to late at night. And the city is never dark, or deserted, or gloomy. You never feel isolated or alone.

And the water in the apartment flows just by turning a handle in the basin, and most have a large tub for bathing in the bathroom. And a room can be lit by just pulling a chain from the ceiling or, in some places, flipping a switch on a wall. And if you are ambitious and not afraid of work, as we Sicilians never were," she added proudly, "you can always find something which will give you eight or ten American dollars a week, even if you have no skill. That's two hundred *lire* a week, Maria, more than our Castellammarese make in six months."

"Oh!, that's wonderful" Maria gushed. "But what about opera or theatre?" Maria asked.

"Opera or theatre?" Dina returned, surprised. "Opera is so popular that our own Toscanini and Caruso regularly perform the works of Verdi and Puccini throughout the city. And there is a place called, 'Broadway' where plays are given six or seven times a week. Maria," Dina concluded, - "This city has more than enough food for the body, and enough art for the soul."

Maria could hardly contain her excitement, and returned home to complete her packing.

They came down the stairs minutes apart into the kitchen where Maria was flipping, a *frittata*, an omelette, and sat at the table.

"*Chi beddu ciauru,* mamma, what a beautiful smell," Carmelo gushed, "Is it almost ready? I'm starved and have to be at the vineyard early today."

Maria turned, and replied with mock petulance, "Yes, *capo*, it is almost ready. But neither you nor your sisters are going anywhere today. Your father and I have something very important to discuss with you."

They looked at each other in wide-eyed surprise, never recalling a time their parents formed a union to discuss anything with them.

Caiozzo came into the kitchen and sat, gravely folding his hands on the table.

"What is it, papa?" Carmelo asked, "you look so serious."

"What I have to say is very serious, Carmelo" Caiozzo responded soberly. "Because of the murder of Pietro Magaddino on New Year's Eve, you, my son, and perhaps the entire family, are in grave danger," he said waving his hand.

"Why papa, what are you talking about? I swore to you that I had nothing to do with Magaddino's death," he protested.

"We believe you, Carmelo," Maria assured him, but..."

"Maria, please, let me finish," Caiozzo interrupted. "I don't believe you would put your family in danger by lying to us, but what we believe doesn't matter. Magaddino believes you are the assassin, and, with Bonanno's approval, he has ordered Turi to conduct a swift investigation, and arrest you within two weeks.

"Arrest Carmelo?" little Maria asked horrified. "But how do you know this? How do you know this is true?" she asked.

"Turi, little one, Turi warned me last week. So, so," Caiozzo continued solemnly, "I have made the decision, and spent the last week arranging for our immediate departure for America. We leave tonight on Santino's boat for Napoli, where we will board a steamer tomorrow for America."

"Tonight, tonight, leave Castellammare?" the children exclaimed agitated and upset, firing questions at their parents.

"But, papa," little Maria asked, "aren't you acting a little hasty? After all, we do have a process..."

"Process? Process?" Caiozzo shouted in anger, slamming his hand on the table. "I'll tell you how the process works. Carmelo will be arrested, and if he is not assassinated while in custody, a jury will surely find him guilty, and he will hang."

They were stunned into silence, broken by Stella's weeping.

"Does this mean," she asked naively, "that we will leave Castellammare forever, never to see our friends again? But where will we live, where will our home be? What will become of us?" she asked through frightened, heaving sobs.

Maria reached down and brought Stella's head to her stomach and stroked her hair.

"*Cara*," she said, "this is not the most important concern right now. Your father..." she hesitated, "your father has made the right decision in the interest of family security."

"Stella," Caiozzo said to his daughter, "I know how insecure this situation makes you, all of us for that matter. But be assured, we will not be alone in America. I received a reply two days ago from a cable I sent to your sister, Grazia. She and her husband, Giacomo, will meet us at the dock in America, and she has already found an apartment for us and furnished it with basic needs. It will do until we get settled.

Carmelo remained unconvinced and was stunned and silent as little Maria protested angrily, voicing what her siblings felt.

"But, papa, why do you wait until the last minute to tell us of a decision which will surely change our lives forever? We have no time to bid our goodbyes or make any adjustment."

"We could not risk telling you sooner. Any one of you could have slipped and given our plan away to your friends, especially if your tongue was loosened by a few glasses of wine," he said glancing hard at Carmelo. "And making you safe is far more important than making adjustments."

Caiozzo went on to give his children a detailed account of the plan of departure for that night.

"Now," he concluded, "go about gathering clothing, warm clothing, and any items of importance to you which you can carry easily. And," he added with a stern warning, "No one, no one for any reason, is to leave this house today."

. . .

Stella was in bed lying on her stomach with a pillow pulled over her head. Poor Stella, little Maria thought, she is like an ostrich who cannot cope and tries to hide from reality.

Giovanna watched her sister pack and asked, "Little one, what is in that small, locked box you just put in your satchel? I have never seen it before."

"That's right," little Maria responded tersely, "you never have because it's very private. It contains my diary, some letters, and other keepsakes which are important to me."

"Well, excuse my nasty curiosity," Giovanna retorted, miffed, "You're excused," little Maria returned dismissively.

She then went to Stella's bed and gently removed the pillow from her sister's head. "Stella," she said softly, "come now and sit up. I'll help you pack your valise."

Stella hesitated then rose slowly and sat on the edge of the bed staring blankly at the wall as little Maria began packing her clothes and personal items.

That evening the family sat quietly around the kitchen table for the last time as Maria ladled steaming *pasta e fasola* into their bowls.

"We will begin leaving in exactly two hours and twenty minutes," Caiozzo announced, looking at his pocket time piece. "It will take thirty minutes to walk the two miles to the dock. I will leave first, followed thirty seconds later by you and the girls, Maria. Carmelo," he said to his son, "you will follow your mother and sisters after thirty seconds more. Keep them in your sight at all times and," he added gravely raising his eyebrows, "make sure that everything you need is at the ready and in working order."

Maria looked at Caiozzo anxiously as she ran her fingers across her mouth.

At ten o'clock, Caiozzo put two packets of wood in the stove and lit them. He then placed lighted lanterns outside the rear and front doors, and looked up at the moonless sky.

Good! He thought. The darker, the better. He walked into the salon where the family was gathered and announced, "It's time." Stella burst into tears as the others quietly dabbed their eyes and wiped their nose.

"Remember, Maria," Caiozzo repeated, "count to thirty before you leave, and Carmelo, make sure you secure the door behind you."

"Yes, papa," Carmelo replied softly.

"Stay vigilant, and I'll see you all on Santino's boat," he said, walking out the door.

Caiozzo never looked back but the salty tears streamed down his cheek into his mouth, and his stomach churned like waves crashing on the shore.

CHAPTER 29

As Santino had predicted, the sky was dark and a light, chilly rain fell but the bad weather with its biting cold and howling wind had not yet crossed the Mediterranean from the north.

Caiozzo's eyes darted left and right as he anxiously made his way down the rocky path toward the top of the village. He turned frequently to make sure Maria and his daughters were following safely behind.

The most direct way to the harbor was straight down Corso Garibaldi, but Caiozzo knew that even at this hour they might encounter a few villagers returning home from a late dinner or a night at Café Pace or the tavern. He led the family across the deserted Via Crispi and entered the village by way of the less travelled, narrow Via Gioberti, which he followed to Via Cappuccini, bringing him to the harbor.

Santino was standing on the deck of the boat waving furiously as Caiozzo turned back to look for his family, who were nowhere in sight. Panicking, he began to race back up the narrow street when the group suddenly emerged from the dark.

"Where's Carmelo and Stella?" he demanded.

"Behind us," Maria answered breathless. "Stella was falling...falling behind...and Carmelo...Carmelo had to carry her halfway through the village."

"Get on board, now," he commanded. As he started up Via Cappuccini, Carmelo stumbled around the corner with Stella clinging to his back and crying hysterically.

"I'll take her," Caiozzo said. "Quickly, get on the boat." Carmelo, panting and flushed, nodded wordlessly and joined the others.

"I'm sorry, I'm so sorry, papa," Stella pleaded between sobs.

"It's all right, it's all right, Stella," Caiozzo consoled, pulling her close and helping her onto the boat.

The thirty foot fishing craft bobbed in the water as small waves rolled and slapped against the side. Santino turned and looked to make sure everyone was on board; then suddenly, the throaty roar of powerful twin engines broke the silence of the night like a raging beast disturbed from his sleep, and the boat moved slowly from the dock, accelerating into the harbor.

"Maria," Caiozzo shouted over the noise, "you and the girls get into the cabin. It will be crowded, but at least you'll be out of the cold and the wind."

Maria went to the trunk and took out two large woolen blankets, then led her daughters inside the cabin.

Caiozzo joined Santino and Carmelo on the bridge, protected by side curtains and an overhead cover.

"There's some canvas in that locker," Santino yelled, pointing. When you get tired, wrap yourselves in it and get some sleep. We have at least 12 hours of open sea ahead of us."

Exhausted, Carmelo took Santino's advice, and immediately fell asleep, ignoring the stench of rotting fish.

"We are fortunate, Giuseppe," Santino called over the engines, "the wind is slight and the sea is calm," he said waving an arm. "We should make Napoli no later than noon tomorrow, in plenty of time for your three o'clock departure."

"Are you sure?" Caiozzo asked skeptically.

"As sure as I know that my spring asparagus will poke their heads through the dirt in seven weeks," he answered laughing.

"All right, then," Caiozzo said, pulling his hat over his ears as he walked to the boat's stern. He wrapped the scarf around his neck and stood with his legs apart, the wind in his face, and his hands tightly clenched behind his back, straining to see the lights of Castellammare disappear where the sky meets the land.

He started at the tug on his arm and felt a small, soft hand slip into his.

"Don't worry, papa," little Maria said looking up at him, "everything will be fine, and someday, we will return to our Castellammare."

"We can only hope, little one, but I'm not so sure," he said sadly.

. . .

Day broke in the east and the sun began to warm the cabin. Maria and the girls woke famished and devoured thick slices of salami and chunks of goat cheese on hard bread, washing them down with cold water. Maria peeled a few apples and handed pieces to the girls.

"Giovanna, please," she said, "take the rest of the food to Santino, your brother and father….and be careful with that knife," she called as Giovanna left the cabin.

"Yes, mamma," Giovanna drawled annoyed.

"You are a lucky man, Giuseppe," Santino said between mouthfuls. "You have a beautiful young wife who doesn't forget to feed her husband. The last time a woman fed me was when I was three months old at my mother's breast. And then she died a month later," he said shrugging his shoulders.

"Why did you never marry?" Caiozzo asked.

Santino thought for a moment and then replied. "I learned early to do for myself, and never felt a man could have more than one great love. God calls some men to marriage or the Church. I believe He called me to the sea."

The bow cut smooth and straight through the blue-green water leaving churning white waves in its wake. The sun burned warmer as mid-morning approached, and Caiozzo put his arm around Carmelo's shoulder, and pointed at the faint grey coastline that began to appear on the horizon. "Napoli," he pronounced.

How strange, he thought, in fifty nine years, this is the first time I have ever seen land outside of Sicily.

Maria and the girls left the cabin and were leaning over the boat's railing, gesturing excitedly as mighty Vesuvius loomed larger and closer. Santino entered the harbor and reduced his speed, cruising among the anchored ships until he saw a pier with a sign that read, 'Star Line Company' and a three stack steamer moored next to it.

"There's your ship, Giuseppe," Santino said pointing, "and here we are, just a few minutes after noon." He backed the boat into a small berth and cut the engines. Maria and the girls thanked and embraced Santino as Caiozzo and Carmelo lifted the trunk to the dock. They returned to the boat and locked in a three way hug.

"Now don't be shy," Santino advised. "You needn't carry that trunk or even your valises. You are travelling first class, and they have porters for that job. Go directly to that uniformed steward and inform him of your status."

"*Grazzii ancora*," Caiozzo said with tears in his eyes.

"*Prego, addio*, and *bona fortuna*, my friend," Santino returned.

Within minutes his boat was back outside the harbor, a small speck on the water.

Caiozzo led the family toward the uniformed steward and handed him the tickets. The man studied them for a moment and then, assuming a palpably false smile said, "Yes, yes, the Caiozzo family. Welcome aboard and enjoy your voyage."

He then pulled the head porter aside and muttered furtively, "Make sure you give them three double berth cabins; we will want to keep the large four berth suite for ourselves."

"I heard that," Maria said, incensed. "Are you saying there is a four bunk cabin available, but that you are saving it for you and your *citrulli*?"

"Well, *signura*, you see, the steward stammered in reply, "it is customary that, if the large cabin has not been reserved in advance, the stewards may make use of it during the voyage."

"Customary?" Maria asked. "Then it is not a company rule is it?"

"Well…no, not exactly," the steward admitted.

"No, not exactly," Maria echoed him caustically. "Well, we are first class passengers who reserved a four bunk cabin and paid a first class fee. I demand the four bunk cabin for my daughters and myself. You can sleep in the lifeboats for all I care."

The steward was visibly shaken and his face turned red in embarrassment.

"All right, all right, *signura, calma, calma*," he said, trembling. He then turned to the porter and officiously ordered, "Take the *signura* and her daughters to the large cabin immediately," "he said twirling his finger, "and then bring them a large bowl of fresh fruit, with the Captain's compliments."

Caiozzo stood gaping and wide-eyed as he watched Maria take charge. He was astonished and a little dismayed.

My God, he moaned to himself, we have not yet left Italy and this woman is already behaving like that crazy American lady, Anthony. Maria is in her prime, while gravity is winning the battle for the cheeks of my ass, and having a good piss is the only thing I really enjoy with my prick.

CHAPTER 30

The stateroom was airy and spacious with two portholes looking out over the water. It had two double-bunk beds, a table with four chairs and a small sofa and smelled like pine trees.

Giovanna looked around anxiously and hurried into the bathroom.

"Mamma," she called meekly from behind the door, "can you come here for a minute, please?"

"What is it?" Maria asked, opening the door.

"Which one do I use?" Giovanna whispered, puzzled and gesturing with outstretched hands.

"Ah *cara*!" Maria answered, suppressing a laugh, "you make in this one," she said pointing to the commode, "and wash in this one," pointing to the bidet.

"But, mamma," Giovanna asked confused, "How do I wash in this,... this little..."

"You'll figure it out," Maria said, smiling as she closed the door behind her.

The lack of sleep and the tension of the previous thirty six hours finally overcame her, and Maria collapsed into a deep slumber on one of the lower bunks.

Caiozzo came out of the bathroom in the smaller, but comfortable berth, scratching his head.

"Carmelo," he called to his son, "go in there and tell me what you see."

"What, papa?" Carmelo asked, turning his lip up.

"Go into the fucking toilet," he ordered, frustrated and confused, "and tell me why they have two commodes."

"Two commodes, papa?" Carmelo asked, walking over to the bathroom. He stood studying the conundrum seriously for a moment and then, anxious to impress his father with his worldliness, announced, "Ah, yes papa! I have heard of this before. He proceeded to enlighten his father. "Now, the one on the left is where you sit and have a shit. The one on the right is where you stand and make a pee pee."

"For Christ's sake," Caiozzo asked, "why the hell do they need one commode for the shit and a separate one for the piss. Everything ends up in the same place," he reasoned.

Carmelo stared at his father blankly for a moment, and frustrated, exploded, "How the hell would I know why, papa?" he said throwing his hands in the air, "that's just the way things are in the 20th century outside Castellammare."

"Ah!" Caiozzo grumbled, pitching his hand forward, "more useless modern bullshit."

"Yes, papa, you're right," Carmelo said placatingly as he walked toward the door.

"Wait!" Caiozzo exclaimed, alarmed, "where are you going," he asked.

"I'm just going to take a walk around the ship, explore a bit," Carmelo replied innocently.

"No, sit for a minute," his father ordered, "that is not a wise thing to do. We do not know who is on this ship bidding their relatives or friends goodbye and who might recognize you and report the sighting to The Friends of Friends."

"But, papa," Carmelo argued, "we are here in Napoli, not Palermo. Who would?" he began.

Caiozzo raised his hands, stopping his son.

"Carmelo," he said calmly, "I have gotten us to this point safely by carefully considering every possibility. Let us not jeopardize our exit at the last minute by a foolish or hasty action. In less than three hours we will be out at sea, and then you can begin your amorous adventures," he said winking.

"Meanwhile, please go down the passageway here to your mother's stateroom and make sure all is well. And tell them to remain in the cabin until we have departed. And you, you, return immediately, *capisci*?"

"Yes, papa," Carmelo complied, "I understand."

. . .

The steward walked up and down the passage barking, "Last call, all ashore who's going ashore."

At 3:30 p.m. the loud, throaty moan of the ship's horn blew three times as the engines revved and throbbed, and the ship moved forward, slipping smoothly into the calm Mediterranean.

Next stop, New York, Maria thought as she stirred refreshed from her sleep. The girls, anxious to get up on deck, fought over the use of the bathroom until Maria interceded, assigning priorities, and strode past her daughters, closing the door.

"Mamma," they protested united in resentment.

Caiozzo woke at the edge of the bunk, holding his crotch.

"C'mon, for Christ's sake," he bellowed, "*Aju a pisciari*, I have to piss."

The bathroom door opened and Carmelo emerged like an actor on cue, clean-shaven, with hair slicked back and smooth like new laid asphalt; a cravat, and a silk scarf foppishly draped around his neck.

"Whata ya think, papa?" Carmelo asked.

"*Beddu eleganti*," Caiozzo responded appreciatively, "you cut a fine figure, my son. But what is that strong scent? You smell like you have just come from a bordello?"

"The cabinet over the wash basin, papa. Everything you need; soap for the body, the hair, skin cream, and small bottles of cologne from Paris," he said excited, walking toward the door.

"*Aspetta*, wait," Caiozzo ordered.

"What the hell is it now, papa?" Carmelo asked impatiently.

"Please," Caiozzo, implored, "sit with me for a moment and listen to what I have to say." He began slowly, measuring his words.

"Be aware of everybody and everything around you," he said, pulling the skin down under his eye and pointing to it with a forefinger.

"Listen carefully to all the conversation around you," he said, flapping his ears forward comically, "and keep your mouth shut," he said, placing a finger over his lips and twisting it. "And, above all, remember, trust no one. This is our way, this is how we Sicilians survive."

Carmelo looked down and then went to his father and embraced him.

"Thank you, papa. We don't always agree, but I think in this respect, you are right. I will carry these words with me forever."

I hope to God he means it, Caiozzo thought as his son walked out the door, but I'm not convinced.

. . .

Neptune was benevolent and, despite travelling on the North Atlantic where the weather could make a voyage uncomfortable at best and catastrophic at worst, it was uneventful, and the ship cruised on across the Atlantic without incident.

The family dined early, at the first sitting at six o'clock, and Maria reveled in the luxury of not having to prepare a meal for her family every night, although, privately, she was critical of the quality of the meal, and troubled by accounts she heard about what the steerage passengers were eating; stale bread and watery coffee for breakfast, and a poor soup or stew for lunch or supper.

She thought about the grey, scab-marked face of the frightened young woman she encountered the previous evening on the steps leading to steerage, who implored Maria not to report her.

"Please, please, *signura*," the woman pleaded, "I am only here for a few minutes to get some fresh air for myself and the little ones here. I don't know if we can survive another day down there in the filth and the stench."

"No, no," Maria replied, "I will not report you. Come here tomorrow night at this time and I will bring you food enough for you and your children."

Maria remembered the day when she and her father returned from Palermo, and she had questioned why so many Sicilians went to bed hungry.

'We do what we can,' her father said. Maria was determined to do what she could.

The next night Maria ordered more than she could possibly eat and wrapped it in a napkin. As she rose for her nightly walk around the ship, little Maria grasped her hand and gave her a napkin with food.

"I heard what you said last night to that woman, mamma, and I want to give this to the *povira signura* and her children in steerage."

"I have never known what to expect from you, little one," Maria said to her daughter lovingly, "but you have done very well this evening, and made me very proud."

CHAPTER 31

On the 21st of January the ship's Captain announced that they would enter American waters the following day at about 6 a.m. and would reach the harbor of New York City no later than 10 a.m. He ordered steerage passengers to remain below until they received further instructions regarding disembarkation.

In a much more respectful tone, he announced; "First class passengers are advised to begin packing their belongings today, and report to the deck by 8 a.m. tomorrow for medical inspections before entry to the country can be approved. Upon approval, you will then be transferred to barges and taken directly to our pier in New York."

First class status afforded passengers the additional benefit of on-board processing, bypassing Ellis Island and the hours of waiting in long lines to answer the brusque, often humiliating questions of the inspectors.

That evening at dinner, the mood in the dining room was festive and electric as well-lubricated passengers who had barely acknowledged one another during the voyage moved among tables, clinking glasses and toasting the successful end of their journey, and the expectations of the opportunities and the adventures that awaited them in the new world.

Everyone at the Caiozzo table was excitedly speaking at once, including Stella, who had emerged from her cavern of fear and uncertainty, and Giuseppe, whose newly acquired taste for gin martinis summoned the sense of false courage.

Maria took her daughter's napkin filled with food and left the dining room to meet the young woman waiting on the steps at the stern of the ship. The night was crisp and clear and thousands of cold blue stars glittered against the black sky and the moonlight shimmered pale yellow on the calm water.

To her surprise, Maria found the young woman on the deck, leaning against the ship's railing.

"*Bona sira,*" the young woman greeted Maria.

"*Sì, na bedda sirata*, it is a beautiful evening," Maria agreed, smiling. "I see you are no longer fearful about being caught on deck."

"No, no *signura*. Many of the steerage passengers are leaving hell's hole to sneak up for a breath of clean air. Surveillance is lax on this last night. The crew is too busy counting their money, celebrating, and getting drunk," she said smiling.

"Will someone be meeting you at the dock?" Maria asked, concerned.

"Oh, yes," she answered with glee, "my Elio, whom we have not seen in two years will be waiting...two years," she repeated, sighing and shivering in the cold.

Maria removed her wool scarf and draped it around the young woman's neck.

"Oh, no, *signura, grazzii* but no," the woman protested.

"Take it, please," Maria said. "I have many others. My daughter, Stella, knits at least one a week," she laughed.

Maria looked around nervously and said, "Well now, I must leave you and return to my family. Here is some food, and take this," she said pressing a twenty dollar bill into the woman's hand.

"No, no, *signura*, thank you but I couldn't, I..., I."

"Please," Maria insisted.

"*Grazzii, signura*," she said, lowering her eyes.

"*Signura*, please, before you leave, you have been so kind, and I don't even know your name."

"*Mi chiamo Maria*, my name is Maria," she replied.

"And you, *come si chiama Lei?*" Maria asked.

"Vittoria, my name is Vittoria," she answered smiling.

"Vittoria," a beautiful name for a beautiful young woman," Maria said.

"*Bona fortuna*, good luck, Vittoria, and *addio*," Maria said as she slipped into the dark.

. . .

Maria's sleep was broken by the creaking sound of the wardrobe door opening. She flipped the light in her berth and saw Giovanna putting her coat on.

"*Bon giornu*," Giovanna said sheepishly.

"*Sì*, yes, *bon giornu*, Giovanna," her mother replied, "But what are you doing" she asked, looking at the clock. "It is just 5 a.m. and still dark. Where do you think you are going?"

Giovanna walked over to her mother and sat on the side of her bunk.

"Mamma," she whispered quietly, "this is a very important time in our lives, one which we will never forget, a new beginning in a land of opportunities we never dared dream of in Castellammare."

"Yes..., and?" Maria queried.

"And, and, mamma, we will be coming into the harbor of the City of New York in about three hours, and I..., I want to be the first in our family, the first on the boat, to see the big statue of our Blessed Lady of the Harbor who stands in the water and welcomes all Sicilians to this wonderful place."

A cackle erupted from the overhead bunk as little Maria leaned over, reached down, and playfully ruffled her sister's hair.

"Oh dear sweet, Giovanna," Maria said, "that statue is not Our Lady of Anything. It is called, 'The Statue of Liberty,' a gift from France to the American people, which welcomes people from all over the world."

"Well, I don't care what you call it," Giovanna said pouting, "to me it's the Blessed Lady, and I'm going to be the first to see her," Giovanna said, walking toward the door.

"Wait, now, just a minute, Giovanna," Maria said, sitting up with her arms folded. She looked at her daughter, smiled and declared, "I understand what you're saying, and you may be right. There are few things in life we do only once; we're born, we die and…and, oh, I don't know what else. But this is certainly one of those once in a lifetime events. I'm coming with you, Giovanna," Maria said, resolved, throwing her blanket aside.

"Me too!" little Maria exclaimed, inspired, jumping from her top berth, landing heavy on the floor. Stella woke bleary-eyed, looked at her mother and sisters, and went back to sleep.

They dressed quickly and, as they followed Giovanna out the door, little Maria remarked dramatically, "And behold, a small child shall lead them."

As they went through the door of the main salon onto the dimly-lit deck, they surprised a small group huddled in the shadows who scattered like frightened sheep at their approach. Even in the cold of the night air, the odor they left behind left no question as to their passenger status, a testament to ten days and nights without a proper wash or change of clothing.

"Who were those people, and what is that smell?" Giovanna asked.

"Those people," little Maria answered coldly, "are the poor ones who have not had the opportunity to pull themselves out of their shit holes, or were too stupid to recognize the opportunity when it came."

"Little one," Maria turned to her daughter, shocked, "where is that sense of Christian charity you demonstrated?" she asked. "There but for the grace of God and good fortune, you might have found yourself among the *poveri*"

"The grace of God has nothing to do with it, mamma," she said, "and, be assured, I will never find myself among them. I will make my own good fortune, and take full advantage of every opportunity, by whatever means necessary," she added with conviction.

"Maria!" her mother exclaimed aghast, as the little one took her sister's hand and walked toward the bow of the boat.

As the sun rose the deck was becoming crowded with excited passengers pressing against the ship's railing. Maria and the girls had secured the most advantageous spot at the bow because of their early arrival, and squinted hard through the sun's blinding rays.

Suddenly Giovanna started jumping up and down, pointing and yelling, "There it is, there it is, off to the right," she said pointing to a small, dim, grey image rising vertically from the water.

As the crowd pushed forward, pinning them against the railing, little Maria suddenly felt some misplaced excitement pressing hard below her waist. She brought her foot down hard on the toes of a panting young man whose screech rose above the din of the excited passengers.

Little Maria turned slowly and looked fiercely up into the eyes of the surprised young man and said through clenched teeth, "*Signore*, you would be better off focusing your attention on the culo of that statue in the water, than on mine, or run the risk of having to swim to the dock when my brother over there," she said pointing to Carmelo hugging their father, "tosses you overboard."

The frightened young man offered no response, and quickly disappeared.

Maria had witnessed the incident and overheard her daughter's warning to the young man. She moved closer and smiling, draped her arm over her shoulder and said,

"Little one, I never do know what to expect from you."

END PART ONE

PART II

LOWER MANHATTAN, NEW YORK CITY
1916-1932

CHAPTER 32

Two barges cut slowly through the green brackish waters of the Hudson River as passengers looked up in awe at the wall of towering steel, limestone and concrete which stretched so high little Maria strained her neck. She felt a curious simpatico with the buildings which seemed to suggest arrogantly that here in America, not even the sky is the limit. On an impossibly narrow island about twenty miles long, a city built on rock and shale defined opportunity for millions of people who lived and worked within it, a place where immigrants found a freedom of speech and movement they had never known.

They lived well enough below the rarefied air of penthouses, in tenements beneath the noisy rumbling of the El where people rushed about and pursued their daily tasks like ants struggling to survive. But, at least, the prospect of improving their lot was always present

The reunion with Grazia was sweet and emotional, bringing a flood of tears and laughter as the family surrounded and embraced her. Even stoney Caiozzo displayed uncharacteristic warmth, hugging, and kissing a surprised Giacomo on both cheeks.

They put the trunk and valises on a flat-bed, gated truck Giacomo borrowed from the work site. Maria and Grazia stepped into the cab and the others, chattering excitedly, climbed onto the bed behind.

"Giacomo," Maria asked as he accelerated down forty seventh street, "where is this famous Borrdaway we have all heard about?"

"Oh, you mean, 'Broadway, *signura*," Giacomo began.

"Giacomo, please," Maria implored, "we are all family now. Call me 'Mamma.'"

"Yes, mamma" he said, smiling, "we are all family now. And I will be happy to show you the great Broadway, if you wish."

Giacomo steered the truck east from the west side piers and stopped where 42nd Street and Broadway converge.

"There it is, mamma," he said dramatically extending his arms. "This spot is called 'The Crossroad of the World' because of the thousands of people from all over who pass here every day." The truck began to roll and shake from the excited activity in the rear, and Maria, awestruck, murmured, "Oh my! Oh my! I could never even imagine that such a place like this existed. Theatres and restaurants as far as you can see. And all the people, and all the motor carriages that make the sound of honking geese. And where are they all going?" she turned in wonder to Giacomo and asked.

"Some to work, some to play and some…, well, who knows, mamma?" he said smiling.

Maria released a deep sigh and shook her head in disbelief, absorbing a frenzied bustle of activity unequalled in her experience.

"Mamma," Grazia interrupted her mother's reverie, "we should continue to your apartment and get settled now. We will return some other time, at night, when you can see all the glittering lights, and all the fine men in top hats and tuxedos, and the fashionably dressed women...some may be wearing my creations," she laughed, hopefully.

The truck lurched forward and Maria turned and looked through the rear window, smiling happily at her children who were laughing and enthusiastically waving to the passing pedestrians. Caiozzo, feeling the effects of the previous night's consumption of gin, sat alone in the corner of the truck bed, groaning with his head drooped between his knees.

Giacomo continued to first Avenue and turned downtown, under the elevated tracks where the steel wheels of a train screeched and clattered on the rails above.

"Oh, yes," Maria shouted poking her head out the side window and looking up, "this is the train in the sky Dina Fontana told me about. Did you know," she asked turning to her daughter with authority, "that you can ride on that train all day and night for only five *soldi*?"

"Yes, mamma," Grazia answered smiling, "I know you can ride the train all day for five cents...five cents, mamma," she corrected. The truck stopped at the curb in front of a plain brick faced four story building at 36 St. Mark's Place. Grazia led Maria and the three ebullient girls through the front entrance to a well-lit hallway smelling strongly of disinfectant, yielding to a flight of stairs. Caiozzo followed slowly behind, steadying himself on the worn wooden banister.

. . .

Carmelo and Giacomo hauled the trunk up to the second floor and stopped in a foyer leading to a small living room where the family stood in disappointed silence.

"I know, mamma, I know what you're thinking," Grazia said to her mother. "But you have to understand, this is a city with millions of people and limited living space. Even in Palermo where *zio* Antonio lived, all the apartments are small. And, actually, this apartment is one of the more spacious in the area, and the building is clean, well-lighted, and well-maintained...not rodent and vermin-infested like most of the others."

The rent was a princely fifteen dollars a month but, as Maria listened to her daughter and looked around, she began to appreciate it was a bargain compared to the ten or twelve dollars a month rent in other accommodations where the tenants suffered loss of flowing water in the winter because of frozen pipes, and the oppressive summer heat which brought disease-carrying insects and rats as large as cats.

Their relatively fortunate circumstance was not a matter of chance. Giacomo's brother, Michelangelo, was a man of great influence in the neighborhood.

He was a *Padrone*, and had the power to determine which family received the best housing and which men would be guaranteed work in his contracting company, in the railroad yard or on the docks as a longshoreman. Michelangelo Vitale was moved more by the ten percent monthly commission he received for his favor and service than by genuine concern for his countrymen. Still, they paid the commission without complaining, happy to have their families safely housed in a neighborhood with the familiar scents and sounds of the old country, and happy to have a weekly payday.

Maria continued through the apartment with Grazia, hands clasped to her chest.

"Oh, *cara*!" Maria soothed, walking into the larger bedroom, "this is more than enough for your sisters and me, and the smaller room will do fine for your father and brother. And," she said turning to Grazia with a wink and a chuckle, "after all, how often can we expect your brother home at night sleeping in his own bed?"

"Oh, mamma!" Grazia exclaimed, relieved and hugging her mother. "Come, come," she said enthusiastically, "come see the kitchen," taking her mother's hand. "Now I know it's small but…"

"Oh," Maria interrupted pointing, "is that one of those stoves for cooking which gives a flame just by putting a match to that…that…"

"Burner, mamma, it's called a burner."

"Yes, a burner," Maria repeated. "And the water really does come just by turning this round…round…"

"Faucet, it's called a faucet, mamma."

"Yes, faucet," Maria confirmed astonished.

Maria turned suddenly and pulled Grazia close to her.

"*Beddu*," she said, stroking her daughter's hand. "you and Giacomo have done very well for your family in very difficult times. We are grateful and proud that coming to America has not caused you to forget and abandon your family. The loss of living space is more than made up for by our safety, the conveniences, and the opportunities we have in America. But, most important, we are all together, once again."

Caiozzo had already conducted his own inspection, left the apartment, and was sitting on the steps of the building entrance with Carmelo and Giacomo, complaining, and observing the pedestrian traffic with disdain.

"Why do they all run around, *pazzu*, like chickens without heads?" he wanted to know.

"Well, all I can say, papa," Giacomo responded, "in Italy we live, *come gli Italiani,* in America *come gli Americani,* the way of Americans."

"Ah!" Caiozzo exclaimed in disgust, throwing his fist through the air.

"Giacomo," he asked, speaking Sicilian, "you maybe got some tobacco and paper?"

"Well, no, not exactly," Giacomo said looking at a grinning Carmelo, "but I have a cigarette, if that is what you're looking for."

Giacomo took a white package marked, 'Chesterfield' from his pocket and handed it to Caiozzo. He looked at it skeptically and said, "Ah, yes, another example of American foolishness. They are so fucking lazy they depend on machines to roll their cigarettes for them."

As Caiozzo drew from Giacomo's match, he became aware of a small figure sitting beside him.

"And what do you want?" he asked the small boy gruffly.

"Nothing! I don't want anything," the child responded. He was speaking Italian, but it took Caiozzo a minute to understand him.

"You are *napolitanu*?" he asked the boy.

"*Sì, sono napoletano,*" the boy answered.

"That's why it took me a minute to understand you. You people speak like the goats bleating in the hills."

"And you are Sicilian?" the boy asked.

"*Sì, ragazzo,*" I am Sicilian, Caiozzo affirmed, puffing proudly.

"Yes," the boy said, "and you Sicilians speak like the dark *mulinciani* people from Africa's deserts," the boy retorted, rising.

"*Aspetta,* wait a minute." Caiozzo said, impressed by the boy's cheekiness. "*Comu ti chiami,* what is your name," he asked.

"My Christian name is, 'Nando' but my mother and brothers and sisters call me 'toilet paper,'" the little boy answered.

"Toilet paper?" Caiozzo asked, confused. "Why toilet paper?"

"Because I am the youngest in my family, always hanging on my mother's leg, and always up her ass," Nando said, tossing his head back, laughing and disappearing up the stairs.

Giacomo accompanied his father-in-law to Ferrara's *pasticceria* on Grand Street early one Sunday morning to meet with his brother, Michelangelo.

"Giuseppe Caiozzo," Michelangelo gushed, embracing and kissing Caiozzo on both cheeks, "wonder of wonders, here we are, *paisanu* from Castellammare now in America together."

"Don Vitale," Caiozzo responded respectfully, extending his hand, "thank you for meeting with me, and thank you for all your assistance on behalf of my family."

"*Nenti, non è nenti*, it's nothing," Vitale said, waving his hand.

"The last time I saw you," Caiozzo said, "you were but a young boy going to America with little more than the clothes on your back. Now, look at you, a grown man with a fine cashmere coat, a tailored suit, and polished nails," Caiozzo observed.

"Yes, well, Giuseppe," Vitale said laughing and nodding, "this is a wonderful country and, honestly," he said leaning forward and whispering, "I have done very well for myself. The streets may not be paved with gold, as we were led to believe, but if a man is clever and not afraid to work hard and dig deep, he may yet find gold under the pavement," he said with a knowing smile.

"Giacomo," Vitale said, turning to his brother, "go and sit with Peppino at the table near the front door, and look for the one or two I am expecting who missed their payment this week."

"But *frati*," Giacomo exclaimed, "according to my records all accounts were settled on Friday."

"Yes, well," Vitale said smiling, "maybe you overlooked a few."

"But...but," Giacomo began.

The smile disappeared from Vitale's face, his eyes narrowed, and he sternly commanded, "Go, go now and sit by the door with Peppino anyway."

"Now," he said turning back to Caiozzo, smiling and pointing to a chair, "let us sit, have some *caffè* and *biscotti*, and discuss your future. Perhaps a little grappa for you?" he asked, pinching his forefinger and thumb.

"Well...ah, yes, *Grazzii*, perhaps a little," Caiozzo responded.

"Niccolo," Vitale called to the waiter, "*un grappa, pi piaciri*."

"You will not join me?" Caiozzo asked surprised.

"No, no, Giuseppe," Vitale said raising his hands, "I limit myself to an occasional glass of wine with dinner. I am a businessman, and drinking and business do not mix well. I leave the drinking to the Irisha in the Second Avenue saloons," he said laughing.

Vitale offered Caiozzo a job as a laborer in his masonry company at $12.00 a week, under the supervision of Giacomo.

"I realize, Giuseppe," he said, "that back home your reputation as a successful vineyard manager is unmatched. But here, in New York, we have no vineyards," he said laughing, "and you have no experience as a mason. But working with my brother, who is an artist, you can learn the trade and, by and by, advance and become a skilled mason yourself, making fifteen, maybe eighteen dollars a week. And," he added grandly, "I will cut my customary commission in half to five percent for the first year. After all, we are family now."

Caiozzo sat smiling but fuming as he thought, twelve dollars a week. I was paid seven dollars a day in Castellammare, and I was once referred to as, 'Don'. Now I will be relegated to pushing a wheelbarrow, loaded with brick and cement, like a common laborer, hired by a man young enough to be my son and under the supervision of a boy young enough to be my grandson. Beneath his tight smile his teeth were clenched but he knew he could not refuse. A refusal would be taken as a sign of ingratitude and disrespect, and also arouse suspicion as to how this poor immigrant could afford to dismiss an offer of steady wages.

"*D'accordu*?" Vitale asked smiling, extending his hand.

"*Assai ginirusu*, Don Vitale," Caiozzo responded, "*d'accordu*".

. . .

Caiozzo left the café spitting invectives and walked into Mare Chiaro on Mulberry Street, the only Italian saloon in the area. Irish cops also frequented the place because of the .75 cent plate of spaghetti and meatballs which was served, with an assurance that the "No Punches Thrown" edict between the Italians and the Irish customers would be enforced. And half the Irish cops who frequented Mare Chiaro made their mortgage payments on attached brick houses in Queens or Brooklyn, to "Vitale Incorporated."

Caiozzo sat seething, sipping a grappa with the same resolve as when he left Palermo; I'll do what I must, I'll dance on the strings when necessary he thought, but I'll never permanently surrender myself to a life making a living dependent on this man and my son-in-law.

Carmelo had no such hubris. Vitale found him a job as a busboy at Angelo's, a popular restaurant on Mulberry Street, frequented by upstanding Wall Street types, bankers, lawyers, entertainers and, most importantly, "*La manu niura*, Black Hand" guys, the notorious criminal organization which controlled the lower east side. There was never any dispute or problem among the clientele who knew their place and drifted comfortably and profitably between their diverse worlds. Powerful and successful men respected each other. Where and how they made their money was irrelevant.

Carmelo did more than just clear tables. His natural theatrical flare delighted diners, and he soon caught the manager's attention.

"You do a very good job young man," Gino complimented Carmelo one night after closing. "Everybody like you, you know." Then he said, pointing to the aging and slow-moving Testa behind the bar, "he getta old an ready to retire. You spenda some time wit him behind the bar. Maybe you learn something, and maybe I makea you bartender. Whata you think?" Gino asked, playfully patting Carmelo on the cheek.

Testa left happily the next month with Gino's generous parting gift of $200.00 in one pocket, and fifteen years worth of what he stole in the other.

Carmelo learned quickly, took control of the bar and soon there were as many beautiful young asses on the stools as there were on chairs at the tables. Carmelo was a natural, in this element. The bar was his stage, and the eyes of the women were on him every night. He chuckled as he recalled his uncle's remarks years earlier about his not wanting to do the work required of an actor, but wanting to be a star. He had fulfilled Antonio's prediction.

. . .

"I have an announcement to make to the family," little Maria said at supper one night.

"What?" Caiozzo asked gruffly, winding the spaghetti around his fork, "have you finally found work?"

"No, papa, not yet. I have not found anything suitable," she said haughtily.

"Oh!, Nothing 'suitable' yet for the *principessa*" Caiozzo echoed her.

"So what is this announcement, little one?" Maria asked with interest.

"That's it, that's just it," Maria petulantly replied to her mother. "I am a young woman of eighteen years, and I don't wish to be referred to as, 'little one' any more."

Heads turned, and Caiozzo put his fork down asking, "What are you saying, little one?"

"Are you deaf, papa?" Maria came back at him angrily. "I am adopting the Americanization of my name, and from now on, I insist on being called, 'Mary,' just Mary," she said proudly.

"'Mary, Mary' is it?" Caiozzo raged, "we have not been here six months and already you want to become an American."

"I want to be my own person and referred to with respect. I am not the cute little family pet anymore," she said defiantly as her eyes filled with tears.

They fell silent at the table until Carmelo came to his sister's defense.

"Let her be, papa," Carmelo said. "She is a woman and has the right to be addressed as she chooses."

"You, now you," Caiozzo raged, "my first child and only son takes sides against his father."

"Ah, papa, stop it, please," Carmelo urged, throwing his hand forward. He turned to his sister.

"By the way, litt...Mary," he caught himself, "the *signura* who has the coat check concession at the restaurant is returning to Italy next week. If you like, I can put a word in for you," he offered. "The salary is only seven dollars a week, but the patrons tip very well, the atmosphere is pleasant, and the work is not difficult."

Mary considered for a minute, then concluded that the job sounded attractive. She could realize ten, maybe twelve dollars a week with tips, putting coats on hangers and only work six months a year. And the prospect of meeting an influential neighborhood man was very inviting. She needed no further persuasion.

On the last night of the *festa* of San Gennaro, Leonardo Contino, a regular patron, came into Angelo's with his cohort, Luigi. Luigi took his coat, silk scarf and hat and handed them to Mary. Contino tilted his head quizzically, looked at Mary and asked, "Are you now here permanently or just a temporary fill-in?"

"Permanently, *Signore*. I was hired last week when the *signura* left and returned to Italy," she replied smiling.

"Good, that's good," Contino said nodding, "Unlike that old *strega*, you, my dear, are a delight to the eyes."

"*Grazzii, Signore*," Mary said, blushing slightly.

She watched as the handsome, self-assured, impeccably groomed man and his associate were ushered to a corner table, and thought, this could be interesting.

The two men sat, looked around warily, then leaned forward toward each other.

"Are you sure everything is in place and ready to go smoothly?" Contino asked.

"Everything," Luigi answered. "The Irishman is a fixture in McSweeney's saloon, and knows exactly where the safe is located. And, as you are aware, he is an expert at his job."

"Well I hope the expert is sober tonight. NO drinking." Contino warned.

He then sat back, folded his arms and looked at Luigi with disdain and said, "And for Christ's sake, after we make this score, go to Santorini, the tailor, and have him cut you a decent suit. You look like a fat manicotti shell, bursting with ricotta."

"Ha" Contino reflected to himself.

"What's so funny?" Luigi asked.

"I was just thinking, tonight the mick steals from his countryman, McSweeney and within a week, he will give it all back, and we will have new clothes and shoes."

McSweeney's was a blue-collar saloon where Irish construction workers from the nearby building site stood three deep every day among a few aging, well-worn whores, drinking half their week's salary before throwing what was left on the kitchen table so the wife could feed the children.

By mid-week, they had spent whatever money they had and drank, "on the arm," on credit, for the next two days. On Friday, they repaid McSweeney, and began the drinking cycle again.

On Friday, McSweeney always stuffed what was owed him, plus that days receipts, into a safe under the wooden floor behind the bar until Monday morning when the banks reopened.

The Irishman had assured Contino there could be as much as $1000 dollars in the safe. Contino calculated that, after paying Don Vitale his fifteen percent tribute, and giving Luigi and the Irishman one hundred dollars each, he could pocket a neat $600 or so.

Contino had no interest in becoming a member of Vitale's family. He was content with "associate status," and pulled enough cons and petty burglaries to keep himself comfortable and keep Vitale satisfied. He also owned two small bungalows in Brighton Beach, Brooklyn, which he rented to Italian immigrants, provided by Vitale for a 15% commission.

When Contino returned to the coat check booth after dinner, he found Mary smiling and holding his coat. She slipped the coat over his shoulders and handed him his scarf and hat.

He turned and pressed $5.00 into her hand saying, "Maybe some night we can have dinner."

"Dinner?" she responded, wrinkling her nose, "I don't need a dinner. I eat here every night for free. But maybe," she boldly suggested, raising an eyebrow, "tickets to the opera or the theatre?"

"Oh!, Oh!," Contino exclaimed laughing and turning to Luigi, "listen to this little one, a real firecracker."

Mary's eyes narrowed menacingly and her lips tightened as she poked Contino in the chest.

"You listen, and listen well," she said firmly, "My name is 'Mary,' not, 'little one,' and don't you forget it."

"Ok!, Ok!" Contino said surprised, raising his hands in surrender, "I'll see what I can do about those tickets...Mary."

"Thank you very much, Mr. Contino," Mary said with a mock curtsy.

" 'Leonardo', Mary, my name is 'Leonardo,'" Contino replied, smiling.

CHAPTER 33

Contino, Luigi and the Irishman stood in the shadows across the street from McSweeney's and watched the bartender lock the front door and then disappear down into the Bowery. The Irishman picked up his canvas bag containing the tools of his trade and motioned to Luigi to take the gas cylinder and blow torch he had brought. Then the three walked across the street, down the narrow alley to the back door of the saloon where he jimmied the lock and cut the secondary padlock with bow cutters.

He led them inside past the men's room reeking of urine and dried vomit, behind the bar, where he removed a wood panel on the floor revealing a small safe, nestled face up in a cut-out compartment, exposing the tumbler.

"Here it is, lads," he announced, pleased with himself, "right where I said it would be. Now, Luigi," he said, "be a good fellow, and pour me a Jameson with a bottle of beer chaser."

"Hey," Contino objected, "I thought we agreed, no drinking on the job."

"Ah, Lenny!" the Irishman exclaimed, pleading, "I haven't had a drink all day. Now you wouldn't be after denying a man a wee drop before he begins his labor would ya?" he asked.

"All right," Contino answered, reluctantly, "give him one, but only one."

"Thank ya, laddie," the Irishman said, draining the shot class and washing it down with the beer.

"Now," the Irishman said, wiping his lips, "Lenny, you go stand by the window and give me a chickie if ya see nosey Moriarity walkin his beat."

Now I gotta take orders from da little leprechaun wit more alcohol than blood in his veins, he thought.

"Yeah, sure," Contino said, disgruntled, rolling his eyes.

"Luigi, stand back, lad," the Irishman said striking a match and putting it to the nozzle of the blow torch with an unsteady hand.

The nozzle spit a blue flame, and the Irishman began his assault on the tumbler. Sparks flew back and singed his eyebrows.

"Ah, shit!" he screeched, "quick, gimmie them goggles in the bag, Luigi," he commanded.

He then resumed his work, bearing down hard with the torch, but then stopped suddenly, realizing too late that he had forgotten an important first step: he neglected to drill a small hole in the safe, into which water could be poured to keep the paper dollars wet and prevent them from igniting.

Contino looked aghast at the flames escaping from the safe, and bolted from the front, followed by the lumbering Luigi, and the staggering, bow-legged Irishman, who had more to drink that day than he admitted to.

"*Vaffanculu*, you someonabitch mick cocksucker," Contino bellowed as the three scurried down the dark deserted street toward the Bowery, tripping over garbage cans and strewing refuse in their flight.

The fire engines arrived quickly and were able to contain the blaze with little damage, but the money in the safe was reduced to a pile of ash.

Old man, McSweeney stood with Moriarity the cop, and the fire chief and muttered, bemused, "Dagos, dumb forking dagos, they can't even make an easy score witout boinin the joint down."

"Well it ain't boint down, is it McSweeney?" the chief said, "We damn well take care of our own," he pronounced, winking and slapping him on the back.

The following morning, Michelangelo Vitale sat with Peppino at Ferrara's, enjoying his breakfast, and flipping through the morning newspaper. A short article caught his attention and he erupted in laughter.

"What's so funny, boss?" Peppino asked.

"What's so funny?" Vitale responded. "It's an article in this here paper about a recipe."

"What recipe is that, boss?" Peppino asked, puzzled.

Vitale looked up, smiling, and said, "A recipe for disaster, which mixes two lame Sicilians with a drunk mick and a blow torch," he answered.

"Oh my, Vitale moaned, "Why, why, does that kid get himself involved with those damn Irisha?"

Word of Contino's fiasco quickly circulated throughout the neighborhood and, although he was the butt of jokes and derisive comments, Mary's interest in him remained firm. McSweeney saw nothing funny about the pile of ashes in his safe but, sensing it would be futile, did not press for an investigation. Besides, he reasoned, if the burglary had been successful, he would have lost the money anyway.

Still, he strongly suspected that the Irishman had a hand in the caper. McSweeney instructed the bartenders that he alone would serve, "the little Mick bastard" with a beer mug from his private collection, flavored with, "a few wee drops from me marnin piss."

Contino put his wounded pride aside and showed up at Angelo's the following week, dismissing the ridicule with good-natured self-deprecation.

"Ah!" he said, tossing his hand forward, "even Babe Ruth he strike out sometime. Next week, who know, maybe I hit a home run."

Mary was delightfully surprised when Contino produced two orchestra seats for Puccini's *La Boheme*, at the Metropolitan Opera House.

"Well, Leonardo," she said coquettishly, "I really am impressed."

Later that evening when the last of the diners left the restaurant, Mary joined Contino at his table for an espresso and an anisette, and the couple had a lengthy and intense conversation about their Sicilian experiences, and their hope for a better life in America.

She patted his hand sympathetically as he related a sad childhood in Siracusa. Orphaned at age three, he grew up in a church-sponsored institution run by The Sisters of Charity, who exercised more cruelty than charity. He left at age fifteen in 1907, and apprenticed as a carpenter in Palermo, sharing a one room apartment with four other boys. By 1912, the frugal Contino managed to save enough money to migrate to America and, with Vitale's patronage, secured employment with a construction company.

"He like me, right from the beginning," Contino said, "and give me leads for other work where I make more money," he said cryptically. "I make enough to buy two small bungalows in Brookaleen from owners who can't make a da payment to Don Vitale. Now, I own, makea the payment to the Don, and takea rent from the paseani."

"Really?" Mary said moving her chair closer and hooking his arm.

. . .

The blistering summer heat broke by the end of September, 1916, and the bedding on the fire escapes of the tenements where many people slept seeking relief disappeared with the autumn chill.

The Caiozzos celebrated their first American holiday in November with a twenty pound, freshly-killed turkey from Balducci's butcher shop, and the usual trimmings of stuffing, cranberry, mashed potatoes and turnips, drowning under an unfamiliar thick, brown gravy.

"This is what the Americans eat on their holiday?" Caiozzo asked disdainfully? "dry, stringy meat and vegetables pounded to mush. Where's my prosciutto, my lasagna? They call this, 'Thanksgiving' but I see nothing on my plate to be thankful for."

Maria and the children rolled their eyes as Caiozzo continued his assault on American food and custom.

"Papa," Mary finally cut her father off, half laughing, "can you please spare us this endless complaining, and let us enjoy our meal in peace. Complain about everything in this country is all you have done since we arrived in America."

"Ah!" Caiozzo muttered as he disinterestedly picked at his food.

Caiozzo was alone in his unhappy adjustment to life in America. Giovanna was mastering English and doing well in school, had made friends, and was on track to be graduated the following summer. Caiozzo and Stella struggled with the language but Maria, Carmelo and Mary were becoming fluent enough in the rudiments to converse. The children were satisfied with their work, and proudly contributed to the household expenses, giving the family a comfortable standard of living not enjoyed by their neighbors.

"Carmelo," Maria called to her son as she cleared the Thanksgiving table, "take this platter of turkey and vegetables across the hall to *signura* Caputo. With five children and no husband to support her, I know she has no money to make a *festa* for her family. And give her this, "Maria said, secretly putting an envelope in his hand. Carmelo smiled and hugged his mother.

"What's that for?" she asked, surprised.

"I know that you have been giving the *signura* money every week..." he began.

"Shush!" Maria interrupted placing a finger over his lips, "God forbid your father should hear."

Carmelo took the platter, crossed the hall and knocked softly.

"Mamma! Mamma!" Nando exclaimed opening the door, "it's Mello, Mello, and he brought us the American bird. Now we can celebrate the *festa* like everyone else."

Carmelo put the platter on the kitchen table as the other children gathered around excited and happy, and Carmelo slipped the envelope into the *signura*'s hand.

"*Grazzii, grazzii tantu*, thank you very much," she said quietly, lowering her head in embarrassment, "and please, please tell your mother..."

"It's all right, it's all right, *signura*, she knows," he assured her with a hug.

As Carmelo walked toward the door, Nando called to him.

"Mello, Mello."

"Yes?" Carmelo said turning and looking down into large grateful, brown eyes.

"Thank you," the boy said in earnest, "and maybe, just maybe," Nando added nodding hopefully, "some day you can take me to the big park that has the zoo with gorillas and tigers...and even Caiozzo can come with us too," Nando added.

"Ha!" Carmelo exclaimed. "Yes, well maybe," he replied.

"What are you smiling about, *frati*?" Mary asked when Carmelo returned.

"Nando, that little, Nando. He has taken it upon himself to shorten by name, and calls me, 'Mello' and," he said, breaking into a fit of laughter, "he refers to papa as, 'Caiozzo.'"

"You see, you see," Caiozzo overheard and growled, "that's what I'm talking about. That kid is becoming just like all the Americans. They always want to change things. They destroy good Italian names and show no respect for their elders."

"Well, I don't know. He seems to like you, papa," Mello said chuckling.

"What?" What do you mean?" Caiozzo asked puzzled.

"He asked me to take him to the zoo and then said, 'and Caiozzo can come with us.'"

"Oh, what the Christ," Caiozzo muttered as he left the room.

. . .

Maria stood on the steps of the Offendorfer Library at 3rd Street and First Avenue, an imposing red-stone, late Victorian building which seemed more forbidding than welcoming to Maria. *Signura* Caputo had told her the library contained a small section of British and American works translated into Italian and, with a library card, she could borrow them for up to two weeks.

She pulled the heavy oak door open, which yielded reluctantly and thought, but this is like entering a vault where you're really not welcome.

Maria walked tentatively toward the counter and noticed the name plate, 'Anna Pastoria'; an Italian name, she told herself and she breathed a sigh of relief.

"*Scusi*," she said and went on in Italian, "I would like to know what I must do to borrow books from the library?"

The librarian looked up and smiled.

"You don't speak any English?" she asked in Italian.

"*No, no, inglese,*" Maria quickly replied.

The librarian looked at Maria skeptically and said, "I think you do understand and speak some English, *signura*. But you're like all of us, all the women when we first come here. Act dumb and pretend you understand nothing. That's when you find out what people really think, and what's going on. I know, I too am Sicilian. But trust me, *signura*. Let us communicate with each other in English.

"So, then, you must first have a library card to borrow books," she said producing an official-looking application.

"What is your name, *signura*?" the librarian asked.

Maria stood silent, anxiously staring at the woman.

"Your name, *signura*, what is your name?" the librarian repeated.

Maria's lips curled in a slight smile, followed by a booming, "My name isa Maria, Maria Pepitone," she replied, prompting a chorus of "Shush!" from the readers, "and I live a numero 3-2-0, Santo Marka Place, New Yorka."

Anna Pastoria smiled broadly at Maria and said, "Good for you, *signura* Pepitone."

Maria left the library with a translation of Flaubert's *Madame Bovary* in one hand, looking proudly at the library card in the other.

CHAPTER 34

The days and months inexorably became years and the unforgiving swelter of the summer of 1920 proved too much for the sixty three year old Caiozzo, who struggled to pull his weight on the job.

"Well, what do you suggest?" Michelangelo asked his brother, Giacomo. "He can barely push six or seven wheelbarrows a day, the other men are complaining, and I don't need this old man dropping dead on the job," he asserted.

"Give him something that doesn't require any physical effort" Giacomo suggested.

"Like what?" Michelangelo asked, annoyed.

"Give him the job of time-keeper, punching the men in and out, and let him bring the coffee for the men on their morning break."

"But that's Caruso's job," Michelangelo protested. "I just can't let a good man go after all these years."

"*Frati*," Giacomo replied "Caruso's seventy eight years old, half blind, and he fucks up the time sheets every day. He lives with his daughter and has no one to support. Give him a pension of fifteen dollars a month. We can easily make that up somewhere."

"Jesus Christ!" Michelangelo exclaimed, "what do I look like, one of those Jew social workers?"

"Please, *Frati*," Giacomo pleaded, "he is my father-in-law."

Michelangelo fussed and threw his hands up disgusted.

"All right, all right," he relented. "But" he warned, "he better not disappoint me."

Caiozzo was delighted with his job change and rationalized it as a promotion, a managerial position more consistent with his skills and status as a former supervisor. And he could disappear for an hour or so every day getting the coffee for the men, leaving him time for a quick stop at Mare Chiaro, and a grappa or two, where he had become a regular and a local character recklessly throwing money around.

. . .

Contino was becoming increasingly upset and impatient with Mary's constant refusal over the years to accept his marriage proposal and was jealous of her popularity and flirtatious manner with the male customers at Angelo's.

"Leonardo," she said smiling and patting his cheek like a mother placating a frustrated child, 'this is all play-acting that I do. It's innocent fun and, more importantly, it guarantees a generous tip."

The explanation did nothing to quench the fire of mistrust and suspicion raging within him, a condition, if not innate, is certainly a cultivated mind-set among many Sicilian men. Despite Contino's insistence upon planning a wedding date, Mary remained steadfast, enjoying her life as an independent woman without wifely responsibilities, but accepting a measure of the security and protection Contino offered. I enjoy the best of both worlds, she thought.

Maria was less sanguine about her daughter's choice and lifestyle. Finally, she confronted her.

"Don't you think it's time you allowed this man to make an honest woman of you?" She went on to accuse Mary harshly. "You're a kept woman, just this side of a *buttana*."

"A *buttana* is it, mamma? Mary retorted angrily. "And how is it that I'm any different from women who marry less for love and more for protection and financial security. At least the choice I have made is made honestly."

Mary's words struck a chord, and Maria reached out to embrace her daughter and apologize.

"I'm sorry, *figghia mia*, for what I said. I worry so, and only want what is best for you."

"I understand, mamma, I do understand," Mary replied.

Things changed quickly for the Caiozzo family. By the end of the summer of 1920, Grazia gave birth to a son, naming him 'Giuseppe' after her father, thrilling him, and ten months later delivered a second son, christened 'Carmelo' after her brother. Caiozzo gave thanks to the Good Lord for continuing his name and bloodline by depositing a nickel and lighting a candle at St. Patrick's Church on Mott Street every day, and spent ten times that amount celebrating at Mare Chiaro.

"Oh!, oh!, here he comes," the barkeep joked. "Do we still call you 'Don' or are you now *Nonnu*?"

"Call me anything you want," Caiozzo responded, "what is important is that Caiozzo blood will continue to flow after I am gone," he said pounding his chest.

...

"So," Caiozzo asked one night at supper, "when are the rest of you gonna get married and have children? Grazia already has one, and the rest of you are still living in the home of your parents," he said glaring at Mary.

"We all pay our share, papa," Stella said. "And I can't even think about marriage now that Grazia has a little one. Someone has to run the shop," she added, proud of her promotion from seamstress to manager at Grazia's clothing boutique.

Run the shop, Caiozzo thought. My quiet Stella has now become a fucking *capo*.

He looked at Giovanna.

"Don't look at me, papa. I still have a year to go in secretarial school, and I'm not rushing into anything. I'm going to take my time, look around, and work in one of those big Wall Street law firms before I decide. Maybe I'll meet somebody there," she said with a knowing wink.

"And Carmelo, what about you? You keep running around the way you do," he growled, "and that thing between your legs is..."

"*Basta*, enough," Maria exploded. "We don't need that kind of talk around the table. Save it for the bums at the saloon."

"Well, mamma, as long as papa brought it up," Carmelo said, "I met my old friend Bartolo Fontana from Castellammare, last week. He bought a barber shop on Kenmare Street and has taken an apartment not two blocks away, and I'm going to move in with him."

"Oh, yeah, Fontana," Caiozzo mused. "His father used to cut my hair in Castellammare. Did a good job, too. But, of course, I tipped him very well," Caiozzo boasted.

"Yes, well, that's not how Bartolo remembers it," Carmelo replied, "But anyway, mamma, I'll be moving out in a week."

"In a week," Maria repeated, putting her hands to her face in distress.

"Don't worry," Caiozzo interjected, snickering, "he'll only be two streets away, and I'm sure you'll see him when he's hungry or when he comes to pick up his laundry."

A *mammuni*, my son is going to become a fucking *mammuni*, still tied to his mother's apron strings he thought.

"And lit..., excuse me, Mary, do you have any surprises for us?" Caiozzo asked, sarcastically.

"Me?" Mary swallowed hard and put her fork down.

"Is there another 'Mary' in the room?" Caiozzo asked facetiously, looking around.

"No, there isn't, papa," Mary answered, raising her eyebrows and pausing. "Leonardo and I are to be married next month," she added casually.

"Married!" Maria exclaimed joyfully, leaving her chair and wrapping her arms around her daughter.

Married, Caiozzo smiled and thought relieved. About fucking time!

Mary reached into her pocket and, grinning, produced a sparkling, two karat diamond ring, which she then placed on her finger and proudly displayed to the family.

"Leonardo proposed two days ago, this time with a ring. And, after all these years, I really couldn't refuse him again, could I?" she asked coyly.

"Of course not," Caiozzo responded caustically. "But tell me, *cara*, are you marrying the man or the ring?" he asked.

"Papa!" Mary responded, batting her eyes with feigned indignation, "what a terrible thing to say!" she replied reproachfully.

"Stop it, Caiozzo," Maria commanded angrily. "And you will have a church wedding?" Maria urged, turning to her daughter, hopefully.

"Yes, mamma, Father Amato has agreed to read the bans this Sunday at Mass."

Carmelo, Stella and Giovanna rose from their chairs and surrounded their sister with hugs and kisses.

"We're all truly very happy for you, Mary. Especially me, little sister," he said smiling warmly. I'll reserve the rear dining room at Angelo's, and we'll have a real family celebration after the service," Carmelo gushed. "We'll talk later, but now, I gotta go," he said. "Bartolo and me are goin uptown to listen to some music in one of them Negro jazz clubs."

"Yeah, sure, go listen to *mulinyam* music, but make sure you bring some rubbers with you. It might rain tonight," Caiozzo said leering, as Maria shot him a disgusted glance.

Giuseppe, Stella and Giovanna retired to their rooms and Mary sat in the kitchen as her mother brewed a pot of espresso. She returned to the table, wordlessly set the pot and two cups down, sat and cradled her chin in her hands, and asked, "So how many months along are you, Mary?"

"Two, maybe three," Mary responded coolly.

"And do you love him?" Maria asked.

"Love him?" Mary repeated. "Oh, I don't know mamma, I guess so. But I don't know how much I trust him," she said shaking her head.

"Trust him?" Maria asked. "Do you think he may be cheating on you?"

"Oh, no, not that kind of trust, mamma. At least I don't think so."

"Then what is it, *cara*?" What troubles you?"

"I don't know if I trust him to let me continue to be my own person with personal interests and still be the wife of a man. He's insanely jealous and very possessive. And I fear Leonardo sees my worth only in terms of fulfilling wifely duties in bed, putting a meal on the table, sweeping the floor and washing his dirty underwear. I don't want to become a prisoner in a cage."

"Mary," her mother said quietly and embraced her, "you can only truly become a prisoner if you give the power of control to someone. Determine what you want for yourself, work hard to achieve your goals, and avoid compromise and dependence."

Maria went to the bedroom and returned with the anthology of English poetry Antonio had given her years earlier.

"Here," she said giving the book to Mary, "read the poem by Richard Lovelace. It makes sense, and the words are true. I found it very helpful and comforting."

Mary looked at her mother quizzically, then began to read.

"Stone walls do not a prison make. Nor iron bars a cage...."

CHAPTER 35

Mary and Leonardo settled into Contino's one bedroom apartment on Broome Street three blocks from Angelo's restaurant. Mary continued to work at the restaurant until three months before she delivered her first child on March 21, 1921. The baby girl was named, 'Angela,' after Contino's mother, a woman he only faintly recalled.

Angela was an alert infant with a pale complexion, coal-black hair and a proclivity for playfully blinking her eyes to the delight of family and friends.

"Be Jesus;" Contino's Irish cohort exclaimed as he looked down at Angela, "she got that light skin, and her blue eyes twinkle like the stars over Erin. She sure don't look like no I..talian to me," he remarked, drawing an angry, suspicious glower from Contino.

Mary giggled at the Irishman's poetic metaphor and began referring to her daughter as, 'my little twinkle,' which soon evolved to, 'Twink,' a nickname by which she would be known throughout her life.

Mary enjoyed the new experience of motherhood but also felt the need for some balance and diversion, and joined the choir at St. Patrick's Church, evoking a furious protest from Contino.

"You don't need this choir thing Mary, he raged. "You're a mother now, and your place is in the home, taking care of the child and managing the household."

"Don't you ever tell me what I need, and where my place is, Leonardo," Mary shot back in anger, waving a finger under his nose. "I know my responsibilities as a mother, and I fulfill them very well. And what time is left over belongs to me, and I intend to pursue my passion for music.

"And as for managing the household, put ten more dollars a week on the table," Mary demanded, "there is another mouth to feed, more clothes to buy, and doctors' visits to pay for."

Contino complained loudly but grudgingly gave Mary the extra ten dollars, five of which she deposited in a secret account at Stabile's Savings Bank on Mulberry Street.

My God, Mary thought, smiling to herself, these Sicilian men are all alike. As soon as they get a woman married to them, their arms suddenly become very short, and their hands can't find their pockets.

Every Sunday after Mass the family gathered at the Caiozzo apartment for a day of food-gorging, wine-drinking and loud, animated discussion and disagreements among the men.

"Look at them, mamma," Mary said, "they are no different in America than they were in Sicily."

"*Veru è*, true," Maria agreed laughing, "the ass, the turkey and the man are still brothers, even in America."

Giacomo was an exception, a quiet, serious man who drank sparingly and was a dedicated father and husband who encouraged and supported his wife's interests. Giacomo and Grazia worked well as husband and wife, and were equal partners.

"Papa," Giacomo said, pulling Caiozzo aside one Sunday. "I need to speak with you privately about a very serious situation."

"What! What is it?" Caiozzo asked laughing. "You are wearing the *facci di mortu*, the face of death," he said patting Giacomo's cheek.

"Papa, this is no laughing matter, and I need to speak with you about it now," Giacomo said seriously. "Come outside and we can talk on the stoop."

Caiozzo reluctantly agreed.

"All right, so what is so important, Giacomo?" Caiozzo asked grinning through bleary eyes as they settled on the stoop.

"Papa, you've been returning a half hour late every day when you go for the morning coffee for the men and…"

"Yeah, well maybe," Caiozzo interrupted, stammering, "but what?…" he began.

"Stop," Giacomo said firmly, putting his hands up, "and listen carefully to me. Friday, I had one of the workers tail you and you went to Mare Chiaro and had two drinks, and then…"

"Well, so what, is that such a big deal?" Caiozzo asked defiantly.

"No, that's not a big deal," Giacomo answered, thrusting his chin forward, "the big deal is you were seen taking and giving money to three or four neighborhood guys who are regular borrowers from my brother's crew. Are you trying to muscle in on my brother's business?"

Caiozzo's face burned red, and he looked away, disturbed.

"*Si' pazzu*, are you crazy?" Giacomo asked, his voice rising.

"It's bad enough that you're lending money out, but you're doing it right here in my brother's neighborhood, under his very nose, and after all he has done for you and your family?" he asked incredulously.

Caiozzo was silent for a moment, then replied, trying pitifully to defend himself.

"Giacomo, I didn't mean any disrespect. I just wanted a little piece of the action to feel better about myself. You know, you know, in Castellammare I was…"

"In Castellammare," Giacomo interrupted, "you fucking managed a vineyard for syndicated land owners. You were not a Don, or even a member of a family. You lived off a myth of your own creation, and now you try to live that myth here in America."

Giacomo rose from the stoop and walked a few feet away, throwing his hands up in frustration.

"What are you going to do?" Caiozzo asked quietly.

"Do? Do?" Giacomo returned, "I'm not going to do anything. But you, you," he said pointing, "are going to stop this rogue business of yours, and then I will collect what is owed you, plus the vig, and turn it over to my brother, with the explanation that I miscalculated last week's take. Pray to the Madonna that he will be happy to have an unexpected earn, and will not ask questions. But I cannot guarantee that he will not find out what you have been up to. This is a small, tight neighborhood where tongues wag freely, and my brother has the ears of an elephant."

"So, my money, my money is..."

"Your money? Your money, papa?" Giacomo asked coldly? "Once you put it on the street the way you did, it was no longer your money. Just be grateful that I am your son-in-law, and you are not floating face-down in the river with rats making a meal of your balls."

...

Peppino pulled the black Packard sedan onto the construction site, and Vitale rolled the window down.

"Giacomo," he called. When Giacomo came over, he ordered, "send Caiozzo over here, now."

Caiozzo walked slowly to the car, dreading the meeting with Vitale. He climbed into the back seat and extended his hand.

"Spare me the pleasantries," Vitale growled, his eyes fixed forward, rejecting Caiozzo's greeting.

"Don Vitale..." Caiozzo began obsequiously.

"What did I say?" Vitale barked so loudly it turned Peppino's head around.

Caiozzo slumped silently back into the seat and folded his hands like a naughty child waiting to be scolded.

"You, Caiozzo, have violated a trust which has sustained us Sicilians for centuries, and stamped a purple patch of dishonor on my name and reputation. You have not only been deceitful, but have disgraced your people with your stupidity in assuming, that, at some point, I would not have found out about your foolish venture. And for this, you must suffer the consequences," Vitale intoned.

Caiozzo's eyes flew wide and he felt a rush of fear so strong it produced a foul-smelling discharge.

Vitale looked disgusted at Caiozzo, and opened the door for relief.

"Don't worry," Vitale said smiling calmly, "I'm not going to kill you. I have already taken whatever money was owed you. But, as of today, you are no longer in my employ, and no longer have my protection. And that goes for your son, Carmelo," he added gravely.

"You and your family have lived well and protected because of my agreement with Bonanno that the Castellammare vendetta would not pollute these shores and disrupt my business, and he agreed. That agreement is now void. You are on your own. *Vattinni*, go now and I wish your family good fortune, if they can find it."

As Caiozzo exited the car, Vitale called to his brother. "I can understand your trying to cover for your father-in-law, Giacomo. But know this, your loyalty is to me and this family. Don't ever, ever, do anything like this again," he warned sternly.

A despondent Caiozzo walked into Mare Chiaro, past the staring eyes and awkward silence of the regulars, nodded wordlessly, and went to the far end of the saloon. Rumors about his misadventure and Vitale's punishment had already circulated through the neighborhood. He placed two dollars on the bar and went into the men's room. When he returned, the two dollars lay, undisturbed, and the barkeep stood at the other end with his arms folded, making snide, aside remarks to the four regulars and glancing sideways at Caiozzo.

Caiozzo looked at him puzzled, shrugged his shoulders, and gestured toward the bar.

"What happened, Vincenzo, you run out of grappa today?" he weakly joked.

"No, Giuseppe," Vincenzo answered, "we got plenty of grappa. There just ain't any for you. Your money's no good here anymore."

Caiozzo looked away and his head dropped to his chest. He reached for the money, stuffed it in his pocket, and walked toward the exit.

"Hey, Giuseppe," a voice issued from the group, "ya shouldn't be leaving money laying around in this neighborhood. Someone just might figure it belongs to him and put it in his own pocket."

Caiozzo heard the raucous, contemptuous laughter behind him, and, humiliated, walked quickly down Mulberry Street. That's the last anyone ever saw of Caiozzo in Mare Chiaro.

CHAPTER 36

Carmelo and Bartolo lay on their backs at the South Street pier, looking up at a cloudless summer sky, their fishing poles askew between their legs.

"You know what I'm thinking?" Carmelo asked.

"How could I know what you're thinking?" Bartolo laughed.

"I read some pages in a book mamma borrowed from the library, a book written by a guy named Mark Twain," Carmelo replied.

"Yeah, so?" Bartolo inquired.

"Well," Carmelo continued, "he writes about two young guys, friends, who go fishing, and run around together, and it reminds me of us when we were kids in Castellammare."

"Yeah," Bartolo replied dreamily after a moment, "I know what you mean. Every time I smell salt in the air, I think of Castellammare, and our childhood, and how innocent and easy things were then. We never had to worry about anything, and…and the only serious decision we had to make was which girl at the Piazza Europa we would try to fuck that night," he said laughing. "Now…, now, everything is complicated and…," he began, sitting up. He turned and looked away. When he turned back to face his friend, Carmelo was puzzled by Bartolo's expression, and could see that something was bothering him.

"Hey, *cucuzza*, what the hell's the matter with you?" Carmelo asked looking at Bartolo. "You look like you're gonna cry."

"Oh, no, nothing," Bartolo said, shaking his head and forcing a laugh. "Sometimes I just get a little sentimental when I think of our childhood in Sicily. Ah!, what the shit," he broke off, "enough of this talk."

"Hey," Bartolo suddenly exclaimed in a eureka moment as he handed Carmelo a bottle of beer, "I got an idea. Why don't we go hunting, maybe next Monday? You got the day off and my barber shop is always slow on Monday.

"Hunting," Carmelo repeated musing, "Yeah, yeah," he answered eagerly, jumping up and smiling. "I ain't been hunting in five years. It'll be like when we was kids in Sicily, running through the woods and…woods," Carmelo paused. "But where would we go hunting, Bartolo?" he asked.

"There's a place in New Jersey, Neptune Beach. I been there three, maybe four times. There's plenty of game, deer, pheasant, fox…"

"What, no *lupa*?" Carmelo interrupted laughing.

"No, stupid, no wolves and no *cinghiali* either," Bartolo joked, playfully punching Carmelo in the shoulder.

"We gotta take the train to this Neptune Beach?" Carmelo asked.

"No, no," Bartolo answered. "One of my customers, he got a car he hardly ever uses. I give him five dollars and he lets me have it for the day."

"Bartolo," Carmelo proclaimed, nodding his head with conviction, "this is the best idea you've had in a long time."

"Yeah," Bartolo agreed, "we'll pack a nice lunch..."

"And a couple of bottles of wine," Carmelo interrupted.

"And a couple of bottles of wine," Bartolo agreed, smiling, "and have a beautiful day in the country."

The two friends embraced, laughing, and began jostling each other playfully, anticipating the excitement of the great adventure they were planning.

Bartolo returned to their apartment and Carmelo went to have dinner with the family as he promised Maria he would every Monday. As they sat eating, Carmelo casually mentioned that he and Bartolo were going hunting the following Monday, and he would not be coming for dinner that night.

"Hunting?" Caiozzo asked, putting his fork down and furrowing his brow. Maria looked at Caiozzo but didn't speak. Ever since the day he was fired from his job, Caiozzo worried, remembering Don Vitale's warning that the family was no longer under his protection.

"Do you think this is a good idea, Carmelo?" he asked.

"Why wouldn't it be a good idea, papa?" Carmelo inquired puzzled, "a day out of the city, romping through the woods with my best friend? What could be bad?"

"Yeah, papa, what could be bad?" Giovanna joined in.

"I guess so," Caiozzo sighed skeptically. "But where would you go hunting in New York? Central Park?" he asked trying to make light.

"Very funny, papa," Carmelo responded. "Bartolo knows some place in New Jersey, Neptune Beach or something. He's been there three or four times and says it's loaded with game."

Caiozzo's concerns lessened. Well, he'll be with his best friend, and at least he'll be carrying a gun, he thought.

After dinner Caiozzo walked with his arm around his son to the door.

"Carmelo," he said with a warning finger, "remember what I told you on the boat before we left Napoli; always keep a sharp eye out, ears keen like the wolf, and stay vigilant."

"Papa," Carmelo replied miffed, "I'm a grown man and I know how to take care of myself."

"Yes," Caiozzo responded, "and you can be a grown man of fifty-years, and I an ancient man of ninety years, and I will still worry about you," he said embracing his son.

"Yes, papa, *capisciu*, I understand," Carmelo said smiling. "I'll see you next week," he shouted back, bounding down the stairs.

...

Bartolo steered the Model T Ford west into the rising sun, up Route 9 into New Jersey. The noisy four cylinder engine competed with the friends as they recalled their childhood in Castellammare and sang Sicilian folk songs. After more than two hours, the paved road ended, and they came to a sign directing them to Neptune Beach over a narrow, rocky path which punished the tires of the car and jostled them about in the cab. The path ended and gave way to an expanse of scrub oak trees and marsh land, baked hard under the relentless heat of the summer sun.

"We're here!" Carmelo exclaimed.

"Yeah, we're here, we're here," Bartolo echoed, but his tone was subdued. They pulled their guns from the rear seat, and Carmelo took the shotgun to bring down any game birds or rabbits they might flush. Bartolo took the high-powered rifle in case they jumped a deer. He threw Carmelo a box of shotgun shells and said,

"I hope you have enough there to make at least one kill today."

"Don't worry about me. I know how to track game. The only thing you could ever sniff out was willing pussy," Carmelo joked. Bartolo ignored the wisecrack.

"Ok, then, let's walk parallel, about ten yards apart so we can still see each other," Bartolo cautioned.

"Whatever you say, great white hunter," Carmelo replied, gently mocking.

They moved forward slowly, the quiet broken by twigs snapping under their boots, ready to shoot any prey they encountered, rabbits, varmints, deer or game birds. Suddenly a gaggle of geese burst honking from the brush.

"I'll get 'em!" Carmelo shouted excited, and raised his shotgun. A single round pierced the heavy summer air, but it didn't come from his weapon and Carmelo pitched forward onto his face.

Bartolo could not believe what he had done. He dropped his rifle and ran over to the fallen figure, went to his knees and hesitatingly touched the spot between the shoulder blades where the bullet had entered.

"Oh Christ! Oh Jesus Christ! What have I done?" he cried out. Bartolo reached out and grasped the shoulder of the friend he had shot, turning him over. Blood gushed from the exit wound, and Carmelo's eyes, wide with surprise but lifeless, hauntingly stared up at him.

"*Diu miu! Diu miu!*" Bartolo moaned through burning tears, cradling and rocking Carmelo in his arms.

"Please forgive me, please forgive me, my dear friend," he wailed, "I had no choice...no choice...they made me do it."

Sobbing, he began a rambling, detached apology, as though the man he had just sent to eternity could hear him.

"It was Magaddino, Magaddino, Carmelo. He demanded justice for the murder of his brother, Pietro, who he said you killed. I..., I don't know whether you did or not, and I wouldn't care. But...but, when they threatened to rape and kill my sister, Dina, oh, God! What could I do?" Bartolo pleaded, breaking down again.

"You know how they work," he said waiving his hands in disgust. "They choose someone close to the mark to do the thing, someone the prey would never suspect. Oh my dear friend," he whimpered, please, please forgive me for this *infamia*."

Bartolo sat dazed for a few minutes with Carmelo's body in his arms, then gently lowered him to the ground. He went to the Ford and returned with a shovel and a large piece of canvas, and dug a shallow grave. He took a string of rosary beads from his pocket, wrapped it around Carmelo's hands, and folded them over his chest. He then leaned forward, kissed Carmelo on the forehead, blessed himself and murmured, "*Addiu*, my dear friend, go with God."

Bartolo covered his friend with the canvas and eased him into the shallow grave, filling it with dirt and spreading leaves around. He picked the shovel up and staggered to the car on legs gone feeble, when his grief turned to rage. He took the rifle from the ground and, screaming obscenities, smashed it repeatedly against a tree, producing a dull echo, and separating the stock from the barrel.

Bartolo then drove ten miles further west where he spent two sleepless, sweat-drenched nights on a filthy mattress in a broken down roadside motel.

On Wednesday morning a frightened and disheveled Fontana walked into Police Headquarters at 40 Centre Street in lower Manhattan, and surrendered to Detective Michael Fiaschetti, head of the Italian Squad for the Department.

The tortured Fontana, weeping and distraught with dried blood under his fingernails, at first claimed the shooting was an accident, and gave Fiaschetti the location where he buried Carmelo. Fiaschetti immediately contacted the New Jersey State Police and, within hours, they recovered Carmelo's partially unearthed, badly mutilated body, ravaged by animals.

But Fiaschetti was skeptical of Fontana's statement that the incident was an accident, questioning why he took the time to bury his friend, and why he didn't contact the State Police immediately. He refuted Fontana's explanation that he panicked out of fear and, after three days of grueling interrogation, the tough-minded, tenacious Fiaschetti broke Fontana, who finally admitted the "accident" was, in fact, an assassination, ordered by an unknown member of the Friends of Friends in Sicily to satisfy a vendetta.

Thirty five hundred miles away in Castellammare del Golfo, a smirking Stefano Magaddino read an unsigned, cryptic, six word cable from America:

"The thing is done! It's over!

CHAPTER 37

With their worst fears about Carmelo's disappearance confirmed, the grieving Caiozzo family had to wait two days to receive the body until the New Jersey coroner's office completed the inquest. The sorry condition of the remains made an open casket unthinkable and Maria, unable to suffer the ordeal of a two day wake, insisted on a funeral Mass with an immediate interment.

She sat inconsolable among her daughters and their husbands, oblivious to Father Amato's eulogy. A pitiful wail echoed throughout St. Patrick's Church;

"*Figghiu miu, poviru figghiu miu,* my son, my poor son," she cried.

Caiozzo sat at the end of the pew, quiet and dazed, with Nando's head gently resting on his shoulder. Carmelo had become Nando's surrogate father, taking him to events around the city and to the stadium where the newly acquired Babe Ruth stunned the baseball world by hammering 54 home runs, leading the Yankees to their first pennant.

"He is one of us, Italian, right?" Nando had proudly asked Carmelo.

"No, no, he isn't Italian," Carmelo replied, laughing, "What makes you think he's Italian?" Carmelo asked.

"Well, they call him the 'Great Bambino' don't they?" Nando said.

Mary's emotions ran from grief to rage at the loss of her brother. How curious, she thought, both my mother and I have lost beloved brothers at the hands of assassins. But this is even more heinous. A murder carefully planned and committed by his best friend. That sonofabitch, Bartolo, should suffer for eternity with Judas in Dante's ninth circle.

During the next few weeks, Mary's behavior became increasingly bizarre. Contino noticed a curious, disturbing habit of Mary constantly washing her hands, and scrubbing the bathroom and kitchen with gallons of Clorox. She also developed migraine headaches and an undiagnosed intestinal disorder, maladies which plagued her throughout her life.

"What the hell's the matter with you, Mary?" Contino demanded irritably.

"What the hell's the matter with me?" Mary shot back. "I lost a beloved uncle, murdered by assassins, and now...now, my brother, an innocent man, is shot in the back by his best friend. What the hell do you think is the matter with me?" she shouted at him.

"Well, with all due respect, and I'm not condoning the assassination, how can you be so sure Carmelo was innocent of the Magaddino murder he is suspected of? I understand everyone in Castellammare heard his boasts and threats of vendetta after your uncle was killed."

"How can I be so sure? How can I be so sure?" Mary raged, thumping Contino's chest, "because he told me he was innocent…he told me," Mary sobbed, "and Carmelo never, never lied to me," she moaned, collapsing into Contino's arms.

Contino reasoned that perhaps Mary's erratic behavior could be attributed to the effects of her second pregnancy, discovered a few days before Carmelo's death.

Shit, he thought, a crazy wife, another mouth to feed, and another bawling kid. Soon I'll be getting those headaches and acting like a lunatic.

The day after Carmelo was laid to rest in that vast grey stone forest just across the East River in Queens, Maria was startled by a sharp knock on the door as she sat in the kitchen. She rose but was stopped by Caiozzo, hurrying out of his bedroom.

"Maria, Maria, wait," he urgently commanded, "let me," he said brushing past her. He put his right hand in his pocket and leaned against the door.

"Who is it?" he asked gruffly.

"*Signor* Caiozzo, it's Detective Mike Fiaschetti from the Centre Street Precinct," a voice replied, in Italian.

Caiozzo hesitated for a long moment.

"*Signor* Caiozzo?" Fiaschetti repeated.

"Yes, I'm here. But how do I know you are who you say you are? Show me some identification."

"Just a minute," came the response, and a photo identification card appeared under the door. Caiozzo studied it for a moment and warily slid the dead bolt to the side, unlocking the door. He cracked it open, leaving the chain link security in place as he compared the photograph to Fiaschetti. Satisfied, he opened the door and stepped back, keeping his right hand in his pocket.

Fiaschetti extended his hand and introduced himself and the uniformed officer, and Caiozzo acknowledged the greeting with his left hand.

Fiaschetti looked hard into Caiozzo's eyes as he grasped the handle of his own revolver holstered on his belt and said, "Before we begin, *signor* Caiozzo, I want you to very slowly, very slowly remove your right hand from your pocket."

"Why? What for?" Caiozzo stammered indignantly.

"Do as I say, now," Fiaschetti ordered.

"Do as he says, Caiozzo," Maria cried out, pressing her hands to her cheeks.

As Caiozzo slowly removed his hand, Fiaschetti grabbed his wrist.

"Get whatever is in that pocket, then frisk him thoroughly," he ordered the uniformed officer. The officer drew a pistol from Caiozzo's pocket. The two men stood wordless, face to face, as the officer completed the pat down.

"He's clean," the officer pronounced.

"You know," Fiaschetti said palming the pistol, "possession of a concealed weapon is a violation of the Sullivan Law."

"Sullivan Law? Sullivan Law, *sta minchia*," Caiozzo repeated. "Fuck you and fuck your Sullivan Law," he shouted.

"I'll forget I heard that, and I'll forget about the pistol too, *signore*, if you'll calm yourself, be civil, and agree to listen to what I have to say," Fiaschetti coolly replied.

"If we may sit?" he asked politely, turning to Maria.

"Yes, yes, of course, please sit. A cup of coffee, perhaps?" Maria asked.

"*No, grazzii, no, signura*," Fiaschetti replied. "I'll come directly to the point. I thought you would like to know, I spent three days grilling Fontana and, finally, was able to break him. He could not contain his guilt and confessed to everything which led him to take your son's life."

"Guilt? Guilt?" Caiozzo responded in anger. "Are New York City policemen so stupid or naïve to believe that this weasel Fontana confessed out of guilt?" he asked. "Yes, he confessed, but it wasn't guilt that made the worm confess. After taking my son's life by their orders," Caiozzo continued, "he shit his pants wondering when the next bullet would have his own name on it and he sought the protection of the police to save his miserable ass."

"You may be right," Fiaschetti said calmly, shrugging his shoulders, "but that is not the reason for my visit tonight."

"Then what do you want?" Caiozzo asked coldly.

"What I want, what I want, is to know what you know about the connection between the Castellammare mob and the Syndicate here in New York," Fiaschetti asked firmly.

"Ha!" Caiozzo exclaimed, "you are more stupid than I imagined. As much as I want these monsters punished, it would do me no good to make my daughters fatherless, and my grandchildren without a *nonno*. *Iu nun sacciu nenti*, I know nothing about any connection" Caiozzo replied.

"You know nothing?" Fiaschetti repeated.

"What did I say?" Caiozzo returned, stone-faced.

"*Allura*, all right, I guess there is nothing…," he began, then stopped suddenly, poking his finger in the air. "Just to clarify one other matter. We heard that you and your family were under the patronage and protection of Michelangelo Vitale. Is that no longer the case? Did you have a falling out with him over some money issue?" Fiaschetti asked probing.

Maria's eyes narrowed as she studied Fiaschetti, then turned to Caiozzo.

"No, no, nothing like that," Caiozzo stammered, putting his hand on

Fiaschetti's shoulder and easing him toward the door. "The arrangement just wasn't working for either of us."

"So he'll fry, Fontana will fry, won't he?" Caiozzo asked, quickly changing the subject.

"I can't guarantee the punishment, *signore*. That's up to the court. But I can tell you that New Jersey, where the trial will be conducted, holds for the death penalty for murder by electrocution."

"Electrocution, a death too merciful for the murder of my son," he said quietly. "I...I apologize for my rudeness earlier but..."

"You don't need to apologize, *signore*. I understand. I also have a son."

"Thank you," Caiozzo replied. "Oh! One last thing Detective. About my pistol that you have in your pocket?" Caiozzo inquired.

"Oh, yes, about your pistol. I'll sleep much better tonight knowing it has been deposited in the muck in the East River, no questions asked. Is that acceptable?"

"*Va beni*," Caiozzo responded, resigned, "*Va beni*."

Fontana was ultimately spared the death penalty because of his cooperation with the authorities, providing them with information about the burgeoning mafia activity in New Jersey. He was sentenced to 19 years in State prison. Following his release in 1941, Fontana disappeared.

CHAPTER 38

Caiozzo didn't sleep any better the night Fiaschetti brought the news of Bartolo's confession. Since Carmelo's death, he was tormented by recurring dreams in which his son appeared, wandering alone in a smoky wood, grey, gaunt and pleading, as he stood helpless.

Caiozzo woke sweating in the dark, and cried out for Carmelo. He rushed to the empty bed and, weeping, buried his face in the pillow. His primary defenses collapsed like demolished structures, leaving a pile of scattered rubble in its wake. The repressed guilt, the conflict of conscience, broke through and took over like attacking vermin claiming its territory. He was forced to face the awful truth; if only he hadn't been so greedy, foolishly competing with Don Vitale's loansharking operation, and abandoned his delusion of importance, accepting his place as an average working man with no status in the pecking order in the neighborhood, Vitale would not have felt humiliated and withdrawn his protection, and Carmelo would be alive... He knew that, sooner or later, his family would discover the reason for his dismissal from his job, and connect it with Carmelo's assassination. Rumors spread quickly and tongues wagged freely in the tightly-knit, lower Manhattan neighborhood, and he could not bear the prospect of the loathing and disaffection he could expect from his family. He felt his only recourse was to return alone to Italy as soon as possible.

Caiozzo's fears were realized much sooner than later.

. . .

Late that afternoon, Maria returned from food shopping, raced up the stairs, and ran screaming hysterically into Caiozzo's room where he was napping.

"You no good bastard, you sonofabitch," she shrieked, pounding his face with tiny fists and elbows, "you gave him a chance for life when you brought us here, and then you took it from him. You told us that we would be safe, protected by Don Vitale. Why didn't he protect my son?" she asked rhetorically through heaving sobs. "I finally found out what everyone in this neighborhood knew. He withdrew his protection because you humiliated him with your stupidity and your greedy quest. Fontana may have pulled the trigger, but you are the one who aimed the rifle, you murdering bastard," she screamed.

Thirty years of repressed rage erupted as Stella and Giovanna watched and listened horrified from the doorway.

"First you took my innocence and my life when I was only sixteen years old. You kidnapped me and forced me into a miserable marriage which drove my parents to an early grave. And now you took the life of my only son. You killed him. Everything about you has the stench of death," she cried, falling back and collapsing on Carmelo's bed.

Stella and Giovanna came into the room and escorted their distraught mother out. Maria collapsed face down on the her bed, quietly whimpering, as her daughters stroked her back and tried to console her.

"What did mamma mean about losing her innocence?" Stella whispered to her sister. "She was kidnapped by papa? How could this have happened?" she asked shocked.

"It happens often in Sicily," Giovanna replied. "It's a barbaric, brutish practice we inherited from the Muslim invaders centuries ago whereby men assumed the right to kidnap the woman they wanted, and force a marriage. Mamma says it happened to her," Giovanna said tersely.

"What?" Stella exclaimed dumbfounded, bringing her hands to her face and crying.

Maria rose slowly and turned to her daughters, painfully recounting the unimaginable circumstances of her marriage to their father, and the gossip she heard in Alleva's *salumeria* associating Carmelo's assassination with their father's reckless activity. The girls sat limp, ruminating over their mother's words.

"I tried to protect all of you from the hideous fact of our marriage, but, as you have discovered, family secrets don't remain secret indefinitely. They descend unexpectedly like a tornado, and leave everything in its path, broken and splintered."

Stella became unhinged and broke down sobbing as Giovanna took control.

"I think we should tell Mary about this, and get her here immediately," Giovanna decided.

"Yes, yes," Maria agreed eagerly, "go to your sister, Giovanna, and ask her to please come."

Mary had always been the intrepid one, the go to person, during a family crisis. Like her father, she had the instinct to quickly assess a situation, not panic, and offer good counsel. She was, in fact, the family *consigliere*.

Despite her own emotional fragility, Mary was not as surprised and less shaken than her sisters and listened stoically as Giovanna tearfully informed her of their mother's jarring account.

They walked quickly on the blistering sidewalks scorched by the summer sun back to St. Mark's Place.

The apartment was tomb quiet as the sisters walked into the kitchen, its faded linoleum floor strewn with groceries.

"Giovanna," Mary ordered, glancing around, "pick up the groceries, and put whatever might spoil in the ice box."

She then went into the bedroom where Maria bolted from the bed with extended arms.

"Mary! Mary! Oh, I'm so glad you're here," she exclaimed with tears streaming down her face. "*Lu mal'uocchiu*, the evil eye once again peers down on this family bringing sorrow which would test the faith of St. Peter himself," she moaned.

"Yes, mamma, yes," Mary said hugging and comforting her mother, "and no one in this family has suffered more than you."

"Stella," she said turning to her sister, "go into the kitchen and bring mamma a drop of grappa."

Maria reached for the glass with trembling hands, swallowed the burning spirit, and fell back on her bed, sighing.

Mary seethed with rage, but remained quiet as she listened to her mother confirm vague, ugly suspicions she had always felt about her parents' marriage and their cold relationship. The separate sleeping arrangements, the lack of any warmth in interacting or civil conversation, and the absence of their grandparents at the holiday table, were always puzzling. Mary chose to dismiss these practices and rationalized them as accepted behavior in many Sicilian marriages where husbands and wives attended to the duties of parenthood, but avoided the intimacy of a man and a woman. They often maintained furtive lives of deception and fantasy; the men did what they willed, the women did what they must.

But when Maria related the gossip she heard at Alleva's *salumeria* about the connection between Caiozzo's folly and Carmelo's death, Mary could not contain herself, rose, and began pacing the room, nervously wringing her hands and biting her lower lip so hard it drew blood.

"Mary, Mary," her mother said softly, "I know how this upsets you. He is your father, and few things can be more painful to a child than to learn of the wickedness their parent is capable of. But I must ask you," she pleaded, "to speak to him, and convince him to leave this house. I cannot bear to look into his face, and you are the only one of the children who has always stood up to him, and whom he would at least listen to." Then her voice rose, and she cried out, "I cannot suffer his presence, and cannot have this man in my home!"

Maria composed herself and said softly, but with determination, "I have suffered long enough with this man, have sacrificed enough for the welfare of my children. Now, I must be free of him, to try to heal myself, and take whatever tranquility may be left to me. Please, Mary," she implored.

"I'll take care of it, mamma," Mary said firmly. "I'll take care of it."

CHAPTER 39

"I knew they'd send for you," Caiozzo said sitting up as Mary stalked into his room. "You needn't bother with the message from your mother. These walls are paper thin and I heard everything she said. I have already made my mind up," he said, slicing his hand through the air in a gesture of resignation, "and I will return to Italy as soon as possible."

Mary pulled a chair to the bed and sat alongside her father, and the small, darkened room assumed the gravity of a confessional. She sat, quietly waiting, as a priest waits for the trespasser to confess his sins.

"So now you know, *figghia mia*," Caiozzo finally said, sighing, "how it came to be that your mother and I were married." He paused, but Mary did not respond, waiting for him to continue.

"I know that this practice may seem ugly and brutal to you, especially since you have become an American woman in the last five years. But I'm also sure, as a daughter of Sicily, you're aware that *fuitina* has been practiced and accepted in our native land for centuries, and survives to this day."

"I'm aware, papa, I'm certainly aware of this savage history," Mary said narrowing her eyes and tightening her jaw, "and I've always had questions and suspicions about the circumstances of your marriage to mamma."

"Well, then," Caiozzo responded with some relief, "then you understand that what I did was not so unusual in our time. Many marriages in Sicily, even in Castellammare, happened this way. I did nothing more than follow accepted custom," he added hopefully.

Mary couldn't contain her rage.

"Even now, papa, even now, you try to justify your beastly, unspeakable action, and give legitimacy to men taking wives by abduction.

"Yes, I'm aware," Mary said, her voice rising in anger. "I'm aware of this loathsome practice, but I'm also aware of the many decent Sicilian men who respected and courted women properly. You had a choice then, papa, but you didn't choose as a decent man would choose. You disgraced yourself, my God, you disgraced yourself," she moaned, "and committed a grievous sin."

"And what sin would that be?" he demanded, tersely.

"The same sin which led to the death of your son, my brother," she bitterly reproached him, "the sin of pride."

"You could not accept mamma's rejection of you, and the fear of humiliation in the village, just as your vanity couldn't allow you to accept your place here in this new world under Vitale. And your vanity resulted in a lifetime of grief for mamma, ending in the death of her only son, because you crossed Vitale."

Caiozzo's head fell to his chest as he pitifully responded.

"He was my son too, and my conscience gives me no rest," he sobbed. "I am haunted by dreams where your brother wanders alone and I am powerless to help him."

"Yes," Mary said turning and avoiding his gaze, "Guilt can drive one to insanity, or worse."

She abruptly changed the subject.

"Where will you go, papa," she asked. "You can't return to Castellammare. It would be too dangerous. Magaddino would see you as a threat, seeking revenge for Carmelo's murder, she wisely counseled."

"Yes, I know, Mary," Caiozzo agreed. "But the end of the war has brought a flurry of activity in the wine business, especially in Toscana. I'm sure I can be safe there, and find work, and labor at what I enjoy and do best. After all," he smiled weakly, "Don Bono always referred to me as 'The Don of the Dirt.'"

"Papa," Mary said rising and walking around the room, "just because you and mamma are separating doesn't mean you must leave the country and return to Italy. This country is young and still growing, and the opportunities are endless."

"Yes, Mary," Caiozzo agreed, "this country is young and growing, but the future here belongs to the young who have the ambition and the patience to take advantage of it. I am old and declining, and America is no place for an old man whose livelihood must come by toiling in the dirt of the vineyards."

I am not comfortable here, Mary. I am a man born and bred in the last century, in a place where, even today, fewer than five or six families have a telephone, and their homes are still lit by kerosene lamps and heated by wood-burning stoves. And strange as it may seem to you, I long to return to that simpler way of life without the complications of modern conveniences. I yearn to hear the sweet music of the mother tongue, to converse with my *paesani*, and end this damn struggle to master the English language.

Of course, I will miss you and your sisters, and regret that I will not see my grandchildren grow up. But I am proud of what you and your sisters have accomplished here in America and confident that you will all continue to do well. All of you are grown up now and, truly, you no longer need me, I'm tired, Mary, he said, shaking his head wearily, and I want to go home. This country overwhelms and frightens me.

When I get settled and feel secure, I'll contact you.

"Now, Mary," Caiozzo said, rising abruptly, "I must go to the Star Steamship Company and book my passage. But, perhaps…you, you might speak to your mother, and ask her if I can remain here until I leave?"

"I will, papa, I'll speak with her," Mary assured her father.

Maria reluctantly agreed, but avoided any contact with Caiozzo the following week.

. . .

The night before Caiozzo departed, Mary instructed her sisters to come to her apartment for a farewell dinner with their father. The husbands, Giacomo and Contino, were conspicuously absent, and the dinner began quiet and tense.

Caiozzo finally broke the painful silence.

"Whatever you may think of me," he said, "I did the best I could for all of you. I don't ask, or expect forgiveness for my transgressions. But I would hope that you would at least understand that I was a product of my time. And whatever you think of the dishonorable way I took your mother, know that I love each of you, my children, as much as your mother does, and tried to provide for and protect you."

"That may be true," Giovanna said," close to tears, "but now I see we were children born out of lust, conceived in rape, not in legitimate marriage. How can you expect us to excuse what you did. We are adults, and suddenly we learn we have been deceived."

"It's true, Giovanna," Caiozzo said reaching for her hand, "the marriage may have been illegitimate, but never think it applies to any of you. Yes, we did engage in deception but, there was always an unspoken agreement between your mother and me about not divulging the circumstances of our marriage, me, out of guilt, and your mother, I suspect, out of shame. We foolishly tried to protect you from a painful truth. Besides," he added quietly, shaking his head, "what good would it have done? What purpose would it have served to tell you the truth? No, no we did what many parents do to protect their children from sordid family secrets. We chose the easy way, the coward's way."

Caiozzo rose slowly, rubbing his hands together, and said, "I'm going back to the apartment now to finish packing, and I'm sure you girls have much to discuss, better said in my absence." He hesitated then added,

"I know earlier I said I would not ask for forgiveness, but, I wonder, I wonder if..."

"Papa," Grazia interrupted, "forgiveness is the foundation of our faith, but it's rare to find in this world. We have been struck like lightening with two painful discoveries within two days, and only time will tell the measure of our forgiveness."

"Yes, yes, of course," Caiozzo replied, resigned. "But when you speak of me to my grandchildren, can you at least find a few redeeming words to offer?"

The girls looked at each other blankly until Mary spoke.

"I read in one of the books mamma took from the library, from the Irish writer, Oscar Wilde. He says, 'Every saint has a past, and every sinner has a future.'"

"Thank you Mary," Caiozzo replied warmly.

They huddled tearfully in an embrace and Caiozzo choked.

"Please, don't any of you come to the dock tomorrow morning. I want to remember that the last time I saw you we were in this embrace, not separated by a body of cold water."

Caiozzo forced himself from them, and his wail echoed in the shadows of the dimly lit hallway as he made his way down the stairs.

...

The next morning Caiozzo rose while the eastern sun was still below the horizon and the apartment was peacefully quiet in the dark. He went into the bathroom, scrubbed, shaved and brushed his teeth, returned to his room, and put grainy, sepia-tinted photographs of the children in his valise. He looked at Carmelo's bed one last time, wiped a tear from his eye and left the room. Then he walked across the hall and gently cracked the door open to peer in at Maria and his daughters, deep and night damp in their sleep. He blew a kiss across the room, crossed himself, and went down the hall to the kitchen where he put five hundred dollars on the table. He then walked out the door and down the stairs to the street.

He was surprised to see Nando, a budding adolescent boy, sitting on the stoop where they had first met.

"So you're leaving now," Nando said as he rose, wiping a tear from his eye.

"Yes," Caiozzo confirmed, "the time has come."

Nando wrapped his arms around Caiozzo and buried his head in his shoulder.

"I'm very sad and feel scared for you, Caiozzo," Nando said between sobs.

"Why, why are you afraid for me?" Caiozzo asked, holding the boy close as he fought back tears. "I am a tough Sicilian man, and I can handle anything."

"Yes," Nando said, pulling back and looking into Caiozzo's face, "but even a tough Sicilian man can fear being alone and dying alone."

"Nando," Caiozzo replied, "the love I have known with my children, and yes, even with you, you rascal, is enough to sustain me. And as for dying alone, Nando, well, we all die alone. At least I'll be buried in my native land."

Caiozzo reached into his pocket and took the rosary which was found wrapped around Carmelo's hands when Bartolo led the police to the grave site.

"Here," he said, "you take this and keep it close to you always. Carmelo loved you like the son he never lived long enough to have, and I, I love you like the *nipote*, the grandson I will never see grow into manhood. *Ciau, beddu*," Caiozzo said as he kissed Nando on the forehead.

"*Addiu, Caiozzo, addiu Nonnu*" Nando shouted as Caiozzo disappeared down the deserted street.

CHAPTER 40

Maria waited a few minutes after she heard the door in the hallway close before rising and slipped into her housecoat. As she passed Caiozzo's room on the way to the kitchen, she peeked in to confirm that he had left. She was surprised to see money on the kitchen table, shrugged her shoulders and stuffed it in her pocket. After she brewed the coffee, she sat at the table, sighed, and began weeping quietly. These were not tears of sorrow or loss, but of joy, and gratitude. Free! For the first time in twenty-nine years, she was free of the oppressive burden of living with a man she detested. And she no longer had to fear that her children would learn the ugly secret she and that man had concealed from them. The thought transported her with palpable excitement and her heart pounded wildly. She imagined she might be having a heart attack and took deep breaths, and the symptoms slowly went away, replaced by the sensation of being in a rapidly descending elevator, somewhat scary, but no less thrilling.

Maria stood at the stove, beating eggs into a frying pan for the breakfast *frittata*, as Stella and Giovanna entered the room, yawning, and rubbing the sleep from their eyes.

"Papa's gone," Stella announced quietly as she sat at the table.

"Yes, Stella, he must have left very early this morning," Maria acknowledged, keeping her eyes fixed on the eggs in the pan.

"He doesn't want us to come to the pier to see him off," Giovanna said.

"Then do as he wishes," Maria said tersely, sliding the plates across the table.

"Did papa say goodbye to you, mamma?" Stella asked with naïve curiosity.

Maria hesitated then sat down.

"Girls," she began slowly, "he is your father, and not knowing the circumstances of our marriage, I can understand the natural feelings you have for him. I'm sure that what you have discovered has been a terrible shock and left you conflicted and angry. You must resolve your feelings in your own time and in your own way. But please allow me to resolve mine in my way, and don't ask me any more questions about him. I want to put the past behind me and begin a new stage in my life.

For the first time since I was sixteen," she said tearfully, "I feel I may yet have a cheery future."

Stella and Giovanna quietly lowered their heads, and picked at the *frittata* on their plates.

When the girls left for work, Maria went into the small bedroom and looked around. Yes, this will do nicely, she thought. Privacy and a room of my own for the first time in nearly thirty years. She went to the closet and smiled as she looked at some of Carmelo's clothing he had not picked up, perfectly pressed trousers on hangers and starched shirts. Always *beddu eleganti*, my Carmelo, she thought, running the sleeve of one of his shirts along her cheek, and inhaling the crisp scent of fresh laundry.

Maria wondered what to do with the clothes, then thought of Nando. He could not possibly fit into Carmelo's trousers now, but he seemed to be growing an inch every six months. In a couple of years, she reasoned, he could have a fine wardrobe. Meanwhile, he would surely make use of the shirts if he rolled the sleeves up and tucked the tails deep into his pants. It gave her comfort to think of Nando wearing Carmelo's clothes.

Maria turned from the closet and her eyes settled on the beds. No, no, she thought, this will never do. I could never sleep in peace in either of these beds. Later that afternoon, Maria and a grateful *signura* Caputo moved the beds and Carmelo's clothes into her apartment.

That night Maria pulled the covers up to her chin in the privacy of her own room, in the comfort of her own bed, and smiled at the thought that Nando had a fine new set of clothing, and the Caputo girls slept well for the first time since their infancy.

With her newly acquired freedom, Maria embraced the 20th Century with the enthusiasm of a child enjoying her first birthday party. Fortune turned to her advantage, and Anna Pastoria, the librarian at the Offendorffer Library, convinced the Board of Directors that she needed someone informed to assist her in ordering Italian translations of British and American reading material, and to encourage the increasing number of immigrant women to learn to speak English.

Maria, eagerly and proudly, accepted the position and danced home with the first pay she had ever earned, a crisp five and two singles. *Diu miu*, she thought as she purchased a small bottle of celebratory *spumante*, someone has given me money for what they thought I was worth, what I could offer, rather than throwing money on a table and treating me as a menial.

But all the old ways did not end easily. Just as priests and nuns eschew the clothes of the secular world for the gravity of black, Maria joined the sorority of grieving Sicilian mothers and widows and gave all her dresses away to la *signura* Caputo. She instructed Stella and Grazia to fashion five black dresses of varying lengths and styles, and was never again seen wearing anything but a black dress, with matching black stockings and shoes, and a coiffure pulled tight around the back of her head in a bun.

Nando became a regular at Mamma Caiozzo's supper table and was assuming the role of family protector in the absence of a male figure. This was confirmed early one summer evening when four of the local toughs gathered under the streetlight, and hurled insults at Stella on her way home from work. She was a plump girl and very sensitive about her weight.

"Hey, *vacca*, cow," one taunted, "be careful, no fall down, he said in broken English, "otherwise we gonna have to get a crane to pull you up."

Nando heard the insult, slid off the stoop and walked slowly over to the group under the street light and approached the tormentor with clenched fists at his side.

"Hey, *stunatu*, you gotta big mouth, "Nando said coolly.

"Yeah, and whata you gonna do about it?" the tough returned.

"What I gonna do," Nando pronounced "is this," driving his knee into the tough's balls, followed by a vicious uppercut which sent his teeth cutting through his lower lip. Blood spouted like the water in the Trevi Fountain, as he lay screaming on his back, with hands cupped to his mouth. The three others scampered like rabbits flushed from the bushes. Stella was always treated respectfully in the neighborhood after that.

CHAPTER 41

The winter of 1922 came early to the city with a ferocity that left the masses unprepared and wondering where the golden autumn of the previous days had gone.

An icy wind whipped relentlessly in and around the narrow streets, and a frigid wall stalled the progress of anyone walking.

Mary, six months pregnant with her second child went past St. Patrick's Church, turned left on Mulberry Street, and battled the wall of wind the four blocks to Angelo's restaurant. With the weather coming this bad, this will be my last week at work, she thought, patting her swollen belly.

Since the pregnancy, Mary only worked Friday and Saturday nights, and of the fifteen or eighteen dollars she made, half was deposited in Stabile's Bank across the street from Angelo's Restaurant. Contino never asked for an accounting of her salary, or the money he put on the table every week. He was a successful, ambitious hustler and ten or twenty dollars meant nothing to him. Times were good, and a man with Contino's talents and lack of scruples, could make the best of it.

Between his virtual no-show job at the construction site, a few burglaries and truck hijackings of liquor commissioned by Vitale, and his rent from the bungalows in Brooklyn, he was doing quite well, prompting Vitale to remark, laughing,

"Leonardo, you're going to have to tell Santorini, the tailor, to make your trousers with deeper pockets, or the money will overflow, and you will lose it on the street."

Contino had little interest in fulfilling his duties as a father but reluctantly agreed to sharing baby-sitting with his mother-in-law, 'Mamma Caiozzo," as Maria came to be called by her children and grandchildren. He sat with Twink on alternate Friday and Saturday nights until Mary returned from Angelo's, then went out on a job or a prowl, and did not return for two or three days. Mary never objected, and, in fact, would not have objected if he stayed away all week, as long as he came home every Friday with a small brown envelope containing thirty dollars.

During the second pregnancy, Contino was gone three or four nights a week, citing obligations to Vitale for his absence. Mary suspected he was engaged in an affair or two but had already lost any interest in him sexually and had no patience for his feeble excuses.

In fact, Contino had met and was seducing an attractive sixteen year old peasant girl, newly arrived from Sicily with dried goat shit still caked on the soles of her shoes and an intelligence quotient barely pushing the dull-normal range. In Contino's mind she was the paragon of what he expected in a woman, and he was the stuff she had dreamt of while herding the family animals in Sicily's rocky countryside.

. . .

On April 20th, 1922, Maria III was delivered at St. Vincent's Hospital in Greenwich Village, kicking and bawling her way into this life like an angry lion cub.

She was as different from Twink in appearance and temperament as sisters could be. She came with coal black hair, a dark complexion, and a nose straight and thin as a needle, strongly suggesting some Arabic ancestry.

She was christened 'Maria' at St. Patrick's Church, which not only delighted Mamma Caiozzo, but settled the score with Contino for his insistence that the first child be named, Angela, after his mother.

Maria attained the milestones early, walking at nine months and speaking in short sentences by fifteen months. She made her wants known clearly in a demanding, assertive manner, was a cantankerous child who rarely smiled and, her facial expression suggested someone who was constantly smelling cow manure.

When Mary enrolled Twink in the first grade at St. Patrick's School, Maria boldly followed her sister into the classroom and sat next to her, clutching the sides of the desk, rocking back and forth, and refusing to obey the commands of the nuns to leave. Father Amato was summoned and finally extricated a defiant, stony-faced child, carrying her screaming out of the classroom, with arms and legs swinging wildly, catching the poor priest in the testicles.

The following year, Mary enrolled Maria at St. Patrick's grammar school where, the usually unflappable Mother Superior, Sister Bernadette, watched anxiously, with her fingers to her mouth, as Maria marched into the classroom like a victorious general inspecting newly conquered territory. Maria spent the better part of the next three years in the principal's office, punished for obstreperous behavior, failure to complete assignments, and provocative questions which the nuns were at a loss to answer regarding the tenets and mysteries of Holy Mother Church.

Twink was the polar opposite of Maria, a quiet, unobtrusive student who maintained excellent grades, knew how to greet the nuns politely and had the good sense to show the sisters the respect they had come to expect. She was the perennial recipient of, 'The Blessed Virgin Piety' award, and was on track to receive a full scholarship to any one of the prestigious private Catholic High Schools for girls in the city.

As the decade of the roaring twenties came to an end, so too was Mary's empty marriage to Contino in its last stage. He was rarely home, and virtually living with Nadia, the peasant girl, with whom he had fathered a child. It was the worst kept secret in the neighborhood, and Mary had known about his double life for years, but feigned ignorance as long as Contino continued to provide for the children and herself. She wanted out of the marriage as much as he, but was biding her time, and had now accumulated nearly fifteen hundred dollars which was on deposit at Stabile's Bank. She also concocted an elaborate operatic scheme which, if played right, could garner her a tidy cash settlement for agreeing to dissolve the marriage.

Contino arrived at the apartment the following Friday, the one night of the week he stayed over. He barely acknowledged his daughters playing jacks on the worn black and white linoleum floor in the kitchen.

"Where's your mother?" he asked looking around, noticing the absence of the usual pots on the stove, bubbling with sauce and pasta.

"She's in the bedroom," Twink answered, without looking up. He then turned and looked down at Maria who greeted him with a grotesque facial contortion accompanied by a nasty tongue thrust.

"Ah, *va al diavolo, ragazzaccia*, go to the devil you ugly kid," he shouted, throwing his hands in the air as he walked toward the bedroom.

Mary was lying on the bed in the dark with her arms covering her eyes and a large, moist handkerchief theatrically dangling from her fingers.

"Mary, *chi succidìu*, what happened?" he asked. "Is it those headaches again?"

Mary rose from the bed slowly, then rushed to Contino, burying her head in his chest and draping her arms around his neck, sobbing.

"Oh, Leonardo, Leonardo, I'm so sorry, so sorry," she whimpered pitifully.

"What? What are you talking about?" he asked wide-eyed and shaken, prying her arms from his neck.

Mary dropped her hands to her side and returned to sitting on the bed. She dabbed her wet eyes daintily with the handkerchief and haltingly began,

"I realize now how I have failed and disappointed you as a wife, and I know..., I know," she said choking back the tears, "that I am to blame for driving you into the arms of another woman."

"Mary, I...I," he started.

"Please, Leonardo, let me finish," she pleaded. "I have heard the whispered rumors in Alleva's *Salumeria*, and at the *furnu* for years, but I just assumed that your dalliances were trivial, nothing more than what many Sicilian women are expected to endure. Yes, it hurt me, but I put my feelings aside for the sake of our daughters. I prayed at the feet of the statue of the Madonna that it would pass, and we would recapture what we felt for each other when we met seven years ago. But now, *Diu miu*, I have found out about the child you fathered with this woman, and the double life you have been living, and my heart is breaking into little pieces like ice when the spring thaw comes," she wailed.

"Mary," he said sitting beside her and gently taking her hand, "let us see if together we can discuss this, make things right, and come to a satisfactory resolution."

She stiffened as an alarming thought came to her. My God! Is this man attempting a reconciliation? But she was quickly relieved as he went on.

"Mary," he continued, "the painful truth is you have not satisfied my expectations of a traditional Sicilian wife, and, no doubt, I have also disappointed you. I think we can both agree that too much has happened over the years, and we now discover we were never right for each other."

Mary dropped her head back and breathed a deep sigh of relief.

Poor woman, Contino thought, shaking his head, I can hear the sorrow in her voice, and see the pain on her face.

"I suppose..., I suppose you're right, Leonardo," Mary said, resigned, looking down and wringing her hands.

"You are still young and beautiful, Mary," Contino tried to comfort, "and I'm certain you will find someone with a common interest, someone who can make you happy. We only live once," Contino said gravely, "and we all have the right to be happy."

Mary had timed her response perfectly.

"As much as it pains me to say it, Leonardo, I believe you are right."

"Good, good," he said, quickly nodding in agreement.

"Now," he continued, "I have no intention to abandon you or leave my daughters penniless. If we can agree on an uncontested divorce, I am prepared to make you a generous settlement of one thousand dollars, and continue giving you thirty dollars a week."

"Leonardo," Mary winced and responded, "you have two growing daughters who, between them, eat more than fifteen dollars a week of food, and outgrow their shoes every five months. And one thousand dollars will not last long in this country."

Contino paused, rubbed his chin and reflected for a moment, then expansively offered, twirling his finger, "Thirty five dollars a week and one thousand five hundred dollars."

Mary didn't blink and countered; "forty dollars a week."

"All right," he yielded exasperated, "forty dollars a week and one thousand five hundred dollars."

"Forty dollars a week," Mary repeated, "and two thousand dollars," she demanded, firmly.

Contino rubbed his hand across his forehead and quietly muttered,

"And two thousand dollars."

Contino left the apartment, slamming the hall door behind him, and stumbled halfway down the staircase, screaming,

"*Vampiru*, I just let that fucking vampire bleed me bone dry."

CHAPTER 42

On October 24, 1929, the exuberant optimism of the jazz age fed by the seemingly endless supply of money made easy and spent just as freely was dealt an unexpected, crushing blow when the stock market plunged 23 percent in one day. The cataclysmic event struck mercurially, like a life-threatening coronary on an unsuspecting victim, and tens of millions of dollars were lost overnight. Still, over the next few months, speculators cautiously moved back into the market, betting the crash was nothing more than an aberrant blip, buying issues of blue chip stock at bargain-basement prices. The lights flickered but did not go out, and, in early 1930, President Herbert Hoover tried to keep the music playing by confidently assuring the nation that, "We have now passed the worst."

His sanguine prognosis was a serious misdiagnosis, and, by 1932, 75 billion dollars in stock value disappeared like dry wood fed to a roaring fire, nearly 5 thousand banks were forced to close, and 86 thousand businesses shut their doors. The unemployment rate swelled to 25 percent, and men in custom-made suits who routinely lit their five dollar cigars with dollar bills were happy to find a respectable butt lying in the gutter.

Giacomo and Grazia Vitale saw orders from uptown ladies for custom dresses decrease by seventy percent; construction in the city slowed to a snail's pace, and gambling on the daily number or sporting events was almost non-existent.

"I can't even make an earn putting my money on the street," Michelangelo moaned. "These people have no job, no income. They can't come up with the weekly vig, much less pay the principle back."

And to make matters worse, some of Vitale's contacts in State and Federal government positions warned him of talk of repealing the 18th Amendment within a year or two. The end of Prohibition did come and destroyed the bootleg industry, a major source of income for the families.

"Christ almighty," Michelangelo lamented to his brother, then went on to joke, "soon we'll all be out of work and have to go on the dole."

But Michelangelo was an astute observer of political, economic and sociological trends. The inside information he obtained from his friends in government, combined with his excellent instincts, led him to the conclusion that Hoover would not be re-elected in 1932 and the New Deal promised by Franklin Roosevelt and the Democrats would usher in a wave of spending on new public works programs stemming the tide of unemployment and injecting much needed currency into the moribund system.

Vitale sensed an opportunity and decided to gamble by expanding his legitimate masonry business to include road paving and highway construction in the outer borough of Queens where city residents with families were flocking by the tens of thousands to escape the dirt, noise and crime of the big city.

Don Vitale had first considered Astoria for his Queens base but ultimately settled on Corona, fifteen minutes further east and only twenty five minutes from Manhattan on the elevated IRT train which ran over Roosevelt Avenue, and ten minutes from the Nassau County border. He was already envisioning a time within the following twenty years when the population of Long Island would explode, requiring highways and wider roads to accommodate the increasing number of automobiles which he correctly anticipated would be bought before the end of the decade. Vitale did not believe the Depression would destroy the country. Vitale believed in America.

He also preferred Corona because of the large number of Southern Italians who began settling there in the early 1900's, rivaling the lower East Side and East Harlem as Italian strongholds.

"And," he confided to his brother, "I want to be in a place where I do business with my own *paesani*, where I feel comfortable. Astoria has too many nosey, ambitious Irisha cops who are hungry."

Before launching his plan, however, he would need the approval of Salvatore Maranzano, the recent victor in the Castellammare War with Joseph Masseria. Maranzano had anointed himself, *capo di tutti i capi*, and had the final say in all family business.

"What you present," Maranzano commented at their meeting, "is an interesting and ambitious proposal, perhaps too ambitious given these bad economic times," he added skeptically.

"Don Salvatore, with all due respect, it is precisely during bad economic times that those who have vision, and are not afraid to act boldly move into the vacuum, expand their empire, and fatten their wallets. My Don," he waxed eloquently, "when one door closes, another opens."

Vitale was a shrewd student of human behavior and knew how to pander to ambitious greedy men with bloated egos. He knew his proposal would whet the Don's appetite and, by the conclusion of their meeting, he had persuaded Maranzano of the plausibility and merit of his plan. Maranzano enthusiastically gave his blessing and instructed Vitale to move forward immediately.

Maranzano did not live long enough to see the plan launched, much less reap any of the rewards. In the Autumn of 1931, he was assassinated in his Manhattan office by two Jewish hit men, recruited by Meyer Lansky, under orders from his friend and associate, Lucky Luciano. With Maranzano out of the way, Luciano moved quickly and seized control of all mob activities in the city, consolidated the five families, and established a commission which shared power and decision-making, minimizing the prospect of another bloody war among the families.

Luciano trusted and valued Lansky's corporate skills and business instincts and listened closely to Lansky's counsel regarding Vitale's plan.

"That kid from Mulberry Street makes a lot of sense, Charles," he told Luciano. "He thinks more like a Jew than a Sicilian. Less muscle and more of this," Lansky said pointing to his head.

"Think about it, a fertile, virgin area on the outskirts of the city, just beginning to reach its peak, and without the meddlesome interference of the goddamn police. If we move now, we can own the Borough of Queens in a couple of years. And his choice of Corona reflects insight, an excellent base for this operation. It is a predominantly Southern Italian population which is familiar with our business and, while many don't subscribe to our methods, they know when to look the other way and keep their mouths shut."

Luciano needed no further prompting from Lansky, and ordered Michelangelo Vitale to move forward with the expansion plan.

On an early spring morning in 1932, Michelangelo and Giacomo Vitale met at Ferrara's *pasticceria* for breakfast before setting off to the hinterland of Corona to explore potential sites for the newly established AAA Road Construction and Paving Company.

They sat at the rear of Ferrara's, facing the entrance, with their backs to the wall. Peppino, the driver and bodyguard was positioned at a window table with a clear view of the street.

"So, little brother, what do you have for me there in that fine new leather case you are carrying?" Michelangelo asked, dipping a *biscottu* into a cup of steaming coffee.

"Well, Mickey," Giacomo replied smiling proudly as he unfastened the straps of the case producing three pages of notes, "the way I see it, what we need to begin, with your approval, of course, is five pieces of heavy equipment; a bulldozer to clear and establish the dimension of the roads, a backhoe, a large truck to haul the debris away, and a grader and a steam roller for the finishing work. And," he added meekly, "a small truck for me so I can get around and supervise the men and the work."

"Of course," Michelangelo agreed, smiling, "a small truck for you Giacomo. And have you estimated the cost of leasing this machinery?" he asked, raising his eyebrows.

"Better than that, *frati*," Giacomo answered. "I obtained three estimates from different companies. The lowest was one hundred and seventy five dollars a month for all five pieces."

"Hum," Vitale grumbled, narrowing his eyes and stroking his chin, "that sounds very costly and…why, why are you smiling, Giacomo?" he suddenly stopped and asked.

"Mickey, when I told the fat bastard who gave me the lowest price that I would first have to consult my brother, Michelangelo Vitale, you should have seen how the color drained from his face, he went limp, and his armpits became wet," Giacomo broke into laughter, "and he began to stammer and said,"

'But in that you are new to the business, and…and we always like to help our struggling *paesani*, for you, one hundred and twenty five dollars a month for everything."

"One hundred and twenty five?" I repeated, making a face.

"Of course that includes delivery and free maintenance" the fat man said, wringing his hands.

Michelangelo smiled weakly, reached over and gently patted his brother's hand.

"I'm proud of what you've accomplished, Giacomo. You negotiated well and got us off to a very good start. But in the future," he directed, "never use my name in any discussions with civilians. Certainly you can imply or suggest an influential connection, but never, never refer to me directly. Let them figure it out and draw their own conclusions, Giacomo."

"I'm sorry, Mickey, I didn't mean…"

"That's ok, kid, you're young and still learning but, all and all, you did very well."

"Now," Vitale said rising from the table, "let us be off to Corona and find land for your field office and all that equipment you leased."

(END OF PART II)

PART III

CORONA, QUEENS, NEW YORK
1932-1980

CHAPTER 43

In the late 1880's, speculators began buying up farms and large, vacant tracts of land in the northeastern corner of Queens County, known as the Old Town of Newtown and, by the end of the Century, The Crown Building Company, aware of plans for construction of a bridge and a tunnel under the East River linking Manhattan and Queens, began residential development. They were anticipating a large influx of Southern Italians from Manhattan to occupy and take advantage of the open space and the opportunities the borough offered.

They guessed right and, when the Queensborough Bridge opened in 1909, followed by the Penn Tunnel one year later, tens of thousands of Sicilian and Neapolitan immigrants packed their belongings once again and made their way across the river, bypassing the Irish and German community of Astoria to settle in, what they would come to call, 'Corona,' crown, in Italian, named after the building company.

Corona was bounded in the west by the trolley tracks of Junction Boulevard and the 'Valley of Ashes' about eight miles east. The name was assigned by F. Scott Fitzgerald in *The Great Gatsby* because of its ignominious role as a receptacle for tons of the city's garbage. From this vast bed of filth and decay, a polluting cloud hovered over Corona emitting the stench like that of a thousand rotting cadavers. The pleas of the townspeople to the City of New York for relief were largely ignored, accompanied by the prevailing sentiment of the day and a callous dismissal:

"Fuck 'em! They're only guineas. They'll get used to it. They always do."

In 1936, the city began making plans to host the 1939 World's Fair, and realized the potential of the Corona Dumps as a site. Its expanse of land, accessible public transportation and the newly constructed highways made it an ideal location, and a massive reclamation program of the land began. When the project was completed three years later, a gathering of the city fathers proudly announced to the public that Flushing Meadow Park was ready to welcome the millions of tourists expected to visit the exhibits of The World of Tomorrow and stroll the pleasant flower-lined pathways and treed grassy knolls. In the town less than a block away, disgruntled early settlers and life-time residents of Corona sat in cafes on 108th Street, sipping espresso or devouring a *panino* with *prosciutto* and cheese on thick-crusted bread from Leo's *salumeria*, and shared a similar sentiment:

"Ah, *vaffanculu*! All these years, they do no thinga for us. They no want to hear about da problem we live wit every day. But then, they makea beautiful new park, makea two new bridge, parkways, and an *aeroporto* in only tree year so the turista cana come and spenda da money. Fucka them, fucka the turista, and fucka da plane they come on.."

. . .

By late July 1932, the AAA Road Construction and Paving Company had purchased an acre lot on Corona Avenue, erected a small wood-framed office, and secured the property and the equipment with a chain-link fence. Giacomo hired ten local men, five with experience on heavy machinery, four laborers and a field work supervisor. Giacomo was responsible for securing contracts from the city, a task made easy because of Don Vitale's connection; many of the city's elected officials were in his pocket. Sealed bids were submitted by competing companies, but the most lucrative contracts, like the Grand Central and Interboro Parkways, were invariably given to the AAA Company, necessitating the hiring of thirty more men and leasing more equipment. The work was steady and everyone prospered, from management to the laborers, a fact which caused raised eyebrows and knowing nods among the locals. Questions were not asked, however, and lips remained sealed, especially with the work crew. They took Don Vitale's dictum very seriously.

"Take good care of your families, live comfortably, but don't flaunt," he advised the crew, "especially in these bad times. Always be aware of your place here and what your responsibilities are. And never, never attempt any rogue enterprise," he warned, a reference to Giuseppe Caiozzo's ill-fated overreaching maneuver years earlier. "Finally," he admonished gravely, pinning his finger over his lips, "always *silenziu*, keep your mouths shut about our business."

Giacomo moved his family to a spacious three bedroom apartment on 42nd Avenue in Corona at the bargain rent of twenty two dollars a month, and Grazia took space on 108th Street in a small shop where she changed her line to children's clothing. "Children always outgrow their clothing, adults don't," she reasoned. She soon convinced her mother and two sisters to move to Corona.

"The cost of living here," she told them, "is almost half of what you pay in Manhattan, and it is quieter and has very little crime."

Mamma Caiozzo, Stella and Giovanna moved into an apartment above the Corona branch of the Queensborough Public Library on National Avenue and, with a glowing recommendation from la *signura* Pastoria, Mamma was hired on a part time basis at the library. Stella continued working with her sister as a seamstress, and Giovanna found work as a legal secretary with the firm of Trafficanti and Chaffe just two blocks from the apartment. After a short, whirlwind courtship, Giovanna married Chaffe, a widower ten years her senior, and settled into his home, a short walk from her mother and sisters.

Stella had shed more than twenty pounds and attracted the attention of Paolo Bonanno who owned an ice delivery business, and the couple eloped, enraging Mamma Caiozzo.

"What were you thinking?" she railed at Stella. "You marry a Bonanno, a man whose cousin may have been implicated in the murder of your brother?"

"Mamma," Stella replied indignantly, "he is a distant cousin, three times removed, and has never even met Don Bonanno. And what was I thinking, what was I thinking?" she responded with tears streaming down her face, "I was thinking that I am a plump woman in her thirties who has enjoyed very little male companionship in my life, and the prospect of marriage grows slimmer as I grow fatter each year."

Mamma Caiozzo found it difficult to refute Stella's argument, and Paolo moved into the apartment on National Avenue.

Mamma Caiozzo rationalized the living arrangement, telling Mary,

"He's really no bother, a very quiet man, and at least he has a profitable business."

"Yes," Mary replied acidly, "he is a quiet man because he has nothing to say. He's so *babbu*, stupid, and unaware, that if he was stabbed in the stomach, it would take him five minutes to say, 'ouch.'"

This very odd man spent his time in the apartment isolated from his in-laws, unapproachably sitting beside the kitchen window, staring vacuously onto the street. Mary wondered if his silence concealed some dark secret or a tragic occurrence in his past. Whatever it was, he took it to his grave five years later, carried off by a mysterious ailment that eluded diagnosis.

. . .

In early 1933, the family was fully reunited when Mary, feeling the effects of the economic crunch, decided to join her mother and sisters in Corona. Contino had moved to New Jersey with his young wife and two small children, and the weekly financial support became erratic at best. Ever frugal, Mary still retained much of the three thousand dollars she had accumulated, but was reluctant to use it for expenses, and her salary and tips at Angelo's Restaurant did not cover the increasing cost of living in Manhattan.

Mary also missed being close to her family and, all things considered, Corona offered a much more attractive prospect.

Giacomo found a one bedroom apartment with a sleeping alcove for his sister-in-law at half the rent she was paying in Manhattan. 100 Street was a quiet, pleasant area within a five minute walk of all the family members. He also hired Mary to keep the books, establish a work schedule and keep time for the workers of the company. She felt the job was as a step down, lacking the allure and excitement of working at Angelo's with its well-heeled, well-positioned clientele. She winced at the thought of having to deal with rough, crude men on a daily basis, and was relieved when Gino, the restaurant manager, offered her work on the weekends whenever she wanted. She could make a few extra dollars and still maintain the valuable social contacts she had developed over the years.

...

Twink and Marie sat in the back of the truck with Mary in the cab clutching her keepsake box, as it moved across the Queensborough Bridge with its gracefully-draped cables linking Manhattan to Queens. They laughed and sang, their voices straining to mimic the shrill pitch of the tires rolling over the steel reinforcement rods on the road. As the van began its descent from the bridge, the aroma of fresh-baked bread from the Silvercup Bakery factory drifted into the van, eliciting a watery Pavlovian response. Sadly, as they would come to discover, this American bread always smelled better than it tasted.

The driver steered the truck east along Roosevelt Avenue under the elevated tracks. The IRT train of wooden cars and wicker seats rumbled and screeched overhead, leaving uniform venetian blind slants of pale yellow sunlight on the dark street below. They passed through Sunnyside and Woodside, home to the rowdy, working class Irish Catholics, to Jackson Heights, populated by lace curtain Irish and haughty Episcopalians.

Less than a half hour after they left Manhattan, Mary, Twink and Marie arrived at the Ann Marie apartment house at 40-40 100 Street, Corona, a place which Mary would call home for the next forty years.

Mamma Caiozzo and the rest of the family were waiting with loaves of bread, cheese, salami, fruit and wine, and they kissed and hugged on the street under the approving scrutiny of *nonna*s at their sentinel posts, hanging out of the windows on folded elbows with pillows comfortably tucked under their chests.

Cousins Frankie, who adopted his middle name, Francesco, after hearing of his grandfather's checkered history, and Mello helped the driver unload the furniture, and, within an hour, it was set up and positioned, and the family crowded around the table in the small kitchen, eating, drinking and laughing as they recounted family stories and the odyssey which brought them to this place.

After the food was eaten and the bottles of wine emptied, Grazia turned to her sons.

"*Ragazzi*," she suggested, "take your cousins for a walk around the neighborhood so they can become familiar and comfortable with their new surroundings. And stay away from that corner candy store where those *cafoni* hang around," she warned as the group made their exit, their voices echoing excitedly in the hallway.

Mamma Caiozzo looked at her daughters and smiled warmly as she took Mary's and Grazia's hands.

"I am now content, complete," she sighed. "We are all here together, with the children, in a place which somehow reminds me of our Castellammare with its *latticini, salumeria, furni* and vegetable market. I feel I am in a Sicilian village, yet, we are in this wonderful country, America, where, if you are honest and work hard, you can accomplish anything. This is the best of both worlds."

"I have felt anger and bitterness for too long, and now it is time to let that go and look to the future with hope for you, my children, and your children, and the generation to follow. *Comu è stranu*, how strange that these many years later I recall exactly the words Padre Marco said to me at the funeral Mass for your poor uncle, Antonio. He said, 'your grandchildren, and God willing, your great grandchildren, will look back on your life for strength and inspiration…do not disappoint them, or yourself.' I realize, now, what he meant, and what our responsibility is. We must encourage and help our children to take advantage of everything this country offers. By the success they achieve in their lives, they will bring pride and honor to a family stained by blood and sorrow."

CHAPTER 44

In June, 1937, Twink fulfilled the expectations of the Nuns at St. Patrick's Grammar School by graduating *Magna Cum Laude* from the prestigious Mary Lewis Academy in Jamaica, Queens, also referred to as, 'Snob Hill' because of its elevation above Hillside Avenue, and pseudo blue-blood student body. It was the jewel in the crown of the Brooklyn Diocese, and Irish-Catholic parents who had clawed their way up the social ladder to respectability and prosperity fought like gladiators to get their daughters accepted to the venerable institution.

Despite vehement opposition from the school's powerful Parent Teachers Association, Twink was afforded the honor of being Valedictorian at the commencement exercise.

"What would you have me do?" Mother Superior, Thomas d' Arc bristled in response to the incensed parents, "exclude a young woman who maintained a straight 'A' average for four years and is fluent in three languages, not including Latin?"

The happy day was attended by all the family members, preening with pride that one of their own had, not only been the first in the family to be graduated from high school, but was also the Valedictorian.

Their presence at the ceremony was greeted by perfunctory acknowledgements and raised eyebrows from comely women in dresses from Bergdorf-Goodman, and their husbands sporting tweedy suits from Brooks Brothers. A thick-starched, button-down man cupped a laugh as he drew his wife's attention to Frankie and Mello in their pin-striped suits.

"Those two chaps over there must have raided Al Capone's wardrobe," he muttered and guffawed.

"Quite so," the wife responded, giggling, her jaw locked and mouth corners turned down, "but what do you expect when you let *them* in?" she sneered.

"And can you believe they have the unmitigated audacity to let the wop girl offer the Valedictory?" she added miffed, raising her chin, disdainfully.

Mary overheard the cruel, biting remarks, put her hands on her hips and sauntered, smiling mischievously, toward the woman.

"*Scusassi, signura,*" she began deferentially, looking up into the face of the taller woman, "but that 'wop girl' you talk about isa my daughter, born in New York City. And she coma to dis school on full scholarship. How mucha you an barrel-ass here," she asked nodding toward the man, "spend to send your daughter to this school?"

"Well, I never," the shaken Brahmin wannabe began indignantly.

"No, no, you never, you never think Italian girl cana compete wit blond in a bottle hair, blue eye and the pale skin of girls lika your daughter. But I tella you dis," Mary continued, "my daughter makea da speech today because she earn da right. She is honor student four years, and…, and she comea from ancestors on the Island of Sicilia who were philosophers, mathematicians an poets two thousand year ago when your ancestors paint their body purple."

"You…you are impertinent, impertinent," the chic lady responded.

"Yes, maybe I am, how you say, impert…, impert, whatever you call. I don know what is impert, but I know I comea from a country dat sing. I think, *signura*, thata your ancestors comea from a country dat burp and fart."

"Eh! Enjoy the day, *signura*," Mary said tossing her hands in the air and laughing at the woman's furious expression. "I sure I will."

The family sat in the second row of the assembly behind the school officials and other dignitaries, smiling broadly and applauding wildly as Twink accepted award after award and delivered a well-crafted valedictory speech. Marie, seething with envy was sullen-faced, twisting impatiently in her seat, and praying the roof would collapse, ending the ceremony and accolades for her sister.

Her own high school career had been as disastrous as Twink's was successful, and even as her sister was considering academic scholarships from some of the best colleges in the East, Marie resolved not to return to Newtown or any other High School in the Fall.

Veronica Damone, her high school music teacher with whom she had developed a relationship, begged her to reconsider.

"Marie, you have not only an exceptional voice, but also a sense of timing and a delivery which I have not heard in all my years of teaching. You can, without doubt, earn a place at the Julliard School of Music, and I can arrange an audition within a week."

Marie was touched by her teacher's interest but remained unpersuaded.

"Thanks anyway, Miss Damone, but sitting in a classroom is not for everybody. It certainly isn't for me," she insisted.

"Then at least," the teacher pleaded, "come to my private studio once or twice a week and let me help you strengthen your voice, and develop proper breathing techniques."

Marie hesitated, but finally agreed and, early Saturday morning and for the next year, took lessons from Veronica Damone before reporting to her job as a waitress at the Automat on 42nd Street in Manhattan.

Mamma Caiozzo, in an attempt to encourage and support her disgruntled granddaughter, paid the one dollar a week fee for the lessons.

"Sing, *beddu*, sing," she encouraged Marie throwing her arms from her chest. "We Sicilians love to sing, and it's good for the soul. Saint Augustine tells us that, those who sing pray twice."

Her faith was rewarded when Marie took first prize in a talent contest on radio, attracting the attention of Murray Green, an agent, who managed two small bands in and around New York. He booked Marie to sing with the band two or three weekends a month and Mary, hesitant at first to allow her sixteen year old daughter to perform in a smoky room to a less than savory crowd, relented under Mamma Caiozzo's scolding. "*Lassatila stari*, leave her alone, and let her go about doing what she loves. Her sister is following her dream two hundred miles away in Amherst, Massachusetts, and you have no problem with that."

Marie began putting an extra five dollars a week on the kitchen table which persuaded Mary that she made the right decision, further comforted by the fact that Mello and Frankie accompanied their cousin on her singing dates. If the boys in the band had any thoughts of compromising Marie's virtue, they were soon discouraged by the icy glare of the cousins who sat stone-faced, arms folded, glaring at them.

Between appearances at the Pepper Pot in Greenwich Village, and the Canary Club under the El in Corona, Green scored a coup and booked the band and Marie in The Rustic Cabin, a popular roadside club in New Jersey, and convinced the management to let Marie sing a duet or two with a skinny Italian kid from Hoboken whose colossal bow tie nearly equaled the width of his body.

The reception was so enthusiastic that management offered a twice monthly gig at thirty dollars a month for Marie to appear with the local heart throb. But by late 1937, the skinny young kid from Hoboken had signed a record contract, and was on his way to much bigger things.

Attendance at The Rustic Cabin fell off and Marie returned to performing in the outer boroughs.

"Shit," her cousin Mello consoled, "what a lousy break. I'm real sorry this didn't work out. I thought you were really great."

"Thanks, Mello," Marie responded, "but I didn't lose anything. I learned a lot just listening to that guy. I mean, Crosby is great, but he doesn't have that sweet, genuine style. He doesn't make you melt," she added laughing.

CHAPTER 45

Nineteen year old Artie Mercer strolled jauntily into the Automat at Forty Second Street and Third Avenue with the confidence of a toreador who felt he owned the day. He was followed by three of his co-workers, each with their pliers, nippers and Lufkin ruler swinging from the leather tool belt fixed around the waist of their denim coveralls.

Artie was in the third, and final year of his apprenticeship in the Metallic Lathers Union, Local 46, a trade responsible for setting steel rods on frames of buildings under construction, and securing them with wire before the concrete was poured. It was an exclusive union which only accepted candidates of Irish or German ancestry and, unless you had a "Rabbi," translated to mean a father, brother or uncle who held a union book, your chances of getting an apprenticeship were as good as your chances of being struck by lightening on Christmas Eve.

At nearly six feet he was tall for the times and stood with Popeye forearms folded, searching for an empty table in the steamy, crowded cafeteria where strangers sat together, still bundled in scarfs and hats against the cold outside. They sat wordlessly at communal tables, greedily devouring baked beans from small brown cups, or scooping up the remains of gooey macaroni and cheese with a Kaiser roll. Thick white mugs of hot coffee dotted every table.

"Nuttin doin here," Artie announced to the crew, motioning them to follow him to the rear, up a few steps, where an elevated platform held a half dozen or so empty tables.

"Today we eat like gentlemen," he pronounced sitting, flinging his floppy peak cap on the table, and resurrecting his sandy brown pompadour with his fingers, "Today we get waitress service."

"Yeah, right," Heaney responded caustically, winking at the other two, "and I suppose you didn't see that empty table near the front door?" he asked.

"Whata think," Heaney went on, "we're stupid or sometin? We seen you eyeball dat Dago waitress every time we come here. The one wit da big tits, and the swell gams," he added, prompting raucous laughter.

"Yeah, and exactly what kind of waitress service did you have in mind?" Grathwhol asked, drawing another round of laughter.

"Fuck you! Fuck you, Grathwhol," Artie replied, red-faced. "I didn't see any empty table in the front. We only got a half hour for lunch and we can't stand around waiting."

"Yeah, yeah, sure," Dougherty said as he bent his arm and drew an imaginary violin bow across his elbow.

Marie and Nula McGuire, the other waitress, turned to each other and giggled as they listened to the sophomoric exchange.

"Well, dearie," Nula said wide-eyed, "go on now, it's your turn, take their order. But be careful of the big guy there," she gestured with her head, "the one with the jug ears who thinks he looks like Clark Gable," she warned. "He's a dangerous one, he is," Nula whispered in Marie's ear.

Marie walked to the table and thought, my God, he does look like Clark Gable, as she greeted the group.

"Hi fellas, have you decided? What'll it be today?"

"Oh, hi," Artie responded with feigned surprise, looking up at Marie, who avoided his gaze. "Well," Artie paused, "well, *signura*, or is it *signurina*. Which is it?" Artie asked.

"Well," Marie returned mimicking with hands on her hips, "whichever it is, it's none of your business."

"Hey, that's no way to treat a customer," Artie responded putting his hand to his chest in mock indignation.

"Then start acting more like a customer than a pick-up artist," Marie responded smartly. "This is an eating establishment, not a Second Avenue Saloon."

"Listen to the mouth on this one, will ya," Dougherty sneered.

"Jeez!" Artie exclaimed, "can't a gentleman even make a little conversation with a lady without havin a pail of cold water dumped over his head?"

"Well, you got half of that right, mister," Marie answered.

"Whadya mean?" Artie asked puzzled.

"You're right about me being a lady. But if you were a real gentleman, your cap would be hanging on one of those hooks over there," she pointed, "not lying on the table where people eat."

"Whoa!" the group groaned in unison.

Artie paused for a moment, tightened his lips, and threw his hands in the air.

"Aw, for Christ's sake," he said exasperated, "just bring me a cup of pea soup and a hot roast beef sandwich with mashed and string beans."

As Marie turned and walked away, Dougherty, suppressing a laugh leaned over and taunted, "Good goin, Artie."

"Wadda ya mean by that?" Artie asked glaring and slowly rising. "Don't crack wise with me, ya dumb Mick."

"Artie, Artie," Dougherty responded to the threat, "ya got me all wrong, pal. All I meant was," he said, desperately reaching, "uh, uh, good goin wit the choice ya made. Pea soup's always good on a cold winters day."

"Yeah, sure, and bullshit to you too Dougherty," Artie snapped back.

. . .

The incident embarrassed Artie and he avoided the Automat for a week, joining the old time lathers at The Blarney Stone for the usual lunch – a corned beef or brisket sandwich, three beers and a shot of Fleishman's whiskey. But he couldn't shake Marie from his thoughts, and at quitting time that Friday, payday, he pulled the three crisp tens, two singles and seventy five cents in coin from the small, sealed brown envelope and quickly headed to the Blarney Stone before the gang arrived. He downed two quick shots of Fleishman's and was on his way out the door as they arrived.

"Hey, where're ya goin?" Heaney asked disappointed, as Artie hurried out the door. "Ya ain't even had a chance to get your load on."

"Ah leave the lad alone," Dougherty quipped, "me thinks tonight he'd rather be sippin the coffee at the Automat, rather than spendin the time with the boys, enjoying the pleasure of Mr. John Barleycorn."

"God speed, Artie Mercer," Dougherty yelled laughing as Artie hustled his way through the crowd on Third Avenue.

. . .

Artie zig-zagged in and around the junior executives, secretaries and mail boys leaving their offices, eager to get home and begin the weekend. The city was especially busy at this time of day and the noise from hundreds of taxi cab drivers leaning on their horns, combined with the hollow rumble of the trains on the Third Avenue El reverberated through the concrete canyons of the city like the discordant symphony of a mad composer.

Artie entered the Automat and quickly walked to the rear where a shabbily dressed, toothless old woman sat alone among empty tables, sucking the last of the pea soup from a bowl.

Shit, he thought, disappointed, maybe she left already. He looked anxiously toward the swinging doors leading to the kitchen, hoping Marie would appear then, dejected, turned to walk away.

"Lookin' for someone mister?" he heard a soft voice behind him. He turned, his eyes brightened, and a crooked smile curled at the corner of his mouth.

"Well…I,…I just uh," he began.

"Back again," she pronounced, "this time without Larry, Curley and Mo. I thought I'd seen the last of you. Thought maybe you went off to charm school or something."

"Aw, c'mon now. Give us a break, will ya?" Artie pleaded. "I just came by to apologize for the way I behaved last week."

Marie placed a hand on her hip, titled her head, and looked at him skeptically for a moment, then said,

"Why don't ya sit down and I'll bring ya a cup of coffee and a slice of apple pie," she suggested. "Maybe it'll help clear those blood-shot eyes of yours."

Artie hung his peak cap on one of the hooks and sank into a chair, breathing a sigh of relief as Marie returned and gently placed the coffee and pie on the table. "Your apology is accepted, mister," she said.

"Thanks," he answered between mouthfuls. "By the way, my name is Artie, Artie Mercer."

"Of course it is" Marie said playfully, "and I'm Marie Contino, Artie Mercer."

"Of course you are," Artie responded, as they burst into laughter.

"Listen," Marie said furtively looking around the cafeteria, "I got a few last minute things to take care of in the kitchen before I knock off. When you're finished, if you like, you can wait for me at the corner of 43rd Street. Management doesn't like us dating the customers," she said, patting his hand. "I promise I won't be long."

CHAPTER 46

They huddled close, walking the six blocks against the wind blowing hard from the West across the Hudson River, and the cold coming off the concrete of the grey stone buildings, to Celestine's, an inconspicuous former speakeasy turned walk-down restaurant on West 45th Street.

It was warm and cozy inside. The smoky air was thick with scents of garlic and basil. Fat men with suspenders, women with bright knit scarves around their necks, and whining bored children twisting impatiently in their chairs occupied most of the tables.

"You like Italian food?" Marie asked, as they sat.

"Oh, yeah, I love it. Ma makes it a couplea times a month, usually on Thursday nights, before payday, when there ain't nuttin else to eat," he said, studying the menu like a child reading for the first time.

"Stay with what you know, what you like," Marie advised, "at least for now."

"Oh, yeah," Artie replied, "I'll have the spaghetti wit the tomato sauce. I know about that," he said smiling.

"So, so," Marie asked, probing, "and how does your mother prepare the tomato sauce?"

"Prepare, prepare? Whadda mean prepare?" he asked, flipping his hands out. "She boils noodles, throws a lump of butter into em, and we mix it up with Heinz Ketchup. And there ya have it."

Marie brought her hands to her mouth, and choked, laughing, emitting a shower of red wine on the starched white table cloth.

"Oh, I...I'm so sorry," she said embarrassed, dabbing her mouth with a napkin.

"Hey, hey, that's OK, everything's jake. But what's so funny?" he asked.

"Oh, nothing really," she replied smiling, "it's just that I never heard of tomato sauce prepared that way."

The waiter placed a steaming bowl of spaghetti with marinara sauce, a basket of warm bread and a side dish of meatballs, which Marie had suggested, in front of Artie. He looked over the table, wrinkled his brow and asked, perplexed, "What, no butter for the bread? And where's da cheese in that little green shaker?" he asked.

"That," Marie replied emphatically, "is not cheese, Artie. This is cheese," she said, spooning freshly-graded locatelli from a bowl over his spaghetti. "And Italians don't usually serve butter with their bread when they're eating spaghetti," she added, playfully chastising.

"Um, um," Artie moaned as he slurped the spaghetti from the plate to his mouth, and speared a meatball.

"Artie," Marie offered, laughing, "try twisting the spaghetti into the spoon," she said turning her wrist. "It'll make things easier, and it looks a lot nicer."

"Yeah, maybe next time," Artie responded, continuing his attack. "Right now, I'm doin OK. Don't know how you Da..., I mean I-talians make this stuff, but it sure eats pretty good."

They lingered over coffee and a plate of cannoli and fruit tarts as Marie related the history of her family coming to America, omitting any reference to the motive associated with her uncle, Carmelo.

"So," Artie asked, drawing deep on a Camel cigarette, "you come from a large I-talian family, right?"

"Not that large, not really," Marie responded. "I mean I have my *nonna*, my grandmother, three aunts and a couple of cousins, with more on the way, but that's about it. My mother and father divorced a few years ago and my mother, sister and I moved to Corona because it was less expensive than living in the city. Besides, we wanted to be close to the rest of the family that was living there."

"Sister?" Artie questioned "funny, you just about got around to mentioning her," he observed.

"Yeah, my sister, Twink. Her real name's Angela, but one of my father's friends, an Irish guy," she interjected, "started calling her 'Twink' when she was a baby because he said her eyes twinkled like the stars over Ireland, or some crap like that."

"Yeah, sure does sound like something a Mick would say," Artie agreed.

"Anyway," Marie continued, "she doesn't live with us now. She's up in Massachusetts, at Amherst College. She got a scholarship, room board and everything. She's the brains in the family," Marie said smiling weakly.

"Jeez," Artie exclaimed, "that's impressive. Ain't many dames, I mean girls, goin to college these days, much less on scholarship. But what's she doin in Massachusetts? There's plenty of good schools right here in the city."

"Well, I don't know, she was always reading, poetry and stuff," Marie said dismissively, "a lot of it by some Emily, Emily, something or other. Twink had her choice of any school but, but she chose Amherst cause of this Emily who lived there."

"So tell me something about your family," Marie prodded, quickly changing the direction of the conversation.

"Well, well, we always lived with my gramps in his house in Astoria, me, my ma, da, and my kid sisters, Doris and Elaine. My gramps...", Artie began.

"Wait, wait," Marie interrupted, "who is this 'gramps' you speak of?" she asked.

"Oh, that's what we call my grandfather, my da's father. People say I'm more like him than I am my own da. Anyway, he came here from Northern Ireland in the early 1900's. And let me tell ya, it wasn't easy for any Irishman to get work back then.

"The classified help wanted ads in the newspapers always included, 'Irish need not apply.' So gramps, being a smart, tough guy borrowed some money from Stammerin Sammy Mullen, a big time Irish shylock from the West side, and bought a moving van."

"Stammerin? Why 'Stammerin'?" Marie asked.

"Well, he had this speech problem and, usually, he couldn't get more than three words out witout stammerin sometin awful unless, of course, he was counting or demanding his money from someone. Then, he had no problem.

"Anyway, Gramps did real good right away and paid the thieving Mick off in six months, and bought two more moving vans. I work with Gramps on the weekends but, like my dad, I'm staying in the construction racket. Good pay, pretty steady and, by the end of the year, I'll have my book, my full-fledged union card. At nineteen," he beamed proudly, "I'll be one of the youngest guys in the union."

"By the way," he stopped and asked, "how the hell old are you?"

"Me?" Marie asked surprised, "well I...I turned eighteen last month," she lied, irritated.

"Eighteen," Artie repeated, smiling and relieved, toasting Marie with the wine, "then I guess my ass is pretty safe," he laughed.

"Oh, I really don't know how pretty your ass is, Artie," Marie returned, staring at him with her face cupped in her hands, "but if I understand what you're getting at..."

"All right, all right, I'm out of line again," he admitted, as they fell back in their chairs, laughing.

As they left the restaurant the frigid wind cracked against their faces.

"I'm not gonna let you walk to the train station in this damn wind and cold," he said, gently kissing her on the cheek and whistling for a taxi.

"That would be nice," Marie said smiling, looking into his eyes.

They climbed into the cab and immediately fell into a clumsy embrace with wet, sloppy kisses, which continued until the cabbie pulled to the curb at the Forty Second Street Station.

"OK love boids," the cabbie said turning, "we're here. That'll be ninety cents."

"Right," Artie said fumbling, pulling a dollar from his pocket and handing it to the driver, "keep the change, Mac," Artie said winking.

"Oh, my, well, thank you very much sir," the cabbie said sarcastically as the couple exited, "I had no idea I had big-spendin sports, real swells ridin in my hack."

They sat in the waiting room on the station platform, a foul-smelling, dirty place cluttered with discarded newspapers, waiting for their trains, Marie's eastbound to Corona and Artie's south to Astoria.

"I don't like leavin ya here alone," Artie said, pulling her close. "Ya sure ya don't want me to see ya home?" he asked.

"No, no Artie, thanks anyway. There's plenty of people around and I'm used to riding the train at night," she assured him.

"Listen," he said staring into her large brown eyes, and holding her hand, "tomorrow I got a moving job with Gramps, but I'll be through by about five. Whata ya say I borrow da's Buick, pick ya up and we can take in a movie or something?"

"Oh, Artie, I...I'd love to but I'm working tomorrow night."

"Tomorrow night?" he asked, "tomorrow night's Saturday. You work at the Automat on Saturday?"

"Well, no," Marie replied slowly, "not at the Automat. She hesitated for a moment.

"I've always enjoyed singing, and about a year ago, I won a contest on the radio, and an agent heard me and booked me with one of his bands. So a couple of times a month, I sing at a placed called The Pepper Pot in Greenwich Village."

"A singer, you're a singer?" Artie responded astounded.

"Well, yeah. I guess so," she said laughing. "I mean, they only pay me ten dollars a night, plus a dollar travelling expense, but it's good experience and we all gotta start somewhere."

"So, you get paid to sing in some joint," he said, narrowing his eyes.

"It's not a joint, Artie," Marie objected. "It's a club where some very fine people come to have a drink and listen to music. I saw Benny Goodman in the audience last month," she added proudly.

"Yeah, yeah, a club with fine people," he conceded. But he was really imagining Marie entertaining a bunch of slicked back, greasy-haired wop gangsters and their molls, and the image made him furious.

"Oh, Artie, here's my train coming," she said rising from the bench and pulling him out the door to the platform where they quickly kissed and embraced.

"Come and hear me tomorrow night. It's The Pepper Pot in Greenwich Village," she managed to shout as the train doors closed.

"Yeah, yeah, maybe," he mumbled, waving weakly as the train pulled away.

Artie never made it to The Pepper Pot that, or any other night.

CHAPTER 47

Marie was staying at Mamma Caiozzo's apartment for the month while her mother basked in Boca Raton's warm sunshine at the winter home of Francesco Crosetti, a landscape contractor Mary had met at Angelo's restaurant three years earlier. The romance, which Crosetti had repeatedly failed to convince Mary to legitimize, enjoyed an uncharacteristic three year tenure due, in no small measure, to his warm winter retreat, the perfect remedy for Mary's persistent complaints of migraine headaches and sinus congestion brought on by New York's cold winters.

When Crosetti's business failed, he informed Mary he would be forced to sell the Florida property, prompting her to terminate the relationship, ostensibly, in his interests.

"Francesco," she tearfully told the stunned, broken-hearted man on their return to New York, "although it pains me deeply, we must end our relationship, for your own sake. You must know by now that I can never accept your proposal for marriage. You are a good man, Francesco, and you need a woman ready for marriage, someone who can make a good home for you, and help you through this financial problem; sadly, I am not that woman, but I wish you happiness and *bona fortuna*."

Mamma Caiozzo's response to her daughter's informing her of the end of the relationship with Crosetti was calm and thoughtful.

"Mary," she said speaking Sicilian, "I once told you I never knew what to expect from you, so, now, nothing surprises me, and I respect your independent spirit.

"But, your failure to remain in a permanent relationship is troublesome. You are approaching forty, and need to think about…"

"Failure, mamma?" Mary interrupted, "a poor choice of words. 'Failure' implies that I have not succeeded in charting the direction of my life. But the opposite is true. I am living exactly as I planned. I am not a fixture in the house of a man. And as for the future, I'll deal with that when it comes and, if I choose to remarry, it will not be because I must; I will never marry out of need."

Mamma Caiozzo put her hand to her chest and sighed, "of course, that is exactly the answer, I expected," she said smiling.

. . .

"So," Mary queried, in Sicilian, over coffee one morning with her daughter, "when does the family get to meet this mysterious young man you have been keeping company with for the past month?"

"What?" Marie asked surprised.

"Please, *figghia mia*, my daughter," Mary laughed, "do not insult me. Your comings and goings every Friday and Saturday night for the past month clearly point to a rendezvous with someone."

"Ok, ok, mamma," Marie admitted shyly. "I should have known that my activities could not have escaped *nonna*'s eagle-eye vigilance and aroused some questions."

"And so," Mary asked.

"And so, yes," Marie said, "I have been seeing someone, a young man I met, a customer at the Automat."

"Well," Mary said, pleased, "that doesn't surprise me. You are a beautiful young woman, and it was only a matter of time before you would attract the attention of a young man. But why all the secrecy, Marie? Who is he and what is his name?"

"Ok, ok, mamma," Marie responded "he's a very hard-working guy, a union construction worker who...who also works every Saturday with his gramps who owns moving vans, and...and..."

"Piano, piano, slowly, slowly, *cara*" Mary said smiling, pressing her palms forward. "But who is this 'gramps,'" she asked, puzzled.

"Oh, yeah, gramps, that's what he calls his grandfather," Marie said quietly.

"Gramps," Mary repeated slowly, "*e chi nomu avi stu picciottu*, what is this boy's name? she asked with mounting curiosity and suspicion.

"His name?" Marie repeated.

"You need hot olive oil to clean the wax from your ears?" Mary asked, impatiently.

"His name is Artie, Artie Mercer," Marie snapped, anticipating her mother's reaction.

"Artie Mercer," Mary repeated, "but this is not an Italian name," Mary pronounced.

"Very good, mamma," Marie answered sarcastically, "I'm so glad you know the difference."

"Yes, I know the difference Marie. I know this is an Irisha name."

"Right again, mamma, he is Irish. And what's wrong with that?" she asked defiantly, placing her hands on her hips.

"What's wrong with that? What's wrong with that? All those people do is drink, fight, make friends and drink again," Mary replied. "What's the matter with you? In all of New York you couldn't find a nice Italian boy?" she asked.

"Well that might be a problem, mamma," Marie cynically replied, "since half the nice Italian boys are dead, murdered by the other half of nice Italian boys, like the ones who murdered your uncle and brother."

"How dare you..." Mary began.

"No, how dare you, mamma, how dare you speak to me of the virtues of Sicilian men. The women in our family, yourself included, haven't exactly been blessed by their relationships with Sicilian men."

"Your own mother, my *nonna* was kidnapped when she was sixteen by a dirty old man twice her age and forced into marriage while her parents stood helpless and the law did nothing, and the Church sanctioned the abomination. Yes, yes, I know that sad story, mamma," Marie said, tears streaming down her face. And my aunt, *Zia* Grazia, marries a guy who makes his living working for his brother, a gangster who, by the wave of his hand, sends men to a watery grave, and *Zia* Giovanna marries a lawyer whose sole practice is defending these gangsters. And *Zia* Stella, poor *Zia* Stella, ends up with a Sicilian mute who, if he's lucky, has the brain of a gamberoni, a shrimp. So spare me the vices of the Irisha, mamma."

Mary sat quietly, listening to her daughter, then raised her head from her chest.

"I cannot dispute that much of what you say is true, *cara*. But you neglect to mention decent, heroic Sicilian men like mamma Caiozzo's brother, Antonio, my uncle, a writer and champion of causes for the poor people of Sicily. Nor are you aware of the risks taken by decent men like Turi, the capitano in Castellammare, and Santini, the fisherman, who jeopardized their lives trying to help us escape a bloody vendetta issued against an innocent man, your uncle, Carmelo."

"Innocent? Innocent?" Marie said looking at her mother intently. "How can you be so sure that your brother was innocent?" Marie asked.

"Never question my brother's innocence again," Mary exploded, with flashing eyes. "I know, for certain, that he was not the assassin because Carmelo never lied to me, never."

An uneasy silence fell over the room until Mary spoke, changing the subject.

"So, this Artie is Irisha. Well, I know some Irisha people who are not so bad. And at least he is a Catholic, right?" Mary asked, hopefully, "right?"

"Well, mamma, that's another issue..." Marie began.

"Ah, no, no don't say!" Mary exclaimed, pressing her hands over her ears, "don't say."

CHAPTER 48

The news of the courtship between Artie and Marie was received with as little joy in the Mercer household in Astoria as in Corona.

"Have ya taken leave of your senses lad?" Adelaide asked her son, pulling him from the kitchen through the house to the front porch. "You're getting serious about an I-talian girl, a Sicilian girl, a Papist, she whined. "By God, you're a good-looking, strapping young lad with a fine future in the union and…and…, you're running about with an I-talian? Can't ya be after finding one of your own?" she groaned.

"Ma, stop it," Artie pleaded, throwing his hands up in protest. "You don't know her. You never even met her. She's a fine girl, a sweet, young, hard working girl, honest as the day is long. And you've no right to judge her. And I don't give a good Goddamn about which alter she kneels at or…"

"Watch that mouth of yours, boy," Adelaide warned sternly.

"…or where here ancestors come from," he continued.

"Well, well, boy, you better give some thought to where her ancestors came from. These Sicilians have ancestors who have ancestors who come from Africa. Do ya want to run the risk of having a darkie with nappy hair hangin round your leg and callin ya, 'daddy'?" she demanded.

"What's all the racket about?" George asked as he walked into the porch.

Adelaide looked at her son and said, "G'wan, g'wan Artie, tell your da, tell him."

"Tell me what, lad, what is it?" he asked, his voice rising.

"Ah, da, ma's upset 'cause I'm keepin' company with an I-talian, a Sicilian girl."

"A Sicilian girl is it?" George repeated, biting the tip and lighting his White Owl cigar "and ma's upset about it?"

"George!" Adelaide exploded, glowering at her husband, "is that all ya have to say to your son about this…this…"

"What would ya have me say, me dear?" George asked, puffing contentedly on his cigar.

"Well, I never…" Adelaide sputtered, placing her hands on her hips, "I never. It's a poor state of affairs, it is, when a man can't find the words to counsel his own son to avoid a scandalous mistake."

"These people," she said through clenched teeth, "are murderers, gangsters and law breakers who contribute nothing of value to this country."

"Ah, yes," George replied sarcastically, "not law abiding folks like your grandda, who surely did his part in the gang wars at the Five Points and cracked the heads of the Dead Rabbits in the service of The Protestant, Bill the Butcher in the late 1800's, or your own da who was the muscle, the enforcer for the shylock, Stammerin Sammy Mullen." George, a graduate of illustrious Peter Stuyvesant High School, an avid reader of history and informed observer of current events went on to elaborate. "No, the I-talians have contributed nothing of value to this country, unless, of course you count the fine art hanging in the museum on Fifth Avenue, or the music of Verdi and Puccini, the voice of Caruso, the reforms of Mayor LaGuardia, and the feats of that young Joe DiMaggio up there in the Bronx."

Artie's mouth gaped then closed as he broke into a broad grin, and Adelaide dropped silently into a chair and folded her hands in her lap.

"Now," George continued gently but firmly, "Artie, you invite that young girl for dinner next Sunday, and tell her we'll be having a fine roast leg of lamb and all the trimmins, which your ma here prepares so well," he said turning to his scowling wife.

"Of all things, of all things," Adelaide wailed, throwing her hands in the air and leaving the porch in a huff.

George then turned to his son, smiled and winked.

"Thanks da, thanks," Artie said gratefully.

. . .

It was a good day for leg of lamb, a crisp golden autumn Sunday when Artie ushered Marie, sporting a tailored suit and a Coty hat, into the porch where they were greeted by a smiling George and the young teenage sisters, excited and giggling as they introduced themselves. Marie's small hand disappeared into George's.

"Welcome, welcome, Marie," George said, fixing his eyes on Marie's hat. "That's a very snappy chapeau you're wearing there," he complimented, "very smart, indeed," he added, nodding approvingly.

"Thank you, Mr. Mercer," Marie replied, blushing.

"Watch him, Marie," Artie joked, "da's got an eye for a pretty woman. He's a shameless flirt."

"Don't pay him any mind, Marie, tisn't so," George laughed.

He then turned and called over his shoulder, "Adelaide, will ya please come out here and greet our guest?"

"I'm basting the lamb," was the brusque reply from the kitchen.

"The lamb's not goin' anywhere. Will ya please put the darn spoon down and come out here?" he commanded.

"She'll be a minute," George said turning back to Marie, who smiled weakly and shifted nervously.

A dour faced Adelaide appeared at the door, wiping her hands on her apron. She hesitated then walked slowly toward Marie, giving her the up and down once over.

"Nice makin' your acquaintance," her face expressionless as she extended a cold, limp hand.

"And so nice to meet you, Mrs. Mercer. I've heard so much about you from Artie."

"Hum, hum," Adelaide grumbled, narrowing her eyes.

"Well, come into the parlor and sit," she directed. "Dinner will be a while yet."

Marie sank into a worn upholstered chair that reeked of tobacco, made worse by the dirty standing ashtray containing a corn cob pipe next to an open tin of Prince Albert.

"Something to drink, Marie?" George asked.

"No, nothing, thank you, Mr. Mercer," Marie replied.

George went into the kitchen to the recently purchased Frigidaire and returned with two frosted mugs and two long neck bottles of Rheingold beer.

He won't need to ask his son if he'll have any Marie was thinking. Artie never seems to pass a beer he doesn't like.

At that moment, Marie was startled by the ghastly entrance of a gaunt grey figure with blood-shot eyes into the room, wordlessly scratching a two day stubble of facial hair with one hand and smoothing a wrinkled, soiled undershirt with the other.

"Gramps," Artie called out, "c'mon in. I want you to meet Marie."

"Marie," the old man mumbled, absently staring at her. "Marie's sitting in my chair," he protested, pointing with a shaking, bent forefinger.

"Oh, oh, I'm so sorry, sir," Marie said, beginning to rise, her voice quivering. She looked at him with the expression of surprised horror seen on the face of someone who has bitten into an apple and discovered half a worm.

"No, no, that's all right, dearie," Gramps said, moving toward her on unsteady legs. He leaned down to greet her extending one hand, and pulling up on the waist of his slipping trousers with the other.

"Hel...hel...hellow, Marie," he said with an idiot's grin, forcing the words and emitting the foul odor of stale alcohol and tobacco. Aghast, Marie leaned back as far as the chair would permit to escape the stench, and replied, "Yes, sir, yes, and a pleasure to meet you, sir."

"Yes, a pleasure it is," he slurred, turning abruptly and leaving the room as mysteriously as he had appeared.

Marie was very grateful for his exit and sighed with relief.

"Well, that was my Gramps," Artie said laughing.

George looked down, then up at Marie, and shook his head, apologetically.

Marie's silent prayer was answered when she didn't have to suffer his company later at the dinner table, or anywhere else for that matter; one week later, poor Gramps fell backwards off a barstool, hit his head on the hard floor, and never regained consciousness.

. . .

Late Thanksgiving afternoon after a quiet dinner with his family, Artie excused himself from the table and climbed into the Buick for the twenty minute drive to Corona. He wore his Sunday best, a dark blue suit, white shirt and striped tie, pinned neatly at the collar, for this first meeting with Marie's family.

As he climbed the stairs to Mamma Caiozzo's second floor apartment on National Avenue, he nervously ran his fingers through his hair and buffed his shoes on the back of his trouser legs. The scent in the hallway carried the residual of the Thanksgiving feast, and he could hear loud laughter and a lot of animated conversation coming from the apartment. Anxious as he knew he would be, Artie knocked three times before a smiling Marie opened the door.

"Hi," she greeted him, smiling with her head tilted back, as Artie kissed her quickly on the mouth.

"Hi, kiddo," he responded, "sounds like ya got a full house here tonight."

"Yeah," Marie agreed, laughing. "Sicilians," she shrugged, "when we're all together like this, it does get a little noisy. Come, come and meet the family," she said, taking his hand.

As they entered the large kitchen, the happy chatter around the table ceased abruptly, and an uncomfortable silence settled over the room as twenty pairs of staring eyes considered the tall stranger in their midst. Annoyed, Mamma Caiozzo finally broke the tension, chastising her family in Sicilian, as she made her way to Marie and Artie.

"I'm ashamed of all of you. You dishonor me. Is this any way for my family to greet a guest in my home, a friend of our Marie?" she demanded.

"Welcome, Artur," she said smiling, extending a fragile, badly gnarled hand. "Please forgivea my family, and forgivea my English. I speak ok, ma no so good."

"You speak fine, *signurina*, much better English than I speak I'talian," he said gently clasping the tips of her fingers between his.

"Oh, Artur," Mamma Caiozzo said blushing, bringing her hands to her cheeks, "I have not been called '*signurina*' since I was a sixteen year old," she said laughing. Her comment broke the chill and the family joined her in a round of chuckles, as she shooed Mello and Frankie from their chairs, inviting Marie and Artie to sit at the table next to Mary.

"Artie, this is my mother, Mary Contino," Marie said.

"A pleasure, sig...sig...*signura*." Artie exclaimed proudly to a round of applause, extending a hand of greeting.

"Yes," Mary responded offering a limp, gloved hand, "itsa good to finally meet da boy my daughter spends so much time with," she said, regarding him warily. Mary reached into her handbag and produced a grey box with a red border marked, 'Regent'. She put an oval shaped, king sized cigarette between her lips, tilted her head, and looked at Arty expectantly.

"Oh yea, scuse me," Artie apologized, fumbling for his Zippo lighter.

"Tank you," Mary said facetiously. Marie then introduced Artie to the other family members, prompting Stella to whisper to her sister, Grazia,

"*Ma stu omu è veru beddu*, but, this man is handsome," she gushed.

"Yes, he is," Grazia replied, "but much too young for you sister," she said laughing and patting Stella's cheek.

"Sometin' to eat or drink, Artur?" Mamma Caiozzo asked.

"No, no, thank you *signura*," Artie said patting his stomach, "I'm full up."

"Mamma," Frankie said, mischievously grinning at Artie, "bring the bottle of grappa and a glass here for our guest."

"Be careful, Artie," Marie warned.

"Ah, for Christ's sake, cousin," Frankie replied, overhearing, "he's a big, strong Irish guy. He can handle it, right Artie?" Frankie challenged.

"Oh, yeah, well...sure," Artie answered.

Frankie filled a large wine glass with the grappa and handed it, leering, to Artie, who drained it in one gulp prompting gasps.

"Jeez," he said swallowing hard and bringing his hands to his throat, "what the hell is this stuff?"

"Well, it ain't mother's milk," Mello offered to laughs.

"Moonshine, Artie, it's Italian moonshine," Frankie replied, bringing the bottle back to the empty glass for another pour. Marie placed her hand firmly over the glass and said glaring at Frankie, "*Basta*, that's enough."

"Ah Marie, don't be a killjoy. We're only..."

"I said that's enough, Frankie," Marie glowered.

"Mamma Caiozzo," Marie called, "please bring a large cup of espresso and a piece of *cassata* for Artie."

"Naw, it's ok Marie," Artie began to protest.

"Bring it please, mamma," Marie insisted.

"Subittu, immediately," Mamma Caiozzo replied, waving a disapproving finger at Frankie.

As the evening drew to a close, Artie waved his goodbyes as Marie walked him to the door.

"Are you sure you're ok to drive and can find your way back to Astoria?" she asked.

"Are you kidding?" Artie boasted, "I've driven wit a lot more booze in me than one shot," he said laughing.

"I'm sure you have," Marie coolly responded.

"Just one thing, though," he said troubled. "I hardly got to talk at all with your ma. I mean, she just sat in a corner with her arms folded, staring at me. It made me very uncomfortable."

"Yes, Artie, I know the feeling," Marie said, looking past him.

"Well, anyway," Artie said kissing Marie on the cheek, "anyway I'll call you during the week."

"Ok, Artie," Marie replied indifferently as she returned his kiss, "talk to you later."

Artie didn't go straight home to Astoria. In his world ten thirty was just the beginning of the night, and he knew the gang would be readying itself for a night of celebrating at the Shamrock, and he was eagerly looking forward to it.

CHAPTER 49

The week following Thanksgiving ushered in the endless, mindless round of holiday parties which lasted through New Year's Day, leaving the revelers with bloated red faces and sloppy fat belies folding over waistbands.

Blue-collar saloons in all five boroughs of the city were decked out in reams of red and green crepe paper, cardboard Santas and flashing colored lights. The "cha-ching" of the ornately crafted, bronze National cash register behind the bar rang from noon to 4 a.m., until the celebrants staggered home, arm in arm.

Mothers had insured that their children would have presents to open on Christ's birthday when they established, 'Christmas Clubs' at the Queens County Savings Bank for fifty cents or one dollar a week. The checks were sent out to the depositors by December 1st, and cashed immediately. The money was safely hidden in the tin of flour on a shelf in the kitchen, or stuffed underneath mom's underwear in the bedroom bureau.

With the holiday season in full swing, the band and Marie were booked for four consecutive weekends at the Pepper Pot, including New Year's Eve, spurred in part, by Marie's soulful rendering of the hits of the day; "I'll Get By," "Embraceable You," and "Body and Soul".

Marie's holiday work schedule conflicted with Artie's social schedule, putting a strain on the relationship.

"For Chrissakes," Artie complained, "you're tied up every goddamn weekend for the next month, and I end up goin' to all the Christmas rackets alone."

"That's just the point, Artie," Marie responded, "there's two or three of these, 'rackets,' as you call them, every week, and you feel obliged to attend all of them. Nothing's stoppin' you from coming down to the Pepper Pot on Friday or Saturday night. I finish my set by 11:00 and we could still enjoy the night together."

"I ain't comin' to no Pepper Pot," Artie snapped, balking like a child forced to eat his spinach. "Ain't my kind of people. I need a place where I can feel comfortable, where I can enjoy myself and unwind after a long week of hard work."

"Artie," Marie lamented, shaking her head, "I've been to these kind of parties with you over the past couple of months, and you don't unwind, you unravel."

"Ah, shit, call it what you want," Artie replied, defensively. "But I'll tell ya what, it's a lot more fun than sitting around an old lady's kitchen table, without a cold beer, eating for three hours, then listening to arguments about who makes a better spaghetti sauce, or if Enrico, what's his name…has a better voice than Pasquale, whoever."

On New Year's Eve at about 11:00 o'clock, Marie finished her set, hurried to the powder room and freshened up. On her way out the door, she wished everyone a Happy New Year and hopped a yellow and red DeSoto taxi to join Artie at the Shamrock Inn in Sunnyside, Queens. She counted the carelessly stuffed mound of dollar bills in her purse and smiled.

Not bad for a 17 year old, she thought. Thirty-eight dollars in tips and salary for three hours of doing what I love. That's more than I make in a week at the Automat, and I didn't even have to carry a tray.

As the cab reached the apex of the Manhattan Bridge, Marie turned on her knees and looked out the back window with her head resting on folded arms. The lights of the city glittered like a thousand white diamonds against the dark cold December night.

God, I love this city, she thought. I only wish Artie felt the same. He can't wait to leave it after his rounds at the Blarney Stone on Friday, and won't return until the work week begins on Monday. Marie chuckled to herself as she recalled the words of former Mayor Jimmy Walker: "Who'd want to be President of the United States when he could be mayor of New York City?"

Walker may have been a thief, Marie thought, but he sure knew what was good.

Marie was pleasantly surprised when she entered the noisy, smoky room where couples Lindied to Glenn Miller's "Pennsylvania 6-5000," to find Artie relatively sober, cavorting and joking with Dougherty, Heaney and Grathwohl.

"Ah, here she is now," Artie announced with Celtic flourish, "my wild Sicilian rose. And have ya ever seen a fairer lass come from the island, lads?" he challenged.

"Right, right, Artie," Marie grinned facetiously, nodding her head up and down. "Is this what's known as Irish Blarney, fellas?" she asked turning to the boys.

"Tis, indeed, Marie, and it's himself here who wrote the book," Heaney said pointing to Artie. "But in your case, it's no less true," he added, planting a long, wet kiss on Marie's cheek.

"Watch yaself there, Mick," Artie growled, "or you'll be needing that ice in your glass to reduce the swelling ya might get under your eye," he said, grinning through clenched teeth.

"Oh, Artie, for Christ's sake, he was only…" Marie began.

"Marie, Marie," Artie protested with open palms, "I was kidding, only kidding. Heaney knows that, don't ya pal?" He turned laughing to Heaney, delivering a savage blow to his friend's arm, knocking him off balance, and causing the drink to spill over his trousers.

"Yeah, sure PAL," Heaney replied, humiliated, and resentful. "Only kidding. I gotta get me another drink," he said disgusted, looking into his empty glass. "See ya later, PAL," he repeated caustically.

1939 was welcomed in with the traditional countdown chorus, "10, 9, 8...," kisses, hugs and glad back-slapping. Dougherty and Grathwohl gave Marie a quick peck on the cheek, and Heaney extended a limp hand and disappeared into the crowd before Artie could approach him.

Waitresses appeared with large platters of cold cuts, heaping bowls of potato salad, coleslaw swimming in mayonnaise, pickles and sliced white bread. The party-goers attacked the food like starving wolves over a carcass prompting Marie to tell Artie, "I'm gonna sit at that table over there until the crowd thins out."

"Yeah, you go ahead, kiddo, I'll fix ya a plate."

"Forget the salad for me," she called after him, shuddering at the thought of cold vegetables dripping with mayonnaise.

"The ham looks pretty good," he said returning and putting a plate in front of Marie, "fresh-baked," he added, "I didn't bother with the baloney or the olive loaf," he said winking and smiling.

"And I thank you for that," Marie replied, smiling weakly. She placed a thick slice of ham between two pieces of white bread, took a bite, and wrinkled her nose.

"What, no good?" Artie asked.

"The ham's ok, but this Silvercup bread is...," she said stopping and shaking her head.

When they finished eating, Artie dragged a reluctant Marie around the room from table to table, proudly displaying her to his other friends and acquaintances, like a trophy with the swagger and bravado of a hunter who had bagged a prize. Exhausted, Marie was finally able to free herself from the tedious introductions and retreated to the ladies room, breathing a sigh of relief. But it was a poorly maintained, dimly-lit, stinky place with discarded tissues and cigarette butts crushed on the floor. She shunned the common bar of Ivory soap lying naked by the sink, and splashed her face with cold water, drying it with her handkerchief rather than using the one filthy cloth towel hanging from a hook on the wall.

As Marie looked into the stained, cloudy mirror, she couldn't fight back the tears beginning to stream down her face. Her legs weakened as she reflected on the unsettling events of the evening, but the tears were stirred by a much more pressing and troubling concern; her period was now five weeks overdue.

When Marie emerged from the ladies room, Artie noticed her pale complexion and swollen red eyes.

"Are you ok, kiddo?" he asked squinting and furrowing his brow.

"No, I'm not ok, Artie. I don't feel well and I want to go home," she said suppressing a sob.

"You mean right now?" Artie asked, perplexed.

"Yes, now, right now," Marie replied, resolved.

"All right," Artie said, scratching his head.

"Good night all," he yelled to the group, waving his arm like a Presidential candidate on the rear platform of a whistle-stop campaign train.

On the drive back to Corona, Marie sat wordless as Artie went on incessantly about how swell the party was, and how everyone complimented him on his great, "catch".

"Your 'catch'?" Marie turned and said, furiously, "I'm not anybody's 'catch', do you hear me? And don't you ever, ever, refer to me like that again."

"Oh, oh. Let's not be so touchy, kiddo. It's just a manner of speaking. It don't mean nuttin."

"Well it means something to me, and I don't like it. And, and while we're at it, knock the 'Kiddo' shit off. My name's 'Marie,' in case you've forgotten."

"Ok...Marie," Artie said and he reached over to pat her hand. He was trying to placate her but was condescending. "But ya know what I think?" he began.

"No," Marie answered sarcastically, "but I'm sure you're gonna tell me."

"Well," Artie continued, "I think your attitude points to the fact that you've been working too hard, you're overextended. I mean, you're on your feet lugging trays at the Automat five days a week, then you're off to that Pepper Piss Club at least every other weekend."

"Very funny, Artie," Marie said dryly.

"Well, alls I'm sayin is Marie, maybe you've taken on too much. Maybe you should be thinkin about giving up..."

"Don't say it," Marie warned, turning toward him, "don't say it. You knew what my plans were when we started seeing each other, and our relationship hasn't changed those plans."

"Hey, I'm not askin ya to change your plans," he said unconvincingly, "but ya gotta cut down on your workload before ya go completely nuts."

Artie pulled the Buick into one of the dark streets alongside Linden Park, across from P.S. 16, and cut the engine. He reached over and put his arm around Marie's shoulder.

"No, not tonight," Marie protested, squirming away, "I told you, I'm not feeling well."

"Oh, ok, now I get it," Artie said pressing his hands forward, "it's that time of the month, isn't it? That explains everything."

"Yeah, Artie, sure," Marie replied blankly, shaking her head, "it certainly is, or isn't that time of the month. Now please drive me home."

The phone rang in the apartment on 100 Street a little past noon on New Years Day.

"Alo," Mary answered.

"Oh, oh, hello, Mrs. Contino," Artie responded, surprised, "and, a happy New Year to you."

"Yeah, yeah, ana hoppa new assa, too, Artur," Mary returned.

"What?" Artie exclaimed, shocked.

"Whatsa matter, you no *capisci 'ngrisi*?" Mary asked.

"I say, 'Happy-New-Years' to you, she repeated, slowly.

"Oh, yeah, yeah, thank you, I couldn't hear you clear. We must have a bad connection or sometin. But, anyway, I was wondering if I could speak to Marie…?"

"No, no, no now, Artur," Mary interrupted. "Marie, she no feela so good. She still asleep. Maybe you calla back tonight," she said, "ok?" abruptly returning the phone to the cradle.

"Who was it?" Marie called drowsily from her bed.

"Arthur, it was Arthur," Mary answered in Sicilian. "I told him to call back later. Now, come, get up and wash your face. I'll make a fresh pot of coffee and prepare a nice frittata for you. And later we'll go to Mamma Caiozzo's for the traditional New Years Day meal of sausage and lentils with the family."

CHAPTER 50

When they returned to the apartment later that evening, Mary suggested a hot cup of chamomile tea.

"Yes, mamma, that sounds good," Marie replied.

They sat wordlessly at the table when Marie turned to her mother with tears in her eyes.

"Mamma…I, I," she began, speaking Sicilian.

"I know, Marie, I know, she said nodding." "Last week I made an appointment for you to see Dr. Panebianco tomorrow."

"Oh!" Marie said surprised. "You knew something?"

"Well, let's just say I had strong suspicions. You pick at your food, you have dark sad circles under your eyes, and running the water in the bathroom sink for as long as you do every morning doesn't drown out the sound of retching. We'll be at his office at seven o'clock tomorrow night."

Richard Panebianco was a dedicated, tireless physician with office hours Monday, Wednesday, and Friday from 9 a.m. to 8 p.m. Tuesday and Thursdays were reserved for his round of home visits, for which his fee was $1.00 more, set at $4.00. He was, "Corona's Doctor," the quintessential healer – tall, dark, handsome, charming – with whom all his female patients were in love, and envied by all their jealous husbands, one of whom caused a memorable incident at Physician's hospital in Jackson Heights.

While making his rounds the second year out of medical school Panebianco encountered the man, an unstable patient, who recognized him as his wife's former boyfriend, accused the doctor of having an affair with her, went berserk, and attempted to run him down in his wheelchair in the hospital corridor.

His flashing smile and comfortably soothing voice had a placebo effect, and female patients often pronounced themselves, "cured," just by walking into his office and being in his presence.

Mary was no exception. She made monthly visits to his office claiming only he could relieve her migraine headaches or sinus congestion. But her shameless ruse went for naught. The good doctor was ten years her junior and quite happily married with two children.

"*Dottore*," Mary greeted him smiling, the following evening, "*Stasira non è pri mia*, tonight is not for me. Ima feela fine, but Marie here," she said seriously, "maybe no so good."

"Ok, Mary," Panebianco said, returning her smile, "have a seat in the waiting room, and let's have a look at your daughter. Come, Marie," he said gesturing her into the examination room.

"What, I no canna come in too, *Dottore?*" Mary asked disappointed.

"No, Mary," he responded, laughing, "your daughter is no longer a child. She is a young woman and has the right to expect some privacy. I'll speak with you when we have finished the examination."

Panebianco completed his examination within ten minutes and, even without a definitive test, confirmed Mary's suspicions; Marie was most certainly, at least six weeks pregnant.

"Do you love him?" he asked, drying his hands and sitting down next to her.

"Oh, I don't know, I'm not sure anymore," she said embarrassed, turning her eyes from his. "I mean when...when it happened," she said, her face brightening, "I really thought I did love him or, or I wouldn't have..."

"It's ok, Marie, it's ok," Panebianco said, patting her hand. "You're a healthy, normal young woman, and dwelling on feelings of guilt will do you no good. You have more important things to think about now. You must take good care of yourself to insure that the pregnancy goes smoothly, and you deliver a healthy child. And you have an important decision to make; do you want to marry this young man?"

"Do I have a choice?" Marie asked surprised. "A child deserves a father and I don't think I could bear the thought of my child as a nameless..., well you know what I mean."

Panebianco reflected for a moment then replied, "I understand, Marie, and that's a valid point. So then marry him, but marry him outside the church," he suggested thoughtfully.

"Outside the Church?" Marie exclaimed.

"Yes." He went on to explain: "Hopefully, after the birth of the child, you may recapture the love you once felt for him and then you can sanctify the marriage with a Church wedding. If it doesn't go well, you can obtain an annulment and be free to remarry in the Church in the future. In either case, your child will legally bear his name and you will have some assurance of child support."

"But that's sinful, deceitful," Marie said.

"Marie," Panebianco replied calmly, "your most important consideration, aside from the health of the baby, is insuring your child carries the name of the father. That is not deceitful. And, as for the matter of sin," he said laughing, "we Catholics are most fortunate. The only thing separating a sinner and a non-sinner in our religion is one good confession."

Marie's mood lightened as she left the doctor's office and informed her mother of Panebianco's advice.

"Ah, leave it to a Sicilian to figure a way out of a difficult situation," Mary commented to her daughter with a wink and a smile.

. . .

Artie was deliriously happy when Marie informed him of the pregnancy. Aside from the happy anticipation of fatherhood, he was relieved by the thought that Marie's duties as a mother would put an end to her ambitions as a singer and keep her where he felt she belonged - in the kitchen and in the bedroom.

Three weeks later, they married secretly within the drab green walls of City Hall, a dreary ceremony attended only by Heaney as the best man, and Twink, who had come down from Amherst to be with her sister. Artie's grin was as wide as a Cheshire cat's as Marie, clutching a small bouquet of early spring violets, smiled weakly through the unceremonious drone of the official's formulaic recitation.

Following the ceremony, they went to Longchamps for lunch where Marie picked at a Waldorf Salad and Artie washed down a Salisbury Steak, more Salisbury than steak, with three shots of Old Bushmills. They walked with Twink to the bus terminal on 42nd Street for her return to Amherst as Heaney disappeared up Eighth Avenue in search of a Blarney Stone bar.

On their way back to Queens on the IRT, they agreed it would be best for each of them to return to their homes separately, inform their parents, and have Artie pick Marie up later that evening where they would spend their first night together as husband and wife in their newly rented apartment in Jackson Heights. The choice of the location suited both of them since it was neutral, halfway between Corona and Astoria; Artie was as uncomfortable living in Italian Corona as Marie was in Irish Astoria.

"So she's pregnant, isn't she?" Adelaide asked her son, resigned.

"Yes, ma, she's pregnant," Artie responded defiantly, "and I'm her husband, I love her, and I'm gonna be a father."

Adelaide clasped her hands, breathed deeply, and left the room.

George walked over to his son, put his arm around his shoulder and said, "Now, now, don't be so hard on your ma. A mother would always rather see her child married conventionally, in a church, with all the accompanying ceremony. But, I'm proud of you, son. You and Marie did the right thing and took matters into your own hands without unnecessary interference by parents who too often screw things up."

He then walked into the parlor where Adelaide was sitting, weeping quietly, put his hands on her shoulders and said, "Well, what do you think of this, me dear? We're not yet out of our forties and we're gonna be grannies."

"Yes, grannies," she said, reaching back and taking his hand, "We lose one child and gain another. I so hope this will turn out all right."

"Dad," Artie called to his father, "we already got an apartment in Jackson Heights, and I'll be needing the car to pack my stuff and pick Marie up."

"Sure, son, take it and keep it as long as you need. I'm thinking ya might, at least, want a short honeymoon somewhere."

"Yeah, well, thanks, da. As a matter of fact, me and Marie was talking about a long weekend at the shore in Rockaway, if that's ok."

"That's fine," George said, hugging his son and placing thirty dollars in his hand.

"Now you and Marie get off to a good start, and have a fine time at the shore. I'll square things with your ma. We'll see ya when ya get back and have a proper celebratory dinner."

CHAPTER 51

Artie bounded down the stairs two at a time at the 80th Street IRT station in Jackson Heights and ran the four blocks to the apartment.

"Marie! Marie!" he shouted, racing from the hallway to the living room, "I got it! I got it!" waving a union book to an empty room.

He called again as a low moan came from the bedroom where he found an ashen Marie lying on a wet bed, clutching her stomach.

"Artie, Artie," she gasped in pain, "my water, my water broke."

Artie moved swiftly and, within fifteen minutes, an ambulance was transporting Marie to Physician's Hospital with Artie holding her hand and swiping her brow with a wet cloth.

He sat in the waiting room with paunchy, older men with bad brown teeth chewing unconcerned on cigars, and young men like himself pacing up and down.

Less than two hours later, a smiling Panebianco entered extending a hand, as he announced in his trademark sonorous voice, "Everything's fine. You have a nice, healthy little boy there."

The cultural divide which had existed dissolved somewhat with the birth of the child. Adelaide was relieved that her first grandchild was a blond, fair-complexioned baby. Mary wondered amused and laughing: "*Ma, chi è chistu, un carusu biondu sicilianu?* But what is this, a blond Sicilian kid?"

Deciding on a name was problematic. Artie was pressured by his mother, who insisted the boy carry a, "good Irish-American name."

"I think it would be a fine thing, indeed, if the boy continued the tradition of 'Arthur', in honor of your deceased grandda, and, of course, out of respect for you, son."

"No, Artie, absolutely not," Marie bristled when she heard, remembering her one distasteful encounter with gramps.

"I want a name that reflects the other half of his family. He already has the 'Mercer' name, an Irish surname."

"Well, it sure ain't gonna be no 'Antny,' or 'Enzo,' or sometin like dat," he declared, scowling.

Mary, who was at the apartment helping her daughter through the first weeks of motherhood, walked into the kitchen. She sat, quietly listening to the debate, curling her arms around her chest and finally interrupted.

"Marie," she asked in Sicilian, "make a nice pot of espresso, please."

Artie and Marie looked at each other puzzled as Mary continued.

"Listen, this a no way to begin a marriage, and no way to begin parenthood. What difference it make what you call da boy? Da namea no change da blood; he isa half *Sicilianu* and half Irisha."

"Yeah, so what are you saying?" Artie asked impatiently.

"What I say, what I say," Mary answered, "is you make a *compromesso*, a compromise."

"A compromise," Artie repeated, "And what compromise would that be?" He asked.

"Well," Mary answered deliberately, "you namea da boy, 'Roger.'"

"Roger" Artie reflected.

"Why 'Roger?'" Marie asked her mother.

"Well, Mary began, "itsa name sound very Irisha and American and," she added smiling at Arthur, "it go very nice wit the name 'Mercer.'"

"Yeah, and?" Arthur prodded, narrowing his eyes, suspiciously.

"And, itsa also very popular name in Sicily because of Ruggero I and Ruggero II, father and son Princes who rule the island in 13th Century."

Artie breathed deeply, crossed his arms across his chest, stroked his jaw and said, "Ya know, I gotta admit, that's not a bad idea. What a you think Marie?" he asked.

Marie swallowed a giggle and said shrugging, "Sounds ok to me, Artie."

"Eh!" Mary exclaimed pinching her fingers together and rotating her hand, "then it's a settle an everybody gonna be happy – *Sì* or *no*?"

And so, with the verve and skill of a *consiglieri mafiosu*, Mary had successfully resolved the problem.

. . .

One week later on September 1, 1939, the issue of naming a child assumed the significance of a lone flea in the galaxy as the festering cyst in Europe burst when the German Air Force mercilessly bombed Polish cities, followed by a massive land offensive across the frontier. Two days later, Britain and France declared war on Germany, plunging the continent into its second round of bloody hostilities in twenty five years. By the Spring of 1940, Hitler's blitzkrieg had swept through Denmark, Holland and Belgium, and on June 15th, 1940, the lights in the city of lights went out as German troops marched smartly under the Arc de Triomphe while casting menacing eyes toward the English coast.

"Jesus Christ," George, a veteran of World War I, moaned, "Is there no end to this madness we are forced to endure? We come out of one world war, suffer through ten years of a depression, only to find we are on the verge of another global catastrophe. Will we never be safe and secure? If there is a God in Heaven, he must be some freaking character."

While America showed sympathy for the cause and plight of the British by sending aid, public sentiment against involving troops in another European war, fanned by the speeches of Charles Lindberg and the anti-Semitic rantings of Father Coughlan, prompted Roosevelt to eschew direct intervention.

All that changed on December 7, 1941, when, on a peaceful Sunday morning, news broke on Philco radios all over the nation that the Imperial forces of Japan had launched a sneak air attack on a place called Pearl Harbor, sinking and damaging twelve battleships, carriers, and mine-sweepers, sending more than 1500 sailors to watery graves or a fiery death in white hot steel hulls of ships.

Roosevelt's, "Day of Infamy" speech roused an incensed America and, within days, long lines formed around recruitment stations throughout the country.

Following a solemn and cheerless holiday season, in late January, 1942, nineteen year old Artie Mercer raised his right hand and was inducted into the United States Army.

"I don't need no telegram to tell me what I gotta do," he said to his weeping, distraught mother.

The night before he was to report to Whitehall Street in lower Manhattan for final processing and the bus trip to Fort Dix, New Jersey, the Mercers, Marie and the child gathered at the family home in Astoria for a farewell dinner.

As Marie sat gently rocking her son in her arms, her eyes were drawn to her mother-in-law's face, laced with fear and anxiety. Despite their acrid relationship, Marie felt the bond all mothers feel when their children face impending danger. Once, in the not too distant past, she thought, this woman held her sleeping son in her arms, just as I'm doing now. And I'm sure she remembers that moment just as I'll remember this one. And tomorrow, she'll give him over to a drill sergeant who will make him a soldier and send him off to war.

Artie had to pry his mother's arms from around his neck, then went to his young sisters, and they engaged in a tearful group hug.

George waited at the curb and held the rear door of the Buick open for Marie and the child. Artie slid in the front beside his father.

"Everything ok back there?" he turned, and asked his wife.

"Everything's fine," she replied. "Pop's got a blanket here," she said, nestling her son between her body and the blanket against the cold January night.

"The heater will warm things up in a minute, Marie," George said looking through the rear-view mirror.

On the drive back to Jackson Heights, George talked non-stop, offering the kind of advice a father would give to his son about to attend his first sleep-away camp. But his light-hearted attempt failed to convince Marie, who heard his broken sentences and the fear in his voice.

When they got to the apartment, Artie turned to Marie.

"Marie...I...I...,"

"I know, Artie," she interrupted, "I'll take the baby upstairs and give you some time alone with your father."

George got out of the car, opened the door for Marie, and looked at his grandson sleeping in his mother's arms. He kissed the child on the forehead then kissed Marie on the cheek.

He looked at her with wet eyes and asked, hopefully, "You...you will keep in touch with us, won't you, Marie?"

"Oh Pop," she said, drawing close to him, "of course I will. I know the importance of grandparents in the life of a child, and I would never keep him from you...or Adelaide," she added.

"Thank you, my dear," he said, choking.

Marie was in bed with the blanket pulled tight to her chin and the room bright with a soft winter azure moonlight breaking through the window shades. She heard the click, then the front door open and close. The toilet flushed then water burped from the faucet and rushed into the sink.

Artie slid under the sheet and the blanket and lay silently staring through the dark at the ceiling, listening to the hissing radiator.

Marie turned toward him and asked, "Are you all right, Artie?"

"This is the first time I ever saw my da cry," he replied without answering the question. "It's the first time I ever saw fear in his eyes," he said, as his characteristic swagger and bravado caved like a sand castle at the water's edge. He put an arm around Marie's shoulder and pulled her close, dropping his head on her heaving breasts. She tenderly caressed his head and felt her own warm, salty tears on her cheek. The torrent of their spring love had abated over the past two years, and Marie knew that the intimacy which followed might be the last they enjoyed. She wept for the young man in her arms going off to the uncertainty of war, but wept also because of the uncertainty of the survival of their marriage.

Artie rose early the next morning and was quietly packing a small valise when he was startled by a rhythmic thumping coming from the living room. He chuckled watching his son in a cowboy hat gallop in a circle on an imaginary horse, holding a rein in one hand and pumping his fist through the air with the other. The boy saw his father and rode toward him, dismounting, and leaping into his father's arms.

"Da goin to work now?" the boy asked, poking and pinching Artie's cheek with tiny pink fingers.

"Yeah, da goin to work now," Artie replied sadly, holding his son tight and smothering his face with wet kisses.

"C'mon now," he said putting the boy down, "help da carry his work valise."

"I do it! I do it!" the child shouted, racing ahead of his father into the bedroom and pushing him aside. He pulled the valise from the foot of the bed to a loud clump on the floor, grasped the handle and tried to slide it, unsuccessfully flopping backward on his can. He looked up scowling and disappointed at his father.

"Ok, da you can help," he relented.

Marie stood at the door, smiling thinly with a cup of coffee in her hand.

"I can make you breakfast, eggs or something," she offered.

"No, no thanks," he said glancing at his Bulova watch. "I gotta be at Whitehall Street by eight. He tried to lighten the tense moment by launching into a soft shoe routine and lyric:

"I'm in the Army now
I'm not behind a plow
I'll never get rich by diggin a ditch
I'm in the Army now."

Or how 'bout this one?" he continued, "We're fighten with a fella who is slanty-eyed and yella and we're gonna beat 'em red, white and blue."

They hugged and kissed for a long time at the door, a scene repeated at tens of thousands of front doors and porches in every part of the country.

"Gotta go now," Artie said fighting tears, pulling back. He turned and walked quickly down the stairs.

Marie took her son's hand and ran to the living room window. Artie emerged from the building, stopped and turned, looking up at the second floor. He smiled and waved at his wife and son, and disappeared down 76th Street.

Marie hugged her son and wept quietly. She knew, whatever happened, things would never be the same.

CHAPTER 52

I don't remember the apartment in Jackson Heights, or galloping around the living room like Hopalong Cassidy on an imaginary pony the morning my father, with other young men not old enough to vote, left to go to war, and I don't remember when I first began putting sentences together or one day, mysteriously, reading the words ballooning out of the mouths of cartoon characters in Gasoline Alley or Dick Tracy in the funny pages of the Sunday Daily News.

But I do remember waking up in wrinkled sweat-soaked sheets on a hot late summer day in 1943, to the dull sound of venetian blinds clicking in the breeze like bad keys on a piano. Everything seemed comfortable and I felt I was where I belonged, but I didn't know why. We were living with *nonna* in Corona.

I looked to the window and stared at a diminutive woman with close-cropped salt and pepper hair, wearing a flower-pattern house dress, doing calisthenics, and grunting like a linebacker.

"Ah, Ruggero," she said turning toward me, "you sleep long time, eight, maybe nine hour."

"Yes, *nonna*," I repeated in broken English, "I sleep eight, maybe nine hour."

"Now you makea fun how *nonna* talk, you bad boy," she scolded.

"No, *nonna*," I replied, earnestly, "I no makea fun how you talk."

"No?" she said smiling, walking toward my bed, pinching my cheek and kissing my forehead. "Ok, c'mon now, you get up, brusha da teeth, washa yaself an get dress. Your mamma she already go to the *marchetta* to buy food. We gotta make a nice *cena* for your farta who come home today on a, on a, how you say?, a 'fourlow', I tink," she said, shrugging her shoulders.

My father, I thought. My father. The guy in the picture wearing an army uniform, holding me in one arm, with the other around my mother's shoulder. He's coming home on a fourlow? Must be a plane with four wings that flies close to the ground, I reasoned.

I washed, brushed my teeth then, still dopey with sleep, walked unsteadily into the kitchen where *nonna* was crushing coffee beans in a wooden bowl. I watched as she went to the ice box and took two eggs out, holding one ritualistically between her slender fingers. I knew what was coming, and I grimaced in disgust. She made a pinhole with a sewing needle on the top and one on the bottom of the shell, put it to her mouth and slurped out the inside.

She then sliced two oranges in half and squeezed each of them over a small pyramid in the middle of a glass dish, poured the juice into a large cup, cracked the other egg, and beat it into the cup with a fork.

Nonna anticipated my attempt to escape and wrapped her fingers around my thin wrists, grabbing my face and forcing the thick goo past my clenched lips down my gagging throat.

"*Bivitillu tuttu*, drink it all," she commanded. "You gotta have an egg every day. Veddy good for you. Panebianco tell me dat."

When the last of it was gone I wiped my mouth with the back of my hand, looked at her with tears welling and cried, dramatically, "you're a strega, a witch, a bad *nonna*. You almost choked me."

"Ah, but you no choke, do you?" she replied laughing, throwing her hand forward.

"No, not today, but maybe tomorrow," I said, grimacing with anger.

"Yeah, yeah," she said, dismissively, "you no choke today, you no choke tomorrow either."

I sat at the chipped white metal kitchen table, dunking a slice of toasted Italian bread into a bowl of warm milk spiced with coffee, when the front door opened. My mother walked into the small foyer, past the sour smelling dumbwaiter, holding a shopping bag in each hand.

"You get everything we need for dinner tonight?" *nonna* asked.

"I got everything HE needs for dinner tonight," my mother replied irritably. "I got a piece of corned beef, a head of cabbage, potatoes, and a quart of beer. He's Irish, not Italian, and he's entitled to his kind of meal after almost two years away in the army."

"Madonna, we gonna eat corna beef and *cavolo* and drink beer tonight," she groaned.

The corned beef sat on the stove in a pot of tepid greasy water covered with limp cabbage leaves. The thick summer day turned to dusk and the street lights went on. The previous night, during a blackout, an eerie siren followed by the shrill pitch of the air raid warden's warning whistle to douse the light coming from *nonna*'s Necchi sewing machine evoked a sharp expletive from her.

"Ah *vaffanculu*," she shouted through the open window.

"Ah *vaffanculu tu*," Armando shouted back, "*astuta la luci subbitu*, shut the light immediately Mary," he commanded.

"*Nonna*, you said a bad thing," I reproached her, waving a finger.

"But how this little one know what I say?" *Nonna* asked, laughing, turning to my mother.

"He knows because he listens and absorbs, my mother had responded, smiling proudly.

"Marie," *Nonna* said in Sicilian, as she paced the floor, looking out the window, "sit down and try to relax. Maybe the plane was late, or maybe he stopped off at his parents' house."

"Stopped at his parents' house when his wife and son are waiting for him? Maybe, but I'd be more likely to find him at that Irish saloon in Sunnyside with those bum friends of his," she responded sourly.

The rasping door buzzer startled us and my mother hurried past me, scattering my collection of toy soldiers and trucks assembled on the linoleum floor battlefield. I looked to the foyer and saw two figures embracing in the shadows, followed by an apology;

"Sorry....plane delayed over LaGuardia airport....had to go to Astoria to pick the car up..."

My recollection from the kitchen floor was the appearance of a pair of spit-shined boots bearing a tall warrior worthy of Homer. I looked up and large, strange hands reached under my arms, raising me to rough face stubble and the scent of witch hazel and tobacco.

"Hello boy, hello son," he said, his voice quivering. "I guess you don't remember me, but I'm your Da."

I nodded in reply and pointed to the photo on the living room table next to the pair of bronze baby shoes, and said, "You're the man in the army suit in the picture with me and my mom," I said proudly.

"Yes, the man in the army suit," he confirmed, smiling.

"You get skinny, Artur," *nonna* said moving toward him, extending both hands and offering her cheek.

"Yeah, well," my father replied, "Army grub isn't very good, especially out in the field."

'In the field,' as I would come to learn was the invasion and capture of Sicily by the American 7th Army, to which my father was assigned. A few days later the force crossed the Strait of Messina and took Naples on the mainland on September 9th, 1943.

"ITALY SURRENDERS, WILL RESIST GERMANS, the headline in the New York Times screamed to the relief and joy of Italian-Americans, whose patriotism and allegiance was never questioned. More than 10 million Italian-Americans served their country proudly during the war.

With victory in the Mediterranean campaign virtually assured as the 8th Army drove the Germans north up the peninsula, my father's unit had been given a five day pass before being deployed to the pacific to join MacArthur's offensive, fulfilling the great man's promise to return to the Philippines and liberate the captured survivors of the Bataan death march.

"I'm not looking forward to this," I heard my father comment to my mother. "These Japs are very mean and treacherous and we know what they do to prisoners of war."

. . .

It was past nine o'clock when my parents tucked me to bed. My new-found sense of security was quickly shattered when I heard the front door close and the apartment became still and dark.

"Ma, ma," I cried out anxiously.

"It's ok. No worry. Your mamma and papa justa go for a walk. They be back soon," *Nonna* assured me from her bed. "Go sleepa now, Ruggero." But they didn't come back that night. I fell asleep to the familiar, comforting sound of the IRT train rattling up Roosevelt Avenue in the distance.

The next morning dark clouds released a brief but welcome shower which cleared the sultry summer air and cooled the concrete on the streets. I walked past the unslept-in sofa bed in the alcove into the kitchen where my parents sat wordlessly on wooden chairs at opposite ends of the table, drinking coffee. My father looked at me, patted his knee, then hoisted me to his lap and kissed the top of my head. My mother dabbed her eyes with a Kleenex and said, "Your dad wants to take you to a baseball game at Yankee Stadium today, Ruggero."

"Oh, wow," I exclaimed as my eyes widened and my jaw dropped, "a baseball game. You comin too ma?"

"No, no," she replied, "I have to work today, "she said turning away."

"But...but," I began anxiously.

"It's ok, you go with your father," she directed, turning and looking at him with heavy eyes, "it's important that your father take you to a baseball game today."

It's been said that a man remembers three milestones in his life with absolute certainty and clarity: his first sloppy kiss in the balcony of some movie theatre, while clumsily groping inside Mary Margaret's blouse and his little man throbbing as his fingers find soft flesh, getting his first car, and attending his first baseball game.

My father and I walked through a short, dark tunnel which suddenly gave way to a burst of sunlight and an improbable patch of manicured green in the middle of the Bronx. The smell of Ballantine beer frothing over the top of the Harry M. Stevens cardboard container mixed with the scent of boiled hot dogs floating in steaming grey water served from a tin in a wicker basket hanging by a leather strap from the vendor's neck. It was

a visceral sensation, simple in its subtle elegance, but the memory stays with me. I don't think I've ever enjoyed a hot dog that much. It's true, the good stuff doesn't quit.

Later that week, we said our tearful goodbyes to my father in the great echoing cavern of polished marble and stone on Forty Third Street and Lexington Avenue. The place was thick with clouds of cigarette smoke made yellow by the slanting rays of the sun piercing the arched windows of the great hall. An invisible man blared over the public address system:

5:15 arriving from Baltimore at gate four.

5:55 departing for Chicago at gate seven.

Young men straining for courage serenaded their wives and girl friends with the popular Andrew Sisters recording of, "Don't Sit Under the Apple Tree, with anyone else but me." Then woosh, he was gone.

The dreaded anticipated invasion of the Japanese mainland came to an abrupt end on August 7th, 1945 when the Enola Gay dropped the first Atomic bomb on the city of Hiroshima. About a week later, Nagasaki suffered the same fate, ending the war in the Pacific and reducing the cities to smoldering sulphur and toxic ash. Within four years, the allies, led by America's fighting forces and overwhelming industrial might prevailed, rising like the phoenix, defeating two world-class powers on three continents.

My father returned on a frigid winter day with hard-blowing snow, in December, 1945. The breech in the marriage which began when he left in 1942 and widened in 1943 during his leave had ruptured.

The brief attempt at reconciliation failed and degenerated into a cycle of vituperative arguments marked by ugly accusations of mutual infidelity, inspired by alcohol and the corrosive effects war and separation can have on an already fragile marriage.

It was a nightly occurrence, which drove me cowering to my bed, burying my head, weeping under the pillow. I had lost and then regained a father. Now I feared I was losing both of them. I felt abandoned and frightened until one night from the bedroom I heard *nonna* railing at them.

"This gonna end, and it gonna end now. Your son, he cry himself to sleep every night and it break my heart. I no stand for it any more," she said firmly.

"Artur, you gotta go stay wit your parents in their new house in Hollis," I heard *nonna* order my father. "Maybe if you have a separation you can work things out. If not, then at least make a good divorce because thisa marriage isa no good, and I no let either of you punish my grandson anymore. An datsa dat, *basta*."

Before leaving the next day, my father tried to explain things to me but I don't remember anything he said.

His departure left my mother relieved, and me confused and ambivalent.

CHAPTER 53

My mother kept her promise to my grandparents, and I spent weekends with them and my father, who was rarely home, in their newly purchased house in Hollis Queens, a pleasant, tree-lined community of tidy homes with well-maintained front yards and tidy people. My playmates had unfamiliar-sounding surnames like 'Whalen, Brownley and Fletcher.'

Hollis was only about a half hour east of Corona, but it was a world away in every other respect. It smacked of Thornton Wilder, and it was like going to a quiet, bucolic Midwest town from busy, chaotic Corona where laundry hung in alleys between buildings and the streets echoed with mothers calling for their children from apartment windows:

"Angelo, ya lousy kid, get up here now before ya father gets home and gives ya a beatin."

On hot summer nights the lights in Hollis went out as soon as The Jack Benny Show ended on radio. But the streets in Corona were alive and crowded with parents walking with their children as they sucked the life out of pleated cups of lemon ice from the Lemon Ice King of Corona on 108th Street. Italian children never seemed to go to bed before 11 p.m. during the summer months.

As Hollis folk slept soundly in their beds, residents of Corona sat on stoops or kitchen chairs in front of their apartments well into the night listening to Mel Allen call the Yankee game over WINS radio or sharing juicy gossip about the fireman's widow, who was suspected of having an affair with Dimitri, the one-legged war hero, who lived alone on the fourth floor of our building.

Friday night was family poker night and *nonna*, my aunts and their husbands gathered around Mamma Caiozzo's large kitchen table playing ten and twenty cent limit poker, intent on beating each other out of eight or ten dollars.

My cousin Mary Ann and I would slip into one of the bedrooms, where I conducted my weekly physical examination on her, playing doctor.

The poker game began promptly at seven o'clock, an oddity since my family was not noted for punctuality. It was suspended at 9:30 when Mamma Caiozzo took two trays of thick, bubbling pizza from the oven. The savory aroma of basil, garlic and tomatoes wafted down the hallway and seeped under the space of the bedroom door. I quickly concluded my physical examination of Mary Ann, affirmed that she was in fine health, and we raced down the hallway into the kitchen.

"Ah look who comes now!" Mamma Caiozzo exclaimed. "Where you two been? What you been doing?" she asked suspiciously, chopping her right hand into her left palm.

"We were, uh, we were...," I began.

"We were in the parlor playing rock, paper, scissors," Mary Ann coolly interrupted.

"Rock, paper...what is this rock, paper...? Mamma Caiozzo asked.

"It's a game, just a game, Mamma Caiozzo" Mary Ann answered. "You wouldn't understand. Can we have some pizza now?" she asked impatiently.

I glanced at her father, my uncle, Giacomo, glowering at me and read his lips.

"Rock, paper, scissor, my ass," he mouthed quietly.

The rivalry among the sisters ceased temporarily as they devoured the pizza and washed it down with potent home made red wine, provided by Carlo the janitor at two dollars a gallon, and engaged in neighborhood gossip.

"So, you hear about the fireman's widow, Mirabella, who's having a little thing with one-leg Dimitri, the *Albanesi* from the fourth floor?" *nonna* introduced.

"Everyone knows about that, Mary," Grazia replied. "You got nothing new to report?" she asked, prompting a round of laughter.

"*Basta*, enough!" Mamma Caiozzo commanded exasperated and reproachful. "Why must you make the lives of two lonely, suffering people the source of your entertainment? The woman cared for her husband for a year as he battled cancer," she whispered, cupping her hand to her mouth. And Dimitri lost his leg at Anzio helping to liberate our people from German oppression. Why can't you talk about the good these people have done? You sound like the busybody *chiacchieruni* who sit in the piazza in Castellammare every day, gossiping and taking pleasure in other peoples' sorrow." *Nonna* and Grazia fell silent and dropped their heads to their chests in embarrassment.

When the game resumed, *nonna* launched into her predictably successful run, winning one pot after another, irritating the other players with her trademark elbow length gloves and annoying challenge, "Make it another," as she daintily dropped ten or twenty cents to raise. She could read a "tell," a giveaway, from the facial or body language of her opponents. She knew when to raise, bluff or fold her hand.

In an effort to minimize the losses of her other daughters, Mamma Caiozzo would stand behind *nonna*, reading her hand and sending signals to the other players. *Nonna*, sensing her mother's presence behind her was vexed, and three or four times a night would turn about abruptly.

"Mamma, again? For the love of Madonna, go stand behind someone else and stop trying to protect my sisters by giving my hand away."

"What? What are you talking about? I'm just standing here," Mamma

Caiozzo replied indignantly, shrugging her shoulders innocently. "*Ma tu sì pazza*, but you're crazy," she added, walking away insulted as my aunts covered their grins with their hands.

Mamma Caiozzo was the only person in the room guaranteed to put money in her pocket that night. After the players anteed up, she boldly removed twenty five cents from each pot, and could realize four or five dollars by the end of the night.

"You know, mamma, you're no better than Spade the bookie." *Nonna* commented. "I lose, you take something. I win, you still take something."

"Ah, you don't like it?" Mamma Caiozzo replied caustically. "Then go to the Sons of Italy hall and play with them and Spade, if they let you in the game." *Nonna* blushed as the others burst into laughter.

Rico Spada, or 'Spade,' as he was known in the neighborhood, was straight out of central casting with his wide-brim fedora, padded-shouldered, pin-striped suit and glossy black pointed shoes. Every other day he had his hair trimmed, nose and ear bristles clipped and nails manicured at Tony's Barber Shop. He then walked across the street, entered Linden Park and sat on the third bench, alongside the still, murky green water of the pond infested with flying vermin, collecting bets lost the previous day on the daily number or slow horses from Jamaica or Belmont racetracks. *Nonna*, however, was a thorn in his side. She collected as often as not, and it wasn't all dumb luck. She never played the daily number; "thatsa for zhadrools," she would say. She knew how to bet, and handicapped a horse from information found in the Daily Telegraph newspaper, the successful horse player's bible. She knew which horse was dropping in class, and which long shot maiden was capable of a come from behind stretch run at the eighth pole, devouring the field. She also paid attention to the horse's breeding.

"Da mamma an da papa isa very import," she instructed me. And she didn't gamble every day, limiting herself to three or four races a week.

Early one spring day, *nonna* bribed me with the promise of a fifty cent piece if I accompanied her to the park to collect eighteen dollars and change from her previous day's winnings.

"You gotta come wit me, Ruggero, because I no wanna run into da cafone, Gregorio. He always give me a big hug and try to kiss me."

We approached Spade sitting on the bench casually blowing smoke rings and calmly listening to Gregorio's rambling explanation as to why he couldn't settle his debt that day. It was clear the man was drunk.

"Ya see, Spade, my friend, I got a temporary case of the shorts. In fact, I owe so much money out, I don't know who to pay first. So, what I do, what I do is, I write all my creditors' names on a piece of paper and put them into a hat. And whosoever name I pull out first, dats da guy I pay dat day."

"Yeah, well," Spade replied slowly with menacing eyes, "that's too bad. But just make sure tomorrow you pull my name out of your hat first, or I'll come looking for ya. And when I find ya....I'm gonna pull your asshole over your ears."

"Tanks, Spade, tanks, tomorrow for sure. I swear on my granddaughter's eyes," he said stumbling backward out of the park.

Spade then turned to us and greeted *nonna* graciously.

"*Bon giornu, signura*. Even though you're a real stone in my shoe, it's always nice to see you again," he said peeling off a ten, a five and four singles, handing *nonna* nineteen dollars.

"Give the change to your body guard here," he joked, looking at me and laughing.

"Yeah, I gonna do dat," *nonna* replied. "An one way or other, I see you again in a couple day," she added.

"Yeah, right, and I hope next time it's 'the other,'" he responded ruefully.

When the bad weather came, Spade conducted business from the last booth of the Plaza Sweet Shop, a convenience for which he paid Abbe and Benny, the owners, forty dollars a month. My mother was a waitress at the busy shop, a five minute walk from the apartment and P.S. 19 where I attended grammar school. I ate my lunch there free of cost, under the vigilant, resentful eyes of Abbe who I heard Spade describe as "so cheap, if it cost him a nickel to shit, he'd vomit," and among a cast of characters which included mob lawyers, "The Turk," who stole more cars in a week than Luby Chevrolet had in his showroom on Queens Boulevard, and Crazy Doc Estratto, the dentist. Estratto had apparently been absent the day they taught tooth filling and reclamation at dental school, and yanked two perfectly salvageable teeth of mine before my mother realized he was a quack and stiffed him for the balance due.

"Hey, Marie," he came in bellowing one day at the height of the lunch rush, "When you gonna take care of the bill? It's been a month now. How much longer do I have to wait?"

My mother turned to him slowly with a tray of sandwiches and coffee and coolly replied, "That depends."

"That depends? Depends on what" he demanded, incredulously.

"It depends on when Christ arrives with the Twelve Apostles and sits down for another Last Supper, you *strunzu*," my mother snapped.

The luncheonette erupted in a round of laughter and a chorus of, "Bravos" as Estratto slithered out and never returned. I saw him eating lunch at the Bickford's Cafeteria across the street and, within six months, a large sign on the window of his office read, "For Rent."

I returned to the luncheonette every day at 3:00 to pick up the key to the apartment and enjoy a soda or sundae in Abbe's and Benny's absence. They were across the street at the Queens County Savings Bank depositing the day's receipts and verifying their balance. When they returned and closed the luncheonette at three thirty, my mother went next door to the Loweeze Plaza theatre to open the candy concession they owned. They gave her an extra $1.00 a day to man the counter until the night lady came on at 5:00.

Nonna and I never paid the 25 cent admission to see a movie or the five or ten cents for a Hershey bar or an Almond Joy. We sat in the dark stuffing ourselves, watching the classic film noir and some real dumb B movies with Doris Day or the ever whining Ann Blyth or Teresa Wright, or the snarling Dana Andrews. *Nonna* was particularly interested in the occasional Italian movie, films like *La Strada* and *Bicycle Thief* or films which featured Italian actors like Sinatra and Borgnine in *From Here to Eternity*, or movies with Italian themes like *The Black Hand* with Gene Kelly. She also enjoyed the films of Bogart and Bacall. One day, she pronounced, authoritatively that she had read in the Italian newspaper, *Il Progresso Italiano-Americano*, that Gene Kelly was, in fact Italian, as were Bogart and Bacall who had changed their names from Bogarto and Bacausa.

. . .

The Plaza Sweet Shop did a brisk business selling boxes of Russell Stover or Fanny Farmer candy, around the holidays. The stocked glass showcase and the shelves behind it always sold out.

One day my mother and I overheard the avaricious Abbe arguing with his partner.

"I tell ya, Benny, that nogoodnik, goy dago gangster is in here every day, collecting money and locking up the end booth in the back. I'm gonna tell him he has to give us $10.00 more a month."

"Let it go, Abbe," Benny pleaded. "Forty dollars a month is enough. Besides," Benny continued, "Spade brings customers in. After they do business, they usually have at least a cup of coffee and a piece of pie." The feisty Abbe was not persuaded and confronted Spade with his demands.

Spade listened quietly, shrugged his shoulders and replied, "Ten dollars more a month? Yeah, sure Abbe, if that'll make ya happy, you got it."

"Ya see?" Abbe said proudly, returning to his partner, "ya stand up strong to these hoods and they back down."

"Yeah, well we'll see," Benny replied crossing his arms over his chest, "we'll see. I don't trust that guy."

A week before Valentine's day, the door to the luncheonette swung open at 3:05 and Spade sauntered in followed by four gorillas carrying large cardboard boxes. My mother was spritzing the head of my egg cream to froth when I saw her jaw drop and her eyes widen as round as a harvest moon. I started to swing the stool around as my mother grabbed at my shoulder over the counter and tried to restrain me. Spade's eyebrows arched and his lips curled into his cheek in a sinister, crooked smile as he placed a forefinger over his mouth.

"In the back," my mother commanded me, jerking her head to the side. Spade and the four gorillas cleaned the showcase out and emptied the shelves in less than five minutes. He then walked to the rear where my mother and I sat huddled in a booth, dropped a five dollar bill on the table and stuffed a single in my peacoat pocket.

"You didn't see nuttin, did ya kid?" he asked.

"No, he didn't see anything and neither did I," my mother protectively intervened, "and we don't want your lousy six bucks." Spade smiled and picked the five off the table.

"You're a tough, smart cookie, Marie, ya bargain hard," he said. "But you're right, six bucks ain't nearly enough" he said, throwing ten dollars down, as he turned and walked away.

"Hey, hey Spade!" my mother shouted after him, waving the ten dollars. Spade just chuckled and kept on walking.

"Shit, damnit!" my mother exclaimed.

"Ma," I said trying to console her, "you didn't do nuttin wrong. And besides, ten bucks is ten bucks."

The next day when my mother came home she told *nonna* and me about the comic spectacle she witnessed at the shop.

"So, so," my mother began between heaving laughs, "the three of them are sitting in the rear booth and I hear Benny say, 'Yes, yes, of course, Spade, thirty dollars a month is more than fair.'

He then goes on to kiss Spade's *culo* and says, 'and breakfast is always on the house.'

"Then, then," my mother continued, "Spade says to Benny," 'Breakfast? Only Breakfast?'"

"And Benny, sweating like a wet dish cloth says, 'Lunch, of course lunch too, Spade,' and Abbe," my mother adds, guffawing and holding her sides, "lets go with a belch and a fart as loud as a fog horn."

Nonna grinned and remarked composed, "Ah, dis no surprise to me. Even da Judisha no can put sometin over on a *Sicilianu*."

CHAPTER 54

By the time I reached my 10th birthday in 1949, *nonna* had given up trying to force the raw egg in orange juice down my throat. At almost five feet tall, I was two inches taller than her and she could no longer physically control me.

However, she remained adamant about the nutritional value of eggs and three or four times a week made a cheese *frittata* for breakfast. The savory aroma greeted me as I awoke, and I was drawn to the kitchen like one of the Pied Pipers followers to sit quietly at the table, fork in hand. I wolfed down the fluffy, lightly-browned omelet as *nonna* sat opposite me, nodding her head and grinning.

The mid-summer sun was already making the air thick and the black asphalt in the street was softening. The day promised to be a scorcher.

Back in my room I sat on the edge of the bed lacing my black ankle-length Keds sneakers when *nonna* came in with a message from my mother.

"Your mamma say no run around today and make sweat." I wrinkled my nose and turned my lip up and scowled.

"No makea dat face to me," *nonna* chided. "You see what happen to poor Greek boy, Nicodemis, who live across street. He is now in *ospitali*, inside a machine because he no can breathe." I had seen pitiful images in Movietone News at the Loweze Theatre of young children suffering in hospitals and the message resonated.

Everyone was afraid of infantile paralysis, the crippling disease which usually struck young children or adolescents. It was the Black Plaque of the 40's and 50's and had parents rushing to the doctor whenever their children sneezed or complained of stiffness in the joints or fatigue. Activities were limited and attendance in public arenas where crowds gathered declined. I lived in the land of, "No!". "No, you can't go to the movies and sit in a crowded, air conditioned place, no you can't go swimming in the pool at the Aquacade in Flushing Meadow Park, don't drink from any water fountains, and I better not catch you running around raising sweat," my mother warned. So we played a game that required very little running, just fast pitching against a brick wall in the school yard with a painted strike zone box. Four guys chipped in a nickel apiece to buy the ham-pink spauldeen at Pete's candy store. It was a twenty cent rubber wonder which, when bounced off the concrete, rocketed up, all the way to Mrs. Tucci's second floor window. Danny provided the bat for the game, a good, thick mop handle borrowed from his mother's kitchen closet.

Before leaving the apartment I asked *nonna* for twenty cents.

"What for?" she asked.

"It's my turn to buy the ball," I lied. The remaining 15 cents was reserved for the after game thirst quencher of Mission Orange Soda. When we'd finished playing, it was waiting rock-sunk at the bottom of Pete's cooler under a large cube of ice floating in frigid water. I struggled to find the elusive bottle as my arm froze to my shoulder. When I managed to bring it up, we sat against a brick wall, in the shade of Pete's awning, knees to our chest, chugalugging the carbonated orange syrup, in serious discussion about by how many games it would take the Yankees to win the pennant, and shuddering over rumors that DiMaggio was considering retiring.

"Shit," Danny queried, "what are we gonna have out there if he goes? Some God damn blond kid from Oklahoma?"

"Hey, dat blond kid is a fuckin powerhouse. He's been hammerin tape-measure home runs down dare in da minors all summer," Richie pointed out.

"Ah fuck him an his tape-measure home runs," Danny replied disgusted.

"Well," Sonny tried to console Danny, "at least us dagos still got Berra an' Rizzuto."

At about 12:30 I walked down 41st Avenue to the Plaza Sweet Shop for my lunch. Abbe greeted me with his usual scowl and I gave him the finger pressed to my chest as I passed him and sat with the lawyers, Joe Trafficante and Andrew Chaffe. Chaffe was my aunt Giovanna's husband.

My mother came over a couple of minutes later with a tuna and tomato sandwich.

"Ah ma," I complained, "I wanted a burger."

"It's too hot for a burger," she said sternly, then leaned forward and whispered, "besides, the chop meat's all brown."

Trafficante and Chaffe were debating as to which Yankee pitcher held the record for single season victories.

"I'm tellin ya, it was Lefty Gomez," Trafficante insisted.

"Naw, naw, it wasn't Lefty Gomez," Chaffe disagreed, waving his arm.

"Chesboro," I announced without looking up between mouthfuls of tuna fish.

"What?" they asked in unison turning toward me.

"Yeah," I repeated, Chesboro, Jack Chesboro. He won 41 games in 1906 or something when the Yankees weren't the Yankees. They were called 'The Highlanders' then." They looked at each other astonished, then at me, then at my mother who had just put a glass of cold lemonade on the table.

"He's probably right," my mother said grinning proudly. "I just wish he knew as much American history as he does baseball history."

I finished my lunch quickly and went to the side of the soda fountain, reached into the bowl on the shelf where my mother kept her tips, and took a quarter out.

"See ya later, ma," I waved.

"Yeah, and no running, ya hear," my mother called after me. As I passed the candy counter on the left, I reached over and grabbed a Hershey bar, knowing Abbe was eye-balling me. I laughed when I got outside and could almost smell Abbe's ass burning.

I got back to the neighborhood around one o'clock and saw the guys standing under a tree, flipping, trading or selling baseball cards, but there was one card which engendered panting excitement and had nothing to do with baseball. It appealed more to the prurient awakening of pre-adolescent boys whose stirring below the waist rivaled their interest in the sports pages of The Daily News. It never made its way to the flipping contest and was excluded from trade, and not for sale, enjoying the same celebrity as the rare Joe DiMaggio card which Junior Caruso was rumored to have in his possession.

Vito Caputo had stolen the Queen of Hearts from his older brother's "French" playing card deck, a scandalous black and white photo of a melancholic, well-worn, naked woman with loins spread, revealing a bush of curly black hair. The enterprising Vito made it available for the usurious assessment of one dollar for a 24 hour period, inducing two guys to kick in fifty cents each, enjoying twelve hours of the wanton lady's company.

"I better not see any scum on dat dare picture," he warned.

"Bless me, Father, for I have sinned... I masturbated six times."

"My son, you masturbated six times since your last confession?"

"Uh...no, no, not exactly, Father. I masturbated six times since last night."

Vito Caputo went on to enjoy a life of prosperity derived from the proceeds of the three porno establishments he owned in and around 42nd Street near Hubert's Flea Museum. He was last seen pitching salacious reproductions of Etruscan art somewhere in the Los Angeles area.

. . .

"You gonna play or what?" Danny shouted as I passed.

"Yeah, yeah, I gotta get my cards first, don't I?" I answered.

As I entered the apartment my nose was assaulted by the daily emission of potent Clorox fumes. *Nonna* was in the bathroom singing an aria from *Madame Butterfly* and scrubbing the sink and toilet with a coarse brush. A wet mop was at her side. She spent half the day in the bathroom attending to her personal needs and the other half cleaning it.

"For Chrissake, *nonna*!" I complained, "will you never stop with this cleaning and scrubbing crap?"

"Hey, hey, watcha da mouth," she responded. "Veddy import to clean da batharoom, an kitchen too, especially in summer. A lot of germs dat make disease around."

"Shit," I mumbled, shaking my head and pinching my nose as I walked into the bedroom and went to the closet to get my stash of cards.

As I dragged the shoebox out with my cards meticulously categorized and neatly bound with rubber bands, I glanced up to the top shelf and, for the first time, noticed a beaten wood box tucked in the corner. As I reached for it, I heard *nonna* bark behind me.

"*No, non tuccari,* no touch dat."

"What is it, *nonna*?" I asked, turning around, startled.

"No thinga, itsa no you businessa," she said nervously, her voice rising.

"Ok, ok, I'm sorry. I didn't know my *nonna* was such a mysterious person," I protested.

"Ah," she said softening, "itsa justa sometin I take wit me when da family leave Castellammare many year ago, somethinga, how you say, 'keepasake'?" as her eyes moistened and her voice trailed off.

The curiosity stayed with me as I left the apartment and walked down the stairs. I giggled, wondering, what could my little old *nonna* have in that box she was so protective of?

By late afternoon, all the cards and pennies available for the taking had been claimed and the winners walked into the lot next to the apartment, overgrown with struggling dry trees and tall, thirsty weeds. The ground was hard and hot.

We found what we were looking for, five guys on line each clutching a dime, waiting their turn to catch a thirty second look at Natale Chicora's ass. We took our place and in less than two minutes we were gaping at Natale, bent at the waist, slowly removing her pink panties below her knees, exposing two fleshy mounds separated by a crack and counting, "One Mississippi, two Mississippi..." By the time she got to "twelve Mississippi," a slight bulge appeared below my waist and I heard *nonna* call from the apartment window, "Ruggero, Ruggero, *veni ccà*." Shit! She's gotta call me now? I grumbled, vainly trying to demote the bulge with my hand.

I stood under the window looking up as *nonna* dropped a quarter wrapped in tissue.

"Go now to Mangiapane an takea da *pani*. An no chew on da end," she warned, as I circled to catch the tissue floating and fluttering like a desperate butterfly trying to elude its captor. Great name for a bakery I thought as I made my way to Mangiapane's on National Avenue; the translation is, "eat bread."

I ignored *nonna*'s warning and chewed one end of the warm, crusty bread, reversed the loaf, and put it back in the brown paper bag. My mother was home by 5:15, just as the water for the spaghetti started boiling and the clams surrendered to the garlic, red pepper flakes and parsley, dissolving in the hot olive oil. A large bowl of arugula, quartered tomatoes and black olives dressed with lemon and olive oil sat in the middle of the table alongside a bottle of chilled white, Sicilian wine, and a basket of bread.

"But why you eat so fast?" *nonna* reproved as I twirled the last of the spaghetti around my fork and swiped a piece of bread across my bowl.

"Because it tastes so good, *li megghiu*, the best," I replied, raising from my chair, kissing her cheek, and turning to the door.

"*Aspetta!*" she ordered, grabbing my wrist. "First you go into da bathroom, washa da face an brusha da teeth."

"Ah, *nonna*," I whined, "what's with you and this washing thing?"

"Do as *nonna* says," my mother agreed. "The scent of garlic belongs in the sauce, not on your breath."

CHAPTER 55

I was down the stairs faster than Jackie Robinson sprinting from first to third base on a single. I hated Jackie Robinson. I also hated Duke Snider, Pee Wee Reese and Carl Furillo. As a Yankee fan, like all neighborhood guys, I was obliged to hate those pretenders from Brooklyn. I think there were only two Dodger fans in the whole school, the Liss brothers, Jerome and Phillip, and they were unmercifully tormented. But when Walter O'Malley, the most despised man in Brooklyn, moved his team to California in 1957, we all felt bad; our best-worst enemy was gone and we missed the Yankee-Dodger rivalry and agreed with the Liss brothers that the scrappy Dodgers belonged to Brooklyn's mean streets, not mellow southern California.

In the evening the guys slowly emerged from their apartment buildings for the nightly on the bounce, street stickball game. The blistering heat of the late summer day had cooled along with our parents' fears that infantile paralysis would be brought on by sweating as we ran the bases or chased a three sewer shot up the street.

The ritual of choosing up sides, 'once, twice, three, shoot,' began and, as usual, being the smallest and youngest with limited skills, I was the last selected, to the chagrin of the team stuck with me. Junior tossed a thick piece of white chauk and ordered me to mark the batters' box on either side of the manhole cover, then draw the bases. Occasionally a car was parked where first or third base belonged, in which case the rear fender of a '47 Plymouth or Ford served the purpose. I was then banished to right field where the action was always limited, and where I would do the least damage.

Fathers, uncles and younger siblings took their places on the stoops or hung out windows to watch the game. *Nonna* was one of the regulars. Surrounded by tall apartment houses, I fantasized I was in Yankee Stadium's great canyon with spectators in the grandstand. I provided my own soundtrack, exhaling forcefully, mimicking the roar of the crowd, and emulating the, 'Voice of the Yankees,' Mel Allen, calling the game, "Going, going, gone. How about that? A Ballantine blast."

Little Teresa was a nightly spectator. Not that she had any interest in stickball, but she knew that two or three times during the game, the ball would find its way down one of the sewers.

"Lott!" one of the guys would call. 'Lott' was an acronym for, 'Little One Time Teresa' because of her uncanny ability to rescue the ball from its' slimy, grey, watery grave with one attempt.

She rose from her place on the curb and came forward wordlessly like the stoney faced hired killer in a western movie, pulling rubber gloves over her small hands, and trailing a ten foot long piece of wire, looped at the end, behind her. With the crowd hovering, she squatted in front of the opening, peered into the dark, smelly abyss of the sewer, and lowered the wire. The loop gently sank under the ball and cradled it as she slowly pulled the wire up with the skill and patience of the old fisherman, Santiago. She reached into the opening and clasped the ball, prompting a burst of applause. She then sprayed it with Clorox, wiped it clean, and held it close to her body with her right hand, and extended the left with her palm up to receive the nickel she had earned. Her face was impassive, and she remained silent. For a long time we thought she was mute until, once, one of the guys began teasing her, thrusting his hand forward with the nickel, then pulling it back.

"Gimme the nickel, asshole, or, after I kick ya between the legs, you'll be lookin for three balls in the sewer," she said, unblinking.

Teresa was able to continue to satisfy her insatiable craving for creamsicles without further incident.

The next day, Saturday, *nonna* reminded me of my weekly charge to pick up two pints of ice, one lemon and one chocolate, from the Lemon Ice King on Corona Avenue and deliver them to Mamma Caiozzo.

I had just settled down to read Edgar Allan Poe's "The Pit and the Pendulum" in Classic Comics, an issue I got from one of the Liss brothers in a trade for three baseball cards of obscure Dodger players.

"Come on, get up, *subbitu*, immediately," *nonna* ordered, putting two quarters in my hand. "You know how Mamma Caiozzo like to havea da lemon ice in da afternoon."

I grumbled as I rolled the comic book up and stuck it in the back pocket of my dungarees, walked up Corona Avenue, bought the ice and returned on the run to Mamma Caiozzo's apartment.

"Ah, you a good boy, Ruggero," she said smiling, pinching my cheek and kissing my forehead. "You hungry?" she asked scooping some ice into a cup for herself and placing the rest in the freezer of the large GE refrigerator her daughters bought her for Christmas.

"Yeah!" I exclaimed, looking up from the comic. "Ya got any of that pizza left over from last night?" I asked.

"Yes, I gotta da pizza from last night," she replied, taking a large beefsteak tomato, fennel, a cucumber and black olives from the refrigerator, and slicing them into a bowl.

"Hey," I said, disappointed. "I wanted pizza, Mamma Caiozzo."

"I hear what you say, Ruggero, but itsa too *caldo*, too hot for da pizza," she said placing the bowl of dressed salad on the table with a hunk of bread.

Jeez, I decided, they all think alike, recalling my mother's comment about hamburgers and hot days.

"So," Mamma Caiozzo asked pointing, "whata you read dare, Micky Mouse or Donald Duck?"

"No," I replied irritably, feeling insulted, "it's 'The Pit and the Pendulum' by a guy named Edgar Allan Poe."

"Yeah, I know dat name," she said. "He also write, how you say? *La caduta della casa di Usher*, The Fall of the House of Usher.'"

My mouth dropped in surprise as I shrugged my shoulders and quietly admitted, "I don't know that one, Mamma Caiozzo."

"Whata you think," she asked smiling, "because I no speaka good inglese, I am illiterate? When I wasa young girl in Castellammare, my brother, Antonio, a writer, a *professore*, may he rest in peace," she paused blessing herself, "bring me many books by English an American writer; Dickens, Austen, Hawthorne an Poe. An for eighteen year, I work in a library. You never see my *collezione* of books in da salon?" she asked, proudly.

"No," I answered, "I never noticed." I was too busy hustling my cousin, Mary Ann, past the large glass bookcase into my examination room.

Before leaving the apartment I walked into the salon and stood in front of the bookcase, surprised by the number of works it contained. I ran my fingers across the titles, neatly alphabetically arranged according to the name of the author. My Italian was limited but, when I came to the letter, "F", I recognized, *The Great Gatsby*, from a movie I had seen with Alan Ladd. Next to it under, "H" was another familiar title, *A Farewell to Arms*, also a film, starring Gary Cooper.

The following week when I delivered the ices to Mamma Caiozzo, an anthology of Poe's works and an abridged edition of Dickens', *A Tale of Two Cities,* sat on the kitchen table, along with a library card.

"What's this?" I asked.

"Those comic books you read wit da pictures is a good start. But you gotta read da real book an, by an by, I promise, you gonna learn more an enjoy more da stories."

...

The autumn of 1949 brought major changes in my life. My father married a divorcee with two daughters, fathered two sons and disappeared into the barren fields turned tract housing developments on Long Island. My mother began keeping steady company with Guido Lanzini, a sales representative for Trans World Airlines, who picked her up every Friday and Saturday night in his emerald green Chrysler sedan with tan leather seats to the hoots and salacious remarks from the neighborhood big guys hanging out under the street light. I got my ass kicked regularly defending my mother's honor.

Early one Friday evening as my mother was tweezing her eyebrows and applying mascara in preparation for her date, *nonna* announced she had two orchestra tickets to Puccini's *La Boheme* at the Metropolitan Opera the following night.

"Yeah? So?" I inquired.

"So," *nonna* responded, "tomorrow you an me, we gonna spend da day in New Yorka, havea nice dinner in Angelo's *ristorante* where I use to work, an go to da opera."

"What?" I exploded throwing myself about, "I'm not going to any opera. I'd rather have crazy Doc Estratto yank another tooth from my mouth."

"You're going," my mother commanded, poking her head out of the bathroom, "a little culture won't kill you."

When I awoke Saturday morning, my twenty five dollar Robert Hall wardrobe, a blue jacket and two pair of slacks, one blue, one grey, hung on the doorknob with a starched white shirt and solid blue tie. Black Tom McCann loafers were parked on the floor. I got out of bed and stumbled into the kitchen where my mother and *nonna* sat drinking coffee, plotting the ruination of my day, and debating which outfit I should wear.

My mother looked at me, smiled and said, "*Nonna* and I were just talking about which pair of slacks you should wear tonight. Whata you think?" she asked.

"Whata I think?" I answered, "I think I shouldn't be thinking about which pair of dumb slacks I should be wearing, going to some dumb opera listening to a fat lady sing who makes aunt Stella look like Heddy LaMar."

"Fine! Then you'll wear the blue slacks with the blue jacket. A solid dark outfit looks much better when attending the opera," my mother resolved.

Like I give a shit, I thought. I left the kitchen and settled on the couch with my book, eager to join the heroic Sydney Carton on his way to the guillotine.

"It is a far, far better thing that I do, than I have ever done; It is a far, far better rest that I go to, then I have ever known."

As usual, *nonna* spent half the morning in the bathroom before I could get in and shower. My pre-adolescent head of hair was cow-licking in four directions and, as I reached for the bottle of Wildroot Crème Oil, the commercial jingle came to mind; and I began to sing;

"Ya better get Wildroot Crème Oil, C-H-A-R-L-I-E It keeps your hair in trim...."

As we left the apartment building I quivered at the sight of the guys gathered under the lamppost on the corner. I knew what was coming.

"Oh! Oh! Look at dis," Sonny taunted as we passed by. "Da kid's all dressed up like a real adult and ready to do da town wit his *nonna*." Nonna ignored the remark and kept on walking as I turned and delivered four furious wrist over bent elbow gestures and mouthed,

"Fuck you Sonny, fuck you."

When we got to the IRT train station at the plaza, *nonna* grabbed my arm as I turned toward the stairs.

"No, no, Ruggero," she said shaking her head, "we gonna takea da taxi." *Nonna* always preferred the comfort and privacy of a cab, made more imperative by the infantile paralysis outbreak and the fear of crowds.

The big yellow and red Desoto with cracked, parched leather seats smelled of Chesterfields and perfume.

"Where to lady?" the cabbie asked, flicking the lever of the meter down which registered five cents.

"We gonna go to Mulberry Street," she answered.

"Shit!" he groaned under his breath, "all the way downtown."

The driver followed the elevated IRT tracks on Roosevelt Avenue, over the Queensborough Bridge, to 5th Avenue and 60th Street. The leaves on the trees in Central Park blazed brilliantly, soft yellow and burning orange, under the warm autumn sun. I pressed my face to the window as the cab turned left onto 5th Avenue past the fountain in front of the stately Plaza Hotel and continued south. As we passed majestic St. Patrick's Cathedral, *nonna* solemnly blessed herself and uttered a quiet Hail Mary. The cab slowed in heavy traffic and rolled to a stop in front of the promenade at Rockefeller Center which led to the ice skating rink under a massive statue, leaning on an elbow, spouting a stream of water. At 42nd Street, two stone lions stood sentinel on either side of the steps of the New York Public Library, an imposing structure which took up an entire city block.

Nonna ordered the cabbie to let us off in front of Old St. Patrick's Church on Mott Street and took my hand, leading me into the church.

"C'mon," she said, "we gonna go in an light a candle. This very special place for our family. I get marry here, your mamma and *zia* Twink get baptized and go to school here an…an my brother, Carmelo wasa bury from here," she added sadly.

As we walked down Mulberry Street, *nonna* reflected nostalgically on her time spent in the area.

She pointed out the building on Mulberry and Broome Street where she lived with her husband, my phantom nonno, Leonardo Contino, and my mother and aunt.

"And dis is where I buy da *salami, prosciuttu, formaggiu*," she noted as we passed Alleva's *salumeria* on the corner of Grand Street.

"An over dare," she said pointing across the street, "isa Ferrara *pasticceria* where we takea espresso an pastry ina da evening."

We continued a few feet further down the street when *nonna* stopped abruptly in front of the Mulberry Street Bar, a venerable neighborhood landmark, circa 1900, in need of some cosmetic attention.

"An dis, dis," she said disdainfully extending her arms, "isa where my papa, Giuseppe Caiozzo, your great granfatha, spenda too much time an too much money drinking grappa. In that day," she instructed, "dis place was call, 'Mare Chiaro, Clear Sea.'"

Angelo's was just beginning to welcome the dinner crowd as *nonna* and I walked in and were greeted by Gino, who warmly embraced *nonna* and kissed her on both cheeks.

"Ma, I no see you for almost tree year. Where you been? *Tuttu va beni*, everything is well?" he asked.

"*Sì, sì, grazzii*," *nonna* responded, "*e tu*, and you?"

"*Beni, beni*. And who is this handsome young man you wit today? But Mary," he said leaning close but not out of earshot, "the older you get, the younger man you find," he said laughing.

SHIT! SHIT!, my inner voice screamed, embarrassed, as Gino led us to a small table by the window.

"I know you always like to sit by da window an watch the people pass by," Gino said as he sat *nonna*. He snapped his fingers and a waiter immediately brought a basket of warm bread, a small bottle of olive oil and a pitcher of ice water with lemon, and placed it on the table.

"The usual, a martini?" he asked, *nonna*, anticipating.

"Yes, Gino, I takea martini, but only one," she answered laughing, otherwise it go to my head," she said dramatically placing her hand over her forehead.

"An for *lu giuvinottu*, the young one, a Coca Cola?" he asked

"Yes, please," I began, interrupted by an emphatic command, "No Coca Cola; water wit lemon," *nonna* answered, pointing to the pitcher.

"Ah, *nonna*," I protested, "am I gonna get infantile paralysis if I drink Coca Cola?"

"No," she said, shaking a finger at me, "but da lining in your stomach could disappear. Ghia, da icea man, tell me he spill some Coca Cola on da fender of his truck and, da next day, he no havea paint dare."

God, I moaned to myself, do these Sicilian exaggerations never end.

But, *nonna* was right about the lasagna. It was the best I'd had outside her kitchen. As I shoveled the thick pasta drenched in meat sauce into my mouth, I noticed *nonna* glancing wistfully at the handsome, young bartender with slicked back, black hair, shaking cocktails for two young women sitting at the bar. She dabbed her eyes with the napkin before returning to her meal. I felt real bad for *nonna*. I knew she had worked with her brother at Angelo's when he was the bartender. She looked back at me, smiled, and said, "God bless, you eat good.

"The lasagna, you like?" she asked.

"Yeah, *nonna*, it's good, but nowhere near as good as yours," I replied, smiling, patting her hand.

CHAPTER 56

As Main Street was pulling in its sidewalks in the outer boroughs and the suburbs, the city was turning its lights on to welcome men in Fedora's, jackets and ties, and women sporting pill-box hats, the throng of people, strolling from east side to west or riding the green and yellow double decker buses along Fifth Avenue, or hurrying up the stairs to catch the el train, which rushed past dimly lit tenement windows on Third Avenue, offering passengers surreptitious glimpses into the lives of the dwellers.

Nonna and I exited the cab at the entrance to the Metropolitan Opera House on Thirty Ninth Street and Broadway. The crowd of men in tuxedos and white silk scarfs escorting lissome women in evening gowns with delicate shawls draped over their shoulders stood under the marquee buzzing in anticipation. Everyone dressed when they went to the opera and I was grudgingly thankful my mother insisted that I wear the dark Robert Hall suit.

The lobby of the opera house wasn't grand but it led to a golden auditorium with a sunburst chandelier, a curved arch separating the stage from the audience and a colorful, patterned curtain. I felt strangely comfortable as I looked around and thought I had been transported back to the turn of the century. In spite of the boom of tasteless post-war construction, as towering, dreary glass apartment buildings replaced the four-story walk-ups, and the artistry of European masons was pulverized and trolley tracks were ripped from the streets, and the gracefully-laced steel of Penn Station was doomed, the old met survived for nearly two more decades.

The maestro walked imperially onto the stage and acknowledged the thunderous welcome with a nod and a smile.

The applause died down as he took his place and tapped his baton on the stand. The musicians raised their instruments and launched into a stirring overture.

I don't remember much about the story, which seemed tedious and confusing, despite the synopsis in the program. And the acting was silly, exaggerated and stiff, lacking Gable's cool:

"Frankly my dear, I don't give a damn"

or Bogart's

"Here's looking at you kid."

But the arias sung by sopranos, tenors and baritones seemed celestially inspired and gave me a new appreciation for the beauty of the human voice as an instrument.

Still, I was puzzled that *Nonna* only preferred operas which had tragic endings; Rodolfo collapsing on the bed of a dying Mimi, Butterfly disemboweling herself on a sword, and Tosca flinging herself from a parapet after the execution of her lover, Cavaradossi. The lissome ladies always exited the opera with black mascara streaming down their pale faces, comforted by their escorts.

"Why does everything end so badly in opera?" I asked *nonna*.

"Ah, datsa life," she responded, fatalistically. "But we still gonna enjoy da good we have;— *famigghia*, love, music, art, blue ocean, green mountain, an...an good lasagna and spaghetti wit clam sauce, an da horse who makea you money at da race track," she added, laughing.

. . .

Nonna never missed an opening day at Belmont Race Track and, in the Spring of 1951, she persuaded my mother to let me accompany her. "I don't know, mamma", my mother had objected, "the track's no place for a kid his age."

"Ah!" whata you talk, Marie?" *nonna* replied, "itsa a sport an he likea da sport, sì or no, Ruggero?" she said turning toward me.

"Yeah, yeah, I wanna go, mom," I pleaded.

Nonna was in the kitchen wrapping two sausage and pepper heroes in wax paper and putting them into a canvas shopping bag along with a jar of escarole, two forks, napkins and a thermos of ice tea.

"What are you doing, *nonna*?" I asked her, puzzled.

"We gotta eat today, no?" she responded.

"Eat? Yeah, we gotta eat but they sell food at the track," I responded, perplexed.

"No, no," she replied, adamantly, "we no gonna eat dat junk, dare, those frankfiefurters."

"Shit!," I groaned quietly, anticipating hard-core, tough-guy gamblers laughing at us bringing our own lunch to the track.

Nonna gave Salvatore, the limo driver, explicit instructions to pick us up at Belmont at 3:30. "No forget, Salvatore, 3:30 exact."

"Ok, ok, Mary," Salvatore replied, irritated, "have I ever left you high and dry?"

I felt ridiculous lugging the stupid canvas shopping bag as we made our way through the crowd to the side of the clubhouse entrance where we were greeted by Seamus, the burly red faced security chief.

"For it was Mary, Mary, plain as any name could be," he erupted in a falsetto tenor with a thick brogue, extending his arms and kissing her cheek.

"Now that you're here, we can we can begin the day's event. Surein it wouldn't be openin' day without you here, darlin," he gushed.

"Alo, nicea to see you again, Seamus," *nonna* replied cordially but with reserve, offering her hand. "Stilla wit da, how you say, baloney?"

"Blarney, Mary, blarney," he answered as he cupped the folded five dollar bill in one hand and swung the VIP gate open with the other.

"And may the luck of the Irish be with you today, love," he called as we passed through the gate.

"He's Irisha, ma no so bad," *nonna* said tossing her thumb over her shoulder.

Thanks, *nonna* I thought, I'm glad you think some Irish people are ok, considering your grandson is half Irish.

Opening day brought out a large crowd but we managed to find seats right on the finish line. *Nonna* took a rag and a bottle with ammonia from the bag and carefully sprayed three seats clean, wrinkling her nose in the process. She placed the canvas bag on the middle seat, sat on one side and directed me to the other. Everything was in place now, and she was ready to handicap the first race.

She took a neatly folded page from the *Morning Telegraph* and, pencil in hand, began reviewing the chart of past performances of the horses. Then she leaned toward me and whispered, "Gino givea me a tip on dis horse, Whitechapel," she said pointing to a grey, 22 to 1, morning line longshot, "Da jockey, Italian boy, isa regular at Angelo's an he say da horse ready to win. I see da workout isa good an I likea da breed. Da horse papa wasa champion.

"You stay here an watcha da seat. I gonna go an make ten dollar bet, eight to win an two to place." *Nonna* always liked to back her first choice up to reduce her loss in case the horse didn't win. While she was gone placing her bets, I was startled by a gruff voice. Turning, I saw a boney, pock-marked face guy pointing to the bag on the seat.

"Hey kid, what's wit da bag on da seat?" he growled.

"It a...it's a ..." I began, just as *nonna* returned.

"Whatsa matter here?" she asked looking up at boney face.

"What da matter is ya can't take an extra seat for a Goddamn bag, lady," he shouted, attracting the attention of onlookers.

"Oh, no, no *signore*, you right. Ma dis seat is no for da bag," she laughed, playing to the crowd. "I save for my husband, Michelangelo Vitale, who gonna be here any minute," she added grinning.

The guy's eyes widened, his jaw dropped and the color drained from his face.

"Vitale?" he repeated. "Oh, sorry, lady, he apologized quickly, and beat a hasty retreat, disappearing into the crowd.

The bag remained on the seat unchallenged, and I dug in for one of the sausage and pepper sandwiches without a trace of embarrassment.

A minute before post time the odds on Whitechapel suddenly dropped to 19 to 1.

"You see what just happen on da tote board, Ruggero?" *nonna* asked.

"Yeah, *nonna*, I see. The odds dropped. That's no good, right?" I asked naively.

"No, no, thatsa veddy good," she corrected. "It mean late money come in on Whitechapel, maybe stable money. Somebody know somethinga," she mused.

Somebody did know something. Whitechapel broke fast from the gate and the jockey, Geraci, immediately moved the horse inside to save ground. He hugged the rail on the backstretch and, on the final turn at the 8th pole, opened up a five length lead, prompting *nonna* to climb up on her seat.

"C'mon Geraci, c'mon, no quit now," she shouted, slapping the program against her thigh, like a jockey urging a horse home with a whip. Whitechapel went wire to wire, crossing the finish line eight lengths ahead of the field and paid a handsome $39.00 for a two dollar ticket, bringing the winning total to more than $170.00.

"Eh! Dat was a good tip," *nonna* exclaimed with a sheepish grin. *Nonna* was a good handicapper, but she also appreciated good inside information.

"Yeah, but *nonna*, even without the tip you liked the horse. Why didn't you bet more?" I asked.

"Ruggero," she instructed seriously, "no be greedy. Givea tanks you put some money in your pocket and no have to tear up a losing ticket. No be greedy an play *cu la testa*, wit da head," she said pointing, "no *cu l'emozione*, no wit da emotion," she said, patting her chest. "An datsa good rule for everything in life," she added.

Nonna made token two dollar bets on long shots in the second and third races, which ran out of the money. But she recouped in the fourth race with a six dollar wager on a favorite which returned twenty one dollars.

"Dat's it," she pronounced, looking at her watch, "*basta*."

Salvatore gonna be here in twenty minute, so we go now." She cashed her winning tickets and slipped me five dollars, bringing the day's total to $182.00, after expenses.

The following week as I sat in the living room listening to Marty Glickman's fifteen minute simulated re-broadcast of the Yankee game, on, "Today's Baseball," *nonna* walked into the apartment followed by a guy juggling a large cardboard box which read, "Philco Television." My heart almost jumped out of my chest as I watched him remove the television, hook up the rabbit ears antenna and adjust the knobs on the twelve inch set until the snow on the screen disappeared, and the picture quit rolling.

"Good evening ladies and gentlemen. This is Douglas Edwards and welcome to the CBS Nightly News brought to you by your local Oldsmobile dealer," followed by the commercial jingle, "Won't you come with me Lucille in my merry Oldsmobile."

"Now," *nonna* said, flipping her wrist, "you no have to listen to da base-aball on da radio, ana you can see Joe Dimaggio every day."

"Good kid," the guy said smiling, "a Yankee fan. You can catch all their home games on the Dumont Television Network, channel five," he winked, thanking *nonna* for the two dollar tip.

We were only the second family in the building to have a television set and, overnight, my popularity took a quantum leap with the guys, and my stickball skills mysteriously improved.

"Put da kid in left field today," Junior ordered. "He's pretty fast and he ain't got that chicken arm no more."

"Ah shit!" Joey began to protest.

"Da kid plays left field today," Junior commanded, and there was no arguing with him.

CHAPTER 57

When the bell for the last period rang at 2:45, I ignored Mrs. Zimminey's call to discuss a book report I had written on Stephen Crane's "The Red Badge of Courage" and bolted from the classroom to the luncheonette, where I got the key, waved a quick hello to my mother and ran to the apartment.

I turned the TV on to WPIX, channel 11, just in time to see Bobby Thompson lumbering up to home plate, swinging three bats over his shoulder. This was high drama.

The Giants, after trailing the Dodgers by 13 ½ games late in the 1951 season had mounted an historic run, caught the Brooklyns, and forced a three game playoff for the pennant, leading to a scenario which could not have been scripted; two outs, two men on base in the ninth inning with the Dodgers leading 4-2 in the deciding game. Thompson waited patiently as the Dodger manager, Charlie Dressen, called time out and replaced his pitcher, Don Newcombe with Ralph Branca, a move which confounded and infuriated the Dodger faithful given that Branca had surrendered a winning home run to Thompson in the first game of the playoffs. But the wicked baseball gods were not finished with orchestrating their cruel joke.

On an 0-1 count, Thompson, swung hard, driving a Branca fast ball into the left field stands and, "The Giants win the pennant! The Giants win the pennant! The Giants win the Pennant..." Russ Hodges, the Giant announcer screeched hysterically over the roar of the crowd. I watched astounded as Thompson jubilantly galloped around the bases, mobbed by his teammates at home plate. I thought of the poor Liss brothers as they watched, what was instantly dubbed, "The Shot Heard Round the World." I figured they were already in mourning, sitting shiva.

The Yankees handled the Giants easily in the World Series, winning 4 games to 2. But the most memorable image for me came in game 6 at the Polo Grounds in what was to become the last time Joe Dimaggio would wear the pinstripes as a player.

In the 8th inning, he lined a double off the left field wall and limped into second. Casey Stengel, the Yankee manager famous for his dramatics, called time out and, as a pinch runner headed toward second base, the ailing Yankee Clipper jogged slowly across the infield and disappeared into the dugout to a thunderous standing ovation from the partisan, but generous, Giant fans. They knew they had just seen the last of one of the greats. An era had ended, but Willie Mays and Mickey Mantle waited in the wings to begin another.

Things can change quickly, and later that week, my mother sat me down at the kitchen table for one of those serious parent-child talks.

"How'd you like to have a room of your own?" she asked.

"What? Whata ya mean?" I asked, puzzled but curious.

"Well, well," she continued smiling as though she was giving me a finely-wrapped Christmas gift from FAO Schwartz, "Guido and I are going to be married next month, and we'll be moving into a house we bought in Rego Park."

"Married? Moving? Rego Park?" the words tumbled from my mouth. I was stunned, hurt, and angry and, after a pause, I exploded.

"I don't give a damn about a room of my own, and I don't want to move to Rego Park or anywhere else." I was terrified at the thought of leaving Corona, my family and friends.

"I'll stay here in Corona with *nonna*. You move to Rego Park with Guido," I replied defiantly.

My mother's smile turned to an icy stare set in a face of granite, and suddenly, I felt a crack so hard across my face it left a red imprint on my cheek, my eyes watered, and my ear droned with a dull ring for an hour.

"Marie!" *nonna* cried out in Sicilian, enough of which I understood, "what's da matter for you? He's just a young boy who's scared to death of giving up his familiar surroundings and moving to a strange place. That's normal for someone his age."

"Stay out of this, mamma!" my mother shouted. "I'm giving him an opportunity to get out of Corona and get a new start in life, and this is the gratitude I get?" I just want what's best for him," she insisted.

"Marie," *nonna* answered quietly, shaking her head, "you have every right to marry and start a new life for yourself. But never assume a decision you make in your interest will automatically sit well with your son. He has the right to his own feelings. Do you really think he could jump for joy knowing he is uprooted and will live in a house in a strange neighborhood with a man he hardly knows, when he has not even seen his own father for more than a year?" she asked.

"Of course, he must go with you," *nonna* continued, "and, by and by, he will make the adjustment. But you must make some compromise with you son, and reach an accord."

Like the good *consiglieri* that she was, *nonna*'s words resonated with my mother. About an hour later I heard footsteps in the hallway leading to the bedroom, and just managed to stuff the yellow and white National Geographic issue with the photographs of brown women with large, sagging breasts, under my pillow before the knob turned and the door creaked open.

My mother sat on the edge of the bed, pulled me close, and apologized for her outburst.

"I just want what's best for you...," she began.

"I know, mom, I know, you just want what's best for me," I replied, mimicking her sarcastically and risking another crack across the chops. But, funny thing, on some level, I really believed her.

About a week later I walked into the near empty Plaza Sweet Shop at 3:00. My mother motioned me to a rear booth as she put a stainless steel shaker under the blade of the green and white Hamilton mixer.

"I have great news" she said placing a malted shake on the table in front of me and sitting down.

"What's that, mom?" I asked between gulps, "Did *nonna* hit the daily double today?" I asked sarcastically.

"C'mon now, don't be a wise guy," she said laughing. "I had a meeting today with the principal, Mr. Charleston, and, because you are in a class for the musically gifted and play in the band, I got him to agree to let you continue to attend the school here until you finish the eighth grade next year. You won't have to transfer to a new school when we move to Rego Park, and you'll see your Corona friends every day."

"You're kidding, mom, really?" I asked, thrilled.

"Really, but you must promise to be on the bus right after school lets out and be back in Rego Park no later than 4:00, every day," she commanded.

"Promise, mom, I promise," I said relieved.

I thought back to a situation two years earlier when my mother insisted I learn a musical instrument and, despite my howling protest, signed me up for accordion lessons, an imperative for many young Italian-American boys.

"Please, mom," I pleaded after three grueling weeks of battling with the cumbersome squeeze box, "I'll do anything, play any other instrument."

"What's so wrong with the accordion?" my mother asked bewildered.

"Mom, did you ever see an accordion player in a band or in an orchestra?" I asked. "Never!" I answered my own question. "The only time you see an accordion player is at Italian or Polish weddings, or picnics when some fat kid hooks those dumb straps around his shoulders and plays, "Lady of Spain."

"Well you're gonna play something," my mother insisted.

"How 'bout the trumpet?" I offered.

"Hum, hum," my mother briefly mused, "the trumpet," she repeated, "like Louie Armstrong or Harry James?"

And so it came to be that my mother's insistence on my playing a musical instrument paid off and ironically allowed me to maintain my friendships in Corona by remaining in the class for the musically gifted in Junior High School 16.

As the eighth grade came to a close, Mrs. Schultz, my guidance counselor, a prim old woman who never guided me anywhere in two years, and

Mr. Fink, the music teacher, summoned my mother and me to a conference.

"Mrs. Mercer," the counselor began.

"Mrs. Lanzini," my mother corrected, "my name is Lanzini."

"Yes, of course," Mrs. Schultz apologized. "Well, Mrs. Lanzini," she continued, "Mr. Fink here, our music teacher, is very enthusiastic about your son's talent. As you know, we here at..."

Mr. Fink, a direct, no nonsense bear of a man mercifully interrupted what was destined to become some bullshit propaganda reflecting the school's attention to each student's educational future. "Mrs. Lanzini, the long and the short of it is I believe Ruggero has enough talent to qualify for an audition for a scholarship and I'd like to recommend him to a colleague, Tom Regan, who is the music director at All Hallows, a very fine Catholic High School in the Bronx."

My mother and I looked at each other dazed and wordless.

What's an 'All Hallows'? I wondered.

"Mrs. Lanzini?" Mr. Fink inquired, redirecting my mother's attention to him.

"Yes, well," my mother composed herself with confirmed conviction, "I've always felt that my son here is talented," she said patting my shoulder. "Must run in the family," she laughed. "I, myself sang professionally for a number of years," she said proudly – "and I know Ruggero is absolutely dedicated to his music. I hear him in the basement of our house practicing faithfully every day."

What a load of crap, I thought. I don't even know how I ever got into a musically gifted class in the first place, and the only thing I ever practiced faithfully in the basement was refining my masturbatory technique.

We left the conference with Mr. Fink's promise that he would arrange an audition and contact us. My mother was delirious with joy and walked on air to the bus stop, chattering endlessly about what a lucky break we got and what great possibilities it could lead to. She suddenly stopped, looked at me and asked, "What's the matter, Ruggero? You look troubled and almost sad" she said putting her hand around my neck.

"Mom...mom, I hate to disappoint you but I...I...I can't read a note of music."

"What are you talking about?" my mother asked, puzzled, "You're in a class for the musically gifted for almost two years and you're telling me you can't read a note of music? How could this be?"

"I, I've been faking it, mom. I memorize a song after hearing it once or twice, and I can play it," I answered embarrassed. "I don't know how it works, but it does."

"Oh! Oh!" she said, putting her hand to her brow. "Let's sit here for a minute," she said, pointing to a bench, "and think this out."

She reached into her pocketbook, took out a Lucky, put it between her lips, and inhaled deep.

"Ok, ok!" she said after reflecting for a few minutes. "Here's what we do. What songs do you think you play best?" she asked, shaking her finger.

"I, I know a lot of them, most of the songs in your record collection. But, I guess, "My Blue Heaven," and "I Don't Know Why" are two that I've practiced most."

"All right, then, you take the sheet music of those two songs to the audition and play them as though you're reading from the sheet. If you do it well, he'll never know you can't read music."

"Mom!" I exclaimed, "that's cheating."

"Cheating?" my mother asked, raising her eyebrows, "What's cheating? Do you know the songs, and can you play them on that horn?" she asked, firmly.

"Yes, I can play them, but...but."

"No 'buts! Put your doubts behind you, and have confidence in yourself," she declared. "Let this Riley guy, or whatever his name is, decide if you're good enough for a scholarship or not. I'll help you rehearse and, by the time comes for your audition, I guarantee you, you'll knock 'em dead."

During the next two weeks, my mother made very helpful suggestions regarding the rhythm, breathing and timing of my delivery.

"How'd you know all this stuff, mom?" I inquired, "you never played an instrument."

"No," she replied, raising her eyebrows, "I never did play an instrument. I was an instrument. Whata you think the human voice is?" she asked. "I did take voice lessons for a year when I was a kid, then I learned more about singing in two weeks than most people learn in a lifetime, listening to and singing with Frank Sinatra," she said proudly, swaying back and forth.

"Frank Sinatra?" I exclaimed, "I...I never knew that," I said with newly discovered respect for my mother. "But anyway, I want to rehearse two more pieces for my audition as a backup in case Regan asks me for more," I said.

"What'd ya have in mind?" my mother asked.

"Well I like, 'Ramona' and it's a pretty easy piece to play," I said, raising the muted horn to my mouth.

"Yeah, that sounds good," my mother agreed, "Anything else?" she asked.

"Yeah, Bunny Berigan's, 'I Can't get Started with You.'"

My mother looked at me, winced, and flatly said, "Forget about, 'I Can't Get Started with You.' That Berigan arrangement is a killer with those high notes. Stay with what you're sure of and what you do well."

On the first Monday in June the call came from Mr. Fink. My audition was scheduled for that Thursday at the school in the Bronx.

"You're not going to the audition looking like a sack of potatoes," my mother said disdainfully, holding a hanger with the ill-fitting, faded jacket and frayed cuffs of the Robert Hall suit. "We're gonna get you a new outfit at Howard's Clothing," she declared.

As we walked down 63rd Drive to the store on Queens Boulevard from our house on 84th Street, a catchy commercial reached me as it had with the Wildroot Cream Oil jingle:

"I'm the little Howard label and I'm proud as proud can be to be sewed in every garment at the Howard factory."

That Thursday I took the D train from 59th Street in Manhattan and got off at the stop where the sign read, "161st Street – Yankee Stadium". What a great omen, I thought. My audition is gonna take place in the shadow of the great ball park.

About two hours later, I phoned my mother from the train station: "Mom, I got it! I got it!" I shouted into the receiver over the rumble of the train in the background. "I got the music scholarship and, I'm going to All Hallows in September."

CHAPTER 58

I struggled to meet the rigorous academic demands of All Hallows, which, unlike the public schools, required Latin, Algebra and Geometry. I managed to pass Latin with a weak 'C' in my first year but spent July and August sweating in Summer School through elementary Algebra and Geometry and barely managed to eke out passing grades. I never could really crack the mysterious code of math, a shortcoming I somehow related to my inability to read music. My subsequent poor grades in intermediate Algebra and solid Geometry kept my cumulative average at a low 'C'.

I was a frequent recipient of corporal punishment by the Brothers teaching these subjects, who firmly believed that sparing the rod spoiled the child. Poor grades and incomplete assignments earned me five cracks across each palm, delivered by fat pink men smelling of piety and celibacy, gleefully wielding a thick snappy leather belt. If the fingers began to close over the palms in a normal defensive reaction during this assault, you got five more whacks, this time across the ass which reduced the anal orifice to the size of a pea. I prided myself in never retracting my fingers and the centimeter of my asshole remained intact.

Studying at home became more difficult with the birth of my two brothers within twenty months. Translating the Gallic Wars, Jason and the Argonauts and conjugating verbs did not mix well with a pair of bawling infant boys in the house. And my 32 year old mother, unaccustomed to the demands of proper and effective parenting was in an emotionally stressed state bordering on mild depression. The atmosphere was not conducive to serious studying.

"That's it, Guido," I heard her hushed, shaky voice in the dark one night, "I don't give a damn if you want a daughter or not. No more kids! I'm not Harriet Nelson or Donna Reed," she said, referencing ideal television mothers, "Motherhood is fine, but I need more out of life."

The music scholarship was good until halfway through my sophomore year. One day after band practice, Brother McGowan, the designated school sleuth who had correctly suspected my inability to read music, collared me.

He swooped down like a hawk spying his mid-day meal, dramatically brushed his flowing black cassock aside, and shoved me into a corner.

"Mr. Mercer," he hissed through yellow, jagged, clenched teeth, as his dark eyes narrowed, "a moment please. Indulge me," he said with a smirk and pointed to a chair on the stage. "I have an issue I'd like to discuss with you."

"Me? Me?, Brother," I asked, innocently pointing to my chest.

"Is there another Mr. Mercer in this empty auditorium?" he asked facetiously, looking around.

"Yes, Brother, I mean no, Brother," I answered, dropping into a chair.

"No then," he began, measuring his words deliberately, "I have been, as I'm sure you know, observing you very closely for the past year, and I notice that you have a most unusual method of playing that horn, that instrument," he said pointing.

"Trumpet, Brother, it's a trumpet," I offered.

"What?" he shouted.

"Trumpet, it's a....."

"I know what it is!" he shouted, becoming red-faced as the veins in his neck bulged over his collar.

"Anyway," he said pausing, "you seem to play that...that trumpet without ever looking at the sheet music, and I find that very curious."

"Well, you see, Brother, I have this thing about memorizing songs, and, I can..."

"Never mind that," he interrupted. "The thing of it, the truth is, you can't read a note of music, can you? Can you?" he persisted, driving his finger into my chest.

"Yes I can, yes I can," I angrily blurted out, foolishly insisting.

"You can?" he asked incredulously, "Good! Good! Then perhaps you'll entertain me by playing this piece," he said, handing me a sheet of some obscure Sousa march.

I stared at the piece as though I was being asked to translate the *Iliad* from Greek to Russian in brail.

I ran up and down the musical scale in a fruitless attempt to forestall the inevitable when Brother McGowan waved his arms frantically and shouted.

"Stop! Stop! Enough! Enough!" He then came within inches of my ear and whispered, gloating, "Just as I suspected," he proclaimed with the satisfaction of Inspector Poirot, who had just unraveled a great mystery.

Within minutes I was sitting in the office of Brother Power, Dean of Students. Brother McGowen, looking smug and pleased with himself, revealed my secret to the Dean and took a seat next to me.

Brother Power tilted his head, looked at him and said, softly, "Thank you Brother, I'll take it from here, you're excused."

"But, but,"...Brother McGowen began, anxious to be present at my humiliation.

"I said I'll take it from here, Brother. You're excused," Brother Power commanded sharply.

The boom of the closing door echoed down the hallway and left no doubt as to his disappointment.

"Ruggero," Brother Power began slowly, shaking his head and grinning slightly, "I guess I have to give you some credit for pulling off this charade for almost two years, a drama in which we were unwitting players. We did, after all, offer you the scholarship, but we were careless. I can't fault you entirely. I don't believe you deliberately tried to deceive us and, for that reason, I'm not going to expel you. Of course, your scholarship will be revoked, but you can remain at All Hallows. However," he continued, furrowing his brow as he flipped through my transcript, "you can remain only if I see an improvement in your grades. You're cutting a very fine line here young man, and, in fact, are in danger of flunking out. I'm going to take a personal interest in your progress. Please don't force my hand," he said earnestly.

"Thanks, Brother," I said, breathing a sigh of relief. "I'll try to do my best."

"No, Ruggero," he said, his voice rising, "trying is not good enough. You'll either do it or you won't. Now, go back to class, get crackin, and don't disappoint me."

Later that afternoon I walked alone through the park on the Grand Concourse, past the old Jewish men and women sitting on benches with their aides, taking in the early Spring sun after a hard winter. I descended into the dark, smelly bowels of the subway and passed the telephone booth where, two years earlier, I had ecstatically phoned my mother to tell her of the scholarship. I got on the downtown express 'D' train and sat looking out the grimy window through the dark at the blurred shapes of the passengers waiting on the platform under muted yellow light as the train rushed by. I was worried sick about telling my mother that my scholarship had been yanked and wondered what her reaction would be. I felt as bad for her as I did for myself, and thought about her apology the time after she smacked me across the face.

"I only want the best for you," she had said, and here I was letting her down.

"Hi," she greeted me, looking up from the sofa where she was reviewing questions from previous real estate licensing exams. "You're home early. No band practice today?" she asked.

"No, mom, no band practice today,...or any other day for that matter," I replied.

She put the papers down, and asked solemnly, "What do you mean, Ruggero? What happened?"

"Mom," I said, choking "I'm so sorry to disappoint you, but they found me out today and they know I can't read music. Brother Power said my scholarship would have to be revoked."

My mother sat wordless, looking at me with a blank stare for minutes, then patted the cushion beside her.

"Well," she said, taking my hand, "at least we got a...a, how do you guys call it?, a free ride for a year and a half," she laughed.

"Yeah, a free ride for a year and a half, then bounced," I responded.

"Wait a minute!" my mother exclaimed, alarmed, "you mean, you mean you got kicked out of All Hollows?" she asked.

"No, no, mom," I quickly answered, "Brother Power said I could stay as long as I didn't disappoint him and pulled my grades up."

My mother breathed deep and said, "Then do what's necessary, but don't worry about disappointing me, Brother Power or anyone else. Do it so you don't disappoint yourself and maybe regret it for the rest of your life."

Money was tight without the scholarship, but between my part time job as a delivery boy at Conte Super Market and what my mother was able to salvage from the weekly budget, we managed the thirty dollar a month tuition cost and, in June, 1957, I was the proudest C plus graduate walking up the stairs of the stage to accept my diploma. Brother Power had a twinkle in his eye and winked as he handed me a piece of rolled parchment delicately tied with a blue ribbon.

Later that afternoon the house was jammed with relatives and the scent of crackling sausage, peppers and onions, drifted into the kitchen from the outdoor barbecue and mixed with the aroma of the baked lasagna *nonna* had prepared. She, and Vittorio LaStarza, her new beau whom I had never met, but greeted me like a long lost grandson, handed me an envelope with a card containing a hundred dollars, followed by Momma Caiozzo with an envelope containing the same amount.

"Thisa for when you begin university study, no for da track wit your *nonna*," she admonished laughing and waving a forefinger.

My mother also had reason to celebrate. That week she had passed the test for her real estate license and was in the process of establishing a small agency on Eliot Avenue in Rego Park. She already had five listings and as many potential buyers.

I was very proud of my mother. She didn't push a sale if she felt a young couple really couldn't afford a house and was always honest about what she thought a seller could reasonably expect. She never over-appraised the value of a property so she could get a quick listing.

In August, 1957 as the Korean Police Action entered its fifth year of a cease fire orchestrated by the Eisenhower Administration, I decided to fulfill my military obligation and enlisted in the Army Reserves the day after my eighteenth birthday. I had no specific plans at the time and patriotically bought the venomous message of the booze-soaked junior Senator from Wisconsin that a Red Wave was sweeping across the Pacific Ocean and the United States government was rotting from within aided by East Coast liberal Commie sympathizers. Besides, the government had issued me a draft card, which meant I could drink legally at P.J. Clarke's on Third Avenue. I figured I owed the government something.

"You're not going anywhere to shoot guns and kill people, or God forbid, get killed yourself," my mother screeched.

"Mom," I shouted back, "I'm eighteen. I can do anything I want, watch," I said, picking up a pair of scissors and racing around the kitchen.

"Besides, there's no war: Nobody's shooting anybody."

"This is shit for the birds," my mother moaned, collapsing onto a chair.

"Yeah, Marie, whata worried about?" Guido chimed in, salivating at the prospect that maybe while I was in the army, I would meet and marry a farmer's daughter from Wrightstown, New Jersey, and be out of the house for good. "There ain't no war and he's goin to a place that's like a Boy Scout's camp," Guido assured my mother.

Not exactly. As the other thirty nine guys and I got off the military bus at Fort Dix, New Jersey, a diminutive, light-skinned Negro guy with Sergeant stripes and battle ribbons extending from his shoulder to his waist roared, banging on the side of the bus with a baton, "Get the fuck off the bus you pussy fist-fuckers. Your ass is now grass, and I'm the lawn mower. You are now killers, hired by the United States Government, and I'm the *Capo*."

Within a couple of hours I was double-timing with a forty pound field pack and an M-1 Rifle into a long wooden barracks with two rows of double bunk beds and an obscene latrine that had no partitions between the commodes and provided no privacy for the early morning or late night deposit.

As I began to unload my gear into the foot locker, I looked around spooked, and realized, shit, this is exactly the same place where guys slept before they went off to war and stormed and fell on the beaches of Normandy, only thirteen years ago.

Sergeant Coles must have read my mind. He walked in, arms across his chest, and reminded us, "You have the honor of sleeping in the same bunk, and shitting in the same latrine as men who gave their lives for their country. The war happened to me twice and it could happen again, this time to you. Listen closely, stay alert and learn everything you can. It could save your life.

"If you're lucky, and I hope you are, in six months you'll be back home trying to unhook the clip on Mary Alice's bra in the balcony of the Bijou theater. If not, you'll be tossing a grenade from a fox hole you dug somewhere in Lebanon. But if that's the case, don't worry about your girlfriend or wife. Your best friend will take good care of her," he sneered.

Oh shit! This guy means it. I could get killed. It's not what I signed up for.

The only thing I had ever worried about was Brother Kelly's leather strap. I just turned eighteen two weeks ago, I groaned. I never wanted to be a real soldier. I just wanted to act, like John Wayne. The Duke never had to worry that the game might be called on account of darkness.

Things got worse. Three weeks into basic training I was devastated by a 'Dear John' letter from Cathy Brannigan, my steady girlfriend throughout high school. She had fallen for a guy wearing a blue uniform and was going to marry an Irish cop from Woodside.

CHAPTER 59

I wasn't surprised when I returned home from active duty in March, 1958 and my mother informed me that she and Guido had decided to sell the house and business in Rego Park and move to a two bedroom cooperative apartment on East 58th Street in Manhattan within view of the Queensborough Bridge spanning the East River with its parade of working barges and pleasure crafts.

I knew of her unhappiness living in Rego Park and was relieved to see the dark cloud of depression lift, replaced by the excitement of anticipating her return to the city, a place which she always viewed affectionately as her home.

"Oh, Ruggero," she confided, bubbling, "I so missed everything about The City, walking through Central Park, seeing the blazing orange and gold leaves on crisp Autumn days, strolling down 5th Avenue in the snow at Christmas time to the tree in Rockefeller Center, and being able to walk to the theatre district to see a play any time I wanted. I even missed the Automat on 42nd Street, where I used to work," she said laughing.

"Maybe it sounds selfish and shallow," she said, "but I love the excitement and glamor of Manhattan."

"No, mom," I replied, "I know exactly how you feel, and it isn't selfish or shallow. You sound happy to be going home," I said. My mother looked at me, paused and smiled.

"You know, Ruggero," she replied, 'that's exactly what Mamma Caiozzo said to me;

'*Va, va*, go Marie, go and be happy.'

My mother reached for my hand with a pained look and said solemnly, "Ruggero, you understand what my move to the city means. It means..."

"I know what it means, mom," I interrupted laughing, "it means I'm finally on my own. I'm not a kid anymore and I don't have to stop off at the luncheonette to get the key to the apartment, and I can run around the streets and get as sweaty as I want."

"You don't feel I'm deserting you, do you?" she asked.

"No, mom, I don't. You know I was always pretty independent, and, really, having a place of my own will feel pretty good," I answered.

"Well, that's a load off my mind," she said relieved. "I've already got some leads on furnished apartments for you," she said eagerly. "And one of them is in Corona," she added, winking. "It's clean and within walking distance to the train station, and Mamma Caiozzo's and *nonna*'s apartments. She was consoling herself that I would have family support nearby.

I was fortunate to get an office job at General Motors on West 57th Street at seventy dollars a week, registered for night courses at St. Francis College in Brooklyn and settled into a fifty dollar a month furnished apartment one block from 'Spaghetti Park' on 108th Street in Corona, where the old men played bocce and the old women with stockings rolled above their knees sat gossiping on benches.

The apartment smelled of Clorox and freshly painted walls where a picture of an expressionless Christ with a burning heart hung, framed by browning palm leaves. The furnishings were depression-era sparse: a worn, faded blue sofa and matching arm chair with a small round side table and a ridiculous oversized cherub lamp. A small wooden kitchen table and two wobbly chairs sat on discolored yellow linoleum across from a pock-marked sink, a small gas range and a Kelvinator refrigerator with a round motor on top. The mattress in the small bedroom was gully-saged but I slept well enough. It wasn't much, but it was mine. I felt like a real adult the day I remembered to refill the ice cube tray and return it to the freezer.

Every Saturday I brought Mamma Caiozzo her two pints of ice from the Lemon Ice King. I spent an hour with her, then walked around the corner to *nonna*'s apartment where I had lunch with her and Vittorio La Starza. At sixty one years old with her beauty fading as quickly as her savings, she had relented and married Vittorio La Starza, securing a means of support from a man who had profited nicely from the sale of his home and his shoe repair business in Whitestone.

"Why didn't you give the apartment up and move into that nice house he owned in Whitestone?" I asked.

"Ah, Ruggero," *nonna* answered, "I no need a biga house to clean an take care. Better, at our age, we use da money to go to Florida in da winter an takea nice *vacanza in Italia*...and, and go to da track once in a while," she said winking.

The love-struck, lonely septuagenarian thought he had found the Hope Diamond and acceded to all of *nonna*'s demands, including the purchase of a five thousand dollar life insurance policy with scandalously high premiums. But Vittorio only made three payments on the policy.

One day at Belmont Racetrack as he watched his 45-1 long shot cross the finish line first, holding a ten dollar win ticket, his heart attacked him and he dropped dead on the spot. My mother and Guido, who had accompanied *nonna* and Vittorio to the track, related the unhappy event to me.

"Your *nonna* is some piece of work, Ruggero," said Guido. "The guy had no sooner taken his last breath when she leaned over him, took his ring from his finger, his watch from his wrist and his wallet from his jacket pocket. Then...then," he continued, unable to restrain himself, erupting in laughter, and grasping his sides, "she...she pried the winning ticket from his clenched fist."

"Well, what the hell did you expect her to do?" my mother asked, defending *nonna*, "wait for the Irish cops to come and steal everything as they dragged the poor guy away?"

. . .

Nonna's grief scene at the wake at Guida's Funeral Home was worthy of a tragic opera by Puccini.

She sat swallowed-up by a large upholstered chair in the center of the room in front of the casket, surrounded by the family, dabbing her wet eyes with a fine silk handkerchief, and accepting the condolences from the line of mourners with the aplomb of a queen holding court.

Nonna's soft weeping suddenly gave way to a crescendo of wailing as she bolted up and rushed toward the casket, requiring my cousin, Frankie and me to intercept and restrain her. Her anticipation and timing was flawless. We got to *nonna* just before she had a chance to throw herself on Vittorio's lifeless body.

As we escorted her back to the chair, she gently freed herself and waved us away.

"*Staiu beni, beni,* I'm alright," she murmured weakly, bringing the room of mourners to tears.

Nonna hooked my arm, pulled me toward her and whispered, "Ruggero, I need takea da air. You come outside wit me, please?" she asked dramatically, bringing her hand to her forehead.

We walked to a small garden in the rear of the funeral home where *nonna* directed me to a bench under a tree.

"We sit here a little," she said sighing as she reached into her purse and took out a long cigarette holder, inserted a Lucky, and lit it with a Dunhill lighter. She inhaled deeply then turned to me with wet eyes, sighed again and said, "Ah, thatsa da way it is. We no cana change what God, He want. And now God he takea my poor Vittorio." The use of the expression, 'take' was common with many older Sicilians when referring to death. People didn't die; God took them, reaching through the clouds with a benevolent hand and lovingly sweeping them up to Heaven and their eternal reward.

Nonna then reached back into her purse, miraculously regained her composure, and produced a document titled,

New York Life Insurance Policy # 947350
Policy Holder: Vittorio La Starza
Beneficiary: Maria La Starza
Amount Payable: $5,000

"Ruggero, what I gotta do wit dis?" she asked.

"Well, it's a life insurance policy for $5,000 naming you as the beneficiary," I said looking it over.

"I know what is," she responded irritably. "But I aska you what I gotta do to...to"

"To collect?" I asked incredulously. "*Nonna*, Vittorio isn't even in his final resting place and you're already concerned with collecting on the policy?"

"Ma shu, Ruggero," she shot back defensively, "I concern about da money. I'ma poor woman. Who gonna pay for da funeral? Whatsa matter for you?" she asked, shrugging her shoulders and spreading her arms.

Continuing the discussion was pointless and I agreed to handle the particulars of the claim for her.

"*Grazzii, grazzii*, Ruggero. You a good boy," she said smiling and stroking my cheek. "Oh! By da way, how long you tink it takea for da settlement?" she asked casually.

"Jeez, I don't know, two, maybe three weeks at least," I answered, shaking my head.

"Eh, *que sera, sera!*" she replied with a resigned sigh as she walked back to resume her performance.

CHAPTER 60

In the Spring of 1961, *nonna* asked me to help her with the preparation of her tax return, a task which even I could handle despite my weakness in math. It was basically a simple one page form.

I noticed a curious pattern of activity in the $5,000 bank account she had opened with Vittorio's life insurance policy settlement; four or five hundred dollar withdrawals were followed by five hundred and fifty or six hundred dollar deposits a few weeks later.

I knew she was receiving a small social security check and another mysterious remuneration from the Garment Workers' Pension Fund where her sister's brother in law, Michelangelo Vitale, was a board member, but the numbers didn't add up.

"*Nonna*," I asked, surprised, "where is this extra money coming from every month?"

"What? Whata you talk?" she asked shaking her head innocently.

"This, this extra $75.00 or $100.00 deposit you make every month," I answered a little irritably.

"Oh, oh,...thatsa no thing. A little businessa I havea wit Spade," she dismissed.

"Spade? Business with Spade?" I responded, aghast. "What business could you have with Spade?" I demanded shocked. "He's nothing but a two-bit bookie and shylock."

Nonna breathed deeply and told me that Spade had somehow gotten wind of her insurance settlement and offered a percentage of the vig or interest on the money he put out on the street if she was willing to back some of his loans giving him access to more money and allowing him to expand his client base.

"*Nonna*, do you know what you're doing? You're in business with a gangster, a connected guy who makes loans to desperate people and gambling addicts. And if they can't pay they get hurt. Their legs get broken or they get thrown through windows. These guys are so rotten they steal from everybody, including each other."

"Ah, whata you know. He lenda money to poor people who no can pay da rent or put bread on da table," she insisted.

"For Christ's sake," I argued, "He's not Robin Hood, *nonna*."

"Eh, no takea da name a da Lord in vain," she admonished, waving a finger. "Besides, he no different from da bank or da credit company. Last week I see men come wit a truck an take da refrigerator an da television from *la signura* Antonelli's apartment while da poor children stand in da hallway an cry."

"Yeah, that's sad," I responded, "but they're not breaking the law. You're involving youself with some very shady characters who live a life outside the law. What happens, "I asked taking her hand, "if Spade welches on the interest he promised, or worse, doesn't return your principal? What are you gonna do? Go to the District Attorney and complain that a gangster reneged on an illegal agreement with you? You're putting your money out there, breaking the law, and, and, you have absolutely no protection for your money."

Nonna's mouth tightened and her eyes widened.

"You thinka Spade maybe steal my money?" *nonna* asked, ignoring the issue of breaking the law.

"He'd steal from his own mother if he needed the money badly enough," I loudly responded.

The following week *nonna* severed her alliance with Spade with Michelangelo Vitale's intervention.

"Jesus Christ," Vitale remarked to his brother, Giacomo, laughing, "there's no mistaking where that woman's genes come from. That sister in law of yours is Giuseppe Caiozzo's daughter through and through."

. . .

By the end of the summer of 1961 I had saved enough money to begin taking classes full time at St. Francis College in Brooklyn. I quit my job at General Motors and worked as a night filing clerk at an insurance company on Queens Boulevard. The fifty dollar a week salary plus what my mother and *nonna* were able to give me was more than enough to cover my living expenses.

But the schedule was grueling, made more difficult by the commuting. I spent two hours on trains getting to school, in Brooklyn, another two hours from school to my night job and a half hour bus ride from my night job to the apartment in Corona. I rarely got more than four hours sleep a night, rising early in the morning to study for exams and complete term paper assignments. I never made the school's Duns Scotus Honor Society but maintained a passing C plus average.

One Saturday morning as I was pounding out a term paper on my ancient manual Smith Corona typewriter, I was startled by a loud knock on the apartment door.

"Mello!" I exclaimed, surprised, opening the door. My surprise suddenly turned to concern.

"What's wrong, cousin. Did something happen?" I asked worried.

"No, no," he laughed. "Jesus, you really got that Sicilian paranoia shit, didn't ya? Everything's fine. C'mon out here, I just want to show ya something."

A shiny black 1953 Mercury sedan was parked at the curb.

"Oh, wow, Mello!" I gushed, running my hand across the door and fender. "Nice wheels. Congratulations, and good luck with it."

"Yeah, well," Mello responded, grinning. "It ain't mine, kid. It's yours," he said, tossing me a set of keys.

"What? What the...holy shit," I stammered, shaking.

"Yeah," Mello continued, "ya mom, *nonna* and Mamma Caiozzo figured the grind of getting to school and then to work every day was gonna be too much for ya and they wanted to make sure ya stayed in college. So they asked me to look around for reliable transportation for ya. Ya know," he said earnestly, putting an arm around my shoulder, "everyone in the family's real proud and we'll do everything we can to help ya out so ya can get that degree. It's a beauty, ain't it? Mint condition wit low mileage, so you'll have it for years. I got it off a guy who had a serious case of the shorts and needed cash in a hurry."

"Mello," I began, suspiciously.

"No, no, kid," he interrupted, "it's all on the up and up. Nuttin fishy. Here's the title and registration," he said, handing me an envelope. "But ya gotta get the insurance before ya drive it around," he warned. "We can go to Graziano's agency on National Avenue. He's a friend of mine and he'll fix ya up right away."

"Jeez, Mello," I don't know how to thank you."

"Ya don't gotta thank me, Ruggero. You know where your gratitude belongs."

Having a car was a blessing and reduced my travel time by three hours every day. My cumulative average rose from a C plus to a B plus, I got a solid six hours sleep every night, and the dark circles under my eyes disappeared.

In June of 1964, three proud Marias, along with other family members, sat teary-eyed at the commencement exercise as I received my Bachelor of Arts degree in English from St. Francis College.

With the ceremonies concluded, the families gathered in the vestibule and flashbulbs popped like lightning strikes. Mamma Caiozzo, supported by my mother and *nonna*, made their way through the crowd to where I was standing. She wrapped her frail arms around my waist, disappeared into my arms, and looked up, whispering, "I givea tanks to God he no takea me before I see dis day. You da first in da family to graduate from University, but I know you no be da last. Dis just da begin for us."

I reached into my jacket pocket and took out a ragged, yellowing library card.

"Remember this?" I asked.

"What you got dare?" she queried through strained eyes.

"It's the library card you gave me when I was ten years old. I saved it as a reminder of how you encouraged me to put the comic books aside and start reading the real stuff."

"*Sì, sìi, iu mi ricordu*, I remember," she said slowly. "So, you say I encourage you? Ah! You make an old lady veddy, veddy happy," as she kissed my cheek through dry, cracked lips.

We then drove over the Brooklyn Bridge to Angelo's Restaurant on Mulberry Street for a celebratory dinner. The family was coming home again, at least for a day, proudly bearing its trophy.

. . .

Three weeks later we gathered around Mamma Caiozzo's bed in her apartment in a gloomy, dimly lit room. Her wispy hair and drawn face had gone white, and she seemed to be fading into the color of the pillow on which her head lay.

"Mary," she called weakly to *nonna*, "raise the shades in the windows," she said in Sicilian. "I want to see the blue sky, the puffy clouds and the sunlight." She then turned her head slowly and scanned the faces of her children and grandchildren and settled on mine.

"Ruggero, *veni ccà*, come here," she whispered, beckoning me to her with frail fingers bent like small twigs. I breathed deeply and went to her bedside, looking down at eyes grown wide in wonder, as though she had already seen that other world and was only returning for a brief respite.

"You do me a last favor, *caro*?" she asked softly.

"Anything, Mamma Caiozzo," I replied.

"I know you no read Italian words veddy good, but you takea all da Jane Austen, Bronte an Dickens leather-bound books for yourself. They are the first books *me frati* give me when I was young girl in Castellammare. I like you to have them so you remember me an, maybe, maybe, some day, you gonna learn to read Italian," she said, struggling but smiling. "The rest, you please send to da library in Castellammare so the children have something good to read."

We didn't wait long, a narrow strip in time, until she closed her eyes and passed peacefully.

A dozen or so young women paid their respects at Guida's Funeral Home and attended the Mass at St. Leo's Church in Corona. As young girls, they gratefully remembered sitting at Mamma Caiozzo's feet in the library every Saturday morning as she read passages from the classics, and encouraged them to find a quiet corner of the house, or a bench in Linden Park, to read and expand their horizon.

CHAPTER 61

After Mamma Caiozzo's death in 1964, it seemed the next fifteen years accelerated with the speed of a run away train leaving blurred hazy recollections along the track. The sense of time had been lost. Funny how the days often seem to drag and go by slowly as the years pass unnoticed so quickly.

By 1980 I was married to the former Anna Maria Cavazzini of Parma, Italy, the father of a fourteen year old daughter, Christina Marie, and an eight year old son, Marcello, and had fulfilled Mamma Caiozzo's prophecy.

"I think this only da first step for you. You no finish yet," she had said years earlier at my college graduation.

Subsequently I had attained a Masters Degree in Social Work, and a Ph.D. in Behavioral Science, and established a modestly successful psychotherapy practice on Eastern Long Island where I lived with my family.

My mother's real estate business was flourishing and she was selling coops and condominiums as fast as they came on the market, and enjoying every day of her life in Manhattan.

My aunt Stella had succumbed to a chronic heart ailment, aunt Grazia left Corona and moved to Pennsylvania to be near her children, and aunt Giovanna divorced her husband and ran off to California with a young jazz pianist.

But *nonna* was obstinate and, even at eighty years of age, with mild, early signs of dementia, rejected the suggestion that she leave Corona for a residential senior citizen facility in nearby Forest Hills.

"I live here for more den half my life, an I gonna die here. I no gonna go to live an eat wit strangers," she insisted.

My mother and I took turns visiting *nonna* on alternate Saturdays to do the food shopping and keep her finances and monthly expenditures in order. But she never required assistance in keeping the apartment clean, and her personal hygiene was flawless.

One week, Spade, the bookie, was found dead in the brush of Flushing Meadows-Corona Park, the victim of severe head trauma.

"Ortiz, the detective who live on da first floor, tella me he think the death wasa murder so they gonna make a topsy-turvy ona da body," *nonna* whispered to me with conspiratorially tight, serious eyes.

"What? What are you talking about *nonna*?" I exclaimed. "A topsy what?"

"You know what I mean," she replied indignantly, "when day cut open da body to see whatsa what."

"Oh for Christ's sake," I exploded laughing, "you mean an autopsy, *nonna*."

"Eh, datsa what I say, no?" she responded, shrugging her shoulders.

Spade's unfortunate passing caused *nonna* a minor inconvenience. She now had to walk four blocks to the Off Track Betting parlor, pushing her way through crude, sweaty, men in a smoke-choked room, to the two dollar window to make her bet and pursue her avocation.

. . .

On a brilliant, warm May Sunday with the air sweet and thick with blooming tulips and Iris, my wife, our two children and I drove down the Long Island Expressway to meet *nonna*, my mother, my two grown half brothers, Giovanni and Roberto, and a reluctant, scowling Guido for a family Mother's Day dinner at The Parkside Restaurant across from Spaghetti Park in Corona. It was one of the last gathering places for a rapidly declining Italian population in Corona, and former neighborhood families came from Long Island and north-east sections of Queens regularly.

Nonna had never been to The Parkside and, generally, was critical of the fare in Italian restaurants, Angelo's on Mulberry Street, aside.

"They makea da sauce so thick you could stand a fork in it. Den they pile it on da pasta wit a shovel," she complained.

But the congenial atmosphere, the presence of her family and a few sips of a very cold, very dry martini, mellowed her and her eyes shone as she studied the faces around the table. She then daintily picked the glass up by the stem, raised it and, smiling, toasted,

"*A nostra famigghia, e grazzii a tutti.*"

"To our family," we echoed in English.

"You know," she said, taking the hands of my children sitting beside her, "you *picciriddi* here da third generation an I sure, like your papa, and uncles, Giovanni an Roberto, you gonna continue to bring honor an pride to da family. I an old lady but I still cana count and I know my tree grandsons havea seven college degree between dem," she beamed. Her eyes were moist as she smiled and looked at me from across the table.

As *nonna* finished her meal, swiping a piece of bread in the remains of the clam sauce, I winked at my mother and wife and asked, "So, *nonna*, did you enjoy your dinner?"

She responded with, what was for her, a five star Michelin review: "You know," she said, dabbing the corners of her mouth with a napkin, "*unn c' è mali*, wasa no so bad," she pronounced, twisting her thumb and forefinger into her cheek.

Two weeks later on a grey, chilly Saturday morning in June, I drove into Corona for my bi-weekly visit with *nonna*. The dirt-baked, weed-infested empty lots of my youth had given way to two and three family brick houses with small, tidy patches of grass in front and children rolling and cavorting in the turf.

As I got out of my car holding a shopping bag of groceries, Julio, a tough, neighborhood Hispanic kid approached me smiling with a stickball bat in his hand. Julio's father had been shot dead a few years earlier, the victim of a robbery in the bodega he owned and he latched on to me like a big brother or father figure.

"Hey, man, how you do today Ruggero?" he asked, slapping his palm over mine.

"Not bad, Julio, how 'bout you? You keeping out of trouble?"

"Shit, man, I never look for no trouble. But if it come my way, I always be ready," he said pumping a fist in the air and laughing.

"Getting ready to play a little stickball?" I asked.

"Yeah, we got a game against da guys from 43rd Avenue. We playin' for five bucks a head."

"Five bucks a head!" I exclaimed, "that's a heavy number."

"Ah, no sweat, we kick their ass regular, but they keep comin back for more. Hey, we could make a place for you if you interested," he said elbowing me in the side.

"Thanks, no, Julio, the day and the game have long passed me by," I replied, looking down the street and recalling the times I drove the ham-pink spauldeen past three sewers.

I pressed a ten dollar bill into his hand and said, gratefully, "Thanks for looking after my *nonna*, Julio."

"Hey, no problem, Bro, your *nonna*, my *nonna*. We look out for da old people in da neighborhood. All da guys like your *nonna*. She a real pisser. We always see her comin' out from da OTB parlor, but she just keep on walkin an pretend she don't see us," he said slapping his leg and laughing.

"Yeah," I said, turning to look up at her window, "she's a character, all right. She still loves the action."

"Hey, dats cool. Nuttin wrong wit dat," Julio reasoned.

"You know," he said, smiling, "your *nonna* like to sit by da window and watch us when we play a game."

"Yeah, I know, Julio, she told me."

"She tell you dat?" he asked surprised.

"Yeah, she said it made her feel good because it reminds her of the times she watched me when I was a kid."

"Well, I have to get upstairs now. *Nonna* will be waiting for her lunch."

"Yeah," Julio said peering into the shopping bag. "I see ya got all her favorites dare, cheese, salami, bread, olives..., and a small bottle of vodka," he added, grinning broadly.

"Quiet, Julio," I mock-warned, shaking a finger at him.

"Ok, man, see ya in a couplea weeks, and don't worry 'bout nuttin."

As I mounted the stairs to the apartment, I was struck by the piquant aroma of Hispanic cooking wafting through the hallway. I smiled and thought, that's nice. Some things don't change. Tonight young children will noisily gather around their kitchen table and scoop up the savory meal their mother lovingly prepared for them.

When I opened the door to apartment 2C I was hit by the familiar smell of Clorox pervading the room. I put the shopping bag on the kitchen table and walked into the living room to the phonograph where Pavarotti's voice was stuck, tediously repeating.

"Nessun dorma, nessun dorma, nessun dorma."

"What are you doing here, *nonna*?" I called, removing the arm from the record. "You're gonna ruin the needle and the recording." My words hung unanswered in the still apartment as I walked down the dark hallway to the bedroom, calling again, "*Nonna?*"

I stood in the doorway and looked to the chair in front of the window where *nonna* was slumped with her arms dangling limply over the side.

"*Nonna*," I shouted, choked, racing to the chair. I took her hand, already rigid with a lifeless cold, and looked into an ashen face of dry, parted lips, and eyes closed tight in eternal sleep. My heart beat rapidly as I sucked in then exhaled air and tasted salty, wet trickles at the corners of my mouth. After a minute or so, my limbs thawed. I cradled her in my arms and gently placed her on the bed, pulling a cover to her chin. I sat stunned on the edge of the bed looking vacuously around the room when the irony hit me. I realized I was in the same room where thirty five years earlier, I had awakened to my first recollection of *nonna*, exercising at the window. The memories built up in my mind until there was no room left and the trickle gave way to a flood of tears as I buried my face in a handkerchief.

But death always brings a myriad of responsibilities for the survivors of the deceased, and I knew I couldn't permit myself an extended period of personal mourning.

The operator connected me to the 110th police precinct and the desk sergeant told me he would dispatch a cruiser immediately and contact the office of the Medical Examiner. I then called Father Michaelo at St. Leo's Church, and Guida's Funeral Home. The last call was to my mother whose immediate shock was replaced by quiet sobbing.

"I'll be there in half an hour, Ruggero. Did...did you?" she began.

"Yes, mom, don't worry, I took care of everything," I said.

. . .

I replaced the phone on the cradle and felt a trembling throughout my body. I went into the kitchen, took the bottle of vodka from the shopping bag and poured one hell of a drink, sending it down my throat in one gulp.

About fifteen minutes later, the door bell startled me, breaking the eerie silence in the apartment. A short, rumpled plain clothes detective and a uniformed officer came in, removed their hats and offered condolences.

"I'm Detective Bracken and this here is Officer Flanigan," he said through tight lips. "Flanigan, stay by the open door and wait for the ME and don't let no busy-bodies near here," he ordered.

He then turned to me and asked, "Did you make arrangements for anyone to?.."

"Yes," I interrupted, "I already called Guida's Funeral Home and St. Leo's Church."

"Good, good," he said, giving me the once over. "Well, lead the way, laddie."

Bracken went to the bed, pulled the sheet down and took *nonna*'s hand, pressing his fingers to her wrist.

"Yeah," he said, turning to me, "this ain't official, of course, but she's passed. This where you found her, in the bed like this?" he asked.

"No, no, she was in that chair by the window," I said pointing.

"Shouldn't have moved her, kid" he said, running his hand through thinning grey hair, shaking his head and grimacing. He then took out a small spiral pad and pen and walked around the room taking notes and asking routine questions.

The ME came into the room minutes later holding a black satchel, extended sympathies and casually greeted the detective by name.

"Keepin busy, Bracken?" the ME asked.

"Yeah, well you know how it is, doc. The eternal footman keeps us on the run. He always calls the game on account of darkness."

"Tell me about it," the ME chuckled caustically, as he pressed a stethoscope to *nonna*'s bare chest, checked her pulse points and looked behind her head and neck for any signs of trauma.

"Pretty straight forward. Looks like death by natural causes," he announced.

"That's how I make it, doc," Bracken agreed.

He then produced a form, made some entries and handed a copy to the detective as he walked toward the door, patting my shoulder.

"Sorry about your grandma, kid. See ya later, Bracken," he said.

"Yeah, don't make it too soon, doc," Bracken called after him, laughing.

The death squad continued with the arrival of Father Michaelo, who, after administering the Sacrament of Extreme Unction, turned, took my hand and drew me to the side of the bed.

"Let us now say a prayer for your *nonna*. You too, Johnny," he ordered, looking at Detective Bracken.

"Our father, who art in Heaven..."

"Hail Mary, full of Grace..."

"May the souls of all the faithful departed..."

"Let me know," the priest said, wrapping both his hands around mine, "when the family has made its final arrangements with Guida so I can schedule the Mass."

Eduardo Guida, lean and tall as a Cyprus tree, and his assistant were waiting patiently and respectfully in the living room.

"*Bon giornu*, Eduardo, "Father Michaelo greeted Guida on his way out.

"*Bon giornu*, Padre," Guida returned.

"The young man here will let me know when you have completed your task," Father Michaelo said.

"*Sì, Padre*," Guido replied. Bracken followed behind the priest and greeted Guida, "How ya doin today, Eddie?" he asked.

"Fine thanks, Johnny and you?"

"Pretty fair, pretty fair," Bracken responded waving his hat as he left.

Jeez, I thought, these guys are like a well-oiled, carefully calibrated machine, each appearing in a timed prescribed manner and discharging his duty with cool, methodical efficiency. If only life was that orderly, I thought.

My mother arrived and we tearfully embraced. She walked to the bed, blessed herself, kissed *nonna* on the forehead, and silently prayed.

"It must have been a sudden, massive coronary," she said turning to me with swollen red eyes. "It's strange. All her life she had physical complaints, but never any sign of a heart problem. Doctor Panebianco always said her complaints were, psycho, psycho something..."

"Psychosomatic," I offered.

"Yes, that's it," my mother agreed.

Guida and his assistant came into the room, wheeling a gurney.

"Folks," he intoned softly, "I think it's best if you wait in the living room while we go about our task here."

My mother and I returned to the living room and sat quietly on the sofa staring at a gallery of generations of sepia-tinted family photographs hanging on the wall, surrounding a portrait of *nonna*'s brother, a mischievously smiling, nattily attired Carmelo.

"How about an espresso?" I asked my mother, rising from the sofa.

"Yes, yes, that sounds good," she answered.

"And maybe a little vodka?" I suggested over my shoulder.

"No, no, I don't need any vodka, and you don't need another," she chided.

"What? What are you talking about?" I stammered.

"Don't shit me, Ruggero, I can smell it on your breath," she replied firmly.

I returned with the espresso and sat, embarrassed, with my head between my knees.

The muffled voices from the bedroom suddenly ceased and the quiet was broken by the faint metallic whirr of a drawn zipper. Guido and his assistant emerged from the bedroom guiding the gurney past us toward the kitchen.

"Wait here for a minute," he ordered his assistant, returning and covering my mother's hand with his.

"I will be at The Home until ten o'clock tonight, Marie. When you feel up to it, come by and we can discuss the final arrangements. And please accept my most sincere condolences," he said in earnest.

. . .

We returned to the bedroom and my mother looked at me and sighed.

"We're gonna have to clear the apartment out," she said walking around the room. "Is there anything you want?" she asked, stopping at a bureau and opening a jewelry box.

"No, no nothing," I began..."Wait a minute, there is something, that old Philco television set in the living room."

"What!" my mother exclaimed, "why do you want that old piece of junk?"

"Sentimental value, mom," I replied. "It's the first TV we ever had. *Nonna* bought it after she had that big winning day at Belmont when I was with her in 1951."

"Oh yeah," my mother reflected chuckling wistfully, "she called you her 'good luck charm.' Anyway," she said fingering through the jewelry box, "there are some real nice pieces here which I'll share with your aunt Twink. But this antique cameo has been in the family for four generations and stays with me. And when I pass, it will go to your daughter, Christina, keeping the chain unbroken."

My mother then went to the closet which emitted the scent of Chanel, and began poking through the row of hanging tailored suits and dresses.

"My God!" she exclaimed. "Look at these labels, will you? Bergdorf-Goodman, Saks Fifth Avenue, Bloomingdales. Your *nonna* never denied herself when it came to clothes. Nothing but the best. And look at the collection of these hats. Every style from Coty to pill-box," she said sliding her hand across the top shelf.

"What's this?" she asked, pulling a beaten wooden box from the back of the shelf.

"Oh, yeah!" I exclaimed hurrying to her side and laughing, "the mysterious keepsake box she carried from Castellammare."

"So this is the box her sister, Giovanna, was always talking about," my mother pondered. "How'd you know about it?" she asked.

"I found it one day by accident, and *nonna* got real upset. When I asked her about it she told me to mind my own 'businessa.'"

"It's locked," my mother said, struggling with the lid.

"Must be a key around here some place," I said, fishing in the corner of the shelf.

"Here's something," I said, pulling a chain hooking a medal of St. Anthony of Padua, and a badly-worn brass key.

"Bring it in here," my mother called as she walked down the hallway to the living room, and sat on the sofa.

The key entered the lock and turned with surprising ease, and the top flipped open revealing a yellowing, frayed card memorializing the death of *nonna*'s uncle, Antonio Pepitone.

"*Nonna*'s uncle and Mamma Caiozzo's brother," my mother pronounced, sadly. "He was a professor at the University in Palermo and wrote courageous articles and stories exposing the collusion between the corrupt politicians, the police and the mafia. And he was running for mayor, and might have won. But he was assassinated by some guy named Pietro Magaddino, who was the brother of Stefano Magaddino, *consigliere* to Don Salvatore Bonanno."

"Yeah, mom, I remember hearing about how *nonna*'s uncle was murdered. This guy, Pietro Magaddino, was never charged. How come?" I asked.

"Because he had connections to powerful, important people in Castellammare, in all of Sicily for that matter, people who saw Antonio Pepitone as a threat to their way of doing business. There was no way the police would arrest Magaddino, even though everybody, including the village idiot, knew he was the assassin," she said disgusted. "But, Carmelo, *nonna*'s brother, was a hot head and swore publicly that he'd avenge the murder of his uncle. Magaddino taunted and laughed at him. Then, then, that same year, New Year's Eve, 1915, they found Magaddino's body in an alley with two bullets in his head. Until the day that pig, Bartolo Fontana, killed Carmelo in Neptune Beach, he swore he had nothing to do with Magaddino's assassination. He had an alibi for his whereabouts that night but Magaddino and his relatives were convinced he was involved and were determined to exact their revenge.

That's when my grandfather, Giuseppe Caiozzo, got the family out of Sicily and came to America."

"So, so...did Carmelo kill Magaddino?" I hesitatingly asked.

"No, he didn't," my mother firmly answered.

"How can you be so sure?"

"I just know," she answered, without elaborating.

"Jesus, mom, that's some story," I said awestruck.

"No, no, that's no story, Ruggero. It's a fact, it's true, it actually happened. Anyway, what's under the tier of that box?" she asked, quickly changing the subject.

I removed it revealing two leather pouches, one small, the other larger. I picked the smaller pouch up, turned it upside down and shook it. A large gold crucifix and a man's diamond ring dropped into my palm. I looked at my mother who was shaking her head and biting her lower lip and asked, "Where the hell did she get these things from and why were they locked up in a box for more than sixty years?"

"Empty the larger pouch," my mother commanded, ignoring my question.

It was much heavier, and, as I slipped my hand into the opening, I felt a handle and pulled out a Beretta pistol and gasped. I was utterly amazed. What was a pistol doing in a box in *nonna*'s closet? My mother seemed completely unfazed. She looked at the weapon in stony silence, nodding her head up and down, then calmly said, "Be careful, Ruggero, it may be loaded." I took the gun into the kitchen away form my mother to the dumbwaiter, opened the door and pointed the pistol down the dark shaft. I slid the clip out of the butt and drew back the slide to make sure there wasn't a round in the chamber. The clip held six rounds, but I noticed there were only four inside it. I picked them out of the clip, went back to the living room and put the Beretta down on the coffee table in front of my mother with the four rounds beside it.

"So whata you think?" she asked me coolly.

"There are two bullets missing from this clip. Maybe Carmelo shot Magaddino and *nonna* hid this gun he used."

"I told you, Ruggero, Carmelo didn't shoot Magaddino," she said irritated.

She then shook her head and looked at me sadly, knowing it was time to share with me the awful secret, one I was beginning to suspect even as I dreaded and resisted hearing it.

"All right," I said, "Then tell me who did. Not..." I couldn't bring myself to voice what I guessed was the truth.

My mother hesitated. "Yes, Ruggero, yes, it was *nonna* herself," my mother confirmed.

I sat down next to her and put my face in my hands. I just couldn't get my mind around it. My *nonna* murdering someone in cold blood. I tried to visualize her as a young girl in Castellammare sneaking upon someone and pulling the trigger of this gun in front of us. It was just too horrible to imagine, but in fact, I realized, it is what happened. My mother would never lie to me about this. My love for *nonna* was undiminished, but, as I looked at the gun, I couldn't help feeling revulsion as well. How could she do something like that?

"She was a freakin assassin," I blurted out in anger.

"She had no choice, Ruggero. And you have no right to judge her," my mother scolded. "What she did was justice, not revenge. She knew that Magaddino would never be arrested, much less convicted of assassinating her uncle, despite the fact that his guilt was the worst-kept secret in the village.

"*Nonna* was a feisty, young Sicilian woman, very much influenced by her uncle, Antonio. She refused to meekly and dutifully accept the mores and customs established by unscrupulous, powerful, self-serving men who never considered the needs or interests of the poor families living in the villages. They had no voice in the politics or the establishment of laws and stood by silently as men behind closed doors determined how the system would run and how justice would be administered and by whom.

"So, she decided to play by their rules and, fearless as she was, took it upon herself to exact justice for Antonio's murder. Vendetta is as common in Sicily as prostitution, and she did nothing more than what men have been doing on that island for a thousand years."

"So you knew, all this time, you knew," I said stunned.

"Yes, Ruggero, I knew but I respected the Sicilian code of *omertà* and never revealed anything, ...until now."

"But how did you finally find out?" I asked astonished.

My mother took a long drag on a Lucky and began: "Many years ago, as a young girl, I became aware of those psycho...psycho, what did you call them...?"

"Psychosomatic symptoms," I repeated.

"Yes. She always complained of headaches and stomach disorders and had bad dreams when she would cry out in her sleep, a pitiful wail..."

One night I woke up to this blood-curdling scream, ran into her room, and turned the light on. She was sitting up in her bed, sobbing and wringing her hands, as though she was washing them, something even you know she did ten times a day.

"Anyway, I held and rocked her back and forth the way you comfort a child awakening from a bad dream. When she finally composed herself, she let go and...and told me how she had planned and carried out the assassination of Pietro Magaddino."

My mother breathed deeply and continued.

"*Nonna* and her brother were always extremely close and everyone in the family said they could probably read each other's mind. Mamma Caiozzo once joked that they came from the same fava bean pod. Anyway, *nonna* told me she was convinced that, sooner or later, Carmelo would try to carry out his widely circulated threat of vendetta and be arrested or assassinated himself.

"For weeks she devised a scheme which she thought was foolproof, making sure that Magaddino would pay for his crime, without implicating her brother: she would kill Magaddino on New Years Eve while Carmelo was celebrating at Deputy Vito's party in the company of his friends, an alibi which could not be contested.

"She left the church dance a few minutes after midnight and waited in the shadows across from the tavern where she knew Magaddino would be celebrating. When he came out, she followed him as he stumbled up Via Garibaldi. As he turned into a dark alley, she took a gun from her purse, that gun," my mother pointed, "and...and shot him in the back of the head."

"My God," I gasped.

"Wait, that's not the end," my mother said, pressing her palms forward. "She then went to the body spread on its back and put another bullet into Magaddino's temple. Knowing my mother, it's a wonder there were any bullets left in that gun," she said nodding toward the coffee table."

"Holy shit!" I exclaimed, bringing my hand to my forehead.

"Oh, there's more, there's more," my mother continued.

"Your *nonna* played this thing beautifully. She ripped the crucifix from his neck, pulled the ring from his finger, and grabbed all the lire from his money pouch."

"Jesus," I asked, "was it necessary to rob him after she killed him?"

"Oh! Smart guy like you, Ph.D. an all, and you don't get it?"

"Whata you mean, mom?" I asked annoyed.

"Don't you see?" she asked, shaking her head. "*Nonna* wanted to make it look like a robbery, something the gypsies would be accused of. But the plan didn't work. Bonanno and Magaddino's brother were convinced that Carmelo was the guilty party and were already planning their retribution.

My grandfather, Giuseppe Caiozzo, was alerted to this fact by Turi, the police captain in the village, who had no love for Magaddino, but plenty of love for Mamma Caiozzo."

"You mean Mamma Caiozzo had an affair with this cop in Castellammare?" I asked, shocked.

"I don't know and I don't care," my mother replied, irritably. "The point is he put his own life in jeopardy and urged Giuseppe to get the family out of Sicily."

And so my mother concluded her exposure of the terrible secret. She paused to let me digest it, and I was consumed with conflicting thoughts and emotions. This woman who I loved and revered had murdered a man in cold blood. I had to condemn what she'd done, but I couldn't condemn her. She refused to be a pawn in a world where men savagely took what they wanted and did what they wanted without regard to standards of decency or the rights or feelings of others. She was a proud, brave woman who acted according to the mores of her culture to exact justice and restore family honor, while trying to protect her brother.

I got up from the sofa and went into the kitchen and poured another stout glass of vodka.

"Again with the damn vodka?" my mother shouted.

I ignored her and struggled to process what I had heard, plunging into an irrelevant, pedantic psychoanalytic explanation of *nonna*'s symptoms.

"You see, mom, here's the deal," I lectured. "All the years you witnessed those psychosomatic symptoms, you were seeing the effects remorse and guilt can have on a person who has committed an unacceptable act. *Nonna* needed to punish herself, to suffer, to expiate the guilt she felt after she murdered that Magaddino guy."

"What the hell are you talking about?" my mother looked at me and asked puzzled. "She never needed to, ex…ex…, anything after she killed Magaddino. Her symptoms emerged for the first time in 1921, a few weeks after Fontana shot her brother. The thing with Magaddino happened in Sicily in 1916… You got the guilt part right but the time-frame wrong. Her guilt had nothing to do with killing Magaddino. It's obvious she blamed herself for Carmelo's murder and that's why she suffered those symptoms all these years."

"My God, you're right!" I exclaimed. "But why didn't she seek relief from a priest or a psychiatrist?" I wondered out loud.

"I doubt she could ever have sought help or confessed to a priest. Her experience with the clergy as a young girl made her very suspicious of them and jaded her faith. As for psychiatry, if those doctors had to depend on Sicilians to make their living, their children would go hungry every night.

"So," my mother breathed a sigh, "now that you know the whole story, how do you feel? Is your memory of her tainted? Do you love her any less?"

"Of course not, mom. I know she wasn't a sociopath or a cold-blooded killer. She didn't do what she did for money or power. She wanted to make sure her uncle's killer paid for his deed and retaliated within a code commonly understood, if not always accepted, by her culture. It wasn't revenge. It was a wild kind of justice."

"I'm very glad you understand that," my mother sighed and said, hugging me and putting her head to my chest.

My mother went into the bedroom and took the jewelry box with the valuables as I stuffed the Beretta and the four remaining rounds into a paper bag.

"What are you going to do with that?" she asked, concerned.

"It's going to find its final resting place at the bottom of the Long Island Sound, where it belongs," I answered.

We locked the door of the apartment and made our way down the dimly-lit staircase. The morbid curiosity-seekers had dispersed, leaving the street virtually empty, except for Julio who slowly approached us.

"Mrs. L. and Ruggero, I so sorry for your loss. I know how it feel to lose a loved one."

"Thank you, Julio," my mother and I responded.

"Me an da guys took up a collection an we gonna send flowers...an...an..., what else can I say?"

"Thanks, my friend, we appreciate your thoughts..."

"Listen," Julio said shuffling his feet, "don't be a stranger. Come 'round once in a while. You always welcome here. Once a Corona guy, always a Corona guy."

"You're right, Julio, I'll do that, I really will," I said touched.

As I walked my mother to her car she said, "Well, I guess I'm now the matriarch of the family, the last Maria."

"I guess so," I replied.

She paused then asked, urging, "Will you make me a promise, Ruggero?"

"Whatever I can do, mom."

"Will you make it a point to come for Sunday dinner once a month or so with Anna Maria and the children? And maybe, when they're on vacation, they can stay over for a couple of days. They're getting older and I haven't spent as much time with them as I would have liked. I'd love to take them around and show them my Manhattan and, and, tell them tales of our family in Sicily," she laughed.

"That would be fine, mom, but I don't know how well Guido would handle having the kids around for a couple of days."

"You let me worry about Guido," she said firmly.

As we embraced farewell, my mother suddenly pulled back and looked over my shoulder to the entrance of the building.

"What's wrong, mom?" I asked.

"Look at the inscription at the top of the entrance of the building. Do you notice anything?"

"No, not really, mom,...oh yeah, jeez! I had forgotten the building is called, 'Ann Marie Court'. So what?" I laughed. "It's your wife's name," she replied softly.

"And, and," she continued, "the building number is 40-40, and *nonna*'s apartment number is '2c'. My building in Manhattan is 440 and my apartment number is '2c'."

"Ok, ok, mom, an interesting set of coincidences that mean absolutely nothing. You sound like a *strega*, a witch, brewing some mystical fate-inspired potion that has its origin in the Sicilian mountains."

"An interesting set of coincidences?" she mused. "Maybe so, but I'm a Sicilian woman and we don't believe in coincidences. It's almost like the past always returns to us in one way or another, to touch us, to remind us, of our link, our connection. Even that kid, Julio, seems to know; 'Once a Corona guy, always a Corona guy,' he said."

"Mom...," I began.

"All right, all right," she said, snapping out of her reverie with raised eyebrows and wide eyes. "Of course, of course, you're right," she said facetiously, patting my cheek.

"*Ciau, beddu.* I'll call you later with the schedule for the final arrangements."

"*Ciau, mamma.*"

On the drive back to my family in Stony Brook, my sense of loss and sorrow began to lift. I looked into the rear view mirror and saw the western sun settle and melt under the horizon and cracked a smile as I reflected on what my mother had said about passing the Sicilian cameo heirloom to my daughter, becoming the family matriarch, establishing a regular routine for Sunday family dinners, and spending more time with her grandchildren.

It never ends well. The Eternal Footman is always waiting patiently, dispassionately, at the door like a faithful servant with coat and hat in hand. But if we're lucky enough, we get to savor the memories and joyous moments of our life with those we love. And if we're wise and prudent enough, we will leave those gifts for our children, grandchildren, and beyond when our time comes to pass through the door.

The family had come to the end of one thing, but the beginning of another.

THE END